DEFIANCE

ALSO BY CATHERINE M. WALKER

Unwanted (Emergence, 1)

Sacrifice (Emergence, 2)

Defiance (Emergence, 3)

Shattering Dreams (The Being Of Dreams, 1)

Path Of The Broken (The Being Of Dreams, 2)

Elder Born (The Being Of Dreams, 3)

NEWSLETTER

If you'd like updates on my progress, promotions and advance notice of when the next book comes out drop by my website and join my newsletter.

www.catherinemwalker.com

DEFIANCE

EMERGENCE
BOOK THREE

CATHERINE M. WALKER

Cover designer: https://www.jcalebdesign.com/

Ebook ISBN: 978-1-925776-19-5

Paperback ISBN: 978-1-925776-20-1

Hardcover ISBN: 978-1-925776-21-8

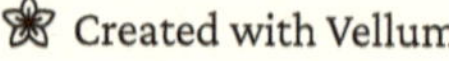 Created with Vellum

CHAPTER
ONE

Ben ran down the road with his young daughter in his arms. Iris was in front of him with their son's hand clutched in hers. If the screams that assaulted not only his mind but his ears were anything to go by, the Sylannian invasion of Vallantia was in full swing. At the rhythmic thud of booted feet, he risked a glance over his shoulder. Sylannians streamed into the street behind him. There was the briefest of pauses before the Sylannians hollered their battle cry and pelted towards him. Ben focused on the looming mess of the Burrow just ahead of them. It was close, but not close enough.

"Iris," Ben called, waiting for her to turn before pressing their daughter into his partner's arms. "Go, get to the Burrow and ask for Lukas. I'll be right behind you!"

"Ben—"

"Run!"

Ben had some relief that Iris stopped arguing with him and did as he asked although he despaired at their slow pace. He unsheathed his sword as he spun to face the oncoming Sylannians. Ben wished he'd had the time to pull on his fighting leathers before they'd fled the bar. Then his blade countered that of the first Sylannian. He drew his dagger with his other hand and struck out at the increasing number of enemies that surrounded him. One woman leapt on him and he pushed her aside. To his shock, the blood that sprayed was not his own. It became apparent these women were attempting to take him down, not kill him. His lips peeled back as more of the enemy grappled with him. Ben's focus narrowed on his opponents. Even the walls of the buildings receded as he made every strike against those he faced count. It wouldn't be enough. There were too many of them, but the longer he detained them fighting with him, the more chance his family had of surviving.

Ben gasped as a sharp pain pierced his abdomen. He twisted as he was pulled to the ground, seeking one last sight of Iris and his children as they disappeared. As his vision darkened, he fancied people were running towards him from the Burrow. The screams that resounded in his ears were from the Sylannians. A metallic taste filled his mouth, moisture spilling onto his lips as he coughed. Fluid hit his cheek and he wondered if it was water or blood. The last thing he saw before darkness claimed him were the eyes of the enemy who fell near him. The eyes that stared into his own went dull as sparks of the veil fled the body, dissipating into the air.

TWO

As Taya and Harry walked into the room, Michael waved them over to take a seat. They grinned at him and took the proffered seats without fanfare.

"Sorry we're late," Taya said.

"You're not. Any problems?" Michael asked.

"None. Our warbands have packed and we'll be ready to head off in the morning towards Vallantia," Harry said.

"Good. We'll remain and wrap up here. I want to make sure we've killed every Sylannian in Callenhain," Michael said.

"Are you sure you don't need more help to finish here?" Taya asked, a frown marring her forehead.

"No, Olivia is discussing some administrative issues with the new overseer. The teams will just do another sweep while that is happening. Besides, there's still Khaliun's tribe if anything crops up." Michael held his hands up to forestall comments. "Which I'm not expecting. Other than some patrols to stop my people getting bored with inactivity, they'll be resting."

"We'll set up and take stock of the situation in Vallantia," Taya said.

"We should only leave here a day or so after you and can catch up on the road, even with Khaliun's tribe with us," Nathanial said.

"Were the prisoners able to give any kind of timeline for this second attack?" Taya asked.

"No, and I'm only guessing at this point that if it occurs, the logical place would be Vallantia."

"The Sylannian commander orchestrated this whole thing to divert our attention," Nathanial said.

"If so, it's a cold-blooded diversion," Harry said.

"The Sylannians must have lost thousands of their people in this attack," Taya said.

Michael!

He held up his hand to the others in the room. Both relieved to hear from Colin and stealing himself for the bad news he knew was coming from the thrum of urgency in Colin's mental call.

Colin, I was beginning to worry about you. Talk to me, what's happened?

Sorry, I had a few issues along the way getting into position.

No need to apologise. If things hadn't gone wrong disrupting the network, Ben wouldn't have needed to send you out.

Do you already know about the Kastlers taking over Vallantia? Colin paused, then hurried on. *Although it's redundant now other than it's why the communication network went down. At least at first.*

Michael surged to his feet. *The Kastlers did what?*

They staged a rebellion and seized control of Vallantia and your family estate, but that isn't the pressing issue right now.

The Sylannians have invaded? Michael closed his eyes, pushing down his instant fury at the news the Kastlers had dared to rise against the Warlord.

How did you know?

I've been expecting it. I'll add dealing with the Kastler's betrayal to my list. How bad?

Ben reached out to Adam a couple of nights ago. Sylanna had just launched their assault on Vallantia. The attack came from within the walls. Ben anticipated that, given the weakened defences, it would fall again by morning. Sorry for the delay. Adam had trouble waking me, then I had to get close enough to contact you.

My family?

Detained but alive. At least under the Kastlers. I don't know yet what's happened with the Sylannian invasion.

Is Ben safe?

He said he was going to ground, Colin replied.

Tell him not to put himself at risk, but I need as much information fed to me as he can.

Now that we have the relay up, we'll feed you everything we find out.

Keep your head down. I expect you're fine where you are, but run if you have to. Otherwise, I'll pick you up on my way through.

Michael resisted the urge to swear and gathered his thoughts as the others in the room all waited expectantly.

"It's official. Sylanna has launched an attack on Vallantia. The city has fallen, apparently for the second time."

"What do you mean for the second time?" Nathanial stared at him as everyone stilled, waiting for his answer.

Michael repeated the information Colin had relayed to him, not bothering to hide his anger regarding the Kaslters.

"So Vallantia is under Sylannian control?" Taya asked.

"Can I just circle back to the Kastlers? As in the Kastler Trading Consortium, attacked Vallantia?" Harry asked.

"So I'm told." Michael ground his teeth. While losing his temper would have been satisfying, it wouldn't change anything.

"They were also behind the re-emergence of the slave trade," Nathanial said.

"I hope we're not going to forget that little detail?" Harry asked.

"If they are still alive after I'm done with the Sylannians, they won't be for much longer than it takes me to string them up." Michael throttled down the flare of anger that bubbled to the surface. "First the invasion. I want the warbands on the road to Vallantia."

Taya stood and bowed her head in acknowledgement. "Yes Warleader."

"They're probably counting on it taking weeks for you to receive word of the attack," Harry said.

"They're in for a bit of a surprise then, but it's going to take us time to get into position," Nathanial said, frowning. "Head to the Smith's place we'll use that as the initial mustering point."

"Now that we have a communication relay up, Ben will inform me if it isn't." Michael turned his attention to his team leaders. "Go, start heading to the Smith's estate and set up. We will do one last sweep here, then follow. Taya, take overall command of the other warbands until I catch up with you. If something goes wrong and you get there before us start reconnaissance when you get in the field. I'll want a full report when I arrive."

"I could keep my team here to help. The last sweep of Callenhain might go faster that way," Harry said.

"No, get on the road. As much as I wish we'd all been there yesterday, don't exhaust your people. It won't do any good if everyone collapses from exhaustion."

They all stood from the table and Michael walked out, heading towards Khaliun while Nathanial briefed the Unwanted. At orders from Taya and Harry, their warbands scrambled.

Michael paused and reached out to Olivia. *Liv, I need you to speed things up.*

What's happened? Olivia's reply was immediate.

Colin got in touch. Vallantia has fallen to Sylanna.

Even under the circumstances, it made him smile as he felt the colourful burst of emotion as she swore.

Do you want me back right now?

An image of a room dominated by a wooden table in the middle, with paperwork scattered over its surface sprung into Michael's mind. Jenna and Theo sat on chairs opposite Olivia. It was one of the many such rooms in the Strafford estate.

As much as it kills me no. Taya and Harry are hitting the road tonight. After the fighting here in Callenhain, the Unwanted can use the extra downtime even if it is only a day or two. I'd rather you settle business, or it will just fall to pieces again before we get back.

Everyone held together well, but the action here pushed us to their limits. You're right. If we're going to ask them to repeat the whole thing, they need the rest. Olivia responded. He could feel her nodding in agreement.

Particularly if this new commander is as competent as Khaliun thinks she is. I fear this could be a protracted battle.

Which is not our strength. Olivia hesitated before continuing. *Should we tell the others?*

It is the Warlord's prerogative to reveal the things he told us to hide. Let's assess the situation on the ground in Vallantia and if I deem it necessary, I'll bring them into our confidence. Then it's on me if father isn't happy about it. Michael shook his head, even though she wasn't here in the room with him.

We'll wear it because I will back you on it. Olivia's tone was firm.

Very well. We'll face up to him if he's unhappy.

I vote we get to Vallantia and assess the whole mess first before we apprise him of the situation.

Or he'll be on his horse and break himself riding across the domain to get there regardless of whether he is recovered enough. Michael grimaced. *Take your time and settle things with Jenna and Theo. We'll talk when you're done.*

The warehouse had erupted into chaos. His fighters were not quite running, but not strolling either. Everyone moved with purpose. Even the members of the Unwanted were up and helping the members of the two warbands who'd received their marching orders to do that last-minute packing. Looking over, he saw Nathanial off in the corner in the sitting area and he wandered over.

The willingness for someone to throw all these lives away, just to keep him occupied, was breathtaking. If that is what the Sylannian commander had done and he couldn't think of any other reason to split her forces. She'd sent two smaller attacks over this side while launching a separate attack on the opposite side of the domain. Michael's lips firmed. This commander was a person he was determined to stop. It showed a cold, calculating ruthlessness that was dangerous to everyone.

THREE

Khaliun packed her gear as did the rest of the Kallith. While she hadn't expected to be going back to their new home anytime soon, the reality of just how long this war might be was settling in.

Most of the Warlord's fighting forces had left already. All heading to a pre-arranged muster point for the battle that was occurring on the other side of the country. It had escalated from a local trader, or so she'd been told, to a full Sylannian invasion. Only the Unwanted and a couple of others stayed, rounding up the rest of the Sylannian forces in Callenhain. However, soon they would also head to Vallantia, the city of Michael's birth.

"It makes me wonder if we would have lost our homeland if we'd been friends with these people years ago when the Sylannians fell on us," Batu said.

Khaliun nodded agreement, grateful that Batu, the senior scout and wolf warrior, had stepped forward on the loss of Tarkhan. "I think some of these people have forgotten more about the art of war than our people have ever known."

"I thought we could hold our own at smaller-scale fights.

These skirmishes, as they called them here in the city, put even that to shame," Batu said.

"All of them use their powers to the fullest to aid them in battle." Khaliun watched the Unwanted where they rested. Even in sleep, the veil swirled around them, although she doubted they were doing anything. She'd learned they had to concentrate more, to not draw in the veil. For the Unwanted, it was like breathing was to everyone else. "Not just the Unwanted, the members of the other warbands do as well. I've learned so much from observing how they fight together."

"I admit it's been astonishing to go into combat with them and see it from this side rather than face them in battle." Batu laughed softly before sobering. "As superior as the Warlord's forces are, I fear they will need more than just our clan fighters."

"From the reports Michael received, the Sylannians have launched a full-scale assault. They think the attacks on us in the Heights and here in Callenhain were a feint. Its purpose was to draw the Unwanted away and keep them occupied while the Sylannians dug in and took as much ground as they could."

"On the honour of the clans, we owe these people."

"What are you suggesting?"

"We go back and raise the rest of our fighters to come and assist."

"We have the right to make the request. If the Warlord's forces lose this war, what remains of the Kallith won't last long in our new land."

"We know you don't need our approval, but we agree. While they were helping us, their homeland was invaded. The honour of the Kallith demands we help them," Batu said.

Khaliun was grateful for the input. She may not need the approval of her wolves, but it was good to have anyway. Particularly since she was without a co-leader to bounce ideas off. It was like a sense check that she wasn't straying too far away from the needs of all, rather than doing just what she wanted. Khaliun pushed aside the guilt over the loss of Tarkhan, her former co-leader. She had a job to do and wallowing in grief over the past was a spiral she couldn't afford to get lost in. It also wouldn't change anything.

"Will some of you be happy to travel with the warleader when he rides? I think I need to go myself to convince the other leaders to send most of the clan's fighters," Khaliun asked.

Khaliun looked around at her warriors and found only agreement. There wasn't a hint of nervousness or uncertainty about the idea.

"Yes, leader Khaliun. The warleader's people took care of our welfare as if we were their own when we rode with them during this conflict."

"Thank you, I will take an escort with me, but the bulk of you will ride with the Unwanted or whoever Michael designates. Think about the choices and if any have a strong preference, speak up when I get done with speaking with the warleader," Khaliun said.

Khaliun strode over to the far corner where Michael and his two most trusted people sat in discussion. Their conversation stopped at her approach and they waved her to a seat.

"What do you need?" Michael asked.

"We have talked amongst ourselves and decided, with your permission, to gather the rest of the fighters from the clans to come and assist your fighting forces against the Sylannians," Khaliun said.

"Are you sure? You know the agreement you reached with the Warlord does not require it."

"You've treated the Kallith with honour. I know the invasion here wasn't our doing, but I can't hide from the fact that Callenhain faced assault while you were assisting us."

"This feint was well planned and certainly not the fault of your people," Michael said.

"Perhaps, but if not for us, you would have been here in Callenhain when they invaded this city. I suspect in that circumstance, the battle you faced would be much shorter. Instead, the Sylannians gained a foothold because I called you away to help us."

"For this commander of theirs to throw all these lives away, just to give herself more time, says much about her and her people's intent." Nathanial shook his head, his expression grim. "I think the attack on the Heights was a deliberate act to draw us up there while they invaded here."

"Or catch us between the two forces," Olivia said.

"Our own experience tells us the Sylannian commander won't stop. If you don't defeat her, what remains of the Kallith won't last long." Khaliun's lips compressed. "I will, of course, leave a handful of warriors to protect those that stay behind, but I intend to gather the bulk of the remaining warriors to fight under your banner."

"Are you sure you want to do this?" Michael gazed at her steadily. "I got the distinct impression you departed with your wolf warriors under strained circumstances. I know from our sharing of minds that there could be repercussions for you."

"I disregarded the other leaders and came to aid you without their consent. At worst, they can banish me. In which case, I'll plead for my wolves. They were just following my orders. Then it will be time to leave the People to tread their path while I take mine."

Pain flickered across Michael's face. "You and the wolves risked much to come to our aid. No matter what happens, in the Warlord's name, I pledge there will always be a home for you among my people," Michael said.

"The bulk of those I brought with me will remain with your

fighting forces and I'll take a small escort with me to fetch the rest," Khaliun said.

"We should head off for Vallantia within the week. I'll send a team of the Unwanted with you and they can guide you on the back roads from the Heights through to Vallantia," Michael said.

"It will save you a great deal of time on the road." Olivia pointed at the map and traced her finger across it, starting from the corner where the Kallith now called home. Then ran along the edge of the mountain range and then down to end up tapping on Vallantia.

"The wolf warriors can stay together as a unit when we travel, under whatever leadership you set up, but Nathanial will nominally keep an eye out for them until you rejoin us." Michael glanced across at Nathanial, who nodded in agreement.

"Thank you. I'll make arrangements and, with your permission, leave in the morning," Khaliun said.

"We'll have the members going with you assigned and ready to ride," Michael assured her. "Forgive me, but I can't come with you myself or spare my seconds."

"I would argue with you if you tried. You have enough to do. The three of you all do. I'll be fine with whoever you assign," Khaliun said.

Khaliun stood and nodded respectfully to Michael, Nathanial and Olivia, who led not only the Unwanted but all the Warlord's fighting forces. Knowing they had their plans to put into place, Khaliun retreated to the wolves. If they got most of their packing done tonight, they could leave tomorrow.

FOUR

His eyes tracked the water as it pooled at the very tip of the lock of hair that fell across his face. As enough gathered, it formed a droplet and plunged downwards towards the grey cobblestones. It exploded, splashing out in all directions, only to fall onto the cold stone and then merge into the growing pool at his knees. The sound ricocheted in his head, yet it was impossible.

A drop of water falling to the ground doesn't make that kind of noise.

Light flickered, diverting his attention from where he knelt and he swayed back, staring up into the gloomy skies. Some storms were the product of power being drawn rapidly through to the world they lived in, rather than the gradual bleed to and from where the energy resided. With this one, it was not the case. He wasn't even sure how he was aware of the difference but, a tiny part of his mind that was still capable of coherent thought did.

Real storm.

A ragged gasp tore itself from his lips as images flicked one after the other in his head. Along with an ever-persistent whispering voice, which he was powerless to block out. He couldn't distinguish if it was his internal monologue or if it came from a source external to him. The visions and words that plagued him were familiar. He'd seen and heard them before.

The body of a man. Motionless. On the floor.

He's dead.

An expanding pool like the one at his knees, but red.

Blood, his blood.

A knife, covered in blood, followed by eyes boring into his own.

Killer, murderer.

They had meaning; he knew they did, yet he was unable to grasp what the significance was or how they connected to him. He lifted his head to see the empty courtyard, ringed with cold stone walls which towered up around him. Everything was the same. There was no one else out here but him. It made sense.

Who'd be out in such weather?

The forbidding fortress that loomed above him hadn't disappeared either. Although a sluggish vibration through the bedrock spoke to him about when and how it had been fashioned. Yet it wasn't familiar to him at all. A vague disquiet settled onto him as it occurred to him that he should know more about why he was here than he did.

His shoulders, arms, and wrists ached from being pulled behind him. Bound so tightly, it was impossible to adjust his position to ease the pressure. He frowned, looking to one side at the chain that ran from him to the enormous pillar. There were four of them. Two at the front and two at the back, each anchoring a chain that shackled him in place. There was some play in the chains, but not enough that he could move to far from where he knelt. Sometimes the guards loosened them, which allowed him to lie down on the cobblestones. High on the pillars, there were metal rings embedded deep in the stone. A reddish-brown stain ran down from just below the binding points. It gave a testament to a past where people were strung up and left until they died. It caused him to wonder if eventually they would haul him up on the pillar and leave him to die. These pillars were ancient and stood in this place longer than the fortress. Pain made itself known, and he staggered to his feet. In this, his bindings helped him stand. He wondered if he was responsible for the dead man that kept reappearing in his mind. If that was why he was out here, chained and bound out in the elements. His head drooped to his chest again as he swayed. Instead, he stared at the ground and the slowly expanding pool.

A rhythmic clattering that echoed around the courtyard caused him to look up from his study of the water. Six uniformed and armed men approached him. Four of them peeled off, going to a pillar each. The guards at the pillars in front of him unclasped the wheels and turned them. He gasped in pain as the small amount of slack in the chain disappeared, holding him in place. The two remaining guards walked towards him. One of them grabbed his hair and jerked his head back. The second uncorked a bottle and poured the contents into his open mouth. He spluttered as the liquid filled his throat, and then he shuddered, muscles contracting. A sudden overpowering need for more hammered into him and he swallowed all that they gave him.

He screamed as pain lanced through him, his body trying to convulse in reaction, causing him to strain against the chains that bound him. He cried out in agony as the bindings that held him upright loosened and he slammed down onto the unforgiving ground, powerless to move as the drug took hold of him. A whimper escaped him as he lay trembling on the cold stones. There was a dark shape in the window of the top tower. He had the impression the person had been there on previous occasions and was observing him. Although he had no idea where the perception had come from. Just as he couldn't even determine how long he had been chained up out here. Or why. As quickly as the pain had hit him, it fled, only to be replaced by wave after wave of ecstasy. Yet it was no less incapacitating. Unable to resist the pull of the drug, his thoughts, what there had been of them, faded. He gave in and allowed whatever they had given him to take the world away. It was better than the misery of standing in the courtyard contemplating the water or what he might have done to earn such punishment.

WHEN HIS TORMENTORS unhooked his arm from behind his back, the agony was immediate. Shafts of pain shot through him. He curled up as he vomited, then pressed his forehead to the cool stones. He only had a brief reprieve before the wheels that controlled his bindings protested as the spikes drove into the links of the chains, pulling them taunt. The manacles bit into his wrists, forcing his arms apart and lifting him off the ground, leaving him suspended in mid-air. Metal screeched against metal and this time they pulled his legs out and down until every muscle in his body screamed in protest. Even muscles he didn't know existed.

He shuddered as the over-muscled guard, walked in front of him and he caught sight of the whip the torturer carried negligently in one hand. It had multiple strips of leather, each with clawed prongs at the end. He flinched as the flail cracked behind him, yet the expected pain to accompany it didn't come. A bark of harsh laughter sounded. Damien trembled, fear racing through him. He would have wilted in relief if the chains that held him suspended allowed such movement.

As it was, the only part of him that could move at all was his head. At a noise from above, he gazed up at the balcony that sat high on the tower. A familiar dark figure stood watching proceedings down below.

"You may begin!"

There was something about that voice that yelled that triggered his awareness. Idle thoughts about who the gloating person was fled from his mind as the crack sounded again. However this time, it was followed by agony. Pain seared in long lines across his back. The barbs bit into his flesh and tore through his skin as the torturer withdrew the whip. He barely had time to scream before the flail lashed his back again. It connected with his already raw back. As the man behind him continued his punishment, Damien begged for the flogging to stop. Blood pooled below him and intermingled with the water on the cobblestones. He was gasping for air, tears tracking down his face as the whipping paused. Uncontrollable shudders shook him as booted feet approached him.

"Some salt, to make sure this hurts as much as it should," his torturer said.

Fetid breath caused him to gag as the torturer breathed near his ear. Then he forgot everything. He screamed once more as the salt was ground onto his back. When his tormentor stepped away, Damien tried to struggle as the whip whistled towards him. The flail cracked, with its barbs tearing into his skin. Damien lost count of how many times the claws ripped into him before the voice above called a halt.

A hand curled in Damien's hair and his head was yanked back. They put a flask to his lips, and liquid spilled into his mouth and ran down his face and chest. His mind registered it was tiscan as he swallowed, gasping for breath in between as they poured more of the poison into him. The pain from the drug hit him as it raced through his body. When the oblivion dragged him down, instead of riding a wave of ecstasy, it was pure agony that burnt through him like fire. It was the double-edged sword of tiscan. One he hadn't realised until recently. The oblivion his body craved could lead to pain just as easily as pleasure. Held in the drug's grip, there was no escape from the torment that roared through his mind.

Isabella curled into a ball on the cold stone floor of her cell, the thin fabric of her gown offering little protection. Alternate waves of nausea and uncontrollable shivering wracked her body. A deep sense of wrongness hung over her, which she couldn't shake. She shuddered as she attempted to reach her brother's mind, only to find herself stuck in her head. It was a circumstance she'd never encountered before. She'd been able to hear and mindspeak others as far back as she could remember. At the rhythmic thud of boots coming closer, then the rattle of keys, Isabella trembled. She had no way of telling how long they'd isolated her down here in the dark prison, but she was aware of what happened when they came here. They'd force her to drink more of the drug.

It was a constant.

Along with pain and fear. It wasn't good for her. Damien had warned her to stay away from the stuff. When she'd started having some violent turns like Damien, and her parents tried to give her tiscan, she'd refused. Yet now, the guards forced it on her. After that first brief spike of agony with the drug racing through her, it was nausea and wrongness that hit. One thing she could be grateful for in this whole mess was unlike Damien, she didn't crave tiscan. While the stuff prevented her from using the veil, that was all it did.

Isabella gasped as a hand grabbed her arm and hauled her to her feet. Instead of giving her the drug like normal, the guards dragged her out of her cell. Neither of the guards spoke to her as they took her with them down the hallway. She lost track of the corridors and doors they went through, but the stairs and subtle increase in the temperature gave her the distinct impression they were heading up. Even the air was fresher. The earthy, damp smell, mixed with the scent of unwashed bodies in the cells, dropped away. She winced as light from some barred windows hit her face, and then she found herself shoved into a well-lit larger room with a couple of stern-looking older women.

"Get her cleaned up and presentable, Ella. The warlord wants her," the guard said.

Isabella slumped to the floor as the guards let go of her and withdrew from the room. She scrambled away as hands reached for her. Ella's meaty hand struck her across the face and Isabella cried out, curling up into herself.

"That'll be enough out of you, girl. Cait and I will have you cleaned up and looking respectable in no time," Ella said.

Tears gathered in Isabella's eyes as the woman stripped her down, discarding the clothing she'd been wearing into a wicker basket in the corner of the room. Cait picked up a wooden bucket and tipped the contents over her. Isabella gasped as the icy water hit her skin and drenched her. She struggled weakly as they scrubbed her with rough sponges, only to have Ella strike her again.

"Enough or I'll order you flogged," Ella hissed

Isabella bit her lip and tried to hold back the tears as the women handled her, alternately scrubbing her and dousing her with cold water. At first, the water that ran off her was black, tainted with the filth they cleaned off her. Then, when it was clear, Isabella smelled the subtle scent of flowers as they switched to a fresh soap.

Ella dried her off with a rough towel and pulled clean clothes onto her. The objection died in her throat as Ella raised her hand. The dress, if it could be called that, left most of her flesh exposed. It plunged at the front. Ella's hand cupped her breasts, pulling them into position as Cait did up the overly tight bodice. It pushed her breasts up even further, not leaving much to the imagination. She swayed a little as she looked down and saw the skirt of the gown they'd put her in had a split up the front. While it covered her, she could see the fabric was see-through and clung to her lower body. It wouldn't take much for anyone to push the flimsy fabric aside and expose her. Ella's hand raised her chin and cruel eyes stared into her own.

"The bodice puts those assets of yours on display and our warlord does like a well-endowed woman. The split in the skirt makes it much quicker and easier should he desire to bed you in a hurry," Ella said as if they were discussing what to have for dinner. "Don't worry though, the warlord will get it off you quickly enough if he wants to. He just has to pull a simple tie at the back, which will cause the whole dress to pool at your feet."

"Can't I just wear a simple skirt and blouse?" Isabella asked.

"The warlord had us make this especially, just for you. It's the type of dress the girls wear in the pleasure houses."

"Please don't do this,"

"If the warlord likes what he sees and you lay back and spread those shapely legs of yours for him, you might just get to keep breathing," Cait said.

"I... don't want to have sex with Aiden." Isabella said, tears rolling down her cheeks as she pleaded with the woman.

"You don't have a choice. Give him what he wants and as

soon as you prove you're trustworthy, your life will improve. Instead of a cell, you'll sleep in the bed slave stable when he's done with you. You'll be housed and fed, all for simply laying on your back."

"But—"

"You don't get to decide anything for yourself anymore. You are the warlord's sex slave. I warrant he'll slap a slave collar around that pretty neck of yours as soon as the smith has finished making them. It's up to you how bad the experience will be."

Isabella started trembling again, although she couldn't tell if it was fear or a reaction from the drug they'd been giving her. Cait dragged a comb through her hair, untangling the mess it had become. They held her hair back with a simple clip. Then they placed a cloak over her shoulders, which wrapped around her and hid her body from view as the dress did not. She looked up at them and Ella smiled.

"Your body belongs to the warlord girl. You're on display for your master, not for the guards to gawk at," Ella said.

After one more inspection, Ella opened the doors and called the guards. The guards entered the room and stared at her for a moment. Isabella froze. The guard was one of the few she recognised. It was Tony. He had been the band leader of one of the Warlord's personal warbands.

"Come on girl, the warlord is calling for you," Tony said.

Isabella swallowed and stepped out into the corridor. She sniffed and wiped her cheeks with the back of her hand. The guards surrounding her weren't the same as the ones who'd brought her up from the cells. They didn't lay a hand on her, but there was nowhere for her to run. She didn't even want to know what they'd do to her if she tried. As they directed her up some stairs, she stumbled when she realised these led to what had been the Warlord's private rooms. Tony reached out and steadied her, his hand withdrawing as she straightened.

The guards on the doors opened them as she approached and all but the one guard dropped off as she entered the suite.

Isabella shivered and tried to shrink back as Tony led her into the room towards the man who stood at the window, looking down at something below.

"Easy girl. Don't give him an excuse to hurt you more than he's going to."

The advice Tony whispered to her made sense, even if it wasn't reassuring and certainly no help in calming her fear. If anything, it heightened them. As Aiden turned to look at her and smiled, her breath stuck in her throat. She understood what he wanted. His desire crawled over her skin, making her feel unclean. Aiden reached out and his hand clamped around her arm, pulling her towards him, his fingers biting into her flesh.

"You're dismissed, captain," Aiden said, reeking of anticipation. "Wait, Damien can't have come here alone and the Unwanted stay outside of villages. Send out some patrols to search the likely campsites around Yalleska. I want that patrol found and taken into custody."

Isabella half turned her head to look as Tony hesitated briefly before acknowledging Aiden's order before he left the room. As the door closed quietly behind Tony, Aiden fixed her with a predatory gaze.

"Please, just let me go," Isabella said.

She flinched as Aiden's hand rose and brushed some of her hair back, then his fingers trailed down the side of her face. Isabella trembled as he undid the clasp on the cloak she wore and took it from her shoulders. He walked across the room to place it on a hook before he came back to her, a possessive glint in his eyes.

"You're built for such attire." Aiden licked his lips as his gaze seemed to devour her. "I have no intentions of letting you go anywhere and you'll learn to enjoy my company."

"No, Aiden please, I don't want this."

"I'm confident you'll change your mind. Come, I have a demonstration for you."

Aiden dragged her with him out onto a small balcony that she hadn't known was there. She shivered as they stepped outside, but it had nothing to do with the chill in the air and everything to do with this man who had hold of her.

"You may begin!" Aiden said.

Isabella jumped as he bellowed his order and followed his avid gaze down into the courtyard below. She gasped and went to step forward to the balcony rail, only for Aiden to pull her back against his body. She tried to ignore the feel of him as he pressed against her. Instead, she kept her eyes on the figure below. It was Damien. Her brother was bound by chains, his arms extended out and up, held in place between two pillars.

Her horror grew as she noticed they'd stripped him of his leathers and a man was standing behind him with a whip.

"Please, no," Isabella whispered.

"They designed it specially with metal barbs to rip through his skin, draw blood and cause as much pain as possible."

The figure below swung the whip, multiple strips of leather striking across Damien's back. The slap of the leather on his back seemed to echo around the otherwise empty courtyard mingled with Damien's scream of agony. She turned her head to one side, squeezing her eyes shut as the whip swung again and again. She shuddered as she felt Aiden grow hard. His pleasure, which he made no attempt to hide, was caused by a combination of Damien being flogged down in the courtyard and having her in his arms.

"You know it's one of the great things about tiscan. It amplifies both pleasure and pain."

"Why are you doing this? You know he didn't kill your father." Isabella pleaded.

"Unfortunately, he knows that as well as you do."

"I won't say anything, I promise. Please, just stop. Let us go and we'll travel far from here."

"Now, why would I do that?"

"Please, I'll do anything."

"You'll not leave this place any more than your brother will, but it is within your power to have his punishment stopped sweet Isa."

"Anything."

"You'll warm my bed willingly. Anytime you give me any defiance at all, I won't punish you, but I will punish Damien," Aiden said.

As he spoke, one of his hands rose and he pushed the flimsy fabric of the bodice aside, exposing her chest. Aiden's hand massaged her exposed breast. His breath became ragged as he did so. She gasped, tears tracking down her face.

"I'll have sex with you. As often as you like, just stop whipping Damien."

He chuckled, the sound coming from deep in his throat. Aiden's arms held her up as her legs faltered and she collapsed against him. As much as she'd wanted to pretend she wasn't concerned about his desire to have sex with her, she trembled against him. His lust thrummed through her, causing her fear to spike. If anything, her response seemed to inflame him more. She'd never been with a man and despite her parents talking to her about sex, it had remained a theory.

"You'll call me master."

"Master," Isabella whispered.

His breath was ragged, and she closed her eyes as his hands stroked her. She bit her lip, trembling, knowing he was testing her resolve. Aiden yelled at those below to stop. That the punishment was sufficient for today. Just as she'd promised, Isabella offered no resistance as he dragged her into his rooms, but she couldn't stop the tears as he pulled at the tie on the back of her dress. Just as Ella promised, it fell to the floor. The flimsy fabric pooled around her feet, exposing her to her master's hungry eyes, hands, and mouth as he pressed her back onto the bed.

SIX

Callan stood up on the roof of the establishment they'd found to stay in while waiting for Damien. It afforded a good view of the forbidding fortress that loomed over the town of Yalleska. The dark clouds that hung over it made it seem even more ominous. That the gates had shut with the only movements being some patrols riding out of town with no one else being allowed to come or go, didn't help the impression either.

"Anything?" Shallan asked.

"No. What is going on in there?" Callan held up his hand to forestall the response.

His squad mates had no more idea than he did since they were all in the same boat. The entire team had spent an unexpectedly comfortable night here in the inn rather than in the Stronghold's barracks. First up this morning, he didn't think too much of it. They'd just been waiting around for Damien. Then some of the team members who'd gone to check out the local markets returned with the news that the Stronghold was locked down. No one knew why. Callan only became concerned when he couldn't contact Damien.

"I've got a bad feeling about this. I think we should get inside and be as inconspicuous as possible," Gavrel said.

Callan nodded. "Agreed. I'm going to have to report to Michael. I just wish I had more to tell him. If anyone's still out in the town, recall them. No one is to go anywhere until further notice."

"I'll check, but I believe everyone is here already," Gavrel said.

Callan returned to the stairs and made his way inside to his room.

Michael? Callan called. Much to his relief, he didn't have long to wait before the warleader replied.

Callan? What do you need?

I wish I could answer that, but I have no idea except there's a problem here in Yalleska.

What's the trouble? Where's Damien?

He's still in the Stronghold. Damien remained to report to the Warlord and planned to bed down in the barracks afterwards. He gave the team the night off and told us to stay in town. Callan held his breath, waiting for the response.

You should have stayed with him, but the Warlord would hardly allow Damien to use. Consider yourself scolded. So what's the problem?

The Stronghold has locked its gates. No one has come in or out. Rumours are flying all over Yalleska, but nobody seems to know what's going on. Callan paused. It was a relief to be unloading on Michael, even if he had little to share except a growing sense of dread. *I can't reach Damien, he's just not responding. I'm sorry. If I'd insisted on at least one person staying with him, somebody would be on the inside and I'd be able to tell you what's happening.*

Someone is inside the Stronghold, Damien. Stay put. I'll get back to you.

Callan breathed a sigh of relief as Michael's presence faded. All things considered, that report went much better than he'd expected.

~

Olivia tightened the girth strap on her horse one more notch, only to stop as Michael groaned with obvious frustration.

"What the powers is Aiden up to?" Michael said.

Olivia suppressed the urge to groan herself. It wasn't like Aiden's orders were difficult. Escort the Warlord to the Stronghold at Yalleska and keep him there while he recovers. However, this was Aiden, so the possibilities of messing up were endless.

"Without more information, that's impossible for me to even guess," Nathanial said.

"The last thing we need is trouble from Aiden. What's happened?" Olivia saw Michael was reining in his aggravation.

"Callan just reported the Stronghold's gates are sealed, with no explanation and no contact with anyone inside, including Damien," Michael said.

"Callan and the team were meant to be with Damien," Olivia said.

Not that she didn't trust Callan's word, or realise that Michael had already tried to contact Damien himself and failed, but she turned her awareness towards Damien, threading her call with his signature.

Damien? Where are you? Olivia called out to Damien in a tight thread, just for him alone. Her eyes flashed to Michael with a hint of concern when Damien didn't respond.

"I can't reach him either. That's not like him..."

"Let's not panic. There are several reasons for Damien being out of communication, being unconscious being one of them,"

Michael said, even though Olivia could hear he was struggling to convince himself of that fact.

"Should we divert to Yalleska?" Nathanial asked. "We've already sent the other warbands on ahead. It's probably something stupid, but for our peace of mind, it might be better to sort out whatever is wrong now."

"We don't need to decide straight away. From here, if we take the upper mountain road, the first part is the same regardless if we are going to Vallantia or Yalleska. Callan can monitor things and call us off if we're not needed," Olivia said.

Michael ran his fingers through his hair, then finally nodded. "I could force contact with Father or Aiden, even from here, but—"

"Father is still recovering, so it's the last thing he needs and it would knock Aiden out for a week. While that might seem appealing if there is an issue they are dealing with at the Stronghold, it's probably not the best option," Olivia said.

"The other band leaders are trustworthy, even if I automatically jump to the conclusion that Aiden is up to something," Nathanial said.

Michael sighed, his aggravation clear. "You're right. Let's get on the road. It's not as if I can do much from here."

Olivia called orders to the rest of the warband around them, who hastened their preparations to leave. She kept a tight rein on the anxiety that formed like a knot in her stomach. While she wanted to believe it was nothing, just a silly little circumstance, none of the reasons she came up with for the Stronghold locking down and cutting communication was silly or small.

CHAPTER
SEVEN

Tony stood a short distance from the other guards outside Aiden's rooms, waiting for the new warlord's pleasure. As a band leader, this was a duty he could have asked one of his team to perform, but more than a sense of duty compelled him to stay here and do this task himself. The two guards on the door had shuffled a half step forward from the normal position but otherwise stood their duty blank-faced. Given Tony could hear the muffled sounds from the other side of the door from where he stood, that half step would make no difference. Aiden wasn't holding back in taking his gratification from the girl, and from her cries, it wasn't an experience she was enjoying.

"Problems Tony?" Derick asked.

Tony cleared his expression, mentally kicking himself that he hadn't noticed the other man's approach.

"Not at all, just waiting for Aiden to finish with the prisoner."

"Surely you don't need to perform this duty yourself?" Derick studied him.

"After the Warlord's death, I'd rather not take chances." Tony

33

hoped the other man believed his excuse. "I'm certain we'd all prefer Aiden didn't put himself in such a position."

"The girl is being kept under control, just like her brother." Derick shrugged and then looked towards the door, a hard smile stretching his lips as the girl's half-pained moan sounded. "Besides, I'm sure she'll learn her place soon enough."

Tony clamped his mouth shut as it became clear the girl's cries had driven Aiden to increase his efforts. He struggled with himself, remaining in position as the other leader walked off. It was hard to appear unconcerned rather than leap on Derick and pound on the man. Or, even better, wrench the door open and prevent Aiden from hurting the girl further.

Yet even if he took steps and tried to stop Aiden, it wouldn't do any good. Aiden didn't have the warleader's abilities but, their new warlord was much stronger than he was. If he interfered and lived beyond such action, he'd probably end up chained in the courtyard below next to Damien, without changing the girl's circumstances. All he could do right now was stand here and ensure the girl made it safely back to the cells when Aiden was done with her. An opportunity would come for him to do some good. He just had to wait for it and hope that neither of Aiden's captives broke before that happened.

TONY TURNED RESTLESSLY on his cot as sleep evaded him. The days of being able to blame sleepless nights on sleeping in a barracks filled with the members of his warband were long behind him. As a leader of a warband, one who'd been the leader of one of those who stood duty on the Warlord himself, he at least had a small room to himself. So it wasn't the inevitable noise of communal living and people coming and going from the barracks at all different times that bothered him. Tony sighed, staring blankly up at the ceiling. If it wasn't Isabella's muffled voice, filled with pain and despair haunting his sleep, or the plight of her brother, it was his brain on repeat going over and over the Warlord's death. A deep sense of failure settled on him. It was reasonable to tell himself that the Warlord's death wasn't his failure. He wasn't present in the room when the blow that killed the Warlord was struck. Just as he hadn't been there when the Warlord was injured in the battle at Callenhain. Still, he couldn't help but feel he'd failed.

Everything happened so fast, there'd been screaming from the Warlord's rooms, and he'd spun and started running back up the stairs and down the hallway towards the Warlord's suite. When he'd burst through the doors, the Warlord was lying motionless on the ground, a pool of blood spreading on the floor. Aiden was grappling with Damien. Then Aiden thrust a bloody dagger into his hand. Aiden yelled that Damien had gone berserk and killed the Warlord, because of his sister's presence in his father's rooms.

It seemed plausible. The tale of Damien killing the baker in his village because he posed a threat to his sister had reached his ears. Yet the band leaders who'd been present told him that the Warlord himself manipulated Damien, and goaded him into the kill. From his experience, if the Warlord wanted you to kill someone, you did it. Unless you wanted to join that person in death. The only individual he was aware of who'd ever gotten away with defying the Warlord's will and survived was the warleader.

Now that he was thinking back over the event, he remembered the girl Isabella protesting, looking towards them, panicked, saying it wasn't Damien. Then Aiden struck the girl with a brutal backhand blow, effectively silencing her, and then ordered her into the cells. Supposedly, Isabella's detainment would last until they learnt what role she'd played in the Warlord's death. There'd been more blood on Aiden than

Damien. The observation meant nothing at the time because it was logical that Aiden got blood on himself. He'd gone to his father's defence and wrestled the knife off Damien.

Damien was insensible and unable to resist the restraint Tony and his fellow guards had used on him. Now that he thought about it. Damien's eyes were glazed. Even before they'd poured the drug, Aiden had given them down his throat. A flask that had come from Aiden's belt pouch. Almost as if Aiden was prepared before going into the room. Knowing he'd need the drug the flask contained. It wasn't as if any of them commonly carried flasks of fortified tiscan brew with them. Aiden possessed numerous faults. Some dark ones. At least if the whispered rumours that ran from warband to warband were to be believed. To Tony's knowledge tiscan addict wasn't one of Aiden's faults. He also couldn't see, given Damien's confused state of mind, how he could have taken the Warlord down. Even in a surprise, sudden attack. Yet moments before, there was no sign of confusion or anger in Damien as they talked while he led him through the halls of the Stronghold. Tony was certain he would have noticed if Damien appeared dazed or under the influence of anything. Then they'd encountered Aiden, who'd dismissed him, saying he'd show Damien the way to his father's rooms. He remembered thinking that was odd. Aiden wasn't known to take on menial tasks for anyone.

He rolled over onto his side and sent a small burst of power to the light stone on the bedside table. It cast a pool of muted light into the room. He frowned, knowing he'd have to take it down to be swapped for a freshly charged one in the morning. The wooden frame of the cot creaked as he sat up, pushing the blanket aside. Despite knowing he was alone in his room, he checked the door was still firmly closed. He stood and walked over and opened the drawer where he'd stuffed Damien's weapons. He should have turned them in at the weapons room.

Instead, he'd brought them to his room and stuffed them in the drawer.

Tony winced at the sight of the blood-encrusted dagger that had been used to kill the Warlord. Any junior guard who'd left a weapon in such a condition would have found themselves on punishment detail for failing to care for their weapon. He picked it up, then turned it over in his hand as he examined it before placing it on top of the cupboard. A uniform and weapon belt remained in the drawer. He'd taken possession of both after taking Damien to the punishment courtyard. Tony frowned. While the sword rested in the weapons rack, the dagger remained in its sheath. Tony grasped the handle of the dagger and drew the weapon. He turned it over, running his thumb over the stylised etchings on the blade. He recognised the crest.

A sword plunging into a flame. The warleader's crest.

It had been a bone of contention between Aiden and his father that Michael was awarded a crest, but Aiden wasn't. On each occasion, the Warlord replied that Michael earned the honour before his tone would turn scathing as he noted Aiden hadn't. Every member of the Unwanted wore the crest. This was undoubtedly Damien's dagger, unmarred by blood. He picked up the bloody dagger and inspected it once more. It was a well-made blade. There was a weapons room in the Stronghold filled with blades just like this one. The Smith and his apprentices crafted each of the blades. Tony even bore a dagger just like this one in the sheath on his belt. They were suitable for any who rode in the Warlord's warbands. Except for a member of the Unwanted. It was a plain blade without the warleader's crest. Their clothing, saddles and blades all bore the crest. All the warleader's people bore it. While the crest on the uniforms of the Unwanted stood out, it made Tony wonder if Aiden ever realised it was etched into the blades as well. It stood out, particularly when the Unwanted fought, but if he could get away with it,

Aiden had a habit of riding to the rear of any fight that occurred. Tony had ridden into combat with such men. In their panic, their vision would narrow until they were almost blinded by anything else around them.

Tony closed his eyes as he realised perhaps Isabella had been correct. Damien wasn't responsible for the death of the Warlord. He had a hard time believing it could have been the girl. So, if this was true, there was only one other person it could have been. One other person was in the room at the time of the Warlord's death. The Warlord's son. Tony's lips compressed into a thin line.

Aiden had killed his father and proclaimed himself the warlord, all while setting up Damien to take the fall for the Warlord's death.

EIGHT

Steven wasn't sure where to look as the enemy surrounded him, divested him of his weapons and prodded him forward towards the long lounge. Even though he tried not to, his gaze kept sliding over to the dead Sylannians on the floor. He couldn't conceive of the possibility that either of his parents was capable of killing any of the invaders of their home. Yet there was the evidence right there on the floor that was hard to deny. There was no one else in the room who could have done so. Not even a servant was present. In short order, Evan was bundled up and unceremoniously shoved onto the next couch.

"Don't worry, Commander Jaclyn won't hurt you," his mother said. "You're far too valuable to her."

The woman whom Steven gathered was Commander Jaclyn spoke to his mother in Sylannian. As his mother replied to the commander, Steven's mouth fell open as the pair engaged in a rapid-fire conversation in Sylannian. He traded glances with Evan and saw his friend appeared as shocked as he felt.

Steven leant closer to his father, who sat passively nearby. "Did you know mother could speak Sylannian?"

"Of course. It's the language of her birth," his father said.

"The language of her... wait, mother's Sylannian?" Steven was struggling to work out if he was intrigued or horrified.

"That's generally what it means, yes," his father said.

"What did mother mean when she said I'm valuable to the Commander?"

"Through me, you have not only Sylannian blood, but the blood of the Monarch House runs through your veins."

"Monarch House? Does that mean what I assume it does?"

"If you think it means your claim for the Throne of a Thousand Islands is just as valid as the current king or Jaclyn's. Then yes."

"Throne?" Steven asked.

"You never told me you were related to a king," Evan whispered.

"If I'd been aware of that little fact, I would have." Steven hissed back, although he wasn't sure why he bothered to keep his voice low. Surrounded as he was, everyone here would have heard him. Then he stared at the Sylannian Commander in her maroon and cream armour. "We're related?"

"Jaclyn is your cousin. Now hush, I'm negotiating with her to keep you safe."

"You seem terribly confident that I'll accept your proposal," Jaclyn said.

"Ah, you speak our language as well. Well done," Steven said, then clamped his mouth shut in an attempt to stop his nervous babbling.

As Jaclyn's eyes swept over him, Steven shifted in his seat. If it hadn't been for the dagger-wielding women surrounding him, Steven would have unashamedly bolted from the room. He breathed a sigh of relief when Jaclyn's gaze moved on to regard Evan.

"What about that one?"

Lady Rathadon sniffed. "He's nobody."

"Detain the nobody wherever you are holding the other prisoners. As for this so-called cousin of mine, search his rooms thoroughly and keep him there for now." Commander Jaclyn turned back to Steven's mother. "I'll deal with you and your claims later."

Steven flinched as two of the invaders grabbed him by the arms and hauled him upright. He twisted to see Evan being dragged from his seat as well. As he was escorted into the hallway, he was taken up the stairs while those with Evan disappeared around the corner, out of his sight.

THE DOOR to Steven's bedroom shut with a solid thunk with a sense of finality. Steven bit his lip as he contemplated the door. Unlike his brother, he could only concentrate on one thing at a time. Right now, that thing was holding onto his mental shield as if his life depended on it. It was unfortunate that he had the sinking feeling it might. He stood and walked to the door and eased it open just enough to peer out into the hallway. His vision filled with maroon and cream, then a dagger being withdrawn from a sheath and sharp words he didn't understand, he slipped back.

"My mistake, I'll stay put, shall I?" Steven said, his empty hands raised in front of him.

The door slammed, cutting off his vision of the Sylannians guarding his doorway. Steven went to his chair and slumped into its cushions.

Evan? Are you alright? Steven called out. He swallowed as the silence stretched.

I'm fine, Evan said.

Steven let out a breath he hadn't been aware he was holding. *Where are you?*

They've put me in the cells below your estate. What have they done to you?

They put me back in my suite. However, unlike when the Kastlers were in control, now I have guards at my door.

Ah, so it's not like you can run and fetch help.

I can't believe no one ever told me that my mother is a Sylannian.

That was a little surprising.

Steven crossed to the window and pulled the curtains open, allowing the morning light to stream into the sitting room. It was shocking. With the events that had transpired, he'd expected somehow that it would be close to sunset or even late in the evening. Yet at most, only a few hours had passed.

What do you think Mother was negotiating with the commander? Steven asked.

I don't know, but whatever it was, the way the Sylannian kept looking at you, I have a bad feeling you're not going to like it.

I was hoping you wouldn't say that. Unfortunately, it's the only conclusion I could come up with as well.

This should brighten up your day a little.

What?

Constance and Peter Kastler are in the cell across from me.

I guess no one told the Sylannians they were allies. Steven chuckled.

Evan was correct. That detail made the day seem a little brighter. Although not by much. A worry that he was the bargaining chip his mother used with the Sylannian Commander was nagging at him. She was his mother, but he still didn't trust her.

They're desperately trying to explain that to the Sylannians. So far, our captors are ignoring them.

Steven took in the evidence of the sheer number of the enemy lining the battlements and massed in the courtyard below.

There are so many of them, nearly a hundred on the walls and in the courtyard.

What about Vallantia? Can you see smoke or anything?

Steven focused in the distance over the canopy of the intervening forest towards Vallantia. Sure enough, smoke billowed from several points in the city.

There are signs of fire, but I would have expected to see more.

I doubt the Kastler mercenaries put up much of a fight.

How do you think they got into the city so quickly? I mean, the gates are usually barred at night.

It can't be too difficult. After all, the Kastlers got in.

Well, yes, but the mercenaries probably just rode into Vallantia during the day or something. How would the Sylannians manage it? I mean, they stand out. Surely someone would have noticed.

Who knows? Maybe you can ask your mother how they managed it. No offence, but she seemed to be on talking terms with them. Or your cousin when you see her next.

Very funny. Steven's stomach rumbled, reminding him he hadn't had his breakfast yet.

Somehow, he didn't think it was a remarkably good idea to open the door again and ask for food to be delivered. At a loss with how he should occupy his time, Steven turned around and searched the outer chamber then snorted at his stupidity. It wasn't like a task was going to appear out of nowhere. Then he caught sight of the stack of reports sitting on his desk in the far corner. His father had servants deliver them to his suite regularly. He'd just never read them. It was a little embarrassing how high the pile was. There was a slant, and he fancied the stack would topple over if any more were added. Most of the reports dealt with routine issues impacting Vallantia and the villages in their district. They'd sounded tedious to Steven, so he'd ignored them. Then there was the other pile. It wasn't as tall as the first, but only because the servants split it in two. Those had been a recent addition to his collection of unread documents. They were about his brother's exploits. Apparently, the records stretched back to when the Warlord claimed Michael's life. Steven had no idea how his parents had sourced the information or how accurate it might be. Needless to say, he'd had no interest in reading those reports either. Steven sighed and picked up the first handful of records from the top of the pile. He looked at the dates and was surprised to see the scribe had thoughtfully placed them in chronological order. Steven flipped open the first page and read the concise words that described Michael's first battle after leaving the family estate. As he eased into a high-backed leather chair and found himself drawn into the account, Steven's troubles slipped away.

NINE

Owen armed himself without even having to think about it. The whole process had become second nature as he slipped back into old patterns from his youth when he'd served as a guard in the employ of the Strafford warlord. It was a life he never believed he'd return to. As his teammates slept around him, Owen picked up his gloves from the chest that sat beside his sleeping cot. He had no loyalty to any of the men and women in the barracks. These weren't his people. Some of them were the type that should have been killed a long time ago. Only the threat of their band leader, Derick kept any of them in line and Derick was Aiden's man. He walked out, careful to make it look casual. Not that anyone paid any attention to him as long as he showed up at his duty shifts. He got the distinct impression Derick had placed him here to keep him occupied and then promptly forgotten about him entirely.

Owen strode down the ancient stone corridor. The Stronghold was from the era of the Smith Lords, with so many passages it was easy to get lost, but he'd trod this path several times before. He'd done this trip enough that he knew the way to the vantage point he was looking for. Life here in the Stronghold had gone from bad to worse since the death of the Warlord. The rumours whispered in the fortress seemed unbelievable, yet he couldn't discount them completely. That the Warlord was dead was an inescapable truth. Unfortunately, he believed Damien would kill to protect his sister. The wrinkle of that proposition is Damien was too smart to be drawn into attacking the Warlord. Damien would have known that going berserk and killing the Warlord in the middle of his Stronghold wouldn't free Isabella but doom them both.

With one glance over his shoulder, Owen took the stairs of the corner tower two at a time. He kept his pace up as he wound his way up to the vantage point at the top. Out of breath, he pushed the door open and walked out onto the turret. He'd found this place early in his exploration of the fortress. It had incredible views over the mountains, forest and the village that sat in the shadow below the fortress, but that wasn't why he'd come here. He walked over to the far side and looked across the Stronghold to see the other tower opposite where he stood. It housed the Warlord's rooms, now Aiden's. If the rumours that the new Warlord had taken her as his bed slave were true, it was also where Isabella spent her nights.

Isabella, please answer me. Where are you? Owen called.

He frowned as he listened, stretching his mind out to its limits, then finally slumped. She never responded. Not on any of the times he'd tried to call out to her. It made him afraid for Isabella because if she was capable of responding, she would have done so. He kept hoping that the whispers he'd heard about her current state weren't true. Below the tower where he feared Isabella spent her nights, Damien was naked, drugged and chained. This time, Damien was lying on the ground. On other occasions, Damien had been effectively suspended between the giant stone pillars that, combined with the chains, held him in several equally painful positions.

Even though there was a fair distance between where he stood and where Damien lay, he could see the bloody rents in Damien's back from repeated floggings. Other guards joked they dropped Damien to the hard stones between the posts, so after that bit of relief, when they suspended him again, it would hurt all the more. Owen gritted his teeth as some guards strutted across the courtyard. He'd had the misfortune to witness the various inventive torture techniques they inflicted on Damien. It had become a daily sport for these men. He squeezed his eyes shut, powerless to help as Damien cried out in pain as the guards tormented him.

Unable to bear it anymore and feeling like a coward, Owen withdrew back into the tower, closing the door, which at least muffled the cries. Owen rested his head against the stone wall and stared at the roof for a moment, wishing there was something, anything, he could do to help.

"I'm sorry Damien, if I could think of a way to get you out of this, I would do it."

Owen pushed off the wall and went down the stairs, wondering why he kept inflicting this journey on himself. Other than the fact, it reassured him that Damien was still alive. Even though Damien begged his captors to kill him on more than one occasion, Owen was glad that the wish hadn't been fulfilled.

TEN

A iden rolled off Isabella, luxuriating in having the freedom to indulge his desires. The slight movement as she rolled over onto her side and curled into a ball caught his eye. He considered pulling her back into his arms to teach her that even pulling away from him without his permission wasn't allowed. Aiden sighed. Just this once, he could give her some slack. Isabella was young and inexperienced but already learning her role. That he was the only man she'd been with, that she would ever be with now, proved to be an astonishing pleasure. Her spurts of fear and pain had made taking her to his bed, particularly her very first time, even more intoxicating. It had also been an unexpected thrill to oversee Damien's flogging.

Aiden decided all around he'd had a remarkably good day, not only when he'd taken Isabella to his bed for the first time, but the days since. He wondered how much better it would be to torture Damien with his own hands. Aiden smiled lazily. He'd never dared indulge in his fantasies when his father had been alive, but now that he was in control, he was free to experiment.

Aiden climbed off the bed and grabbed his robe, pulling it on as he walked to the sideboard where a row of vials that contained the tiscan that kept Isabella's abilities with the veil in check sat. They were lined up in order, the dosage increasing and becoming stronger with each subsequent day. He picked up the smallest of the vials, although the healer assured him it was twice as strong as her previous dose. As he removed the stopper, he sniffed the stuff, noting the earthy undertones. He'd tried it a few times when he'd been younger, but unfortunately, he never could work out what all the fuss had been about. Still, he couldn't deny the effectiveness of it on people like Damien. The healers advised him even if Isabella didn't succumb to full addiction, the daily dosage would keep her talents in check. He walked back to the bed and sat down on the edge.

"Sit up Isabella," Aiden said.

He lay a hand on her shoulder, noticing the tremors that spasmodically ran through her. Aiden realised with satisfaction that her shivering was her body's response to her tiscan levels becoming low. There was a certain extra level of thrill for him with her being aware while she was in his bed, which is why he'd withheld her dose until he was finished with her. Aiden put the vial of tiscan on the small side table and pulled her upright. She whimpered, but otherwise did nothing but tremble in his arms.

"Please Aiden..."

"What do you call me?" Aiden turned her face up, so she was staring into his eyes.

"Master, please, it makes me feel sick..."

"Ah my sweet Isa. Until you learn to fully accept your place in life, the tiscan helps to control you. It's been too long since your last dose. It's why you can't stop trembling." Aiden grabbed the vial from the side table. "Open your mouth or I'll call the guards to come in, restrain you, and pour it in."

A tear traced down her cheek, her lips trembling as she

complied and opened her mouth. He brought the vial to her lips and tipped it. She grimaced, but swallowed it all. Satisfied, he tipped the whole vial into her mouth, watching carefully as she drank the full dose. He eased her back down to the mattress, putting the empty vial to one side. His eyes narrowed as her back arched and her face screwed up, a gasp of pain coming from her. It was a pity she wasn't like Damien. The healers advised him they didn't think it was likely she'd ever sink into oblivion. He was told they needed to raise her dosage levels carefully, so she didn't overdose. As her body relaxed back into the bed, he leant forward and kissed her on the temple.

Don't worry, soon, once you accept you belong to me, there will be no need to keep you detained in the cells. Aiden whispered to her.

He smiled as her eyes barely flickered in response, although he had no doubt she'd heard him. Aiden yelled for an attendant. As he expected, it didn't take long before the doors to his rooms opened and Ella and Cait, the two of the older women he'd selected to ensure Isabella was presentable before she was brought to his bed, entered.

"Warlord?" Ella said.

"Make sure she's covered up. I'll not have others leering at her. She belongs to me," Aiden said.

"Perfectly understandable warlord," Ella said.

Aiden caressed Isabella's shoulder, then stood and walked over to the balcony and let himself out, looking down at the pitiful huddled figure of Damien below.

You've failed. Your sister is mine, Aiden taunted.

At a throat clearing behind him, he turned to see Ella had pulled a loose linen shift over the girl and backed off from the bed. Isabella stared up at the ceiling above her, moaning softly as Cait brushed a stray lock of her hair to the side of her face.

"You did a remarkable job of presenting my bed slave. You're both excused from any other duties. As my bed slave's handler, you'll have full control of her and my new acquisitions when they arrive, as soon as the bed slave stable is refurbished. You'll see she's fed, watered and punished when necessary to keep her in line. For now, make sure she's suitable to be in my presence and bed every evening."

"It will be done as you order, Warlord," Ella said, her chin raised and her eyes narrowed as she swept Isabella with her gaze. "Would you like us to train your bed slave in her duties?"

Aiden allowed himself to wallow in his gratification. "With the others when they arrive certainly, as you'll see when they get here those slaves are younger so should be easier to mould. I'll break this one in myself. See that she's taken back to her cell for the day."

At Aiden's wave of dismissal, Ella and Cait bowed respectfully. Cait opened the doors and called for a guard. It surprised Aiden that the guard who walked in was Tony.

"Band leader, how convenient that you were loitering outside my suite. Come and take the girl to the cells. I'm done with her for now." Aiden ordered, a smile curving his lips as he set eyes on Isabella, who was mostly insensible on the bed.

"You wouldn't have to wait so long for her to be escorted to your bed if Isabella is installed in her old room, warlord. I can have guards stationed at the door easily enough so she can't escape," Tony said.

"No, it's not appropriate. She's a bed slave. Once the slave stable is cleaned out and secure and I'm satisfied she knows her place, she can be put in her stall. As band leader, I have an additional duty for you. Ensure she is taken to her handlers every evening," Aiden said, gesturing to Ella and Cait, who stood by the side of the bed where their charge lay. "Then when they've finished presenting her appropriately for me, you will ensure my slave is escorted to me."

He stared at Tony, half expecting the man to argue before he thought better of it. Instead, much to Aiden's irritation given the efforts he'd made to elicit a reaction from Tony, the man simply scooped Isabella's unresponsive form into his arms without commenting. Not a flicker of emotion passed across Tony's face. He'd been hoping Tony would react badly. The band leader was one of his father's men, and Aiden doubted the sincerity when Tony uttered the title of warlord.

"Do you require anything else, Warlord?" Tony asked, his voice was smooth, without a hint of concern.

"Bring me one of those Sylannian women. At least they are accomplished and know how to satisfy a man," Aiden smirked. "Oh, I almost forgot. Wait a minute."

Aiden strolled over to a chest by the wall and withdrew two slave collars from the top drawer. He turned and walked back towards Tony and had the satisfaction of finally eliciting a reaction from the man as he recognised the collars. He passed the slave collars to the band leader.

"Warlord?"

"You'll collar both her and her brother. They are both condemned to slavery," he smirked, "for their actions in killing my father."

The guard's lips thin at being told to collar Isabella and her brother, but again Tony wisely kept his opinion to himself. The band leader simply nodded before he turned and walked out of the doors. Aiden chuckled as the doors closed behind Tony's retreating figure. He'd always dreamed of what it would feel like to hold this level of power over people. Yet his imagination had fallen way short. It was even better than he'd dreamed it would be.

ELEVEN

Tarkhan closed his eyes as his keepers bathed him, luxuriating in the warm water. He'd struggled when they'd first imprisoned him here, but he could now admit some aspects were enjoyable in this new life. Not long after his capture he'd come to the rather startling conclusion that the king of Sylanna must be sterile. He could think of no other reason he'd be here, with the king's wives attempting to successfully breed with him. It was his only function now. The person he'd been, a warrior, a leader of the clans, seemed like the life of another. A life he'd had to let go or risk sending himself into a spiral of depression and loss. At least that is what he kept at the front of his mind.

The pressure of the whispering voices urging him to calm acceptance was inescapable and much easier to bear when he dropped his resistance and gave himself to them. His compliance brought small luxuries into his life. Better food and drinks, all fed to him by the hands of his keepers. They still didn't allow him to engage in such activities by himself. After all, he could use a knife or goblet to harm himself, and that was something his keepers wouldn't allow. The bed he slept in had a more comfortable mattress, sheets, and pillows. This was the most recent addition, a soaking bath, rather than a sponge bath. Even this they did for him, although he had to admit the days where he might have tried to escape by drowning himself were gone.

"I am very pleased with your progress, Tarkhan."

"Thank you. I'm trying to obey you all."

Tarkhan shuddered as a burst of pleasure flooded his mind as she stroked his temple. It no longer shamed him he not only looked forward to such rewards but actively tried to earn them. Although he kept his motivations buried deep in his mind. This was hard to achieve, particularly of late as the keeper had taken to rummaging around in his memories, although it had been a relief that she'd confined herself to dredging up forgotten memories of his childhood. To live again, he had to survive long enough to seize opportunities when they presented themselves. Those moments would never occur if his keepers still believed he fought against his new life. It was slow, but bit by bit they were giving him more leeway with the promise of greater freedoms to come.

"I judge you'll be ready to be bound soon. Then you won't have to live with such constraints," the Keeper said, her tone matter of fact.

"Bound?"

"Hush, don't fret." The Keeper waited until the muscles he'd inadvertently tightened relaxed. "Once I deem you are fully compliant and accepting of your life, a control bond will be forged into your mind."

Despite his best efforts, Tarkhan tensed again, and he took a deep, settling breath, and allowed the Keeper to soothe his agitation. While he wasn't sure what being bound meant, he was certain it wouldn't be good for any hope he had of freedom.

"What will happen to me? With this control bond?"

"There's no need to worry. All Sylannian men are bound in such a way. If your mother hadn't fled to a foreign land, your firstwife would have forged a mate bond with you long ago. As it is, a wife of this house will bind you to them."

"It's certain then? I'm Sylannian? You know who my mother was?"

The Keeper nodded. "You wouldn't be here if we didn't believe you to be Sylannian."

"Who was she? Why did she flee her home?"

"Given your age and the memories of your mother, she was indeed Sylannian and fled her father's court," the Keeper said, her hands continuing to bathe him as she spoke, and the soothing pulse coming from her increased. "Our record keepers tell us that when our current king's mother seized the throne from her father, her purge was unsuccessful. Several of her siblings fled the cleansing of the court and remain unaccounted for. We believe you are a child of such a one. Our archivists are digging in the royal records to determine which of the daughters who escaped is your mother. Even without that information, our people in your former homeland should recover evidence to confirm your heritage."

"What evidence could there be?"

"When your mother fled the purge of the monarch house, she would have taken her daggers with her. Each blood dagger is inscribed with the daughter's name and parentage. Our agents are seeking to retrieve them from her final resting place."

"So it's true. I'm Sylannian," Tarkhan whispered.

"We go to significant efforts to reclaim our lost ones when we locate them. Accept the training I'm giving you and once a wife takes your mind, you'll live a life as close to that which you should have had all along."

Tarkhan felt a sense of loss as if a part of himself he'd held dear had been ripped away exposing a lie. He was aware that this was because of the whispering, separating him from who he'd been, but a tear traced down his cheek in response.

"Yes Keeper. What do I have to do?"

The keeper moved position, pulling him to her so he was resting on her shoulder.

"Relax, you are not at fault with any of this. Your mother should never have run from the court. Drop your mental barriers, allow me to guide your mind, to show you what we've learnt," the Keeper whispered to him, urging him to calm and to drop his shields.

Before he could respond, between one breath and the next, his keeper slipped into his mind and on this occasion, he noted his mental barriers didn't react to her intrusion at all. While his keeper had done this before, on each of the previous occasions, it hadn't taken long for his unconscious mind to fight such intrusion and his shields had reasserted themselves pushing her out. The pulses of calm that accompanied the whispering urging his compliance were much stronger now she was inside his mind. Tarkhan heard a distant moan and realised it was his own. A part of him was aware he should push the Keeper out. She might see things he didn't want her to know. This time, he found he could not do so. Something that at first had been entirely alien to him, somehow after all this time he'd spent under their control, now seemed natural.

That's it, lost one. Relax, the Keeper soothed.

I don't understand what's happening, Tarkhan said.

All is as it should be. Your training is working. Reassurance pulsed through Tarkhan and the tension drained from him. *It feels normal for me to take control of your mind because it is. This is one benefit of the control bond. You won't have to struggle to be calm and accept your position. The wife who takes you will do it for you.*

Tarkhan found he was struggling to separate her whispered voice from his internal voice. While one part of him relaxed as she took control, another part of himself that he hoped was buried deep enough she wouldn't detect, was horrified. Tarkhan felt like he was two people now, his old self and this new persona that they were conditioning in their ways. Right now, it was this new self that rather happily conceded control of his mind to the keeper. While his old self watched on like a voyeur.

Memories of his earliest childhood rose at the keeper's bidding. They were his memories that he hadn't been aware he'd remembered. Or so the keeper whispered to him. Tarkhan focused on the images of his mother as the keeper drew them to the forefront and wondered how he'd never seen it before. With her dark eyes, long black hair and flawless complexion with no sign of any tattoos, without even a hint of the characteristics of the People. He was undoubtedly looking at his mother. He was looking at a Sylannian.

"We suspect your mother was already pregnant when she fled the Monarch Court," the Keeper said.

"But that means..."

"It was a rare circumstance in our history, but the sovereign who sat on the throne was a king. Madness caught hold in the Monarch House and the daughters, all of them with the blood of the Monarch, were desperate to bolster their claim. The race for power is not so bad when a queen is on the throne since only the children she has birthed carry the monarch's blood. The king had many daughters but no sons, so the daughters were vetted and checked for their suitability to be the next queen. If they could also breed successfully with the king, it would prove they were fertile and double their claim to the throne."

"You're saying my mother bred with her father?" The shock of her words caused Tarkhan's normal self to reassert itself.

"It is not such an unknown thing for children of the high court families. They like to strengthen their bloodlines. Particularly in the Monarch Court." The keeper sent a wave of reassurance. "I know it is strange to you having been brought up in different ways, but if it helps, you are not related to any of the wives you are breeding with."

Tarkhan sighed, admitting that she was correct. That was exactly what his issue had been.

"But if my sister was on the throne, um, I'd be expected to, well…" Tarkhan broke off, his face heating and he squirmed until his keeper forced calm on him again.

"Hush, none of the women here are that closely related to you. Cousin several times removed at best. Besides, the king's daughters are too young to breed with you as yet. When they have their first flow and cleared to breed, we shall see, but that is not this day."

Tarkhan's eyes widened at the implication and he desperately wrenched his attention back to the conversation regarding his parentage.

"But my father was of the People."

"It matters not who your father was. Only that your mother was a daughter of the Monarch House with the blood of the king, meaning you are a son of the monarch's blood by direct descent."

Tarkhan's eyes flashed open as the door to the bathing room was drawn aside and Chelsie walked in. His breath caught, but with the Keeper within his mind, urging him to remain calm, his momentary fear fled, and he stared at Chelsie with a hint of anticipation. As best he could work out it had been months since he'd bred with her. With complete honesty, the emotion he recognised as desire was his own and not brought forward by his keeper. As much as Tarkhan hated to admit it, he'd enjoyed the week he'd spent breeding, as they called it, with Chelsie. If he'd understood his role here, it must be Chelsie's fertile period and she'd come to breed with him again.

"Now, do you understand why we've taken such care to

protect you, my warrior?" Chelsie asked as her silks pooled around her feet and she stepped into the bath.

"Yes mistress," Tarkhan said, finding he could not take his eyes off her. During sex, he'd found she enjoyed it when he used her name. At all other times, he addressed her as mistress to show he was subordinate to her. She liked that even more,

Chelsie slid down next to him, taking the keeper's place. "Go."

As the keeper withdrew from his mind, Chelsie slid in to take her place. Chelsie expertly took control and then forced him to relax. A part of him mourned this loss of self. That he did not stop her as he once had. However, he admitted that if he displayed defiance of their wishes, in particular Chelsie's desires, his world would be much worse. Still, he wished he was deliberately complying with her wants instead of her forcing it on him. The future of living under this level of control terrified him.

"It's been so long since you've come to my bed, mistress, I was beginning to fear I'd displeased you," Tarkhan said.

Delight danced in Chelsie's eyes. "Your body is giving away your pleasure at seeing me again, even if your mind is conflicted."

"I'm sorry mistress—" his words halted as her fingers pressed against his lips.

I'm inside your mind's barriers now. Eventually, you will fully accept my presence and I will bond you to me permanently. Chelsie grabbed his hand, placing it on her abdomen. "Do you know how to sense a new life in another?"

Tarkhan's eyes widened, and he broke eye contact with Chelsie to stare at her abdomen, switching to his othersight. There he saw it, that spark of new life within her.

"You're pregnant mistress."

"I am. It's why I've been absent these long months. I waited until the underwives could assure me the child is healthy and I will not miscarry. You have performed your duties extremely well. You'll be moved to better quarters on my orders. I'm willing to give you time to accept your new life. You have until this child is born to become accustomed to the mind bond and give yourself freely to my full control."

"Thank you," Tarkhan said. "I'll do my best to comply with your wishes."

Tarkhan's back arched as Chelsie rewarded him. The pulse of pleasure burst through him unfiltered since she was within his mind barrier. He was aware when she withdrew from contact with his mind and in this moment he wanted to protest her loss as she left him to be replaced by his keeper. A small pulse told him she'd noted even this reaction to her leaving him and it pleased her greatly.

You are mine now, warrior. You know this to be true.

Chelsie's parting words rolled through his mind. With his shields sliding back into place that part of him that remained defiant reasserted itself. He shuddered, panting as the remains of the burst of pleasure that had been her parting gift wore off. Incapable of doing anything else, but she was aware this would be the case, as were his keepers. Everything they did was deliberately designed to break him down, bit by bit. And it was working. Chelsie's demonstration had proven he'd have no chance of escape once Chelsie seized control of his mind. Tarkhan had to gain his freedom before Chelsie's child was born, but at least that gave him a timeframe.

CHAPTER
TWELVE

Tarkhan spun around on the spot, slowly taking in all the details of the room. The Keeper and underwives had gone to a lot of trouble to make him comfortable. Multi-coloured silk panels draped from the middle of the ceiling to the wall, hanging down to the floor. A woven basket stood in the corner, filled with rolled-up blankets. Cushions of all different sizes and colours were piled up to one side. They'd even gone to the trouble of sourcing a small stove, complete with a pipe stretching up to the roof. Tarkhan drew in a thread of the veil, pushing it out to wash over the stove. The smile froze on his lips, it had been a vain hope he'd be able to make his kaf of a morning when he woke. Then, aware his keeper was watching, he walked over to a shuttered window. He reached out and pulled the lever. Tarkhan gasped as light spilled in. A vast canopy of giant green leaves filled his vision. Soft puffy white clouds marred the otherwise perfect blue sky. As the warmth of the sun brushed over his face, he closed his eyes.

"You've gone to a great deal of trouble," Tarkhan said.

"Chelsie ordered us to make you as comfortable as possible," the Keeper said.

"I don't suppose I'll ever be allowed outside?" Tarkhan asked. Unable to help the wistful note in his voice.

"Perhaps, if you continue to prove your loyalty and worth to Chelsie, something might be arranged one day…"

"But?"

"It's too dangerous right now, but once issues have settled, it could be a possibility."

"Admittedly, I've been locked up since I arrived here, but I haven't heard any signs of trouble."

"I'm aware it's not what you're accustomed to, but Sylannian males are always wrapped in layers of protection. Even our king, who has more freedoms than the average Sylannian male, lives a life far more restricted than the one you are used to. Besides, we're at war. You, better than any, should know this."

Tarkhan kept the frown from his face. He could hear the lie in the echo in the keeper's mind. At least a partial deception, hidden among the truth.

"A war that you've won. I promise I won't cause you or Chelsie any problems."

"Your behaviour has been exemplary, otherwise you wouldn't have been moved here." The keeper's hand reached up and brushed his temple. With the light touch of her fingers, calm washed over him. "It is not as extensive or as outdoor as I think you mean but, this compound you share with the other mates has a secure private garden area. Which you will be able to use during the day. Come, let me show you."

Tarkhan's breath caught, and he smiled in anticipation. He didn't know which part of her surprising announcement he found more exciting. That there was an outdoor area he could access or that he'd finally get to meet some of the other males that lived there. Tarkhan allowed the keeper to usher him out of the door. He was a couple of strides into the new room when he stopped dead in his tracks. His mouth fell open as he took in everything around him. Tarkhan's mind grappled with what he was seeing, trying to make some sense of his surroundings. This place was ringed by some of the biggest tree trunks he'd ever seen in his life. Birds sang in the branches. Dappled light filtered through the leaves to spill onto his skin. There were pools, surrounded by ferns and flowers, and a longer narrow pool off to one side. Chairs were arranged in groups and piled with cushions, while others were off by themselves in private little grottos.

"We're up in the trees?"

"Of course. Only the serving class and collared workers live below." The Keeper sniffed. "That is where you'd be if you hadn't proven yourself. You'd only have a narrow cot crammed into a long house with hundreds of other collared servers."

"How is this possible?"

"This is the Court of a Thousand Islands. It is as old as our people. The trees have been cared for and strengthened for generations."

"But there are pools and everything up here." Tarkhan didn't bother to hide his astonishment.

The Keeper's eyes sparkled in amusement, clearly enjoying his delight.

"Of the possible fates awaiting you after you were captured, belonging to the Monarch House is hardly the worst thing that could have befallen you. Even if your life is far more restricted than you would prefer, there are many benefits you will enjoy that even those Sylannian born and raised will never see, let alone acquire."

"Thank you for this," Tarkhan said, hands raising in the air as he gazed around his current surroundings, the smile dropping from his lips as he faced her. "All the luxury in the world doesn't pay for what I've lost."

There was no other description he could come up with other than pain flickered across the keeper's face. "Your unhappiness at the loss of what you once had is understandable, but you will adapt."

"You mentioned sharing this area with others. Will I at least be able to meet them?"

"I will permit for you to interact with the others in a couple of days once you've settled in. For now, it's time for you to return to your rooms and rest."

The keeper gestured back towards the open door. With one last look around the garden, Tarkhan returned to his living quarters. The prospect of gaining access to even this limited promise of freedom was something he didn't want to risk.

CHAPTER

THIRTEEN

S amuel lay on his stomach on the massage bench, content to stare into nothing.

"What would it be like to be a normal husband with no kingdom to run, no cares at all in this world?" Samuel whispered.

"Did you say something husband?" Fiona asked.

Samuel turned his head and focused on Fiona, who sat on one of the lounges nearby. He hadn't meant to speak aloud, not that it mattered. She'd likely catch a sense of his mood even if he'd just uttered the words in the sanctity of his mind. As bound as they all were, it was hard for any of them to keep anything to themselves.

"It's nothing. I was just wondering out loud what it would be like to be a normal husband in a normal house without the weight of caring for the kingdom."

"For you? Much the same, I suspect," Fiona smiled as she regarded him. "Except you wouldn't have the court appearance to deal with. For us, your wives, it would be a lot more relaxing since we'd only have a house to run instead of a kingdom. Now I must go or I'll be late."

"For what? Where do you all disappear to?" Samuel asked.

"Wars don't run themselves and neither does the kingdom."

"Is this something I should attend to?" Samuel asked, pushing himself up.

Fiona shook her head and waved him down. "No, you'd find it tedious. It's just one of our regular meetings. The senior wives of the Monarch House always take on the function of running the kingdom when there is a king on the throne."

"Perhaps I should..." Samuel paused when his eyes caught sight of a bowl with a black residue and a brush near it on the table close to where Fiona sat. "What is that?"

Samuel pushed himself up and crossed the room to pick up the bowl. Fiona leapt up from the chair, snatching it from his hands.

"Nothing, I'm sorry the servitors should have cleaned this up."

Samuel's eyebrows rose. "Clearly it's something or you wouldn't be so agitated."

"Please, don't mention it, Samuel. You'll embarrass some of the other wives. They use it to hide the grey hairs that have started to appear."

He reached out and ran his fingers through her hair, then grabbed her free hand and pulled her gently towards him. Fiona blushed, handing the bowl out to one side. One of the hovering wives dashed forward and took it from her.

"There isn't a single grey hair in your head. I also think I'd have noticed before now if you were dying it."

"I don't, but some of my fellow wives have a few greys appearing. They want to look good for you."

Samuel resisted as Fiona pushed at his mind, trying to get

him to turn away from the topic. If anything, that made him even more suspicious.

"If they didn't want me to discover such a secret, why would they dye their hair in here?"

"They don't. One of your wives probably came in here, distracted by something, and accidentally left the bowl behind."

Samuel caught an image from Fiona's mind before she could bury it. A child running through the room. An underwife in pursuit, with the bowl in her hand. Fiona picked up the giggling child and handed her to the underwife. Samuel gasped and stepped back, unable to hide his reaction. The girl in Fiona's memory had a black smudge on her forehead.

"Whose child was that? Why were the underwives dying her hair?"

Fiona laughed, her hand pressing to her lips. "Samuel, that was one of your daughters. She doesn't need her hair dyed but sometimes the children want to be included. I'm sorry, I just should have told you. I didn't want you to be upset."

He mustn't find out what we've done.

Samuel maintained control over his facial expression and made soothing sounds to her. If Fiona realised he'd caught the echo of her inner thoughts through the bond they shared, she'd shut down. He pulled her into his arms and her head nestled into the side of his neck. With his mind wide open, the contact between them intensified his awareness of her and their mutual bond. Samuel pushed aside the feelings and thoughts he'd expected to sense from her and concentrated on the level of emotion buried beneath the surface. His questing mind paused. There it was, a vibration, all close together and spiky. Regardless of the fact that she appeared relaxed in his arms, it spoke to him of her sudden fear. It spoke of the lie in the words she'd uttered. What perplexed him was why she was lying.

He'll order our deaths if he finds out.

It took every inch of control Samuel possessed not to react. There was only one reason, beyond being out of his mind, that as the king of Sylanna, he'd order the death of his wives. His wives were engaged in treason against Sylanna. Against their king, their husband.

Against him.

SAMUEL HUMMED to the immature silk spider, and it scampered from his hand. It climbed up his arm to his shoulder, where it hopped to the top of the couch to scamper over to its brethren. He waved at the nearby spider herder, who half bowed. Then with a hum, she took charge of the spiders and led them from the room back out to the trees they belonged in. Samuel stretched. A handy distraction that allowed him to check his surroundings one final time. None of his senior wives were present. Fiona had claimed they were dealing with the tedious administration details involved in the war effort and the kingdom. It was only Fiona's stray thoughts and her sudden fear that caused him to suspect there might be other reasons for them to be absent from his presence.

He walked out of the room down familiar hallways, heading towards the inner sanctum. Even if it hadn't occurred to him to come this way for a long time. Samuel frowned. He couldn't remember the last time he'd visited the children's dayroom. He prodded at his memory, yet didn't discover even a hint that he'd ever bothered to attend the nursery. The children had been brought to him occasionally, but as far as he could tell, he'd never gone to them. Now that was another oddity he couldn't reconcile. Samuel added it to the growing list of things he'd begun to notice. It had taken all the patience he possessed to sit, lounging around, waiting until his firstwife, primewives and secondwives left.

Samuel slid the door open and strode down the hallway, deeper into the heart of the Monarch Court. He snorted softly as he remembered running down this same passage in one of his failed attempts to escape the underwives who'd cared for him. His child self had been determined to visit his mother. The smile faded from his lips. It was one of the few wonderful memories he still possessed from his childhood. Before he realised that when he grew up, he would cleanse the court. A memory that his wives decided was safe for him to remember. Childish laughter floated down the hallway as he approached the day room. An underwife that came out the door, who stopped abruptly, caught Samuel's attention. Her eyes widened.

"Husband, we weren't expecting you."

"I decided to visit the children. It was a spur-of-the-moment decision, but one I think is long overdue."

"Really, we haven't prepared—"

Samuel raised his hand, dismissing the concern, and went to walk forward, then his eyes narrowed as she made a half step to block his path.

"I'm not only your husband, but your king. Get out of my way, or I'll order your execution."

The underwife swallowed and backed up before prostrating herself on the ground. Samuel pushed the door aside and walked into the dayroom, only to pause just inside the entry. He was uncertain why he'd come. Children were running around in the outdoor area, while others sat quietly in the corner as an underwife read to them. Some were practising their use of the veil under the sharp eyes of an instructor. There was nothing here that he didn't expect to see.

One of his small daughters, sitting on the mat listening to the story, looked over at him. Her mouth opened as she stared up at him. Samuel felt as if his heart stopped mid-beat, much like the room stilled around him and the childish laughter receded. Samuel walked forward and knelt in front of the girl. He reached out and tilted her head up and brushed his fingers along the distinct dye line that hadn't quite faded from her forehead.

As the child's green eyes stared back at him, Samuel's heart hardened.

FOURTEEN

Ben stared up at a wooden roof above him. It was a well-constructed roof without any of the nooks or uneven lengths that would allow all manner of insects, wind, smoke and, worse, smell to seep in. He was fairly confident he recognised exactly where he was since he'd stared up at such a roof before. It was the trapdoor, complete with a ladder to allow the occupant to scramble up to the roof above, that gave it away. Ben turned his head and found a similar trapdoor on the floor. Partially open shutters allowed filtered light into the hut; the mismatched wooden planks of the huts opposite were on display. If he leant out of the window, he'd be able to touch the buildings on the other side. If someone stood on the outside looking at this place, they would see what looked like a mess of a building. Something that resembled tiny box-like huts, jammed on top of each other, made of mismatched bits of lumber and tin. That was the last clue that let him know his assessment of the roof had been correct. He let out a sigh of relief. Against all odds, he was in the Burrow. Even more surprising, he was alive.

"So you're awake at last," Lukas said.

"So it seems, I take it I have you to thank for pulling me out of the mess I was in?" Ben turned his head in the other direction.

The corners of Lukas's eyes crinkled. "Some who are aware we serve a mutual master did and sent word to me."

"Ah, well, send my thanks to them," Ben said. He moved on the bed and winced as his injuries pulled. "I need to get moving."

Lukas lay a hand on his shoulder in light restraint. "Things are in motion. We have evacuated your family and the Smith out to the Smith's country estate. Adam advises Colin finally contacted Michael and passed on your message. You will lie there and let yourself heal."

"Ah, so that dagger thrust was as bad as I thought it was."

Ben grimaced. His benefactor was correct. As much as he wanted to be out and about to and check on the current status here in Vallantia, he had to heal first. Even if he didn't think he had time to allow that healing to take place. At least his family had made it to the safety of the Smith's residence, which was on the very outskirts of Vallantia's district, up towards the mountains and well away from the rivers. He also needed to act as the anchor of the relay and to pass back information about what was occurring to Michael. With his power level, Michael could reach out directly to him, no matter where he was without an intermediary. That wasn't the case with the rest of them. Ben remembered the splitting headaches he'd suffered as Michael tested their communication limits to work out where to position each of them in the relay.

"Worse, but you'll heal. The Smith was most displeased and has sent back some leathers for you."

"I didn't have time to dress appropriately. If I'd delayed, I wouldn't be here at all."

"If it helps, you killed quite a few of them before they took you down, and your family is alive because of it."

"How did I get in here?"

"You were seen. A few of ours finished the Sylannians you left behind and dragged you here to our den."

"Ah. Thanks for my family's life and mine."

"No need. If we all survive this, Michael would have killed us anyway if we'd sat back watching and let you die."

Ben couldn't help but chuckle even though it made him wince as pain lanced through his abdomen.

"I take it you have someone with healer's talent in here?"

"Not as talented as the one who rides with Michael, but yes, it's why you're alive."

Ben's eyebrows rose. "When did you set eyes on the Unwanted's healer? Michael is awfully protective of her."

"Some issues drew me to Callenhain. I got sloppy and ended up in a rather unfortunate situation. Fortunately, those who'd detained me made the mistake of taking Michael's healer and one of his men." Lukas smiled thinly.

"I doubt that worked out well," Ben frowned, thinking about it, "for them."

"That recruit of Michael's lost control, which resulted in everyone he perceived as a threat dying."

"So that meant all of them, I take it?"

"Every last one."

Ben stared at Lukas. He couldn't believe anyone would be that stupid to lay a hand on any of Michael's people. Not if they expected to live, anyway. Most sane people went out of their way to avoid a negative interaction with the Unwanted. Yet while Lukas was known for being quite inventive in certain areas, he wasn't the type of person to get creative and make that kind of story up. His long-time friend had no need to. The life the man normally led was hair-raising enough not to require embellishment.

"How's it going out there?" Ben asked.

"The city and the Rathadon estate have fallen again," Lukas said dryly.

"The Burrow?" Ben knew the answer to that one or neither of them would be here, but asked anyway.

Lukas laughed in genuine amusement. "They tried to take this place a few of times, but as always, the Burrow proved a little problematic for them. I'm sure they'll try again sometime, but for now, we're safe enough."

"They haven't kept trying?"

"Oh, sometimes a group of them gets brave and makes a run." Lukas shrugged, his eyes going cold. "They also died while they were at it. Several times over. We've had years to get the Burrow to resemble a maze, ready to kill any we didn't want to have access."

"That was industrious of you."

"That was Michael's orders."

"Did he explain why he wanted you to do that?"

Lukas laughed. "For the exact circumstance that happened. He reasoned the Burrow stood out and anyone who tried to invade wouldn't be able to help themselves. They'd die in substantial numbers until they learnt better."

Ben flicked his eyes over to regard Lukas. "How have you been, besides recent events?"

"Well. Busy doing business, not always my own. I'm sure you are aware of what that's been like."

"Did you ever think this would result from four boys seeking adventure into the Burrow?"

"Did I believe I'd call those lads I stumbled on, lost in the maze, friends? No, those born of your station didn't associate with the likes of me. But that is where we all learnt to run in the shadows."

"You mean you taught us about the underground world hidden in the shadows? I'm not sure moving in the shadows is a gift Michael possesses. If anything, he's always been the one everyone watched and was drawn to. Even back then, when we were children."

"He, more than all of us, is a master. So much so he can walk out in the light with no one suspecting he leads the shadow path." Lukas laughed.

"We all gained from our friendship."

"My people became more than they were because of the friendship that grew with those four boys."

"Do you think Michael knew what was to come?"

"No, but he is a true child of the Rathadon warlords. Even as a boy, he gathered people to him, started laying the foundations for survival. Although I suspect he wasn't aware he was doing it."

Ben shifted his position on the bed slightly and closed his eyes. There was no way Lukas was going to let him get up until he healed properly. The resident healers of the Burrow would need to recharge before they could finish healing him. It was unfortunate that even his own assessment of how he was feeling was telling him it would take a few more sessions. Only then could he resume his duties. For now, it was up to the others to fill in, although he was sure Lukas and the Smith between them would do a fine job of coordinating efforts here in Vallantia.

FIFTEEN

Evan sat with his back pressed against the rock wall behind him. All things considered, he had to hand it to the Rathadon's. It was a very fine cell. However, given a choice, he had to admit this wasn't where he'd pick to spend his idle hours. It was cold, damp, dirty, and lacked any bathing facilities or other amenities he'd grown accustomed to. It also possessed its own distinct odour. A musty, stale smell that mixed unpleasantly with the rankness of unwashed bodies. He picked up the small metal mug and grimaced. Water. He was reduced to drinking water and unpalatable food. If you could call what they gave him to eat food. It consisted of hard, dry bread that seemed to grow with a life of its own and some kind of runny, greyish slop in a bowl. Evan decided he should be grateful it was tasteless as well.

Evan? Ben said.

Ben? Evan started looking around.

He snorted softly at his stupidity. Of course, Ben wasn't down here. If he had been, Ben would be in a cell just like he was.

Did you get out?

Out of my room? Absolutely.

Are you drunk?

Now you're just teasing. I'm locked up in the cells below the Rathadon estate.

Speaker and Lady Rathadon? Steven?

They aren't down here. Speaker and Lady Rathadon are being detained in their rooms. Steven is being kept in his rooms. The woman is keeping him segregated from the rest of us.

Which woman? In case you hadn't noticed, there are quite a few of them in town.

Evan couldn't help the chuckle that came out of his lips. As one of the Sylannians walked down to peer at him through the bars, he smiled blandly. The Sylannians didn't appear to have a sense of humour. At least those assigned down here didn't seem to. Then again, if he was them, he wouldn't be happy either. They were stuck down here as well, with the only light filtering through from the narrow barred windows. The entire view consisted of a wall, and occasionally boot shod feet that walked in the outer courtyard. Not even so much as a blade of grass or a patch of sky was visible from them.

I can only imagine what it's like in town, I'm afraid, but the enemy in charge here is their commander, Jaclyn. She was giving all the orders and Steven says she calls on him regularly, pumping him for information on Michael. Full maroon clothing with what appears to be a spider web pattern in cream traced through it. All of hers wear her colours, so watch out for them.

He hasn't divulged much about Michael, has he?

No, Steven says he's trying to bore her with ancient history.

Do you want me to try to get you out?

Evan was tempted to beg Ben to help him, then he sighed. Unlike in the past, when there was hardly anyone down here, the cells were full and there was always a group of the Sylannians on guard duty.

I'd owe you for the rest of my life, but no. It's too dangerous.

They keep guards down there?

Night and day. I think they've found the tunnels, so keep out of them. If you manage to get in here, and they let you live, you'll probably end up in the cell next to me.

Is everyone in the cells except the Rathadon's?

No. A few of the Kastler's thugs that survived the attack are here in the cells, the Kastler's much to their dismay, and me. The house staff are kept under tight watch but are still serving in the house.

Right, keep your eyes and ears open, not that I'd expect you'll hear or see much down there and I'll keep in touch.

Wait, did you know about Lady Rathadon's heritage?

What about her heritage?

Powers. Michael will have to be warned, or it'll be a nasty shock.

What will be a nasty shock?

Lady Rathadon is a Sylannian.

How could she possibly be Sylannian?

I have no idea, but she admitted she was.

Is that it?

No. It gets worse.

Well, spit it out. What else?

The Sylannian Commander's mother and Lady Rathadon were sisters.

Michael is related to the Commander of the Sylannian invasion?

Apparently.

Did it seem like Lady Rathadon had something to do with the attack? Like she arranged for it just to get rid of the Kastlers?

I don't think so. Lady Rathadon didn't appear at all pleased to see her former countrymen. She even killed some of the Sylannians.

She what?

Well, I don't see how it could have been anyone else. The only other person in the room was Speaker Rathadon.

Anything else I need to know before I go?

No, that's about it. Ben, where's Michael... wait, don't answer that. They don't pay any attention to me, but it's probably best if I don't know. Be careful out there.

Evan sighed as Ben withdrew. That was the most interesting conversation he'd had since he'd been shoved down here. He was glad to learn Ben was still out there somewhere. Although Evan wished he was as well. It had been long enough since he'd had contact with Ben he'd been afraid the barkeeper was dead. Evan picked up the bowl of slop they'd given him and gulped down a mouthful of the stuff. If he didn't think about it and swallowed fast enough, it wasn't so bad. At least that's what he told himself. He looked up to see the Kastler's staring at him from across the walkway that ran between their cells. Not that any cell was better than any other, but he would have preferred they weren't opposite him.

"Who were you talking to? Can they get us all out of here?" Peter hissed at him.

Evan glanced around as if attempting to find someone, then gave them a thin smile and said in his driest tone. "Does it look like there's anyone else in here in this cell but me?"

"Stop trying to be funny." Constance glared at him sullenly.

"I might not have been able to overhear you, but you were mindspeaking with someone." Peter insisted, his face screwing up in a scowl.

A couple of their Sylannian guards edge closer and Evan rolled his eyes.

"Steven and I are friends. He was checking in on me," Evan said.

"Why isn't he down here?"

"The Sylannian commander seems fascinated with him. Everyone always wants a piece of him. Steven's just lucky like that, I guess," Evan said.

He widened his eyes pretending shock at the idea, although as he gazed at the Kastler's he realised it was a wasted effort.

"Where is the warleader when he's needed?" Peter said.

Evan couldn't help but laugh. "You've changed your tune. Besides, you'd best hope he doesn't catch up with you. What he is likely to do to you will be far worse than being in this cell."

"What's that meant to mean?" Constance said, her eyes narrowing.

"Did you seriously forget about that bit where you invaded his family home, took over Vallantia and styled yourselves as some sort of overlord?"

"Well, so have the Sylannians," Peter said, his back stiffening.

"The Sylannian hold no allegiance to us at all. They are trying to take over the Warlord's domain for their king. You, on the other hand, betrayed your own people. You sold them for your own financial gain. Then attacked Michael's family. I don't know if you've noticed, but Michael takes all of those things a little personal."

"Steven sided with us in case you've forgotten," Peter said.

"You really think so?" Evan's eyebrows rose.

"Of course, he was right on board the entire time," Peter said.

"You weren't here every day. Steven even took part in our meetings on how best to proceed." Constance appeared smug, as if the little detail might save her.

"You mean the sessions Steven attended where you came up with all your plans that Steven promptly fed back to his parents?" Evan smiled at them, aware it was insincere.

"He couldn't have, he doesn't have the brains..."

"He was acting on his father's orders."

"Either way, it's not like his brother could know any of it."

"You just keep sitting here in the dark thinking the warleader has no knowledge about any of your activities before the

Sylannian attack. It might give you solace while you wait here for your death to catch up with you," Evan said.

Evan went back to his bowl of slop. He picked up what passed for bread and dunked it in the grey sludge to soften the hard lump, then he gnawed at it. It was sad when the food was a far better proposition than continuing conversation with his neighbours.

SIXTEEN

Tony trembled as barely suppressed rage ran through him. Muted as they'd been by the doors, the sound of her cries each night filled with fear and pain, rather than pleasure as Aiden took her, had been unmistakable. He hadn't missed the trace of blood on the sheets. All of it gave testimony that Aiden had not been gentle when he forced himself on Isabella. Using coercion by torturing her brother was not consent. Only the guards on the door, picked from Aiden's warband, had stopped him from charging into the warlord's suite at Isabella's first cry. Aiden may not be as strong as the warleader and the rest of the Unwanted, but their new warlord had far more power than he did and surprisingly Aiden's warband seemed loyal to him. If Tony had tried to break in and stop Aiden, he would have been dead before he entered the room. His death would not help the girl. One thing held him and gave him hope.

"Easy Isabella, you just need to survive. Aiden's people found no trace of the rest of your brother's squad." Tony kept his voice soft, even though there was nobody near to overhear him.

"Damien had other members of the Unwanted with him. I know he did."

"Michael?"

The guard smiled sadly at the thread of hope he detected in that whispered word.

"The Unwanted who escaped will find the warleader. He won't tolerate this. Any of this."

It would take time for the warleader's people to find him, to pass on news of what had happened here, and he didn't want to give the girl false hope. But he wanted her to have something to hold on to, so she'd get through the rough days to come. While she might have this respite from Aiden's cruelty, she would be brought up from the cells and be back in Aiden's bed tonight. Tony ignored everybody as he continued his path down to the bowels of the fortress. He didn't have to say a word to those on duty who opened the doors for him. He could see it in their eyes. News such as this had a way of running like fire and spreading from person to person.

With the only glow thrown by the light stones, Tony walked the remaining distance down the dark stone corridor until it broke into an open area. The cells were down a a passage on the other side. Tony paused, looking at the cell guards who sat clustered around a table.

"The warlord wants the girl and her brother collared," Tony said.

The cell guards were a team separated from the rest of them. On duty or otherwise, they spent most of their days down here in the dark. Rumour had it they owed allegiance to no one, except the Stronghold itself. In a small otherwise unremarkable village, the Warlord had stayed up late drinking one night and told him a story. As such, Tony was one of the few who knew the rumours weren't true, but it was a trust he'd kept. The cell guards were loyal to the Warlord and answered only to him. There'd been a time when the young Paul Olenna, before he'd become the Warlord, had been imprisoned down in these cells. Paul had escaped the cells and took those imprisoned down here with him the night he'd killed his father and become the warlord in his place. The former prisoners became the core of the cell guards. Trusted to keep not only those who the Warlord imprisoned, but the escape route out of the Stronghold safe.

The cell guard's trade glances before one of them stood and took the two collars Aiden had given him from his hand. The cell guard stared down at them, a vein in his temple jumping. He placed one on the table next to them and stepped closer. Tony kept his gaze to the side, not wanting to catch the other guard's eyes while doing this. It was a distasteful task the warlord had ordered. The girl whimpered as the cell guard snapped the clasp of the collar, locking the mechanism with a small thread of power. They had been designed in such a way that anyone could lock them onto a captive's neck, but once on it either took a smith with an affinity for metal the equivalent of a Smith Lord of old, or chopping off the head of the slave to remove the thing. Tony was grateful that Aiden hadn't demanded they brand Isabella and her brother as well. It was a nasty little detail that he hoped their new warlord didn't remember.

"I'll send one of the other guards to collar the brother," the cell guard said.

"No, I'll do it. The warlord wants one of the Sylannians brought to him as well," Tony said.

Tony was careful to keep the inflection out of his voice as he spoke. The cell guard glanced at him sideways but otherwise said nothing as they walked through the door down the hallway to the cells. As they walked in, the conversation stopped as those in the cells watched their approach. As Tony walked with Isabella towards an empty cell, Allani, an older Sylannian he'd been informed was a leader among these people, stepped forward.

"Please, don't put the poor child in there alone."

He paused, waiting on the cell guard's response, who finally shrugged.

"I'm sorry, but the warlord has requested one of you to be brought to his bed," Tony said.

Allani gazed at him and nodded before turning to look at her fellow Sylannians. They uttered not a single audible word, but he was certain they talked it through among themselves. One of the younger women came forward and stood to one side of the cell door, waiting calmly.

"What's your name?" Tony asked. He had a feeling this was going to become a regular occurrence and names were easier than 'hey you'.

"Jana," Jana's eyes tracked to the three peaks on his shoulders before rising to meet his gaze. "Captain."

Tony tried not to show surprise at the evidence Jana had enough knowledge about their ranks to decipher his position. He pushed his concern aside, then nodded at his fellow guard, who stepped forward with the keys to the cell door.

"The rest of you step back now, except for Jana," the cell guard said.

A rustling of silk sounded as the women moved to the back of the cell they were held in without a word of protest. Just inside the door, Jana laid one hand on Isabella's head and whispered to her in Sylannian. Tony frowned and was about to growl at the woman when she took a step back, hands raised. He wished, not for the first time, that he spoke their language. He walked into the cell, and kneeling, placed Isabella on the ground.

"I'm sorry," Tony said.

"It's not your fault." Isabella's words were soft and slightly slurred.

Isabella's eyes were glazed from the drug she'd been given and she slumped against the wall as if unable to hold herself upright. Isabella pulled her knees up to her chest and buried her head in her arms. He looked up in time to catch a silent exchange between Jana and Allani, before the older Sylannian woman switched her attention to Isabella.

Tony gestured to Jana, who stood by the cell door and she walked out, her face impassive.

"Please, help Damien. He didn't kill the Warlord," Isabella said.

As Tony walked out, he paused and took on trust that the Warlord's story that night so long ago had been truth rather than a made-up tale to pass the night away. He stared at the cell guard as he spoke.

"I know Isabella. It was Aiden who killed his father. I'll do what I can. Just stay alive."

The cell guard's face went pale, but otherwise he didn't react.

"Could we get a bowl of water and a cloth? We can at least clean her up," Allani asked.

"I'll arrange it," the cell guard said, his gaze holding Tony's as he spoke.

As Tony turned to walk away Allani's hand rose to cup the side of Isabella's face. Then as the girl burst into sobs, Allani gathered Isabella into her arms. He drew a breath as his heart twisted. He could almost like the Sylannians after this, since they seemed determined to do what they could to help Isabella. Even if it was just to be a shoulder to cry on. Tony sent a wish out into the veil that one day soon, he'd get the chance to plunge a blade into the new warlord's heart.

SEVENTEEN

Tony walked back through the fortress after dropping Jana off at Aiden's rooms as he'd been ordered to do. It was unfortunate Jana was unarmed, or he'd hold the hope that the woman would do them all a favour and kill the usurper. Still, his momentary pang of guilt over escorting Jana to Aiden fled as she seemed to have no hesitation in what she was about to do. Unlike Aiden, however, he wondered at Jana's motives. He'd caught the flicker of anger on her face at the state Isabella was in and the exchange Jana had made with Allani. He certainly wouldn't trust one of the Sylannians in his bed. Although since he wished Aiden ill, he didn't feel compelled to point out his gut feeling the Sylannians were up to something. If anything, he hoped for Jana's success in her plans.

Tony grimaced at the slave collar in his hand wishing he had the power to destroy the thing. He couldn't though because Aiden would likely watch from his windows, high in the tower, to make sure the task was completed. As Tony passed an open door, he saw a squad of guards with the one in the lead holding a flask.

"Is that the drug for the prisoner?"

"It is. He gets dosed every day," the guard carrying the flask said.

"Here, I'll give it to him if you like."

"He's dangerous. You can't do it by yourself."

"Oh please, while I appreciate all the theatre, we all know he probably can't even remember his own name right now. Suit yourself, but I have to collar him," Tony brandished the slave collar, "orders of the warlord, so I'm going out there now anyhow." He shrugged as if it didn't matter to him at all when, in reality, a seed of an idea occurred to him the moment he'd seen the flask. However, the plan, if it could be called that, centred on getting his hands on the drug they were dosing Damien with.

The guards looked at each other, then with a grin, handed over the tiscan. These men were mostly those who'd been permanently based here at the Stronghold. They were lazy and would get out of any task if given half a chance.

"Thanks. The chore is getting a little tedious," the guard said.

"No problems, and I hear you." Tony rolled his eyes and waved one hand in farewell as he continued down the hallway.

Tony waited until he'd turned down several back corridors before he paused and glanced around. With nothing but an empty passageway, he went into a small side corridor and ducked into a rarely used communal bathing room. Situated down here, it was inconvenient to get to. So he should be safe. He moved across to the drain, and opening the flask, he poured most of the drug out. Then he placed it down carefully and topped it up with water. He'd never been addicted to the stuff himself, but he'd had plenty of experience with those who had been. While the watered-down tiscan would probably be enough to knock him out, it would have little effect, if any at all, on someone like Damien.

Tony walked back out of the bathing area, resisting the urge to check for the presence of anyone else in the corridor. To his relief, he didn't encounter anyone as he made his way to the small door that led to the punishment courtyard. As he passed through the entrance and strode into the enclosure, Tony noted he'd been correct. He was being observed by his new warlord from the tower that loomed over the punishment courtyard.

With the pretence of being unaware of Aiden's scrutiny, Tony walked across to Damien, who stood slumped, held up by the chains that ran to the four pillars. Tony's jaw clenched. He hadn't needed the images of the Warlord's death to know Damien wasn't guilty of the crime Aiden had accused him of committing. Thankfully, he'd worked that out himself before Isabella had thrown her memory of the event at him. Otherwise, he might have thought Isabella was messing with his head. Damien had done nothing other than be in the wrong place at the wrong time and have a sister that Aiden desired to possess.

He walked to the closest of the pillars and placed the collar and flask to one side while he released the wheel. Slowly, so as not to hurt Damien more than he already was, Tony eased more slack into the chains, bit by bit until Damien was lying on the ground rather than suspended as he had been.

He stooped over and picked up the collar and flask, resisting the urge to stare up at the balcony above. Tony crossed the short distance to Damien, then knelt and pulled Damien up, who moaned even though he was barely conscious. Careful to keep his face impassive, Tony snapped the collar around Damien's neck, fusing the catch with a small burst of power. It was such an easy thing to do, yet he hated himself for doing it because of what it meant. Tony winced in sympathy at the mess the flogging had made of Damien's back.

I'm sorry, you don't deserve this. Stay strong.

Why?

Tony froze, the pain in that one word striking him to his core.

A simple question that he couldn't answer. At least not in the time he had. He also didn't think Damien could understand any kind of response he might give right now. He picked up the flask and drew out the stopper and raised it to Damien's lips.

Listen to me, you've been drugged with tiscan. I've watered this batch down. I'll try to get this duty reassigned to my squad. Derick's warband hasn't located the team that you brought with you.

Tony realised he'd tried to convey too much too soon. He doubted Damien could comprehend much of anything right now. Still, he hoped enough had sunk in that Damien wouldn't give away that he hadn't received the full dose the local healer brewed to contain Damien's powers. Otherwise Tony feared he'd be keeping Damien company chained up here in the punishment courtyard. If that happened, he'd be no help to anyone.

CHAPTER

EIGHTEEN

Jaclyn turned, frowning as a daggerwife appeared in the doorway. It wasn't common for them to interrupt when they were aware she was busy with other tasks.

"What is it?" Jaclyn asked.

"It's the prisoner. First, she's demanding to speak with you," the daggerwife said.

Jaclyn looked at Myra, who appeared as astonished as she felt. She didn't need to see Ricardo's face to know he was as stunned as they were.

"That caused you to come running straight here because?" Ricardo asked.

"She is most insistent husband."

Jaclyn's eyes narrowed as now even the daggerwife became confused and a little less sure of herself.

"Which prisoner?" Jaclyn asked.

"The old disfigured lady." The daggerwife at least sounded certain again.

"Did you drop your guard around the old one?" Myra asked.

"No! At least, I don't think I did Primewife Myra."

"Go," Jaclyn said.

"But she said you will really want to hear what she has to say."

Jaclyn eyes widened as the daggerwife still stood there, arguing with her, after she'd been dismissed. Her temper flared, but Jaclyn withheld her reprimand as Myra held up her hand and crossed the room to the daggerwife. Myra's fingers brushed the woman's temples.

"Go to your assigned sleeping quarters and rest," Myra said.

Jaclyn sensed the compulsion Myra used on the daggerwife, who took a hesitant step to the door, then paused again. Myra pushed at the daggerwife once more, reinforcing her order. As the door opened Myra turned her attention to the two dagger-wives who entered.

"Someone has tampered with her mind. Escort her back to her assigned sleeping quarters and make sure she stays there until one of us permits otherwise," Myra said.

The daggerwives took charge of their fellow daggerwife, who appeared bewildered but did not protest as they carefully removed her daggers from her as a precaution.

"The old one tampered with her mind?" Jaclyn asked.

"She did. I, at least, want to have a chat with that one and explain to her what is going to happen if she tries it again." Myra's lips compressed.

Jaclyn stood and walked over to the small wooden box on the mantle and then opened the lid. She retrieved the daggers that had been taken off the old woman.

"We are secure now and I've put this off for long enough," Jaclyn said.

Ricardo's arm snaked around her waist. "Those blades do not mean the old woman has the blood of the Monarch House."

"I can't think of a reason a Sylannian fleeing our homeland would stop long enough when running for her life to steal

Monarch House blood-knives and robes. If anything, they would get her killed before anyone worked out she was a commoner. At least if it was anyone but me."

"A dagger can quickly end any threat the woman poses," Myra said.

"No. Both the old woman and man may yet be useful leverage against their son."

"I take it you mean the dangerous one we keep hearing all about, rather the one who's already in our possession?"

"The more I learn about Michael Rathadon, the more I want to meet him. At least after we are fully secure here." Jaclyn placed the dagger and robes back in the box. "For now, given she went to such lengths to send that message to me, I find I'm curious."

Jaclyn walked out the door with the others following in her wake. They'd left the old Rathadon's under guard in their rooms, keeping them separated from the rest of the prisoners they'd taken. There had been a surprising number of household staff in this place, not to mention the trader family and all their people that had been trying to hold the estate and the habitation before their arrival. One of the daggerwives on duty opened the door on her approach, allowing her to sweep in without pause. Lady Rathadon stood with her back to the door, looking out the windows at the garden beyond. The old woman turned, her expression indecipherable. Jaclyn just regarded her for a moment, before a faint smile touched the other woman's lips and she sat near her husband in the long, straight-backed leather chair.

"Thank you for coming so promptly, niece. It is kind of you to humour an old woman's request," Lady Rathadon said.

"Such an address is a barbarian custom. It doesn't have any hold on me."

"Only because we Sylannians have the habit of killing each

other. Old age is a rarity among the aristocrat families of our people."

"You weren't always Lady Rathadon. What was your name?" Jaclyn asked.

"Adra."

"So Adra, you were a child of the Monarch House?"

"Please, I've been known as Lady Rathadon far longer than I was Adra. My sister, your mother, enacted the dance of daggers for the Monarch Throne, killing our father and his wives. An opportunity to run presented itself and I took it."

"Only to end up here in the barbarian lands."

"It seems surviving the dance of daggers is something we have in common. I'm curious about how you still manage to live in Sylanna. Or have things changed that much?"

"Not so much. I was too young when my older brother, our king, initiated the dance of daggers. I ran and mate bonded to Ricardo."

"Ah, by the time your brother's wives found out you were alive, it was too late?"

"Precisely. So they sent my house to war instead." Jaclyn shifted in her chair, aware Adra, Lady Rathadon, was getting more information from her than the other way around. "How did you go from Adra, a daughter with the blood of the Monarch House to Lady Rathadon?"

"I washed up here. Edward Rathadon was the younger son of the Rathadon warlord. I took his mind to make him mine. Then killed his siblings to assure my safety," Adra said, waving her hand, her tone distinctly matter of fact. "Easy enough to arrange here. Everyone believed they died of a condition they call veil sickness."

"Mother claimed her father had ordered his daughters be brought to his bed and was breeding with them before mother killed him." Jaclyn looked squarely into Adra's eyes. "Were you, is your oldest son…"

"Your mother did not lie about the depths our father and his wives had descended to. I was pregnant when I ran from the Monarch House, but that child is not Steven."

"Where is that child?"

"When I washed up here on the outskirts of Vallantia, a group of men set on me. Edward came along and killed them. It's how we met. Ease your mind, I lost that ill conceived child."

"So Steven…"

"Has the blood of the Monarch House running through his veins, but only from me. Steven is not the result of me being forced to breed with my king. The other half of Steven's heritage is Rathadon."

Jaclyn sank back into the cushions of the chair she was sitting in regarding Adra. In part she was horrified, but she could hear the truth in the words this aunt spoke.

"You went to great lengths to ensure I received your message. What do you have to say that is so important you'd risk my anger?" Jaclyn asked.

"We both know if you were going to kill me or my son, we would already be dead. My other son must concern you greatly to let us live. You intend to use us as hostages against Michael, I take it?" Lady Rathadon spoke bluntly, not taking her eyes off Jaclyn. "I think this is a conversation that should remain between two daughters of the blood. Of course, it is totally your decision, niece."

Jaclyn gritted her teeth, then forced herself to relax. She wished she could refute the old woman's statement as to why they were still alive, but unfortunately, Lady Rathadon was correct. A situation that she couldn't remedy in the immediate future since none of them would be very useful as bargaining tools if they were dead.

"Go." Jaclyn didn't even look at the daggerwives as she dismissed them.

The old woman waited serenely, as if she wasn't being held hostage in her own home, waiting as the guards filed out. As the door closed behind them, Myra moved subtly to shield Ricardo, who'd come with them. Jaclyn wished she'd asked him to stay behind, but it was too late now.

I don't know what her game is, but I think it's unlikely to be an assassination attempt. She knows she couldn't beat us, Jaclyn said.

"You are correct, Jaclyn, and it would be a pointless exercise given the number of your people that are here in my home. We'd all end up dead, regardless of how many of yours I killed first," Lady Rathadon said.

Jaclyn's eyes widened at the knowledge that the old woman had overheard her mindspeach with Myra and Ricardo.

"My patience grows thin. What do you want?" Jaclyn stared at the old woman, taking in the olive skin and hair that had been black before she'd aged.

"As old as I am, I have the blood of the Monarch House flowing through my veins." The old woman smiled, eyes glittering. "As a result, my sons have just as much claim to the throne of the Monarch House as you do."

If she's telling the truth about her heritage, she's right, Myra whispered.

I sense no falsehood in the woman's words, Ricardo said.

Neither do I. She's deliberately left her mind open as she spoke so I could see her truth. Her claim is as strong as my own. Or it would be if she was still fertile, Jaclyn said.

"You need to stop manipulating the minds of my people," Jaclyn said. "Or relative or not, I'll end your life. I will still have possession of your husband and Steven to influence Michael."

"You'll have even more pressure to bring on Michael if you bind yourself to Steven and breed successfully with him."

If you mate successfully with Steven, the child will have an unmatched right to ascend the throne, Ricardo said. *With the blood of the Monarch House from both its mother and father.*

If we are lucky, that child will inherit the fabled strength of the Rathadon's, Myra said.

You would have to mate bond him of course and elevate him to husband for that. We'd have to check with the record keepers, but I think it would be a first for any house to have two husbands, Ricardo said.

Jaclyn was astounded Ricardo had made the comment and that the others seemed to agree with him. Admittedly, there was nothing that stated she could not do so. It was just unheard of.

Only because we have so few men. Myra shrugged. *Her sons are Sylannian regardless of whether they know it. Sylannian and with the blood of the Monarch House.*

Sylannian women have been permitted to run previously but not males. Sylannian males belong to Sylanna. Always, Ricardo said.

She threw an irritated look up at the others, who didn't even appear embarrassed about the conversation they were having between themselves about who she would breed with.

After all, my love, it is you who has often said we will do what we can, anything in order for our house to survive, Ricardo said.

It's another path we can take. It is better to have multiple options rather than be forced into only one, Myra said.

The old woman sniffed, and Jaclyn returned her attention to this newfound relative.

"It might be ancient history now, but having two husbands in a house has occurred in our past. Even three or four if old records were to be believed. Sylannian blood has weakened as the years turn and pass," Lady Rathadon said.

"Why would you want me to make Steven mine? You know what the likely result will be," Jaclyn asked of the woman.

"I am simply doing the same thing your husband and fellow

wives suggest. Opening up multiple paths for survival," Lady Rathadon said. "Besides, I'm perfectly willing to give one son to you to save the other."

"This will not change the fate of this land. We will continue to conquer it piece by piece. But you are correct that it may just allow you to live, at least a little longer." Jaclyn stood.

"Unlike his brother, Steven is much like Sylannian men. Prey to the influence of others. To prepare for you to take my place, I have removed my maternal protection from Steven's mind." Lady Rathadon's stare was a challenge.

Jaclyn gritted her teeth. She couldn't even refute Lady Rathadon's certainty of what the likely result was going to be. She turned away from the old woman, this aunt, and walked towards the door.

Be gentle with Steven when you collar him. He's irritating occasionally, but he is my son and he did not know his heritage until you invaded our home.

The old woman's voice whispered in her head as she strode out of the rooms and down the hallway to the foot of the stairs that led to the suite they had taken over for themselves. She couldn't even deny that was exactly what she was going to do. Even if she was undecided on the wisdom of mating with him herself, regardless of what the others urged her to do. Still, this wasn't her fertile period just yet, so she had time to consider the issue. Besides, she had a war to fight, so the last thing she needed was to be pregnant as well.

You don't need to be on the front line. Our youngest son was conceived and born in the trader lands after all. Your brain will work perfectly fine planning and controlling this war, even when you are with child, Ricardo said.

I will not be rushed into this decision, but I give you all my word. I will consider it, Jaclyn said.

Jaclyn felt them all settle, content to allow her time to think the issue through, although she could tell they were all in favour of her taking this man as her husband. Instead of returning to the rooms they were using, she opened the door on the left, where they had detained Steven. Grateful she'd left him isolated in his chambers as well. It would certainly make things easier going forward if she did as her family was urging her to. As both Myra and Ricardo followed her, she ignored the satisfaction she sensed from them both.

CHAPTER
NINETEEN

Jaclyn walked into Steven's room. He stood up as she entered and swallowed. She smiled at the hint of nervousness he displayed. She wondered how she'd missed the telltale signs that gave away his Sylannian heritage. Of course, his eyes were full barbarian, but it's not like he could help those bright blue eyes of his. He tensed as she walked up to him, but didn't move as she placed one hand on his chest. Her other hand rose, and she rested her fingers on his temples. His eyes widened as he gazed back at her.

Hush Steven. I won't hurt you.

Without a direct mate bond forged into his mind, she could not fully compel him, but he relaxed readily enough under the soothing pulses she sent him. She lowered her eyes, noting his buttons were only half done up. Jaclyn pushed his shirt aside and ran her hand over his chest. She smiled appreciatively. Unlike the average soft and pampered Sylannian male, Steven had well-developed muscles. Coming to a decision, she grabbed one of the silken ties from around her waist. She reached up and wrapped it around his neck. At her prompting the silk wound around itself twisting, its ends disappearing as it formed into a solid collar.

You will take him as a mate? Ricardo asked.

I haven't decided yet, but you are all correct. His bloodline is too valuable. Just in case I decide to mate him myself, could you see if you can start preparing him to accept a mate bond? It will go easier on him if he is willing and opens himself to it. Jaclyn glanced over at Ricardo, who nodded.

Of course Jaclyn, Ricardo said. *It will be a novelty having a second husband in the house. I miss the times I spent with your brother before you became my firstwife.*

There was hint of sadness in Ricardo's mindvoice. It wasn't something she'd realised until they went to fight against the clans and now here. Despite never being alone, always being surrounded and having at least one of their wives in their bed from the time they became a husband, Sylannian men lived lonely lives. Severed from male friends or companionship from the instant they selected their firstwife. Almost every moment of their lives controlled from that point forward. Except for interactions when they were at functions. Even then, they were in a pool of safety protected by their daggerwives.

Regardless of my decision because of his heritage, Steven will at least be a member of our household. Should it be safe and you enjoy each other's company, I see no reason you can't be friends in the future. Jaclyn smiled at the spurt of happiness that came from Ricardo.

Jaclyn looked back at Steven. She was cautious. Steven's mother obviously realised that if she didn't collar Steven straight away that she would.

"You belong to me now, Steven. I will decide what to do with you in the coming days," Jaclyn said.

She sensed his confusion. Touching his temple, she soothed him again and smiled in satisfaction as he responded as she wished him to. It seems Steven's mother was correct. He had that much in common with the average Sylannian male. They were ridiculously easy to manipulate without a wife to protect their minds. Without saying more, she turned from him and left his quarters. Before Jaclyn went back to her suite, she gave orders to the daggerwives regarding his change of status. In response, a team of daggerwives entered his room, this time to protect Steven from any potential harm, rather than as prison guards. It was a distinction that Steven didn't need to be aware of, at least not yet.

TWENTY

Ben glanced around the dank underground tunnel. These things were ancient and previous feet had worn a rut before him. There were some advantages to living in a city that had long been home to marauding warlord's and smugglers. They didn't stretch everywhere in Vallantia, but they covered most of the old quarter, coincidentally aligning with both the poorer sections of town and the traders' quarter. Most of these he was familiar with. He'd explored these tunnels with Michael and the twins before Vallantia fell to the Warlord. When Michael had asked him to lead his network, he'd reacquainted himself with them.

That didn't mean he wasn't surprised by some of the newer offshoots he'd discovered. It seemed some of the wealthier players had found all sorts of reasons to attend places that might raise eyebrows. Particularly if they'd just strolled into certain less reputable areas and through the front doors. Although it suited his purpose, since it gave him access to more of the city. Unfortunately, this network in Vallantia itself didn't extend all the way to the Rathadon Estate. Those Rathadon warlords of old had been too canny for that. While they'd wanted secret ways in and out of their home, they took exception to the common folk to gaining access to their fortress. Of course, he was aware of those ways in and out as well, but few did, and he'd have to travel well out of the city to gain entry to them.

Ben looked back at the team that followed him and motioned for them to take care. They were approaching an area where some locals had been herded into. Everyone was well versed in their role this night, so they maintained silence as much as they could. While he could talk one on one with an individual without risk of anyone else overhearing, if he broadened it to include the entire group, any who happened to be in the vicinity could potentially overhear them. Certainly not an entire conversation, but possibly enough to realise there was something wrong and come to investigate. If that person was Sylannian, which was probable, it would get a little messy. That was something they'd all rather avoid. So they resorted to the old-fashioned method.

One of his people pressed forward, climbing up the stairs to the door, resting her hand on it as she closed her eyes and concentrated. Michael and all the Unwanted could each perform whatever skill they wanted to with the veil. They had talent in bucket loads and then some. Of course, they paid a price for what they could do, but that was also something he was more than happy not to pass on to anyone. Let everybody think they were all powerful. It played into the reputation of the Unwanted and meant less risk for them and everyone else. For the rest of them, they had to collect the right group with skill sets that complimented each other. They needed to combine skills in order to help them complete the task they set for themselves.

After checking that no-one was on the other side, she eased open the door, then deftly undid the latches that held the wooden shelf in place. Finally, she pushed on the shelves and the entire cabinet swung into the room. Ben winced at the scraping noise, which suggested an object had been placed on the other side of the shelving unit. His team quickly made their way up the stairs and into the room.

Ben entered, and the others pushed the shelving unit back into position. A muffled clunk gave away that the latches had clicked into place, securing the shelf once more. He glanced around the boat shed they'd come out in, seeing evidence the smugglers' den was still in use. This was a risk given Michael had briefed him that it was probably smugglers who'd ferried the Sylannian's into Vallantia. Even if they were using this place in some capacity, they weren't staying here. The Sylannians had taken over some of the better appointed houses in the city for themselves. Which meant the bulk of them were well away from the poorer quarters and the series of dockside warehouses, favoured by traders and smugglers alike. He made no judgment on which was which, other than he suspected most of the traders engaged in some business that was underhanded.

They fanned out, checking their surrounds. Ben ran on light feet up the next set of stairs, with a handful of his people following him. A hand reached past him, once again touching the door. He glanced at her and she shook her head, then held up five fingers. He eased his sword out of its sheath. There was a slight shuffling as the rest repositioned themselves and those who came forward drew their weapons. When the others indicated they were ready, he pushed the door open, breathing a sigh of relief that the hinges didn't squeak and give away their presence. A group of Sylannians lounged on some chairs off to one side and Ben broke into a run. Ben grinned fiercely as he realised two of their enemy had made the mistake of falling asleep. They were upon the Sylannians before their realise the threat they were under and surged up. Daggers flew from either side of him, taking out the two who'd had the misfortune to be sleeping on the couch. Sword rising, Ben took on the Sylannian closest to him, hoping there wasn't any more of their kind close enough to hear the noise and come to find out what was going on. As one of his opponent's blades struck his chest, he grunted but the blow didn't draw blood. This time he was grateful for the Smith's ability at crafting fighting leathers. While he'd have a bruise from the strike, he'd survive. The enemy gasped and froze for the barest moment, but that was all Ben needed. He pressed his advantage and struck, forcing his opponent on the defensive. Another of his people leapt on her from behind. An arm wrapping around her neck before they jerked the blade they wielded across the Sylannian's throat.

In the sudden stillness, he breathed deeply. They'd learned in this fight so far it was much easier to overwhelm the enemy with numbers if they found them in small groups. The Sylannians also seemed to have a few flaws in their fighting style. Strangely enough, they were far more difficult to bring down in cramped circumstances than in a big open space. When in the open, it was as if they forgot about all the space they had to manoeuvre in. Of course, now that they had pushed their campaign out of Vallantia to conquer the surrounding farmland and towns, there were far fewer of them in the city itself. Not that they seemed to be short of people. Until recently there had been a constant shipment of Sylannians pouring into Vallantia, then out to join those already battling to take and then secure even more land.

Unfortunately, the citizens of Vallantia were mostly cowed. Not that he could blame them after first being subjected to the Kastler's thugs, then to have Sylanna invade. It hadn't taken too many public executions for most people to comply with what the Sylannians wanted them to do. Which was to work to supply the Sylannians with the food and resources they needed to keep fighting. That was something Ben was determined to do his best to hinder.

TWENTY-ONE

"Khaliun," Batu said.

It was one word. Only her name. Yet the warning and horror conveyed caused her to frown. She followed the direction of Batu's hand as he pointed off to the side of the encampment. Khaliun's breath caught as her mind finally registered what she was seeing. Row upon row of death markers marred the rolling hill. The symbols carved into the stones gave testimony that the deaths they marked were clan.

Despite the early hour, no children were laughing and running around. The camp was still. A chill ran down Khaliun's spine. The guards noticed their presence on the road. It could hardly be missed that the bulk of the wolf warriors did not return with her. A thread of tension jumped from one perimeter guard to the other on her approach.

"Khaliun, what news?" A sentry asked.

"The wolves ride with the warleader," Khaliun said, threading the words she spoke with reassurance. She was rewarded as relief flowed from the camp guards, closely followed by concern. "Send word. I've come to call a conclave."

The perimeter guards stirred, moving from one foot to the other. None meeting her gaze.

"Be careful. Things have changed since you and the wolves departed."

"Things were changing before the wolves left to fulfil our blood debt or our departure wouldn't have been contested. Should the warleader and the entire Warlords domain fall to the Sylannian threat, what remains of the People will be next."

"What will you do?"

"About?"

"If Erden doesn't agree?"

The guard's word choice gave Khaliun pause. She had no doubt the guard had excluded the other leaders, who together made up the conclave on purpose.

"I and those with me will turn around and ride back to rejoin the rest of the wolves and the warleader," Khaliun said, then spurred her horse forward at a trot, heading into camp towards the meeting hall.

"Protect your co-leader. Don't allow her to face Erdan alone," the perimeter guard said to Batu as they rode past in a barely audible whisper.

Khaliun stiffened in her saddle at the warning as the wolves with her traded glances and then close ranks around her, with two of the scouts taking point. She shivered as a breath of cold from the veil washed over her. As Khaliun switched to her other sight, she saw the shimmering shield that had been thrown around their group. The Unwanted who rode with her may not understand their conversation, but they certainly understood the body language of their companions. Her entire team dropped their reins to draw weapons. It was unheard of in their own territory. Khaliun sensed the underlying tension in the camp as well as they did. When combined with the caution the camp guards felt compelled to give her, she found she couldn't fault her small band of wolves or the Unwanted.

Confident behind the shield the Unwanted had thrown up, Khaliun opened her mind shield, grateful she'd spent time while away practicing her abilities under the guidance of various members of the Unwanted. One and all the warleader's people had no issues with offering their knowledge and helping her practice. As a result, she was, if not stronger, more capable than she had been when she'd left. Whispers ran from clan member to clan member. As they rode by, spoken word of mouth and mind raced ahead, spreading news of her arrival throughout the camp.

She'll stand up to him

The wolves were always formidable, they'll protect us.

Even a reckoning of the clan will be better than what we've become.

As Batu stiffened next to her and threw a worried look at her, Khaliun gathered he'd picked up the stray comments as well. For her to go against the decision of a conclave would cause a reckoning of the clans. Khaliun scanned those around her as they rode past, trying to see if she could spot those whose thoughts she'd overheard. Even though they'd been phrased as if they were random, idle thoughts, she had a sinking impression that the speakers had intended her to hear them. They were a careful warning, just as much as the camp guards had been.

"They're afraid. They believe the conclave will refuse," Batu said.

"It's more complicated than that. It's as if they think there is no longer a conclave," Khaliun said, keeping her posture relaxed but ready to act. "That we've returned gives them hope, but they also fear it won't be enough."

"What could have happened?" Batu said.

"I don't know, but I fear I'm about to find out."

"We. We will find out. You won't go in alone. Not after that warning," Batu said, his tone flat and uncompromising.

Khaliun decided against objecting that the precaution wasn't necessary. The alarm and general feeling of the camp had her unsettled as well. She squared her shoulders and, even though her fingers twitched to draw a blade, she resisted the urge. Instead, she concentrated on radiating assurance. Or rather, the dangerous confidence that the Unwanted gave off to those not of their ranks. First, she would find out what had occurred. There was no point in second guessing or coming up with contingencies until she discovered why the perimeter guards had considered it imperative to warn her.

As they pulled up outside the circular meeting tent right in the centre of their camp, she could see word had reached the other clan leaders. Or at least two of them. Erden strode towards the meeting house, his face closed. The only emotions Khaliun could sense from him were a mixture of anger and pride. Orghana walked from the opposite side, her face pinched, two burly clansmen following in her wake. While Orghana didn't say a word to her, Khaliun caught a complicated mix of fear, anger, and defiance as the woman stared straight at Erden.

Tension bounced around the camp. Khaliun shivered but resisted the urge to slam up her mental barriers in response. Right now, the extra information she might glean from those around her might help. The Kallith in the camp believed war was coming. Not from Sylanna, but among themselves. Khaliun reined in her horse and dismounted, taking the opportunity to scan her surroundings. The crows, Eden and Organa's clan, were prominent. After the wolves, they were one of the strongest fighting tribes of the Kallith.

"The other co-leaders aren't here," Batu said, disguising the fact he was scanning those nearest to them by turning to hand his reins to one of their team. "I'm getting a really bad feeling about this. I don't want to give up our weapons, but I know on entering the meeting house, we have to."

"Try to remember everything we've learned while fighting with the warleader and the Unwanted. Even without weapons, the skills we possess enhance our physical strength," Khaliun said, as more of the crows appeared. They stood scattered among the huts surrounding the meeting place. Some of the more prominent crow clan members pressed in closer, hands resting on their weapons.

Erden gasped as Khaliun turned her back on the other leaders and walked into the tent. As Batu followed her lead, she smiled grimly. Tradition held that as the supplicants of the conclave, she should wait and be the last to enter. What she'd done showed she condemned her fellow leaders before any of them uttered even a single word in conclave. Khaliun pulled out her weapons, ignoring the sudden shaft of wariness from Erden to place them on the weapons rack.

"Have you been away so long you've forgotten our ways?" Erden asked, gesturing towards Batu, his voice dripping with contempt. "Batu isn't a leader. He doesn't belong here."

Khaliun glanced over her shoulder, flicking a quick hand gesture to Batu, and walked across the room to take a position on the other side. Batu simply complied and fell in beside her. Although Batu appeared calm and unconcerned, Khaliun sensed the continuous draw on the veil as he filled himself to capacity. Khaliun did likewise, then relaxed as a flow of power came in a stream to her from the Unwanted. They might be outside the meeting house, but they could read the tension as well as she could. While she hoped force wouldn't prove to be necessary, she had an uneasy sense it would be a vain hope.

"He does. The wolves voted for Batu to stand up as temporary co-leader until times are more stable and we make a more permanent appointment," Khaliun said, deliberately keeping her tone pleasant.

Khaliun kept her amusement firmly behind her mind barrier at the shaft of aggravation coming from her fellow leader. Moments passed by as Erden glared at her before he broke eye contact and stomped over to divest himself of weapons. Orghana was subdued compared to her co-leader and already had her weapons in her hand to place on the rack. As two of the crows followed close on Orghana's heels into the meeting place, Khaliun's eyes narrowed.

"Your clan members, however, are not co-leaders of the Kallith. They have no right to be in here."

Erden's back stiffened. "They're here for security. You, after all, have gone against the will of the clan."

"That's not how this works. Not even if you get the vote of a full conclave," Khaliun said, deliberately channelling calm. She wouldn't be any help to anyone if she lost her temper. Instead, she directed her attention to the two crow clan members. "You two do not belong in here. Leave. Wait outside, if you must."

The crows hesitated, their gaze sliding over to Erden.

"Khaliun is correct. Neither of you have a place in here. Go," Orghana said.

The crows didn't even look at Orghana, let alone acknowledge the order from their co-leader. Instead, they steadfastly ignored her to focus entirely on Erden. For his part, Erden's lips thinned as he regarded his co-leader. Khaliun kept her own expression blank with considerable effort.

"They're with you because I can't trust you," Erden snapped, swinging his glare to his co-leader.

"Which is it?" Khaliun asked mildly. "I thought you said they were here because you think I can't be trusted?"

Khaliun kept her stance relaxed as she gathered more of the veil and spun a light shield around her fellow leader. Orghana's eyes widened as the shield enveloped her, but she gave no other reaction other than the hint of defiance directed at Erden. As Orghana went to take her place in the meeting circle, she hesitated, then her back stiffened as she stepped aside. Khaliun only just prevented herself from gasping as Orghana took a position not only away from Erden, but on the wrong side. Co-leader tattoos were meant to flow from one to the other, creating a unified whole. Instead, their co-leader tattoos were broken.

"Not that it should be necessary, but it's the will of two leaders of the clan against one." Orghana turned her icy gaze on her clan members. "Get out unless you wish banishment."

Erden growled deep in his throat and waved his hand. "Go. Keep an eye on the rest of the wolves out there."

Orghana, I'm going into this blind. What has happened in my absence?

Won't he hear us? Orghana asked, her eyes widening.

No. Michael and his Unwanted have taught me a great deal while I've been riding with them. My control is much more focused these days. You're stalling. What's caused this?

It started with minor disagreements on the daily business of our tribe. This is my fault. I let him have his way rather than stand up to him. Then it got worse.

Worse?

He argued Yangir and Narantuya, as our strongest healers, had to go into seclusion. For the good of the clan.

What? They have talent, but it has never been necessary for those of their skill level to go into seclusion. That's why the joint leaders of the Kallith approved their elevation to co-leaders of their tribe. They rode to war with us and acted as field healers.

I know, so do they, but rather than spark an argument, they complied.

Who has taken their place? Why isn't the new co-leader here?

Their tribe refuses to nominate or accept anyone else.

Ulagan and Tuya? Where are they? Khaliun asked, her stomach sinking as she waited for Orghana's response.

Stood down. Erden argued they were too old to be of use in leading Kallith through these times.

You didn't stand against this idiocy? It took every ounce of self control Khaliun possessed not to grind her teeth.

I was going to once I realised things had gone too far, but the other leaders urged caution. They said without strong leadership, the Kallith would fracture and the People would scatter and be no more.

"Have the pair of you finished conspiring with each other?"

Khaliun allowed the silence to stretch between them. She took in Erden's stiffness and closed expression with his mental shields wrapped so tightly they smothered any ability he had to sense her concern.

"What have you done, Erden?"

"I don't answer to you."

"Ah, but you do. As leaders of the clan, we answer to each other and all our people. We don't possess absolute rule. Or have you forgotten?"

"You're unfit—"

"My tribe does not agree with you, but this isn't about me right now. I called for a conclave. We need to send for the other leaders of the Kallith."

"I've stood them down for the good of the clan."

"You don't have the authority without the full conclave and you know it."

"Decisions had to be made. You weren't here, so you wouldn't know." Erden said, his pitch increasing, spittle spraying from his mouth. "You and the rest of the wolves ran off and left us all defenceless."

"You felt vulnerable because I and the rest of the wolves left to fulfil our obligation? Our blood debt to the Warlord? I understand your concern after all we have been through, but you and the remains of our people are safe here."

"You understand nothing! The Sylannians will come after us again and that Warlord you're so fond of will fall on us. You left us with no protection."

"Has another mountain pass to our old homeland been found?"

"No. There's been no sign of the Sylannians. Or any other attack here," Orghana said.

"Someone had to preserve our ways. We are the last of the People," Erden said.

Erden has become filled with hate and fear, but many of our tribe follow him. I don't understand it, but they soak up every word he utters.

Khaliun realised Erden was still speaking while she'd been distracted talking with Orghana. She wasn't entirely sure of what he'd said, but she wasn't impressed with the latter half.

"...for the good of the People you will stand down and the wolf tribe will prepare to disband," Erden said, his head high and his chest puffed out.

As he drew in a breath to continue, Khaliun interjected, determined to take some of the wind out of his ego. "You don't have the authority to do this. Any of it."

She reeled and walked towards the door, Batu at her heels. A thump of feet gave away that Erden was closing the distance between them. Not wanting conflict, but aware it was coming, Khaliun snatched her weapons from the rack and was barely clear of the tent before she spun. The team of wolves she'd brought with her tensed, drawing more power to themselves yet held at the ready.

"Take her and contain her in the cells! She's a risk to us all!" Erden snarled.

A group of crows stepped forward only to pause as her wolves and the Unwanted placed themselves in front of her.

"Stand down," Khaliun said, pitching her voice so it carried across the growing crowd that had gathered. "I accuse Erden of a serious breach in the Way. As a leader of the Kallith, I call for a reckoning. Fetch the other leaders of Kallith."

Erden lunged forward, only to find himself restrained by a group of clansmen. In the struggle that followed, Khaliun marked the clan tattoos of those who assisted. It was a slight relief to see representatives of not only the eagles and snow cat tribes, but a handful of crows as well. Reason hadn't fled everyone.

"What are you doing? You can't let her get away with this!" Erden said, as he writhed ineffectually under the restraint.

"You lot, go! Release the leaders from wherever they have been confined."

"But Erden—"

"Erden stands accused and until this matter is settled, what he wants is immaterial. Under threat of banishment from the Kallith for any who interfere, free the other leaders." Khaliun nominated a handful of wolves. "Go with them. The safety of the leaders is paramount. You have my permission to place any who hinder you under restraint. You may use any tactic you need, up to and including lethal measures if necessary."

A collective gasp sounded from the watching clansmen at the last order, but none stepped forward to protest. As her team and other clansmen rushed off to do her bidding, Khaliun stood, trying to exude calm. As the wolves disappeared, a group of crows moved toward her. At a scrape of metal and the two members of the Unwanted moving to bracket her, the Crows stopped and took a noticeable step back. All she hoped was that her exterior was calmer than the seething anger that kindled inside.

CHAPTER
TWENTY-TWO

Allani watched as Tony, the captain who seemed to take it as a personal responsibility, carried Isabella back into the cell. She kept her expression neutral, although her heart ached as Tony knelt and lay Isabella down on the makeshift bed. The usual guards had brought it in without explanation, but Allani suspected it was the work of this man who at least found Isabella's fate *distasteful*. Even the food the regular cell guards supplied them had improved since they'd placed Isabella in with them.

Jana bent over and brushed Isabella's temple with her fingers. "Sleep child, I will help bring what vengeance I can to the monster that torments you."

The captain flicked his gaze from Isabella to Jana. His confusion mixed with suspicion was clear. While Tony seemed to suspect they were up to something, Allani could sense from his mind that he didn't want to press them for any details. He also couldn't speak so much as a word of Sylannian, making these interactions easier.

"The warlord requests Jana brought to him again," Tony said.

Allani nodded, then transferred her gaze to Jana. "Are you sure you're up to this?"

"Of course First. The girl's life would be easier if you would let me insert a control bond in his mind. I can do it," Jana said, as she rose smoothly to her feet.

"Perhaps, but with all the guards here, we are severely outnumbered. It would be impossible for us to defeat them all, and I'd rather not risk Isabella or Damien. We'll do this my way. Drain Aiden as much as you can without being detected."

Jana's face screwed up, and she looked down at the ground for a heartbeat before her head rose. Her expression blank. "I was alone here for so long before you came and since then you've treated me as one of your own. It will be as you order."

"I know you want to do more. We all do, but trust me on this. Weaken the new warlord. It will be enough," Allani said.

"I trust your judgement First," Jana ducked her head, "it's just Isabella suffers so much under that monster's hands."

"We are helping her in the best way we can. Go. Exhaust Aiden so he's incapable of dealing with even those weaker than he is in power level, but don't get caught."

"That's enough. I'm sorry you don't have a choice," Tony said.

"Of course Captain Tony, I apologise for keeping you waiting. I was conferring with my firstwife. I'm ready now," Jana said.

Tony's eyes flicked between them both before he finally gestured for Jana to proceed him. Allani watched as the cell was locked once more and Jana disappeared, her head high as Tony escorted her out of the cells to the warlord.

Allani pushed Jana's task from her mind. The wife would do as she was ordered to do. Either Jana would survive or not. Her fate was with the powers. Allani moved over to Isabella's side and sunk down beside the girl, snapping her fingers. One of the lesser wives came scurrying across with a small bowl that had contained their bathing water that morning but was now empty.

"Is it safe?" Isabella whispered.

"Yes child, they are gone," Allani said, sending a wave of reassurance to the girl.

Sweat beaded Isabella's entire body as she trembled in an effort to contain herself.

"Please, I can't bear for anything belonging to that man to touch me." Isabella pushed ineffectually at the cloak she wore.

One of Allani's daggerwives assisted Isabella in removing the cloak and the thin slip she wore. At the sudden movement, Isabella lurched to one side and Allani positioned the bowl as Isabella retched up the contents of her stomach. Allani glanced over at the group of wives over to one side of the cell, who started up their high, wailing chant. As they'd been doing at this hour of late, as if it was some custom. When, in fact, it was simply to mask the noise of Isabella throwing up the drug. While some of the poison passed into Isabella's system, caging her emerging powers, it was nowhere near as much as these people believed. If they'd known how little the girl was truly being affected by it. That she seemed to be allergic to it. They'd be terrified.

Allani waited until Isabella slumped back onto the sleeping cot. Before leaning forward, her hand resting on Isabella's temple.

"What happened, child? Show me," Allani said.

While Isabella's body remained listless on the bed, her eyes were intense as she gazed up into her own. Allani was swept up in Isabella's recall of the events that had happened to her from the moment she'd been taken from the cell until Aiden had poured the vial of tiscan down her throat. The memory was sharp right up to the point, then it was fragmented and confused between Aiden's rooms and the cells.

"I'm sorry Allani, I should have been stronger," Isabella said.

"Nonsense. You did a superb job. Aiden will never suspect you are not falling under his sway," Allani said, then gathered Isabella into her arms, rocking her gently.

"He'll transfer me to the stable soon. I don't think I can stand against him without your help."

"You are stronger than you believe yourself to be, Isabella. Besides. I'll help you reinforce your mental shields against his intrusions as you sleep."

"But he's already able to manipulate me. I can't seem to stop him but I know it's him," Isabella's voice caught, and she wiped the tears from her eyes.

"For small things, yes, you are prey to others as everyone can be without good shields. I guarantee you, your inner mind is your own and he will not break through, no matter what he tries."

Isabella's eyes were full, brimming with unshed tears. "Promise?"

"I promise. I'm much better at such things than this Aiden who seeks to possess you," Allani said, stroking Isabella's head while she soothed her. "Now, let us help clean you up and you can sleep."

Allani snapped her fingers at her fellow wives, who came forward. One removed the bowl Isabella had been sick in and discarded the contents into the waste bucket in the corner. Another wife brought a basin to help wash the girl. As little as it was, Isabella would feel better after they helped her wash, like they were wiping away the taint of the man that had pawed at her all night. When they were done, they threw a length of spidersilk over Isabella and Allani hummed at it, coaxing it to envelop the girl. Isabella sighed, curling up onto her side and drifted off to sleep.

As the girl lay locked in the drug that persisted in her system, Allani threw her personal shield around Isabella, then gently probed her mind. Allani pulled further details from Isabella. The entire scene where the old warlord had been killed, complete with sight, sound and smell. Right down to the last detail. For anyone who shared this memory, it would be like they were Isabella, at that moment in the room when disaster hit. When she was done, Allani went to work, helping to reinforce the girl's mental barriers against Aiden. Not too much. He'd get suspicious of his lack of progress if he couldn't manipulate her at all, but he'd not capture her mind, no matter how hard he tried. Any bond he attempted to insert to control Isabella would slide off her reinforced internal shields. At least while Isabella remained here in the cells. Soon she feared Isabella was correct and Aiden would move her out of Allani's direct reach. That made the work she did on Isabella's mind now even more important.

Allani had no sense of the passage of time while she worked. She sank back, pinching the bridge of her nose. While the idea of sleep was enticing, there was still one more task she had left.

"Lend me your strength. I fear I don't have enough power to reach the individual I must find."

The wives didn't question her order, they simply complied by sending their energy to her. It didn't take long to replenish her flagging store of the veil.

"You've found someone suitable First?" the primewife asked.

Allani nodded. "There is a man here, Owen. Isabella knows him well. He was her protector, of sorts. He shouldn't be hard to find. Keep watch, but don't pull me out unless necessary."

TWENTY-THREE

Owen's eyes flared open, his breath catching in his throat as he stared into the darkness. Other than the soft snoring of one of his fellow guards down the far end of the barracks, and the regular breathing of those that slept near him, it was quiet. He could have sworn someone called his name.

Owen.

Yes?

Owen eased himself up, glancing around to make sure none of the others had been disturbed.

Find the warleader. The woman ordered.

Owen gasped as the compulsion settled in his brain, sweat beading his forehead as he stopped himself from leaping to his feet immediately to obey her order.

Who are you?

My name is Allani, I'm a friend of Damien and Isabella.

Owen frowned as he caught the slight hesitation before she'd answered him.

Why do you want me to go to the warleader?

Aiden has taken Isabella to his bed, using the threat of Damien's life. The warleader needs to be told it is Aiden who killed his father. Not Damien.

I know I've heard Aiden has taken Isabella in his bed and I've seen Damien chained up in the courtyard. Owen wanted to believe this woman, yet he had a small part of his mind that doubted. *Damien would kill for Isabella,* Owen said, his voice hesitant.

He would, but he didn't. Isabella observed it all. It was Aiden who killed his father and then planted the blade in Damien's hand. Damien's mind is fogged by tiscan making him less than he is and unable to fight back, Allani said.

Aiden plans to kill Damien's team. Go. Find them, then go to the warleader.

I can't leave here without Isabella and Damien.

Don't be foolish. You can't free either of them by yourself.

If Michael finds out Damien killed the Warlord, he will kill Damien.

Tell the warleader it's Aiden. Isabella was there and saw it all. This is what happened, show the warleader.

Owen stiffened as Allani seemed to grab his mind. Images, words, and sounds flashed in his mind. It was disconcerting. He gripped the edge of his sleeping cot as what he was actually seeing with his eyes was superimposed with the memory the woman had shoved in his head.

Aiden whispered lies in Damien's mind.

Wait, what? Damien's strong. How could Aiden do such a thing?

I don't know. He boasted to Isabella he'd been in the back of Damien's mind since he joined the Unwanted. That Damien is his unwitting puppet. Aiden said he'd done it all right under the warleader's nose.

Owen bit his lip and ran a hand through his hair.

I don't want to leave them like this.

Aiden is now the warlord, his men are in control. Isabella believes the warleader is the only one who can beat Aiden.

Oh please, Aiden isn't that strong in the veil.

He is stronger than he appears in certain ways and the guards here follow him. The best way you can help Isabella and Damien is to find Damien's team.

Owen ducked his head and squeezed his eyes shut. He didn't want to believe her, but it made more sense to him than Damien going berserk and killing the Warlord.

Where is his team?

I wish I could tell you, but that isn't something Isabella knows, but you must try.

Promise me you'll look out for them both.

Owen swallowed as the silence stretched. He could feel the woman shut down and as she considered her reply. The knowledge didn't make him happy in any way, shape, or form.

Just get to the warleader.

Owen sent his silent assent to Allani, although his heart ached. A part of him wanted to stay here, in case he was needed. Although with her order pushing at his mind, he doubted he could resist what she wanted him to do for much longer. He grimaced. Logically, the likelihood of an opportunity to break both Isabella and Damien free was slim. In all honesty he had to admit someone else was better skilled at sorting out this mess than he was. Grateful he'd never been a packhorse, he gathered his bag and weapons. Without a backward glance, he eased the door open and walked out into the corridor. He kept his pace to a normal stride, his expression neutral. Just another guard among all the others that followed the warlord, reporting somewhere for duty. The last thing he wanted anyone to think was that he was sneaking out of the castle.

Owen paused on the edge of the courtyard, contemplating the gate. The compulsion pulsed at him, urging him to leave the castle. He gritted his teeth and ignored it. Once set by Allani, it made no distinction that the gate was locked, making it impossible for him to leave. As dawn tinged the sky, Owen heard good natured joking along with grumbling as a team of guards started massing. Some were on foot, while others clattered in on horseback to wait with their squad.

"Listen up! The traitor's team is suspected to be camping somewhere in the forest around Yalleska. You all have your assignments. Remember locate them and send for reinforcements. The Unwanted are believed to be complicit in the old Warlord's death and are dangerous." A tall band leader bellowed from the front of the massing search party.

As the gates groaned open and the squad marched or rode forward, Owen stepped out and merged into their ranks. Even though his heart pounded, no one so much as sent a stray glance in his direction as he walked out of the Stronghold with them all.

OWEN STARED AT THE TAVERN, then glanced once more around the quiet streets, grateful it hadn't been difficult to slip away from the search party. At least it wasn't once they'd finished their unsuccessful search of the forest and returned passing through Yalleska on their way back to the Stronghold. It was just as well there weren't many such places where the members of the Unwanted could be staying. Even so, it had taken him the whole evening to stumble upon where they were staying. The solitary member they left on guard duty, even here in Yalleska, also gave away their presence. A handy thing under the circumstances. He doubted the woman had understood the task she'd given him. Yalleska might not be the size of Vallantia or Callenhain, but it certainly had more than one lodging place. His guess regarding the type of establishment they'd be in paid off. This place was quiet and out of the way. Another thing to the warleader's credit, he kept a tight rein on discipline over his people. Even when he wasn't around to enforce it.

Not wanting to try his chances with the man on the door, he turned and made his way down a side street. Even if he was believed by the guard, his presence would draw the man's attention from the street. With Aiden's men out looking for them, it was the last thing they needed. Owen ignored the side door to the tavern. While it was likely unlocked, it was also more than probable that the kitchen hands were bedded down in the corner. They would be up early to get breakfast ready for those that lodged in the upper rooms. He climbed carefully up on some ale barrels stacked near the back entrance to the taproom. Then he jumped, grabbing the edge of the balcony, using his momentum to propel himself up, then he swung his foot over the edge. He used his arms and legs to haul himself up and over the edge, then clambered over the rail. Owen suspected, this room, the largest, would house whoever led the warleader's people within. He doubted they'd tolerate anyone else staying in the place while they were here, and he'd already discovered the owner and his family slept in rooms to the back. Grinning, he cracked the door open and eased inside to find cold metal pressed against his throat. A voice as cold as the steel spoke to him out of the darkness.

"Tell me why I should let you live."

Owen froze, his eyes widening as he swallowed with his mind shockingly blank for a moment.

"You're one of the Unwanted? You came with Damien?"

"I'm Damien's second, Callan. What of it?" Callan asked.

"Damien and Isabella are in trouble."

Light flared in the room without the man who stood at his side having moved and the light stones still being shuttered on the table beside the bed. Owen swallowed again. On the positive side, this was clearly one of the warleader's men. His eyes slid sideways as he tried not to move.

"His sister? What is Isabella doing here? What trouble?"

"Ranlith was sacked by Sylanna. The Warlord brought us with him when he passed through what was left."

"What the powers was the Warlord doing in Ranlith? They were meant to travel directly to the Stronghold." Callan grated, then shook his head. "Never mind. I doubt you'd be aware of the reason. Go on."

Owen slowly let his breath out. "The Warlord is dead."

"How?" Callan growled. Anger from Callan rolled over Owen in waves, and he squeezed his eyes shut as the emotion battered at him.

"Damien killed him, or so Aiden says. It's why the Stronghold is locked up."

"Damien what?"

Owen let out the breath he'd unconsciously been holding as the overwhelming anger cut off.

"I don't know all the details. I wasn't there. Aiden accused Damien of going mad and killing his father. They chained Damien up in the inner courtyard and Aiden had Isabella thrown into the cells. He's accused her of being her brother's accomplice."

"Why would Damien do that?"

"It's said he found his sister with the Warlord and Damien snapped and killed him."

Callan withdrew the blade that had been held at Owen's throat and started swearing.

"That would be a stupid thing to do, and Damien isn't stupid. He's enough of a tactician to work out being in the middle of the Stronghold and doing such a thing, he'd die and then his sister would as well."

"I was told to tell you it wasn't Damien. It was Aiden who killed his father."

"Who told you?" Callan bit out.

"She, she said her name was Allani." Owen shook his head. "I don't know anything about her, but she placed a compulsion on me. I couldn't refuse to come here."

"Wait, who did you say?" Callan somehow became more intense than he had been previously. So much so Owen was reminded why normal people avoided the Unwanted.

"She said to tell you her name is Allani. She said she's in the cells with Isabella. That Isabella is being kept drugged as well to control her. That Aiden is in Damien's head, but she's doing her best to keep Aiden out and shelter Damien's mind as much as she can." Owen shrugged, hoping Callan believed him. "I'm sorry, but I don't understand even half of what that means."

"Never mind, I've got a fair idea. What else did Allani say?" Callan asked.

"Aiden desires Isabella. He has forced her into his bed by threatening Damien." Owen frowned.

A flash of pain crossed the other man's face and when he opened his eyes Owen couldn't help but flinch back as fire seemed to dance in them.

"There's more..." Owen whispered against his best judgement.

"What?" The fire reduced in the other man's eyes.

Although Owen wasn't sure he found it anymore reassuring, since now those eyes with the hint of flame in them were gazing straight at him, he shuddered. It was like the man was staring through him.

"She said Aiden plans to send men out to kill you all. He knows some of you must be here somewhere. He also knows the warleader isn't, or else he would have gone to the stronghold rather than Damien. Allani said we need to get to the warleader."

"How would Allani know all this from the cells?" the man asked.

"Isabella knows, because Aiden calls her to his bed every evening, after he's done..." Owen stopped and pushed down the helpless rage that boiled inside. "He likes to tell her his plans, what he's going to do to her and everyone. Then sends her back to the cells drugged with tiscan. So Allani knows. Allani said he wants Isabella, but he fears her power. Isabella can't use her abilities, but Allani can since no one has thought to drug them."

Callan swore softly again before sheathing his blade.

"If you are lying to me, you will not live long enough to enjoy your prank."

"I'm not lying, besides they assigned me to one of the warbands. They've been scouring the likely campsites on the outskirts of Yalleska all day. It's how I got out of the Stronghold. New orders have come down to search the town. They know you wouldn't have left without Damien," Owen said, hoping it was enough to convince Callan, then remembered the memory that had flooded his mind. "Allani showed me what happened to the Warlord, she said it was from Isabella who was there when Aiden killed his father and planted the blade on Damien."

Irritation flashed across Callan's face, his jaw clenching before he took what Owen could only describe as a calming breath. Unfortunately, Owen wasn't entirely sure it worked.

"Why didn't you start with that?" Callan bit out.

"Um, sorry I'm a little, I don't know. No one has ever shoved another person's experiences in my head before," Owen said.

Callan sighed, rubbing his face with his hand, growling deep in his throat.

"Show me," Callan said.

"I don't know how," Owen said, swallowing again.

The silence between them lasted long enough that he thought he was about to be killed out of hand for his stupidity. If he was honest right now, he wasn't sure he'd blame the warleader's man. If he was in Callan's shoes, he'd kill him as well.

"If you are telling me the truth, we don't have time for me to get it out of your mind now. The fast way would kill you or leave you mindless. If you aren't telling the truth, when I discover you've been lying and trust me, I will get it out of your head. I'll kill you," Callan said.

"I swear to you I'm not lying. I protected Damien as best I could in Ranlith before the Warlord claimed him and did my best for Isabella." Owen's head dropped and he gazed at his boots. Right now he didn't care if the other man killed him. "I've failed to protect them both."

Hearing movement, he glanced up to find Callan had turned and was in the middle of pulling his leathers on. Owen hadn't heard the alert that Callan had sent. He just guessed Callan had woken the rest of the Unwanted since he could hear those in the rooms around stir. They weren't loud, but in the stillness of dawn, it stood out in the otherwise quiet tavern. It impressed Owen despite the circumstances. They were up and moving, herding him along with them and he headed out of Yalleska town with veil drawn mist hiding their path.

TWENTY-FOUR

Callan set a hard pace, drawing the veil to himself in a continuous flow, not only obscuring their passage from any who might look but muffling any sound they made. This wasn't something they habitually did in a population centre and if they did, it wasn't usually him who decided on the course of action. It was unfortunate that right now it was him left in the leadership position, despite the lengths he'd gone to avoid it. Procrastination wasn't a habit he wallowed in, so he made the decision. They needed to get out, and he'd make it up from there.

With a small pull of energy, he gathered moisture from the wells and bodies of water into the air, thickening the surrounding mist. A small use of the veil, utilised to great effect. Early morning mist was a common occurrence up here in the foothills, which was how it would appear if someone glanced out their window. If the information Owen had passed on was correct, it was best if there weren't people who could helpfully point the warbands who tried to track them down in the right direction. Despite Yalleska being the Warlord's home village and being at the base of the mountain that the fortress sat on, Yalleska wasn't big. Prosperous yes. Very. But smaller than anyone who hadn't been here before would expect. It was somewhere in between the sizes of the sprawling cities of Vallantia and Callenhain and tiny little villages like Ranlith.

With the village waking from its slumber, Callan breathed a sigh of relief as they left Yalleska behind without a hint of disturbance or being pursued. Callan had already received reports that warbands had searched around Yalleska, although he hadn't realised Aiden's warband had been searching for them. After the teams finished checking for them in town, Callan guessed they'd spear off toward Vallantia, seeking signs of them further afield. With a light mental signal to the team, he turned off the road and headed cross country, heading for the nearby forest. All followed him without hesitation, even their informant. Not that he had much choice, since they tied a guide rope to Shallan's horse to make sure he stayed with them. Callan ranged out with his mind as they hit the trees, but discovered no other sign of life in their vicinity. Still, he didn't drop the concealment he'd generated. Finally, he slowed and came to a halt by a small stream. Callan dismounted, as did the rest of the squad.

"Isn't this a little close to Yalleska?" Owen asked, as he glanced around.

"You said they've already checked the closer campsites. We should be safe enough for now."

"Oh, of course," Owen said.

"Besides, we have plenty of cover here, and I need to see the memories that Allani sent to you," Callan said.

Callan detailed Shallan to get a crew together and keep watch towards Yalleska. She promptly selected a couple of people and they ran off back the way they'd entered this forest. The rest of the team spread to take up defensive positions in case needed.

"What do you need me to do?" Owen asked.

Sit down, relax, and make sure you are in a comfortable position, Callan said, gesturing to a rocky outcrop near the small bubbling river.

Simple enough for you to tell me to relax, not as easy to do. Owen took a shaky breath before sitting down.

As Callan walked up behind Owen he sent a wave of reassurance to the other man.

The more relaxed you are, the easier this will be for you. You'll end up with a splitting headache anyway, but if you can remain calm and go with the process, you won't be begging me to chop your head off to ease the pain. Callan explained.

That explanation doesn't make this easy. Owen chuckled, although Callan could hear the tension in it.

Get comfortable, close your eyes and listen to the babbling of the stream, the wind rustling the leaves, and concentrate on your breathing. Breathe deeply but slowly, pausing before the inhale and again before the exhale. Ignore everything else. Callan placed his fingertips gently on Owen's temples and felt him flinch. *It's alright, I won't start without you being aware of it. This method is longer, but easier on you than the other way.*

Owen assented, but to his credit, he didn't speak. Instead, he simply tried his best to follow the instructions and relax. Callan closed his own eyes and slowed his breathing down, mimicking the pattern he'd suggested to Owen. He smiled faintly, as it didn't take long for the other man to follow his example. Time passed, but he paid it no attention. He simply monitored the state of Owen's mind.

I need you to drop your shield. Don't worry, the rest of us are maintaining strong shields and we are far enough away from town for the constant chatter not to be problematic for you, Callan said, keeping his tone soft and calm.

Owen's tension increased a notch, but it was still much lower than it had been when he'd started trying to get the man to relax. Callan waited patiently, noticing when the tension left Owen once again, as nothing untoward happened. He suspected Owen often ran with his shields down when he was out hunting alone without being aware of it.

This is what's going to happen. Soon I'll ask you to remember what Allani said to you, to remember what she showed you. Stay as relaxed as you can with your mental shield down. There will be a spike of pain as I enter your mind. It's what will cause your headache. Try not to panic, it will just be me creating a small connection with you. From there, I'll take the memory Allani shoved into your head.

Callan kept his link to the veil loose, allowing it to flow around and through him, waiting for Owen's tension to decrease further. Finally, he started drawing in power, although he didn't really need much. It was the sad thing about the ability he was about to use. It could be so destructive, but so easy to accomplish.

Think of what Allani told you. Repeat it in yourself. Remember the memory she sent you.

With only a subtle push, the conversation took a life of its own. It was like he was there. Owen wasn't just trying to remember and mutter the words to himself. He relived the experience once again, as if he was back there with Allani whispering in his mind. Taking care not to tense himself, which Owen would feel and respond to, Callan used the power within himself and punched a connection into Owen's mind. Callan ignored Owen's ragged gasp and scream as he ruthlessly battered down Owen's automatic response to fight and kick this intruder out of his head. Callan wasted no time in seizing hold of the memory. The words Allani'd said, whispering again on replay in his head. Then the part he was waiting for, where she'd flung Isabella's memory of the attack on the Warlord. This time there were images, feelings, sounds, all of it replaying. The memory, the raw emotion, horror and fear Isabella suffered in that moment sent Callan to his knees. As the replay finished, Callan withdrew from Owen's mind, pausing just before he left.

Sleep, Callan urged.

Owen could not resist his compulsion. Particularly since he was still right there in the other man's head. Callan supported him as he slumped, easing him to the ground. Nodding as two of the other team members who'd been waiting for that moment came forward to assist carrying Owen off to a sleeping cot. Finally Callan fully withdrew from the other's mind and, as gently as he could, cut the bond between them. Owen moaned as the snapped connection rebounded back at him, but otherwise didn't stir. Callan squeezed his eyes shut, trying to ward off the overload of emotions that had accompanied the harrowing memory. These weren't his feelings, they were Isabella's. After a few steadying breaths Callan looked up at the members of the team, who stood in a ring around him.

"It's true, the Warlord is dead by Aiden's hand," Callan said.

Callan held up his hand and allowed Gavrel to assist him up as shock resounded through everyone. The Warlord had been a like a permanent fixture in all their lives. The thought that he was dead was inconceivable. While Callan knew he needed to contact Michael, he also needed to rest a few hours himself. It was another reason he'd gotten them out of town.

Callan? Shallan tugged at his awareness.

Yes? Callan asked.

As you predicted, riders, a team, on the road from the stronghold down into Yalleska town, Shallan said.

Very well, stay put and alert me if anyone heads in this direction.

Shallan acknowledged his order and Callan sensed the woman return her attention back to watch the approach.

"Stand watch over him, but he'll sleep for hours. Short of tying him to a saddle, we won't be going anywhere for a bit. Set up a rough camp, but keep in mind we might have to depart in a hurry." Callan ordered.

"Yes Callan, rest before you try to contact Michael. A little sleep won't make much difference at this point." Gavrel chastised.

"I know, I intend to," Callan said, sending a small wave of reassurance to the team members.

Not much shocked the Unwanted. The knowledge of the death of the Warlord was one thing that had done so. As Callan checked the clearing he took off his cloak and bundled it up as a pillow then settled down under the shade of a tree. He didn't think he'd sleep, but he could rest a little before contacting Michael.

Callan opened his eyes as a hand touched his shoulder, startled to realise he'd fallen asleep. A steaming mug of tea, one that had properties to ease headaches, was presented to him. He nodded his thanks, before adjusting the temperature of the drink so he wouldn't scald himself, and gulped down the contents. He grimaced, wondering why such things had to always have a bitter taste in them. It wouldn't totally relieve his headache, but it would dull the ache, and his own body's ability to heal would take care of the rest. It was an unfortunate side effect of the tie he'd forged between Owen and himself. When it snapped, it snapped back both ways. At the one who'd forged it, and the one who'd received it. He'd cushioned his own mind, but still suffered the impact as it snapped. Although Owen's head would be much worse, suffering from not just the rebounding bond snapping into him, but from what Callan had done to punch into the man's mind that way.

Gavrel gestured to the cot they'd set up next to him. Callan was about to chastise them but realised they'd wouldn't have set it up if there had been any sign of search parties heading in this direction looking for them. They were safe enough for now and from here they could return to get back into Yalleska if Michael ordered them to do so. Finally, he eased himself up enough to roll into the cot. He raised his hands and massaged his temples lightly with his fingertips. He could contact Michael just as easily lying down as he could standing up.

TWENTY-FIVE

Steven sat, his fingers playing over the collar they'd placed around his neck. He knew there must be a secret to it. It had been as soft as silk when Jaclyn had placed it around his neck. The silken strip had brushed against his skin, causing him to shiver as it wound and twined itself into a collar. Then it had hardened to its current form.

Despite the years he'd spent strutting around thinking he was Michael's equal, if not better, he'd come to the conclusion he wasn't as smart as his brother. Even he wasn't that stupid. He'd seen the clothing the women wore. It went from long flowing silken material that seemed to hiss with a life of its own around them, to solidifying into their strange battle armour. The only conclusion he could come to was they were controlling this stuff using the veil. Somehow. He may not be the most talented practitioner, but he was still a Rathadon and the one thing he had plenty of right now, was time. To work out what triggered this stuff, he spent his time watching and listening, with his other-sight on as much as he could. His current attempt to get his collar to go from its rock-hard form was to send pulses of power at different levels through it. His fingers played over the collar and he concentrated on trying yet another combination of power. Steven tensed at the barest of shivers running through the collar. Then slumped as the collar stilled. It was hard and unresponsive. Then he straightened. It was the first reaction he'd had from the thing.

"Don't fret. It means you belong to me. None will dare touch you," Jaclyn said, her dark eyes not giving away even a hint of emotion.

Steven jerked his fingers away from his collar and plastered a smile on his face, trying desperately to think of something to divert her attention. He really needed to be taking more notice of what was going on around him when he tried his experiments. He turned his focus to Jaclyn, who stood just inside the doorway. For the first time, he wished fervently that the hinges squeaked.

"I can't help it. Do you know what it is to be collared here in the Warlord's domain?" Steven asked.

He twisted in his chair, watching as the commander's guards filtered in and spaced themselves around the room. Jaclyn was never alone. Never. There was always a horde of dagger wielding women with her. Not that it would matter all that much if she showed up alone. He was under no illusions of who would win if he'd been stupid enough to try to pull a weapon on her. Unlike the Kastlers, they had scoured his entire suite and removed everything that could conceivably be used as a weapon. At least for him. He fancied his brother and every member of the Unwanted could find plenty of uses to use what remained as a weapon. Steven tried to be indigent about it, but unfortunately, he understood why they'd do so. The Sylannians didn't even allow him to have a knife or fork for his meals when they fed him. They didn't allow him anything sharper than a spoon.

"Why don't you tell me?" Jaclyn asked.

Steven recognised that tone. She was being not only condescending but hoping once he started talking to divert the conversation onto his brother. Jaclyn was quite adept at getting him onto that topic. He smiled. It was just as well he actually didn't know enough about his brother to compromise him. Let alone in Michael's role as the warleader. That was a minor detail where his past arrogance was paying off. Steven had to admit, this game he played with Jaclyn was also a much better diversion for his mind than fantasising about her touch on his skin. Which, much to his disgust with himself, was something he did with alarming frequency. Steven clenched his teeth. Commander. Sylannian Commander. The enemy. He couldn't even afford to think her name.

"Slavery is not unknown here."

"So I'm led to believe, and yet you all have such a hard time adjusting to your new life." A hint of a smile curved Jaclyn's lips. "As I've told you before, you are not a slave. Your life will be restricted from what you know, but it is not slavery as you think of it. I will decide on your fate soon and then you shall know what your life will be going forward."

Steven shuddered. The commander was beautiful. He'd give her that, but she was deadly. Every instinct in him screamed at him when she was near. Which he had to admit was unusual for him. It was that abnormality that made him pay attention to his instincts for once. Of course, they screamed two different things at him. He seemed to flip-flop between fearing her and then wondering when she'd visit him again and fantasising about her long fingers brushing his skin. Which she seemed to do a great deal. Her fingers would touch his arm, face, or brush his temple. He found himself shuddering again, although this time as he imagined those fingers of hers caressing his temples again. With effort he pushed aside the feelings for this woman, this enemy, he reminded himself, that assaulted him and concentrated on his story. Mostly in order to stop himself from thinking about Jaclyn the way he was. He had to keep firmly in mind how dangerous she was. He had a sinking feeling that it was an endeavour he was failing at.

"We were once many regions controlled by different warlords. When they conquered new territories, they took those that fought them as slaves. Those taken had no rights. They were prey to whatever anyone who was free wanted to subject them to. The only way out was death."

"As I told you. That collar tells all that you belong to me. No one would dare interfere with you if they want to live."

"Except your king?" Steven said. Then instantly regretted it as her formally opaque eyes flashed in anger. Increasingly, he hated it when she was unhappy with him, even if it confused him why he'd feel this way. He'd been learning bits and pieces about them as well. Not that this Sylannian gave away much about her homeland, but occasionally even she slipped.

"Except my king, but you needn't fear. My brother and his wives are far away. The daggerwives of this house will kill to protect you," Jaclyn said, that rare flash of something smoothed away.

"Then the Warlord rose. There are so many rumours that abound about his past, of who he was before he became the Warlord. It's hard to tell the truth from fiction. He swept through the regions controlled by the different warlord's one after the other. All were left dead or kneeling with bowed heads pledging to accept his rule." Steven continued on with his story. It was something he'd known since childhood, even if he hadn't had the opportunity to retell it before.

"So fascinating. This is the same man that your brother, the warleader, now follows?"

Steven lifted his eyes and contacted hers. While he rarely met her eyes, somehow he had the feeling it gave her power over him. He made an exception this time. He shuddered. It was like he was losing a bit more of himself every moment he looked at her.

"There is only one Warlord now. Just like there is only one rule you can never argue your way out of, it will result in a death sentence."

"Which rule is that?" Jaclyn asked, her tone pleasant, but he could tell she wasn't happy.

He wasn't being suitably deferential to her. She hated it on the rare occasions when he showed so much as a hint of defiance towards her wishes. She expected to be obeyed in all things.

"Enslaving another person is strictly forbidden. You can lock people up, kill them even, but you can't own people. Some believe he's most unreasonable about it, but you can guarantee that this." Steven plucked at the collar around his neck. "Will not please him and you won't be able to argue your way out of the trouble you're going to be in."

"I believe your Warlord will kill me if he gets the chance, anyway. I am, after all, invading your country,"

"You'd think so, wouldn't you? But I don't know. You might have gotten away with invading. The Warlord might even be persuaded to forgive it. After all, my parents are alive and they defied him. Taking slaves though, I don't think he's ever forgiven such a thing. At least not since he's come to power."

She'd been pecking away at his mind and it irritated her immensely that she hadn't made it past his mind barriers. While that particular failure surprised him, he was certainly happy about it. It seemed Ben's advice for him to practice his mind shields had an unexpected benefit. Even though he'd followed Ben's advice, he never would have believed that with practice, he'd actually get reasonably good at the skill. He allowed himself a small little internal cheer. Steven was grateful Ben's assessment had pricked at his ego, particularly since it had proven to be important. Of course, he had the sinking feeling if she really put her mind to it, he'd fall into her arms willingly enough. He seemed to spend enough time day dreaming of doing exactly that.

"You expect your brother will try to enforce this law on behalf of his Warlord?" Jacklyn asked.

No matter how hard Steven tried to keep the discussion about the past and the Warlord, his brother always came up. Jaclyn was quite adept at bringing the conversation around to Michael. Or rather, he was just bad at trying to avoid the topic.

"I don't just think he will. I know it. He's done so in the past."

"Ah, but sadly for him, your brother will end up wearing my collar just like you are before this war is out."

Steven burst out laughing at the idea that this woman, or anyone, would manage to take, let alone keep, his brother as a slave. Even if they mistakenly managed the first part. As her eyes narrowed, he held up a hand, wiping the tears of laughter from his eyes with the other.

"You've clearly never met Michael. I wouldn't judge his capabilities by me if that is what you're doing."

"I'm not. Your father and mother, however, give some insight."

"Ah, but that's where you're wrong. You've never met his true father." Steven had the satisfaction of seeing confusion flicker across her face.

"Given your father is right downstairs in his rooms, we both know that isn't correct."

"I can understand as an outsider why you might assume that. You see, while we share the same birth mother and father. You need to take into consideration how young Michael was when he was taken. The warleader's father is that man who raised him. He is more that man's son than the Warlord's own flesh and blood. His father, the one who trained and taught him, is the man who dominated this entire land and ruthlessly conquered it, eliminating all resistance to his rule."

"What does that have to do with your brother?"

"Who do you think it was who did most of the conquering and eliminating in his father's name?" Steven asked, giving her his most pleasant smile. "The exploits of what Michael did, what he became in those first few years riding for the Warlord are chilling."

Jaclyn's eyes narrowed as she regarded him. "I've seen the map of this domain. Your Warlord's home territory is up and closer to the other side, so how could your brother have done all that? Surely this place was one of his last acquisitions?"

"You'd expect so. If all you took into account was the map and distance. The Warlord, although despised by many in that day, wasn't stupid. Many considered that my family was the strongest among the warlord families of that era. Our family history had a bit of a a notoriety for brutality that could challenge the Warlord's reputation. Other than a few small places that fell rapidly, he cut across the mountain trails and took Vallantia first. He didn't want the Rathadon warlord to have time to fortify. My brother was one of the first he claimed into his ranks. Another little piece of surety, not only of our parents' good behaviour. Once news flew that the Rathadons had fallen, it struck fear into them all. When others became aware this upstart had the Rathadon scion riding for him, they didn't care that Michael was only thirteen. Their terror spiked even higher. People whispered behind closed doors that the Rathadon scion, Michael, was like the Rathadon Warlord's of old. That he possessed unnatural strength in the veil. It did most of the rest of the work for him. It is said the Strafford warlord at Callenhain threw his own daughter out of the gates as a sacrifice just to appease the Warlord and Michael rather than face them in war." Steven was conscious he was babbling and closed his mouth.

Jaclyn sat looking at him for such a long time he feared for a moment he'd revealed too much. His strategy was always to talk about those early years rather than the present. It was obvious, even to him, it was details about Michael that she wanted. He was terrified that she would start these sessions with his parents. Unlike him, they had far more information to divulge about Michael, who he was now, what he did and, not so coincidentally, his communication network. That is why he talked with her, just giving her enough that she kept coming back. He played the oblivious fool. Pretended he didn't realise she was trying to get intelligence out of him about Michael. To be honest, it wasn't exactly a hard role for him to play. He was determined, however, that she would not get the current information that she could use against Michael from him. Of course, this might have been easier if he hadn't grown up before this latest mess hit them. The depths others would sink to in the pursuit of money had sunk in. Before the Kastlers and their little invasion had hit, he really hadn't known anything about who or what his brother was. For once, he was determined to be that big brother he always should have been. That little knowledge he possessed, these women wouldn't find out from him.

As her hand moved, Steven found himself diverted, his breath catching as he wondered if those fingers would brush his chest, arm or lightly play over his temples. He looked up to see her smile. He watched her as she paced towards him. Her hand cupped the side of his face, and his resistance crumbled as he leant into her touch. Her lips softly brush his own, and he responded to her before he was aware of what he was doing.

Jaclyn backed up, her eyes gazing at him with what he could swear was a possessive glint. His breathing was ragged, and he craved her touch. She turned and walked out of his room. As the door closed, his desire for the commander's touch cut off. Jaclyn had manipulated his emotions again. Steven swore softly and reinforced his mental shield.

TWENTY-SIX

Steven stood up as the doors opened, hating himself a little as a surge of happiness hit him at the thought it might be Jaclyn. He was both disappointed and relieved that it wasn't Jaclyn, but one of the other women. While there were so many of them, it was difficult to tell them apart. This one he recognised. He was finding it challenging to maintain a suitable anger at them. His captors had kept him isolated from everyone since Jaclyn had placed her collar on him. He only ever saw them now. The Sylannians even brought him his meals rather than the servants. More often than not, if it wasn't Jaclyn paying him a visit, it was this one primewife Myra. It was sad how eager he was for their visits. Although if he was being fair to himself, the reaction was probably due to his isolation.

"Steven, I'm glad you're up."

"Well, it's not like I'm free to go anywhere, but even I can't just sleep all day."

"Ah, poor man, come I shall take you for a walk in the gardens."

"Are you sure it's safe?" Steven asked as he stood, smiling blandly as she looked at him. "For you I mean?"

"It's sweet you care for my welfare, Steven, but please don't worry about it. This estate is now fully secured, as is Vallantia itself."

Steven winced. He really needed to learn to guard his tongue. These people did not appreciate it when he didn't show them the deference they obviously expected. It was something about her treating him like a pet that she had to take out for a walk that grated. Not that he was going to turn her down. It would be pleasant to be out in the fresh air after being cooped up for so long. Steven sighed. His mouth always got him in trouble, and he was way too eager to accompany her. That galled him as well.

"How exceptional of you all. It hasn't been a skill set we've been good at recently. Everyone seems to just breeze right in without breaking a sweat."

There it was again, his mouth going off before his brain kicked in. It was like he was channelling his brother's attitude, with none of Michael's ability to smack down anyone who might take offence. Steven blinked. He swore her lips twitched in response. Perhaps Myra wasn't as cold as she pretended to be. It was a piece of information he filed away for future reference. The possibility also made him blush.

"You are terribly amusing. No wonder we're going to keep you," Myra said as she turned a smile on him.

"Keep me?" Steven asked, aware his eyes widened but unable to help it.

She was silent for a moment as the doors were opened for them and she led him out into the gardens. The other Sylannians surrounding them and spreading out through the enclosed private garden.

"Do you not understand what Jaclyn's collar means? It's not common for her to make a personal claim."

He reached up and ran his fingers over the maroon and cream collar he wore. Once again, he wondered how it could be so cool against his skin.

"How could I know? You've all kept me isolated from everyone since before Jaclyn put this thing around my neck. I noticed it is in her colours," Steven said carefully.

"When we conquer a land, the lives of the bulk of the population go on much as they have. It is just that they and all they produce belong to us. Sylannian houses will move in and take ownership of the various regions and the people in the name of our king."

"I think I've got that part."

"Some men, those especially talented, are taken to a breeding house in our homeland. We don't take many, despite what it appeared like with what your traders tried to do. On the king's order, we dealt with the traitor houses who traded with them and lowered their standards to breed uncontrollably with those who are lesser than us. We must protect our bloodlines. I'm sure you understand."

"Of course." Steven nodded, although right now he didn't have a clue, but a certain amount of dread settled on him.

"But you, with your bloodline, are unique." Myra reached out and brushed her fingers against his temple, causing him to shiver. "No matter what, Jaclyn decides we will take you back to our homeland where you belong."

"What do you mean?" Despite himself, Steven found himself fascinated. In a horrified kind of way.

"As your mother proved, while rare, females can leave without consequences if they have the capacity and as long as they never return. The scarcity of males makes it forbidden for them to leave. All Sylannian males belong to Sylanna. Even those born to those who've fled our homeland."

"What does the commander intend to do with me?"

"Jaclyn has not decided yet, but I believe she will mate bond to you and take you as a husband. If she breeds successfully with you, that child will have an undeniable right to the throne of the Monarch House."

Steven swallowed, looking at her, trying to work out if she was serious. Unfortunately, he got the distinct impression she wasn't joking at all.

"The breeding part I think I understand, but mate bond? Why do I suspect I won't like that part?"

Myra turned to face him, her fingers brushing his temple again. A wave of calm crashed over him.

"Jaclyn will forge a permanent control bond with your mind. Your life will be different from what it is now. As a primewife, so will I, but you are lucky. In Jaclyn's house, no other will be permitted to seize control of your mind."

"Control? Only two of you?"

"As soon as you prove you are trustworthy, it's likely we'll withdraw and allow you the peace of your own mind. We believe it is the longstanding practice of all wives of a house forging a control bond with their husband that brings on madness."

"So, um, I take it I will have no choice in this little adventure?" Steven asked, trying to keep his tone light.

It was an attempt he failed at. The notion horrified Steven that these women intended to force their way into his mind so they could control him. That it might send him mad didn't sound all that appealing, either.

Her hand stroked his temple again, and despite himself, he relaxed. Steven swallowed, knowing she was soothing him. It was something Jaclyn did to him as well, yet even though he was aware they were doing so, he couldn't withstand them. Particularly when one of them was touching him. It didn't help that he not only responded to their touch but fantasised about it. It was frequent enough he recognised when they were doing it. That knowledge was terrifying.

"Everyone, particularly men, finds change stressful, but you don't have to worry anymore. It is our duty to protect you now and we'll make the correct decisions for you. While Sylannian men usually choose their firstwife, I'm afraid that will not be the case for you." A hint of concern was in her eyes as her hand rested lightly on his arm. "The selection of the other wives that you breed with will be carefully done. The underwives will consider future matches and breeding possibilities of the offspring."

"Those bloodlines you spoke of?" Steven said dryly.

"Exactly, I'm glad you understand."

Steven swallowed and he understood how some of his peers who'd had their partnerships arranged for by their families felt. Except those were normally contractual, with an end date in place. All for the good of family fortunes. He'd never been subject to such things himself since the Warlord had forbidden any new Rathadons to be born on the threat of death. It was an order he and his parents had taken seriously. This arrangement, however, did not sound like anything of the sort.

"What if I can't perform?"

"Don't be concerned. One benefit of the mate bond means you won't have any problems with your performance." Myra's eyes sparkled, and this time, he was certain she was amused.

"I don't suppose letting Jaclyn know I'm flattered, but no thanks is an option?"

"Great strength in the veil runs in your father's family line that now combines with the Monarch House bloodline in you. No, refusal isn't an option."

"Then it's my brother you want, but as I explained to commander Jaclyn, I don't think you'll have much luck collaring him or keeping him if you have the misfortune of doing so."

"We will deal with your brother, but like you, he belongs in Sylanna. We will do our best to collar him and keep him safe. Even from himself. Although forgive me for saying so, but you are much easier to control than we think your brother will be," Myra said, her fingers brushing his temples again.

Steven closed his eyes, wishing he wasn't so susceptible to his emotions being manipulated by these women as, once again, his little burst of horror at what she'd said was pushed aside. He knew he'd been disturbed since Myra hadn't wiped that knowledge from his mind. The emotion itself didn't upset him anymore. Instead, Steven found he was wondering when she was going to touch him again. Steven only just restrained himself from groaning as he realised he desperately wanted her too. The knowledge his emotions in that regard were due to Myra's manipulation did little to ease his mind.

"I see what you mean. I don't think this would work on him."

"As you are finding out, we are skilled at mind gifts." Myra continued to soothe him.

Steven didn't bother to even try to fight what she wanted. He'd learnt quickly he had no ability at all to stop Jaclyn, and it seemed Myra had the same capability. He wondered if his susceptibility to being manipulated emotionally was one of the reasons he'd kept falling in with the wrong people, who sought to use him for wild schemes against his brother.

"When will..." Steven stopped and swallowed. "When will this happen?"

Myra responded to his emotions and his fear was washed aside. A sense of wellbeing swept over him again, although it was Myra that compelled him rather than him being at ease with their plans for his life.

"Your place is with us now. In the meantime, we will continue to work with you to help you adjust to your new life."

"Is that why others can scream, yell, and cry, but one of you always soothes me when I'm upset?" Steven asked, stopping to look at her. "You're all training me."

"We will never allow you to hurt yourself. With the veil potential you carry, you are far too valuable," Myra said softly. "You need to get used to the idea you belong to our house. Soon, if I am not mistaken, Jaclyn will take control of your mind and you will be hers. Come, it's time to return you to your rooms. If I don't have time to walk you tomorrow, I will make sure another does. We want you to be happy, Steven."

"Thank you." Steven licked his lips and relaxed as her soothing touch washed over him once more.

"You are doing well. You accept our promptings for you to return to calmness already. Some men we've taken fight for months before they succumb to the inevitable. There is no point fighting."

"Can I speak with my parents before I retire to my room?"

Myra looked at him with a hint of a smile on her lips before she nodded.

"Of course, you are doing well and I am pleased that you are already curbing your instinct to fight against my promptings. You deserve to be rewarded. I will take you to visit them and assign another to take you to the safety of your rooms after."

Steven concentrated on staying calm as she walked him back across the gardens. The other women, as always, saying nothing but were vigilant for any threat and followed closely. He'd never been conscientious at practicing the mind exercises his mother had taught him all those years ago when he'd been a child. Now he tried to remember the old drills. He'd rather be relaxed because he forced it on himself. Not because these women were controlling him.

CHAPTER
TWENTY-SEVEN

Aiden rolled off the bed, still indolent, and he reached over and grabbed Isabella's hand, tugging it gently. She came to him, standing next to him without him having to use any more force. He wrapped his arms around her as she stood, and without having to be prompted, she pressed her body up against his. He sighed in pleasure, kissing the side of her neck, which in turn caused her a thrill of pleasure. His ability to exert such control over her to cause pain, fear or pleasure when he wanted her to, caused her to slip increasingly under his control.

"As a reward for your performance tonight, I'll spare your brother his whipping in the morning."

"Thank you, master," Isabella whispered.

Of course, other methods of torturing Damien would continue, but Isabella didn't need to know that little detail. Owning her was far more pleasurable than he'd even dreamed it would be. Regardless of her motivation, Isabella had chosen to be his sex slave. This was the first step in breaking her.

Aiden had taken a tremendous amount of satisfaction in

teaching Isabella that she'd rather be pleasured than suffer pain. She'd found out the hard way he could inflict pain without her passing out or her skin even being broken. Regardless of how fast or slow she learned, causing her to suffer or not, he got a great deal of gratification from the act, and that was all that mattered.

Aiden wondered if Isabella's increased skill this night was the influence of the Sylannian. He smirked, making a mental note to have the Sylannian women rewarded. Now that Isabella was more compliant and accepting of her status, soon she would be where she belonged in the refurbished slave stable. Soon enough she'd be sharing the stable with other sex slaves and by then Isabella could give the new slaves pointers on how to please him. Aiden grabbed Isabella around the neck and squeezed. Isabella gasped but didn't break his hold. As panic flared in her, Aiden licked his lips. Isabella's hands rose to grasp his own as she feared her impending death. Just as she was about to slip into unconsciousness, he released her. Aiden chuckled as Isabella slumped to the ground, gasping for breath.

"You're a lot like her," Aiden said.

He walked over and languidly grabbed his robe off a hook on the wall. There was nothing quite comparable to a chaser of torture after sex with his slave.

"Who master?" Isabella whispered.

"Michael had a sister, Nera. She wasn't quite as powerful as him and wasn't a fighter, so father kept her here at the fortress." Aiden's eyes narrowed as he gazed back at where she still lay slumped on the floor.

"Is that why you think I'm like her? Because your father brought me here to protect me?" Isabella asked.

Aiden smiled fondly as he remembered Nera. "Unlike you, she had dark hair, but your eyes are as blue as I remember hers being. Of course, you are older than she was."

"She was too young to be ripped away from her family," Isabella said.

"I was the first to take her as well. It was when I learnt the pleasure of causing another person pain," Aiden said, a thrill running through him as Isabella stiffened. "She didn't learn her place as fast as you have. She wouldn't stop wailing as I had sex with her. I was afraid the guards would hear, so I took a pillow and pressed it against her face to muffle her screams until I was finished."

Isabella gasped as he returned to her, a small burst of fear emanating from her as she trembled when he came up behind her.

She looked at the ground, her voice a whisper. "Did they catch you?"

Isabella shuddered, Aiden found her fear intoxicating, although he'd learned several valuable lessons from the time he and Nera had spent together. He'd discovered he liked being in control and dominating another. To force them to do what he wanted. Particularly when they had no ability to fight back. It was the first time in his life he'd felt so formidable.

"She suffocated as I had sex with her. It was such a waste." Aiden grasped Isabella's chin, forcing her head up so her eyes met his gaze. "I had to make it appear like she'd killed herself, of course. My father would have killed me if he'd known what I'd done."

"Please, master, don't kill me," Isabella whispered.

Aiden threw his head back and laughed. "Ah no sweet Isabella, as much as discovering I'd killed Nera gave me an unexpected thrill. There are others less valuable that I can sate that desire with. You'll not escape me through death as easily as Nera did." Aiden squeezed his hands around her neck again, cutting off her air, his breath quickening as she grasped desperately at him. "I've had more practice. I know how far I can go before a woman dies now."

"Thank you, master."

"You've inspired me, you know."

"Master?"

"It was an entirely unexpected thrill to discover I'm the first and only man you'll have sex with. Somehow, it makes my possession of you even more satisfying. Would you like me to tell you the orders you're responsible for?"

"Yes, master."

"My warband has orders to capture more sex slaves for me. They are to ensure the girls they collar are virgins. Just like you were before you agreed to fall into my bed."

As Isabella's eyes widened, Aiden released her, causing Isabella to slump to the ground. In a way, he'd learnt as much as Isabella had. He'd found he quite enjoyed taunting her. To hurt Isabella when combined with those bursts of Isabella's fear gave him almost as much pleasure as having sex. While it was galling that he still couldn't get past Isabella's mind barriers, he could now manipulate her in other ways. He turned from her and threw a robe at her so she could cover herself prior to her handlers coming to take her back to her room. The other servants should be grateful the girl put him in such a good mood for the morning. It meant he probably wouldn't feel the need to have any of them punished or killed for their failures.

TWENTY-EIGHT

Ben leant back against the smooth stone of the outer city wall. The Smithy was an impressive sight. A single-story building with no appreciable joins between the stones that it was fashioned with. Not that it was an unusual building style, it was a mark of establishments that had been around since the era of the Smith Lords. What stood out was where once there had been windows and huge double doors, there was nothing but smooth metal. There didn't even appear to be a seam between the stone of the building and the solid metal plates. There was a mound of freshly dug-up dirt near the wall of the building and discarded digging tools nearby. The newly revealed stone wall extended into the bedrock.

"I knew the Smith's abilities were incredible, but this is..." Lukas said.

"Is impressive. From the looks of it, the Sylannians have given up trying to get into the place," Ben said.

"I don't blame them. I think I'd give this place up as a lost cause as well. Even knowing what's inside," Lukas said, his sharp eyes scanning their immediate surroundings as some quick hand gestures sent members of their team to lookout positions. "We're clear."

Ben scanned their surroundings for any sign of someone nearby with his othersight then reached out.

Smith? We're in position, Ben said.

I'll open the door. Let me know when you're all inside, the Smith said.

With a muted metallic groan, the doorway disappeared into what had appeared to be a solid rock wall. Ben ran across the intervening space. He hit the release on the wooden doors that swung open effortlessly and led their crew inside. Ben spun, counting heads as everyone followed him into the building.

We're in, Ben said.

A metallic ringing sounded from the doorway as the metal portal slid across to seal the entrance once more.

The armoury is through the archway to the left, and down the stairs, the Smith said.

Ben was about to ask what archway when the ground shifted beneath his feet. The stone floor seemed to undulate like waves rippling over the open water. It was a decidedly unnatural way for stone to behave. What had appeared moments before as a solid wall glowed. Heat rolled over him, causing him to flinch back. A rumble accompanied the heaving of the floor. Dust was thrown up to hang in the air as the stones comprising the wall sunk down into the ground. Consumed back into the earth from which they'd been dug.

When the dust settled, an archway stood with steps leading down. As he walked towards the entranceway, glow stones flared to life, lighting his way down into the armoury.

"Remind me never to annoy the Smith." Lukas muttered as he walked down the stairs behind him.

"I haven't seen anything like this, but the twins are the same. Or so Michael assures me," Ben said, then stopped as he hit the ground floor and light flared around the armoury. He whistled in appreciation. "Now this will come in useful."

"Just as well this place is inaccessible unless the Smith grants access," Lukas said.

Ben regarded his friend. "Otherwise, some of your less than honest crew might try to come back?"

A wolfish expression lit Lukas's face. "They wouldn't be able to help themselves. Everyone load up, although not more than you can carry easily."

"We can always return for more if we need them."

Their team scattered, collecting an assortment of daggers and swords. While others stuffed fighting leathers into bags and slung various sheathes and belts over their shoulders. Ben eyed the array of different weapons along the racks and regretfully decided to leave the battle axes behind. It wasn't like he had time to learn how to fight with them.

"Who knew this even existed?"

"The Warlord, Michael and I did. I'm certain Olivia and Nathanial have been told about them as well. Michael ordered the Smith to set up stockpiles in case of emergencies."

"You mean there is more than just this secret armoury?"

Ben nodded. "Quite a few. They're stashed across the Warlord's domain. Michael didn't want to risk only having one vault of weapons in case that was the place that fell to the enemy first."

"That's enough, you lot. Let's get moving. Remember, you still need to be able to fight if we encounter the Sylannians."

As their team filed back up the stairway into the smithy, Ben had one more glance around the armoury before he took the stairs two at a time to the top. He communicated with the Smith, sending an all-clear. Ben watched in fascination as the stairs collapsed on themselves. They disappeared and seemed to flow, filling up the archway until once more it was nothing but a solid wall.

While he'd known intellectually that the Smith could lock down all his holdings, it wasn't something he'd ever seen before.

TWENTY-NINE

True to her word, Myra took him to his parent's rooms to call on them. It was the first time the Sylannians had allowed a visit since they'd taken the estate. As Myra spoke to the guards who'd accompanied them to the garden in Sylannian, Steven wished he spoke the language. As the doors opened to his parents' suite, the Sylannians flowed into the room with that smooth grace they seemed to have. They placed themselves around this chamber in much the same fashion as they did in his suite.

"Sit Steven." Myra gestured to a chair over to one side.

Steven kept a tight rein on his tongue as he walked over to the seat and sat as the primewife ordered him to. She didn't just control his life right now. If Myra was to be believed, the Sylannians intended to manage every living, breathing moment of his existence from this point forward.

"Yes, Myra."

"Others will fetch your parents and these daggerwives will stay to protect you, then return you to your rooms after your visit."

"Thank you for this trust. I understand the restrictions on me and I won't cause any trouble." Steven swallowed, staring up at her, then took a breath and deliberately tried to calm himself.

"Everything will turn out for the better, Steven, you'll see," Myra said, then after one more soothing touch she left the room sweeping past the daggerwives that stayed to watch him.

He closed his eyes, reminding himself he had a purpose in appearing to accept their control over his life. Even if Myra's ability to change his emotions, with a brush of her fingers and a thought, was frightening. The effect didn't last long once he was out of the Sylannian's presence. For Myra to say Sylannians were exceptionally good at mind skills seemed to be an understatement. Steven twisted around to stare at the daggerwives who stood calmly with no indication they perceived his disquiet. It gave a different meaning to their presence now that he knew they were there to protect him from himself and from others. To make sure he couldn't escape from the fate they had in store for him.

Steven fidgeted in his chair, trying to keep his emotions firmly behind his mental barriers and not give away how tense he was. As the latch clicked, he swung his head expectantly towards the internal door. Relief hit him as his parents entered the room. A household servant assisted his father rather than one of the Sylannians. He'd wondered if the Sylannians had them under constant surveillance and took up station in their rooms when he wasn't here as well. His mother paused as she took in the presence of the daggerwives, but it was barely perceptible. Steven waited as they settled into the long couch, and as the servants produced coffee and sweet bread, before they all retreated to the wall. The shuffling as the servants tried to stay as far away from the daggerwives as they possibly made him smile.

"Steven, it's good to see you," his mother said.

Steven wished he had his mother's skill. It was the tone and pleasant expression of someone who didn't have a care in the world. As if their home hadn't been invaded and there weren't bloodthirsty Sylannians with very sharp daggers willing to kill them if they so much as looked at them the wrong way.

"You too. I hope they are treating you well," Steven said.

"As well as we can expect," his father said.

"I think they're afraid to do much against us in case they can't defeat your brother. At least that is the sense I get from them." His mother's gaze rose and scanned the daggerwives who lined the room.

Steven relaxed. That was his mother. He was learning she was fearless. It was something he wished he'd known years ago. That it hadn't taken their current circumstances for him to work it out.

"It's astonishing how frequently they turn the conversations we have onto Michael and the Warlord. Just as well I can't actually tell them what they want to know."

"It seems there is a reason for everything." His father's lips twitched as his gaze swept over the guards. "You've brought friends to visit with you."

"Not so much." Steven plucked the collar he wore around his neck from beneath his shirt. "They put this around my neck a few days ago and I found out what it means."

"It means Jaclyn has followed my advice and claimed you," his mother said, her eyes narrowing as she gazed at the daggerwives speaking to them in Sylannian.

While he may not have understood his mother's final words, they sounded like a command. The guards shifted, a fleeting expression of confusion passing between them. The reaction astounded Steven. He'd never seen any of them look uncomfortable before. Lady Rathadon stood, her gaze fierce. Steven shuddered as cold washed over him. Then an unbroken string of words left his mother's mouth, her tone cutting. He was about to tell his mother it wouldn't work but sat there dumbfounded as the daggerwives backed off and fled the room. He stared at the women, his mother, that he realised he'd never known.

"Wait, what do you mean by your advice?" Steven asked.

"I spoke to the commander about taking you as her husband and breeding with you. Regardless of the results of the war, it's a contingency that may save your life."

"You told her to take me?"

"Try to keep up, Steven. The daggerwives of Jaclyn's house will defend you, the underwives will care for you. You'll want for nothing."

Steven went cold from head to toe at his mother's assessment of his fate.

"You didn't consider that I might want to have a say in any of this?" Steven asked, entirely outraged at the offhand manner his life had been dismissed.

"Through my blood, you are a Sylannian male. Once Jaclyn learned of your heritage, any choice you had up to that moment ceased to exist. I would think you'd rather be Jaclyn's husband and breed with her than transferred to some breeding house in Sylanna."

"Or here's an idea. Michael might actually win this war. Then there'll be no need for me to belong to anyone."

"If your brother wins, he'll be sitting on the throne in the Court of a Thousand Islands."

"Through me, your brother's right to claim the Monarch Throne is as strong as Jaclyn's," his mother said with a smile that didn't reach her eyes.

Steven's thoughts were spinning. "You expect Michael will claim the Sylannian Throne?"

"Exactly. In the meantime, mate not only with the commander, but all the wives they order into your bed. It will keep you safe and, if we're lucky, distract her from the war." His mother sounded like she was discussing nothing more important than the weather.

"Wait, you set all this up? You set me up?"

"Calm down Steven. It was all I could do to potentially save your life. Granted, it will be a different life than you ever thought you'd lead, but you will live. I have removed the protections I've held over your mind. Or at least that I held when you weren't running off into town. Jaclyn will not find it hard to bind you to her."

"Father, are you just going to sit there?" Steven asked.

"You've always been upset about the Warlord's edict against you forming a permanent relationship and producing heirs," his father said in a bright tone. "It should resolve both those issues. You're about to have hundreds of wives and father quite a lot of children by them."

Steven stared at his parents, horrified that the pair of them could be so casual and dismissive about trading his life away to the Sylannians.

"What if I don't want hundreds of wives, let alone have children with all of them?"

"Stop being difficult, Steven. The sooner Jaclyn claims your mind and takes you to her bed to mate with you, the safer you will be. Even better if the breeding is successful. Male children are highly prized since there are so few Sylannian men, but you can hardly control that part." His mother sounded almost thoughtful.

"Mother!"

"Practice your calming exercises, just as I've taught you all these years. Once Jaclyn takes control of your mind, there will be nothing you can do to stop her. It will go easier on you if you relax and don't fight the procedure." Lady Rathadon stood, her hand making a shooing motion towards him before she snapped her fingers at the servants to assist his father. "Go, I'm sure

Jaclyn will not wait long before she concludes my advice is the correct action for her to take."

Steven stared at the closed door his parents had walked through. It was like he was seeing his mother for the first time. As the absurdity of his life hit him, Steven did the only thing he could. He sunk back into his chair, laughing.

CHAPTER
THIRTY

Evan's eyes flashed open to meet the darkness of the cell. There was nothing that immediately screamed out to him that should have woken him. He'd been in the cells long enough that even the snoring and heavy breathing of his fellow prisoners didn't disturb him any more. Evan rolled over onto his other side, twisting his arm to make a more comfortable surface for his head, and closed his eyes.

Evan! Steven said.

Steven? What's wrong? Evan eased himself up to lean against the rock wall.

The Sylannian guards sat down at the far end of the cells near the doors that lead up to the rest of the estate. They'd long since stopped their patrols. The only time his captors walked down to peer into the cells at their prisoners was when they pushed the bowls of food under the door and threw the bread between the bars onto the ground.

My mother has ordered me to breed with the Sylannian comman-der, Steven said, a hint of panic in his mind voice.

If Evan hadn't been wide awake before, he was now. *She what?*

She's told me the sooner one of the Sylannians is pregnant by me, the safer I'll be, Steven said.

Evan rolled his eyes. *Could be worse, you could be down here in the cells.*

Would you be serious? Mother said she's removed the protections she's held over my mind. Myra said—

Who's Myra?

The primewife. She said Jaclyn will forge a mate bond in my mind, which will give them control over me. Everyone is saying it will be easier if I accept it. A hint of desperation threaded through Steven's words. *If they install this permanent connection, well, what if more information sunk into my head, despite myself, than I'm aware of? Ben said I had poor control.*

Wait, just give me a moment. Evan rubbed his face, and focused his sleep fogged mind, reaching out across the veil towards the one person, near enough he had the strength to contact that might have advice. *Ben!*

Evan waited tense, expecting the Sylannians to come and investigate as his calls to Ben grew increasingly louder into what could best be described as a holler at the top of his mental voice.

Evan? Are you aware of how early it is? Ben said.

The mental connection between them strengthened as Ben took over the effort of maintaining it. Evan slumped in relief. These days, with as meagre rations as his captors fed him, even calling Ben had been exhausting.

Sorry, Steven has an issue, and I don't have the experience to advise him, Evan said, then quickly filled Ben in on what little Steven told him of his situation. Evan winced as Ben's rolling exasperation flowed through the veil.

At best, I'd say tell him to just have sex with them and keep his ears open for any of their plans and feed them back through you. Wait for a moment. I'll seek advice on something and get back to you.

As the mental connection faded, Evan checked on the sleeping forms of those in the cells around him and their guards. Thankfully, no one else down here seemed to have shifted, let alone been paying attention to him.

Well? Steven asked.

Sorry, I'm waiting for Ben. He said he was seeking advice. Just wait, I'm sorry, but it might take some time, Evan said.

Evan didn't know why he felt sorry for his friend. After all, Steven was still up in his luxurious suite of rooms, complete with its own bathing room. He was the one stuck down here in the cells. Evan sniffed, then instantly regretted it as the rank, unwashed, odour filled his senses. He wished he believed the smell was coming from the other residents of the cells. It was unfortunate he was contributing his own stink to the stale air. On the bright side it was relatively cool. He fancied if it was hot, the stench would be even worse.

A faint rush of sound that Evan recognised as Ben signalled the mental connection being established moments before the man spoke.

Evan?

I'm here. Not like I've got anything else to do, Evan said and winced at his dry tone. Not that Ben was here to observe his reaction, but it would still colour his mindspeech.

Tell Steven that his brother will reach out to him shortly, Ben said.

I'll let him know.

Evan squeezed his eyes shut. If Michael was going to speak with Steven directly, it meant the situation was far worse than he imagined.

∼

STEVEN EASED himself onto his bed while keeping firm control over his nerves. It wouldn't do him any good at all if his captors came in to investigate why he was agitated. Since he'd been warned to get comfortable, he judged his bed was the best place. Then he felt it. Like eyes were boring right into his very skull and the weight of the veil pressed him into his mattress.

Steven? Breathe, or we'll have to connect again if you pass out. You'll be fine. Ben has kindly agreed to be the focus of this conversation, Michael said, his smooth, assured mental voice filling Steven's head.

I don't know what that means. Focus?

It means I'll have a terrible headache and probably be cursing Michael's name for a few days, Ben said.

To sustain the mental connection when we're so far away takes a great deal of energy. It's fine for me, but for Ben, as strong as he is, it's a stretch.

We decided it would be better for me to be bedbound than you under the circumstances. The Sylannians might get suspicious if you're unconscious for a few days.

Oh, I didn't realise. Thank you. This means I'm in trouble. Doesn't it? Or you would have just replied the long way, bouncing the message through your relay.

There's no simple solution. The commander can't forge the control bond in your mind unless you agree to it.

But, I'm not you. I'm weak.

No, you're not. You've just been told you are your entire life and didn't practice.

So I was lazy.

It wasn't your fault. You were always the obedient son as a child. Allowing mother to smother your mind.

You didn't.

No. I was difficult and strong willed even before the Warlord claimed me. Now focus Steven. We can talk about old times when I'm done with this war.

Right. So, don't agree to the control?

If you agree and lower your personal mind barrier, she will own your mind. Jaclyn will be able to control every breath you take, erase your memories and recreate you into whatever it is she wants you to be.

That doesn't sound pleasant. What am I meant to do?

Agree to sex with them if you're inclined to. Convince them you're willing, but whatever you do, don't consent to the control bond.

Myra said I won't have a choice.

Technically, they can force bond you but...

But? But what?

Your mind would likely be mush afterwards. Play them. Convince them you will breed with them, but are afraid of the bond.

How?

You've had men and women over the years playing that game with you. I know you have.

Steven's face heated. *I didn't realise your reports on me were that detailed.*

People took a great deal of delight in informing me of your exploits, Michael said, his tone dry. *So do to the Sylannians what all those people tried to do to you over the years. Convince Jaclyn and however many of them they want you to sleep with that you love them. Just ask her not to take your mind. Tell her it's not our custom. Whatever you need to do to buy yourself time.*

Myra said only the two of them would take my mind because their custom was causing madness among their people. I could press that issue.

If she really wants change, she can start with you. Play on her fear of madness. Convince her you'll be loyal without the need of a mind bond. You need to know, if you submit, with this type of bond, not even Kesha can reverse it. You'll be bound to Jaclyn for the rest of your life.

Did you know about mother's heritage?

No. Safe to say that was as much of a shock to me as it was to you. I'll be having words with her when I see her.

I could have misunderstood mother. I don't have the under-standing of these matters that you do, but I get the distinct impression mother wants you to keep going once you deal with the Sylannians here.

What do you mean?

Our mother wants you to kill the king of Sylanna and take his throne. That whole blood of the Monarch House thing.

Michael groaned in frustration, and Steven caught the fleeting impression of Michael rubbing his face with one hand.

I don't even want this realm, but I seem to be stuck with it, let alone to be the king of Sylanna as well. I can see a chat with our mother is long overdue. Michael said, a growl in his tone mixed with frustration and fatigue.

Steven brightened a little since, for the first time in his life, it seemed his brother's anger was directed at someone other than him. Then he sobered as concern for Michael hit him.

You sound tired.

I'm fighting a war. Tired, kind of goes hand in hand with the responsibility.

I'm sorry Michael.

For what?

For being such an idiot all these years. You showed more restraint with me than anyone gave you credit for. Including me.

The past is the past. If I was inclined to hold a grudge beyond its usefulness, there wouldn't be many people left alive in the Warlord's domain. Michael paused, a distinct sense of humour transmitting through the connections they shared before Michael sobered. *Ben has filled me in on some of your actions during the Kastler's coup. I could have wished you'd shown more responsibility earlier, but I'm glad you're stepping up now.*

I, I had no right to expect you'd reach out to help me after every-thing I've done. Many wouldn't. So, essentially just roll with the situation and try to stay alive long enough for you to win this war?

Essentially. I'm sorry I can't be more helpful. Practice your personal mind shield.

I have been since Ben told me I should. That it was dangerous.

Good. He's right. I think you're stronger than mother wants you to believe. Remember, we share the same parentage. From what I'm advised, the minds of Sylannian men are smothered and controlled from birth. It's no wonder they never learn to protect themselves.

You really think so?

I do. Hold on to your shields and be aware of the influence they'll constantly try to inflict on you.

Like mother does, when she wants me to change my mind on something. They always brush my temple and it's like I don't have a choice but to calm down or accept what they want.

Exactly like that, but take heart. You at least recognise this as something projected on you by another person. There was a time you did not recognise the emotions belonged to someone else.

Steven flushed at the unexpected praise. For once, he was perhaps doing something right.

I'll practice and try to remember.

Ben told me you summoned and held light while in the caves under the estate?

Well, but I've always been able to summon light. It's no big deal.

It takes more ability and power to not only call but to sustain light than you think. You're not me. You never will be, but you are not as weak as you've been taught your whole life.

I've just been lazy?

Unlike me, it wasn't in you when you were younger to question and push the boundaries. You never learned anything different or had to fight to survive, before now.

Steven started hearing the outer door to his suite open. *I've got to go. One of them has just entered my rooms. Thank you, Michael, for everything.*

Take care. Practice! Michael said, his final injunction before his presence disappeared between one breath and the next.

Somehow his brother filled a room, even when he wasn't physically here. Now that Michael had gone, the room was distinctly empty, and he'd never been more alone in his life.

THIRTY-ONE

Allani stirred, aware she'd fallen asleep while waiting for the drug to pass from Isabella's system. She checked her charge to find Isabella was awake and watching her. Although her heart broke to see the emptiness in the girl's eyes. She no longer wept every time she was brought back to the cells, or begged the guards not to deliver her to the warlord when they came for her.

"They're going to come for me again soon," Isabella said.

"I wish I could take your place."

"At the moment, he's determined to cause me pleasure rather than pain. Once he's had sex with me, most of the time he tends to fall asleep."

"Jana leeches strength from him as much as she dares when she's with him."

"Thank you," Isabella said to Jana, who sat near Allani.

Jana simply sent a wordless wave of reassurance. "I wish I could do more for you, but he's fixated on you."

Isabella shook her head, then levered herself up and crawled the short distance between them, leaning into the older woman's shoulder.

Allani wrapped her arms around Isabella as she rested against her shoulder, allowing comfort to flow between them. While Isabella expelled much of the drug they gave her, she was always lethargic when she first woke. Allani stroked the side of Isabella's head.

"Take heart. Owen will find Damien's team and help will come."

Hope glimmered in Isabella's eye. "They'll call the warleader." A hard expression flickered across Isabella's face. "Michael will come, and he'll kill Aiden."

"Remember the lessons I've taught you," Jana said, her hand reaching out to stroke Isabella's temple. "He should be tired enough that he won't play his usual games with you. He'll still probably insist on mating with you, but he should drop off to sleep easily."

"He can possess your body and force you into his bed, but your heart," Allani said as her hand rose so her fingers brushed Isabella's heart before settling on her temple, "and mind are your own."

"That thing who calls himself a man can force himself on you, but you do not belong to him. No matter what he tells you, keep the knowledge close to your heart that you are your own person. Not his possession."

Isabella stirred. "The attendants told me the stable, where they used to house the bed slaves who belonged to the warlords of old, has nearly been restored back to their original purpose. They said Aiden will transfer me there when it's done."

"You need to keep your hopes up."

Isabella shook her head. "I'll try, but until the warleader comes, it's easier to be what he wants me to be."

"Isabella—"

"I haven't given up, but right now, he's my master and I'm his bed slave." Isabella pushed herself to her feet and then grabbed the discarded cloak. "He can have my body, but thanks to your help, my mind is my own."

Allani nodded and hummed to the silk which slid to the floor, pooling at Isabella's feet.

Allani hugged Isabella to her and whispered fiercely. "Don't forget who you are."

"I won't, but it will hurt less if I don't resist." Isabella's eyes went dead as she buried the spark of defiance and her fingers rested on her chest. "After all, this body is built perfectly for a master to take his pleasure from. In a past era, I would have been sold and trained much younger. Aiden is just restoring the old ways. I was born to belong to him, or so he told me. I only have to lie back and let him do whatever he wants. If I tell myself that, over and over, that is what he hears from my thoughts. Rather than the fact that at the first opportunity I get, I'm going to kill him."

At the sound of a metal door opening and boot shod feet marching down the corridor towards them, Isabella wrapped the cloak around her shoulders, doing up the clasp to hide her body.

"It's time Isabella," Tony said.

"Do you know if the workers have completed the stable, captain?" Isabella asked.

Tony hesitated. "They finished it today."

Isabella turned back to her, plucking at the cloak she wore. "At least once they take me to him, I won't have to wear this again. The clothes they dress me in for Aiden don't cover much. They say I won't be allowed clothes at all once installed in the warlords stable. It's a measure, along with the slave collar, to prevent me from running away. Only my master and the attendants who tend to me will ever set eyes on me again and live. Just like in the old days. Or so they say."

Allani covered her mouth, not even bothering to wipe the tears that trickled down her cheeks as Tony led Isabella away. Then she sent a plea out into the veil that the warleader would receive her message and fall on this place with vengeance in his heart.

CHAPTER
THIRTY-TWO

Isabella watched as Aiden left the bed and put on his robe, then pulled a cord off to one side. A bell rang faintly, a summons for her handlers to come and collect her. She'd learned not to leave his bed until she was given permission to do so. As the tremors in her muscles started, she knew they'd dose her with tiscan again when he was done. At the sound of a latch, she turned her head to see an internal door open. Her eyes widened a little since it had never been used before while she was here. On every previous occasion, the guards only escorted her in and out of the main doors to his room. Isabella's heart sank at seeing Ella and Cait. It was always those two who had the responsibility to bathe and dress her before she was brought to her master. She had the sinking feeling Tony had been correct about the stable being ready to house her.

"Take my pet to her stable now and make sure she is dosed before she takes her rest." Aiden ordered. "You'll not use her name to address her anymore. It gives her a grounding to who she was in the past and a sense of worth."

"Of course, Warlord, we have everything prepared," Ella said before crossing the room towards her. Ella connected the chain to her collar and tugged on it.

"You'll both be her primary handlers in the stables, along with the other bed slaves as well. No one else is permitted to see or lay hands on my property from now on," Aiden said, then waved his hand dismissively.

"As you will, Warlord. Come on girl, up you get," Ella said.

"Oh and Ella, when you've bedded my prize pet down, bring in my recent acquisitions for a viewing," Aiden said.

"Of course, Warlord, we have the new bed slaves washed and ready for the viewing," Ella said.

Isabella stood as the woman tugged on the chain leading her to the door. Cait stooped to pick up the flimsy gown and the cloak Isabella had been wearing on entering Aiden's rooms and followed. She shuddered as the possessive brush of Aiden's mind on her own. The door closed behind her with a heavy thud as Ella led her down the long, cold, stone corridor. Cait opened another door and stood to one side as Ella took her through into an open area that looked like a sitting room with several doors along the wall. Weak sunlight trickled through the shuttered windows, revealing a collection of hard wooden stools. Isabella stopped as she saw a handful of young girls huddled in the corner of the room. All of them naked and chained.

"Come on, you'll meet the others another day," Ella said, tugging on the chain.

Isabella stumbled and followed on behind Ella, twisting to take in one last sight of the children before she was half dragged into the next room. Ella secured her chain to the wall.

"Well, you won't be needing clothes again," Cait said as she put the flimsy dress she'd been wearing away in a cupboard against the wall.

"Who were the girls?" Isabella asked.

"New bed slaves seized from nearby villages."

"But, they're so young. Surely Aiden—" Isabella gasped as Ella struck her.

"The likes of you don't get to use the warlord's name. He's your master," Ella said, her face screwed up in an ugly scowl.

"Yes Ella. Surely my master wouldn't force the girls to his bed. They're children," Isabella said.

"They're only a little younger than you, but the younger they are, the easier they are to train. Like you, they're bed slaves now. They'll go to your master's bed when he calls for them."

"Which, for one of them, will probably be after the viewing later this morning," Cait said, smirking at her.

"This is your entire world now. Your stable and the warlord's bed," Ella said as she threw a bucket full of water at her.

Isabella gasped as cold water drenched her, but refrained from protesting. She just stood there trembling as both women washed her down before throwing yet another bucket of water over her. Although the water was cold, it had nothing to do with her trembling. That was because of the knowledge they'd give her tiscan again soon. She shuddered at the thought of being forced to have more of the stuff. She still wasn't used to the drug, and it did nothing but make her feel sick. The women dried her off efficiently with rough towels, then Cait took her chain and pulled her back out the door.

"Come on girl, we'll get you fed, then bed you down in your stable and dose you as the warlord ordered before you sleep," Cait said.

"So, this is where I'll be kept now?" Isabella dared to ask.

"This is where you'll stay unless you are in the Warlord's bed. It's referred to as the stable. In the old days, this is where the bed slaves that belonged to the warlord, as you do now, were bedded down in between servicing the warlord's needs," Ella said.

"There were more bed slave's back then. When the warlord had to go on the road, we loaded a selection of bed slaves into windowless carriages. Your master has commissioned a bed slave carriage and ordered the loading vestibule restored to its original use. By the time everything is in place, the stable should have its own guards to protect the warlord's property. Both here and on the road," Cait said.

"Guards?" Isabella asked. "I thought my master said no one else was to see me?"

"The warlord is waiting for some guards to displease him. It shouldn't take long. They'll be transferred from their current warbands to form the stable guards. If they're male, he'll order the healers to castrate them, of course," Ella said, her eyes glinting with amusement.

"You were the first new bed slave the warlord has taken, but there are several more already. Once you've settled down and proven you can be trusted, you'll have some company when you aren't sleeping or entertaining your master," Cait said.

"Take a seat."

Cait secured her chain once again on a ring attached to the side of a heavy wooden table. Isabella sat on the bench the woman indicated. Ella moved around the small dining area and soon enough, she had a plate of food placed in front of her. She stared and picked up the lump of dried bread to nibble on the corner.

"There are advantages to belonging to the warlord girl. Don't doubt you'll be well kept, particularly since you're giving him the sport he wants," Ella said as she placed a goblet of water on the table in front of her as well. "Those, as get claimed by regular folks, won't have their own bed in a comfortable stable like you've got. Or their own handlers to care for them I'll warrant."

"So it's not just me and Damien. Slavery has been reintroduced?"

"It never really went away, girl, it was just hidden. Cait and I found work in a pleasure house in Callenhain, looking after the boys and girls that were kept there while slavery was banned. It's where our new warlord found us and had us recalled back here specially to look after you and his other bed slaves. Now that the warlord has reintroduced slavery again, those as own them won't have to hide the practice," Ella said.

Isabella picked at the food they gave her, trying to fool her stomach that there was more of it than there was. Even in the cells, they'd been given a bowl of soaked grains with the lumps of mouldy bread. As she finished her meal, sweat prickle her whole body, and she shuddered. She tried to hide her reaction as her stomach twisted. Not from the food or drink but from the lack of tiscan. She wanted to be left alone so she could curl up in a ball of misery.

"Come on girl, I'll take you to your stable and give you your drug, then you can sleep." Ella unlocked Isabella's chain and led her out of the room.

Isabella didn't protest, although she wished they'd lock her up without the drug. She couldn't understand how people like Damien became addicted to the stuff and took it willingly. From her perspective, she'd never been so sick and miserable in her life as she was when they dosed her.

Ella opened a door and pulled her into a small room. It was only big enough to house a wooden bench for a bed with a small table beside it. Her stomach clenched again as she recognised the tiscan flask and she took an inadvertent step back. The chain clinked against metal as her handler secured her chain to the wall. The woman pushed her down onto the hard bed before taking the stopper off the flask.

"Please, I'll behave. I won't do anything," Isabella said. "I've accepted I'm a slave now."

Ella ignored Isabella's plea and pulled her head back, and tipped the contents of the vial into her mouth.

"You don't get a choice, girl, you're only a slave. Your master has said you are to be dosed every day. There's a good girl. Lie back now before it hits you. It's full strength now. The healer said it should help make sure some of the drug has the desired effect even if you can't keep the full measure down." Ella pushed Isabella down onto the bed, her hard eyes staring at her. "Don't be sick now. You know we'll have to give you more if you don't keep that dose down."

Isabella sunk back onto the bed, clutching her stomach as overwhelming nausea hit her. Not able to help herself as her stomach rebelled, she rolled over and heaved. Ella made a tsking sound as she held her hair back and shoved a bucket across.

Ella pushed her back, wiping her face with a damp cloth as she lay there shuddering. Isabella shook her head as another vial came into view.

"No more, please..."

Isabella cried out in pain as a meaty hand slapped her across the face.

"Learn your place, girl. It doesn't matter what you want anymore. Now open up, we'll try it a sip at a time," Ella said.

Isabella remembered her promise to herself not to fight them and accept this life, burying the hope of rescue deep in her mind. Although she made one vow to herself. She'd learned exactly what Aiden enjoyed, and she'd ensure he didn't even think about the younger girls. Isabella simply opened her mouth as the flask was held to her lips. She swallowed the mouthful she was given, tears springing in her eyes. Mouthful by mouthful, Ella ensured she drank the tiscan. As her muscles contracted and pain lanced through her, she was unable to help but scream.

"That's better. We'll give you a bit more to replace what you didn't keep down, but it's an excellent sign you're hurting from it." Ella opened a second bottle and tipped the vial into her mouth again. "Go on, swallow it all now. The pain will be over soon and you'll sleep."

Wave after wave of nausea rolled over her, followed by excruciating agony. Tears dampened her cheeks as her muscles contracted and released. Her whole body was on fire. As the light globe was shuttered, she was vaguely aware of the door thumping and a key rattling. Isabella paid no mind to the resounding thunk as the bolt slid home. She didn't know why they'd bothered to lock the door. She was incapable of doing anything except lying there in agony on the hard bench until the torment finally subsided and she fled into the darkness of sleep.

THIRTY-THREE

Steven sat cross-legged on the rug in his outer room, eyes closed as he concentrating on his breathing. Ricardo sat nearby, engaging in his own calming routine. Much to Steven's surprise, Jaclyn's husband had started joining him for meals, sometimes just for a chat or walk in the garden. Meditation had become a daily practice and despite himself, Steven found he was warming up to the other man. He'd even gotten used to the ever present daggerwives that surrounded him. Even more of them were present when Ricardo came to visit. Yet now they seemed like a fixture. So much so Steven found he almost forgot the daggerwives and underwives were positioned around the room. He had the vague idea that if he could foster a friendship with Ricardo, it would come in useful. Exactly how was something Steven was still working on but regardless of that it couldn't hurt.

"You're doing well with the meditation exercises. You are much calmer now than you were."

Steven was more than willing to allow Ricardo to believe it was the calming exercises his mother had taught him that had caused his apparent calmness. The Sylannians didn't need to know it was because he was also practicing his mental shielding. Just as Michael had advised him. Despite what Ricardo perceived, he was just as agitated as he had been since this whole drama unfolded. He was, however, much better at pushing his concerns aside and hiding behind his mental shield.

"I am more relaxed," Steven said, knowing it was the absolute truth and Ricardo would hear that certainty. Even if it wasn't for the reason, Ricardo thought.

"Yet you are still nervous?" Ricardo said, studying him.

Steven wracked his brain for an explanation and mentally kicked himself for allowing too much to leak through his shield. Once again, he decided the truth, or at least a partial truth, would serve him for this purpose.

"It's this mate bond. It terrifies me." Steven licked his lips and allowed some of his fear to leak through his shield. He knew it worked when Ricardo looked troubled. "I didn't realise the extent of it, but my mother enforced strict control over me my whole life. The only time I was free of it was when I was away from her influence. That resulted in me being far more susceptible to others than I realised. My mother didn't have a choice in that. It would have caused people to talk and question why if she kept me locked away here."

"That makes sense. She would have been at risk if anyone discovered her Sylannian heritage. Both from your Warlord and our king," Ricardo said, nodding as he considered the excuse.

"I finally get to be myself and now this has happened. I've come to terms that instead of my mother dominating my life, it is now Jaclyn. The breeding thing, well, it's not that much different to the contract arrangements some of my peers are bound by." Steven ignored the little internal whisper that at least contracts between families and individuals had end dates. "Jaclyn doesn't need to force me. I'll breed with her or whoever the underwives decide I should. She doesn't even need the mate bond to sway my emotions. Jaclyn and Myra do a frighteningly good job of getting me to do what they want without it."

"I won't lie to you. The forging of the mate bond hurts. That is why you need to learn to come to terms with the mind bond and give yourself freely to her control."

"Easier said than done. Myra told me you all fear the mind bonds you forge cause the madness suffered by Sylannians."

"We can't be certain, but yes, Jaclyn believes this to be true. It was Jaclyn's first decree when I accepted her as my firstwife that we would return to the old ways. We believe the practice works since unlike other houses who formed at the same time there is no sign of the deterioration in our house. Other than being away fighting wars all this time, it's the only difference. It's why she won't allow any of the other wives except our primewives to bind me, or you. Once Jaclyn takes the throne, she'll order an end to the practice."

Steven gave a little internal cheer at the lengths Ricardo was going in his attempt to explain. It meant, in part, that Ricardo was at least not automatically dismissing the concerns he'd raised.

"Then why not end it now? Why forge yet another mind bond when you fear it will cause madness?"

"It's..." Ricardo trailed off, looking even more troubled than he had been at the start of the conversation.

"It isn't necessary. Whatever Jaclyn does with me, I'll do my best to obey her. Regardless of if it's taking me as her second husband or to put me in one of your breeding houses. Your ways were strange to me at first but I've been doing my best to comply with the directions of the underwives and daggerwives." Steven mentally kicked himself as he realised how much desperation had crept into his tone.

Compassion flared from Ricardo. "All the underwives and

daggerwives assigned to your care report you've been doing well. Jaclyn is pleased with your progress, even if she hasn't shown you that."

"I won't cause any trouble," Steven whispered.

"You raise some valid points. I can't guarantee anything, but I'll speak with Jaclyn regarding your concerns."

Steven rose to his feet as Ricardo did and bowed his head. "I didn't mean to whine at you. I'm afraid, but I know my place."

Ricardo's hand squeezed his shoulder. "Things won't be as bad as you fear. Instead of the daggerwives or underwives standing guard while you sleep, you'll be breeding with them. Other than that, you'll have more freedom once Jaclyn decides what is best for you. Particularly if Jaclyn takes you as a second husband. Now try to relax rather than stress about issues that, as a reclaimed Sylannian male, you have no control or say in. It is Jaclyn's issue to worry over."

"Yes Ricardo, thank you. I'm trying to learn your... our ways."

Steven kept a tight control over his satisfaction as Ricardo reacted positively to his word choice. He'd rehearsed some of the conversations and reasonings he could present in case opportunities presented themselves, but was still shocked that it seemed to have worked. Steven had sensed the compassion and understanding from Ricardo that he'd wanted. He just hoped between the conversations about the same topic he'd had with Myra and Ricardo that they'd both been feeding it to Jaclyn.

THIRTY-FOUR

Ben paused, pressing against the wooden walls in the darkness. Normally, even in this part of the city, there would be lamps to push back the darkness in the depths of the night. Now, because of the Sylannian's, darkness held sway every evening. Those who normally kept the lights fuelled up and going at night just didn't bother and since the Sylannians said nothing, it stayed that way. It certainly made stealing their way through the streets at night an easier prospect.

A creak of timber sounded as the wind, blowing in off the broad river, blew through the city. He wrinkled his nose as the smell came with it. The ambient light thrown from the moon and stars, peaking through the scattered cloud cover, was just enough to see the dark outlines. Four bodies were suspended from a beam that stood in the broad square. Even though the bodies had rotted the Sylannians left them there. Birds of prey circled throughout the day and came in to feast despite the noise of carts, horses and people that persisted in a city the size of Vallantia. The Sylannian rule in those first few days had been absolute and brutal. Executing any that defied them quickly and efficiently. They left such reminders of what would happen to any who defied them scattered throughout Vallantia. With the rotting evidence of what would happen to them if they didn't comply, hanging in the open spaces with the city, it didn't take long for people to stop fighting.

Ben moved on, trying not to taste the decaying flesh that was in the air as he breathed. He cautiously rounded the corner, then ran carefully down the dirt alley. Granted, it was compacted through years and years of use, but this was the poor quarter. No one bothered to cart in stones. He doubted they would care enough to do so even if the streets were broad enough for carts. The only work done on these winding narrow maze of lanes that wove through this quarter was to throw buckets of sand into potholes when they developed. Now and then, someone would throw stones into one. A wolfish smile spread across Ben's lips. Of course, they'd probably procured them from the merchant quarter. Not stolen, of course, simply relocated.

Ben looked up and caught the fleeting movement of one of Lukas's people who ran across the rooftops above. They kept watch on them all. He had no idea how they managed to leap from roof to roof, keeping pace with his own group without making a sound.

The warehouse is just around the next corner, Lukas said.

It didn't take us as long to get here as I thought it would, Ben said.

Show caution. There are two guards about to come around the corner of the warehouse towards the front doors, Lukas said.

Ben paused, signalling to those that were with him that their target was ahead. The Sylannians kept the bulk of the local population they'd enslaved that worked the farmland closer to Vallantia locked up together. A huge warehouse served to house the group of captives during the night. Just before dawn, the Sylannians roused their captives and sent them out by barge or cart. The workers would tend the crops and herd stock under close supervision, only to be brought back to the city in the evenings to be locked up again. While Ben had contemplated hitting the barges or carts to or from the city, or even the farms they worked at, he'd quickly discarded it. Interestingly enough, there were more guards on the convoys to and from the farms and at the farms themselves, than on the place where the captives were detained for the night. Right here, while it was still well before dawn, was the time where there were minimal guards on duty. He'd assessed it was the easiest time to get them free. Of course, then they had to get all the people they freed clear of the city, but that was the next problem.

He watched as he received signals back from his team that they were in position. This was always the worst part. Waiting. Somehow, at this point, time seemed to go on forever, although in reality they hadn't really been here too long. Soon enough, the two guards walked back to the front of the warehouse from their circuit. Ben watched, alert as they all were, while the guards leant against the wall near the doors looking bored as they talked. Probably more to keep themselves awake than because either of them was actually interested in the conversation they were having.

It didn't take long before they pushed off from their position on the wall and walked around the perimeter again. Lukas had his people watching this routine all week, and it was a pattern they hadn't diverted from at all. As they passed his position, he pounced, taking his target cleanly from behind. He lowered the body down to the ground and removed the keys from the belt of his victim. Standing, he sprinted for the doors, allowing others to drag the bodies of the sentries out of sight and dispose of them in the nearby river. As these next few hours were the ones that mattered the most, he didn't waste any time in opening the doors. As the key turned in the lock, he was relieved to hear the solid thunk. Ben pushed the doors open and slipped inside, his team members following close behind. The noise of the doors opening had woken those nearest the doors despite it not being as loud as his imagination had told him it was. Those curled up on the cots surged up, only to come against their bindings. Ben held his finger up to his lips, then went to work, hacking through the Sylannian silk bindings. The stuff had properties that made it far stronger than fabric ever should be. Thankfully, the blades forged by the Smith were one of the few things that could cut through the Sylannian bindings.

"Come on, move, get everyone up and out of here. We have little time," Ben said.

His people went from cot to cot, waking those who'd somehow slept through their entrance before cutting them loose. Men and women alike they all wore the same thing, loose fitting grey trousers and long sleeve loose tops, with flat sandals on their feet. Ben's jaw clenched at the sight of the grey, seamless collars around their necks. Those would have to be dealt with later. This was all taking longer than he liked already. The stronger among the captives needed no urging to help those among their number who were older or carrying injuries. As the last of the workers streamed out of the warehouse, he pulled the doors closed and carefully locked them again. It would only give them a little more time, but he'd rather give their group as much of a head start as he could.

He turned and broke into a light jog to catch up to the tail end of the group they were rescuing. Noting that some of the fitter members had held back monitoring their fellow captives' progress, but also checking on him and his remaining people. He pulled one of his daggers out of his belt and passed it to one of the more competent-looking women in grey. Her eyes shone in the dim light as she grasped it.

"Thank you, whoever you are," she said.

"No thanks are necessary," Ben said.

With a group this size, it made the underground network beneath Vallantia impractical. Lukas had reasoned it would be quicker and easier to get those they rescued out of sight into the Burrow, rather than one by one down into the tunnel system. In particular, with the injured. Once within the relative safety of the Burrow, they could extract those they rescued out of Vallantia to safety in locations outside Sylannian control. One benefit of their current location being between the poor and merchant quarters was the water wasn't far. Not the traditional docks. That would be suicide to attempt them. The Sylannians kept them well guarded day and night. The mess of multi-storey wooden buildings of the small section of the poor quarter affectionately called the Burrow loomed ahead of them. He, for one, was relieved to see it, although he could feel the trepidation coming from those they'd just rescued. They recognised the place just as easily as he did. It was unlike anywhere else in Vallantia. It resembled something a child would build with a bunch of mismatched blocks precariously placed on top of each other. They fronted onto a small section of the river that was like a dump. The residents of the Burrow threw everything into this small section of the river. They emptied toilet bowls, discarded scraps of uneaten food, and dead bodies weren't exactly unheard of either. These residents lived by their own rules, beholden to no one. The Kastlers left those who lived in the Burrow alone. Of course, the Kastlers were after money, and everyone said there was no profit to be had in the Burrow.

The Sylannians hadn't bothered with them again so far either. Not after their first few efforts to clean them out had resulted in their own people disappearing into the depths of the Burrow, never to be seen alive again. They'd learnt it was much harder to intimidate a bunch of people who didn't actually have much to lose. He didn't doubt that burning them out occurred to the Sylannian invaders; he was equally sure they'd come to the realisation they'd probably lose the bulk of the city and their base as well. So they'd pulled back and left this corner of Vallantia and its occupants to themselves. The residents, for their part, ignored whoever governed the greater city. Or at least they appeared too. The Burrow contained hidden strength, and when it came to poverty, appearances can be deceiving.

Despite how disreputable and poor this sector appeared, not all who lived here in these ramshackle buildings were poor. Disreputable certainly, some of the best who walked the shadows had their hideouts nestled within this mess. They made it their business to support those who acted as their front and protected them in their midst. Some of those who worked for Lukas ran with his group, helping to protect the former captives, while more of their number kept watch from the rooftops. Not that the bulk of the people they'd rescued would realise that little detail.

Lukas continued business as usual when the Kastlers took over Vallantia. Under the Sylannians, it was a different story. With the arrival of the invaders, Lukas had put a stop to most of their operations. Still, the Burrow had come to life, now serving its second function, hidden within its decrepit exterior. People cheered that this little enclave survived to all extents outside of the Warlord's rule. They operated in the past on staying well away from the Warlord and his interests. As long as they didn't bring too much attention to themselves, they continued to operate in the shadows. To all appearances, the warleader looked the other way.

Or so everyone thought. Incorrectly, as it turned out. Lukas and his people paid their share of tithe to the Warlord and unbeknownst to the greater part of the population, Michael was well aquatinted with Lukas. These few people were perfectly aware who not only they really worked for, but who he worked for as well. Even so, they'd done their best in the passing years to keep out of his way as much as he'd done to keep out of theirs. Many of the residents of a certain age remembered the association between him and the warleader. The need to be circumspect had all changed when the Sylannians had taken over and he'd run to ground within the depths of the Burrow. Or rather, they'd rescued him since he'd fallen just short of their home.

Ben saw those they'd rescued hesitate as they approached the winding, narrow alleys that lead into the depths of the Burrow and he swore.

"Forget everything you've heard. If you want to live go, our path lies within the Burrow," Ben said, emphasising it with a mental shove at those ahead of him.

As those they'd rescued continued to hesitate, another member of his team hissed in frustration. "Take your chances with the Sylannians if you prefer!"

As if a dam burst, they ran forward. It seemed even the Burrow was better than the Sylannians. The groups spread out, funnelling down the narrow alleyways between the building structures, each group led by one who knew this inner network of alleyways. A whistle from the rooftops caused him to glance up to find Tina, the lookout, on the walkway that ran between the buildings.

"It's all clear," Tina said.

"Thanks."

Without waiting, the lookout scaled up the side of the building until they hit the roof and ran, mirroring their progress above as they moved towards the river. While he couldn't see the weapons, the woman was armed to the teeth. Ben resisted the urge to hold his breath as they reached the river. The refuse reeked.

"How do they stand this?" the woman said.

"It serves its purpose for those that live here and now for us as well," Ben said.

He stood guard as the team ushered those they'd rescued through a doorway into what had been a storage facility Lukas used for his operations. Ben had refrained from inquiring exactly what Lukas normally stored in the long multi storey building. Or where they'd found to store the goods. It wasn't his business. One of the handy things about this facility it had several ways out if they needed to flee. It had access points to the roofs, the river, and an underground tunnel that led under Vallantia's outer wall.

THIRTY-FIVE

Jaclyn acknowledged Ricardo as he entered the room before turning her flat stare back at Sasha, the firstwife of the sister house that she'd put in charge of Vallantia.

"No excuses. Track down the rebel elements in Vallantia. There can't be that many of them. Make an example of any you capture to deter others from joining their ranks. Now go. I expect to hear you've secured the city on your next report." Jaclyn snapped, allowing her displeasure to be conveyed in not only her words but through a complicated mental pattern layered through them.

Sasha and her fellow wives backed up and knelt, pressing their foreheads to the ground before standing and backing out of her presence. If anything, it showed they were aware they'd failed, and she was displeased with them.

"Still not going well?" Ricardo asked, holding his hand out to capture hers.

Ricardo tugged her arm gently, and she complied, sinking down onto the chair with him. Ricardo's strong fingers kneaded the muscles in her shoulders. She hissed as his fingers found a tight knot, but didn't pull away from his ministrations.

"No. There is a group of locals opposing our efforts. Our forces in town are struggling to track them down."

"Much trouble?"

"Groups of the collared workforce are going missing, never to be seen again. Worse, whole patrols are ending up dead. I'll give it to the rebels. They are quite inventive."

"In what way?"

"They leave the bodies of the daggerwives they've killed in prominent locations. On display to the newly collared."

"Ah, it gives our new acquisitions the belief there is hope for them."

"Exactly." Jaclyn ground her teeth, then pushed down her frustration. It's not like it would achieve anything useful. "How did your session with Steven go?"

"I agree with Myra. He's gone to considerable effort to hide something." Ricardo paused, and he proceeded more slowly. "Although I judge, Steven is genuinely terrified of even the thought of the mate bond."

"Your advice?"

"Take Steven as a husband and breed with him. The mate bond can come later once he's more settled in his new life and knows us all a little better."

"You don't think it's a risk?"

"How? If these rebels you speak of can get in here and extract Steven from the centre of daggerwives and underwives that surround him every day, then we have bigger problems. It means we've lost this war already."

"If you'll permit First?" Arianne asked.

"You have some insight into this?"

"Steven has been fully compliant with the underwives and daggerwives assigned to him. No sign of any defiance." A hint of a smile curved Arianne's lips. "At least not in words or behaviour. One of the underwives mentioned the other day that the practice of mate bonding to a husband before any children have been born to the house is a more modern practice."

Jaclyn's eyebrows rose, and she glanced over to the underwives. "Is this true?"

"Yes First. In ancient times, when we had more Sylannian men, the mate bond was only conducted once the male had proven he wasn't sterile by producing children with not only the firstwife but other wives as well."

"I also agree with our husband. There is no way Steven could escape by himself, even giving him space in his rooms by himself for some time. If the rebels can get in here and take him. Then we are all dead. I'd suggest in that circumstance we run and find safe territory for ourselves and our children," Arianne said.

"Go to him and speak with your future husband about it." Ricardo held up his hand as she went to protest. "See for yourself. Regardless of what he is hiding, Steven is terrified of the mate bond. It's your fertile period. You said you'd decide Steven's fate before now. I understand your hesitation, but this delay is causing him more fear. Kill him or take him as your husband. It is your decision, but he shouldn't have to suffer this way."

The rebuke in Ricardo's tone was clear and, even though she wanted to argue, Jaclyn found she couldn't. Not only was Steven a Sylannian male brought up in a foreign land, he had the blood of the Monarch House flowing in his veins. He'd had to face pressures and decisions alone that no man should ever be forced to endure while residing in this barbarian land.

"You're right. All of you. It's a constant struggle between not losing our ways and doing what I think is right for our people. I will take Steven as a husband, but defer my decision on the mate bond," Jaclyn said.

THIRTY-SIX

Steven kept his eyes closed and his emotions as level as he could when he sensed Jaclyn walk into the room. He didn't even flinch as Jaclyn knelt near him. Although he couldn't help the shiver that ran through him as her fingers brushed his temple.

"I have made my decision regarding your fate. I am claiming you as my second husband."

Steven opened his eyes and took a steadying breath. "I won't cause you any trouble. I'll breed with you and whoever you say, which I'm told is your..." Steven grimaced, "our custom."

"You fear the mate bond."

"I'm sorry Jaclyn, yes I do, but I think..."

"You think what?"

"Forgive me, it's not my place to think such things."

"Tell me."

"I think there is a part of you that fears forging a permanent bond with another mind as well. Or you would have captured my mind already."

Steven held his breath as Jaclyn sat back, a frown creasing

her forehead, then she reached out and grabbed his hand. Calmness washed over his mind with the contact and Steven allowed his relief to show.

"If you accept the mate bond, then there wouldn't be misunderstandings like these. I'd know what you're thinking without you having to explain. It works both ways. You'd know my mind as well."

"The fact that I can hear the mindvoices of random people in my head occasionally is horrifying enough. If you can't even have privacy in your own head... ever... no wonder our people go mad." Steven shuddered. He didn't even have to pretend that he was horrified on her behalf, on Ricardo's behalf. Or even a king he didn't know. "Wait, do I understand correctly the king, your brother is bound to all his wives?"

"He is only bound to the wives who have given birth to a child. Not all his wives."

"How many wives is that?"

"I'm not precisely certain. The inner sanctum where the children live is not open to anyone outside the house. Of the wives who've given birth, only those who've given birth to a male child appear in court. A hundred, possibly more." Jaclyn shrugged.

Steven thought he was horrified before. As it turned out, he was wrong. Now he was outraged on behalf of someone he didn't know. Worse. He was fuming about the fate of a king who'd ordered the invasion of his home.

"How does the poor man keep straight where his own thoughts begin and end?" Steven stood abruptly, taking a step back from Jaclyn. "All these years, Sylanna has been watching everyone go mad. Justifying the mass murder of entire family units. Generation after generation and you're trying to tell me it didn't occur to any of you, before now, that the cause was this practice of binding all your minds together?"

"Of course, I believe that's the cause. It's why I won't allow all the wives to bind Ricardo, or you. Please calm down," Jaclyn said, her hand reaching out to make contact with his temple.

Steven stepped back, allowing all his hurt, fear, and anger boil up to breach the mental shields he'd been holding onto this whole time.

"Yet you still insist on forcing a mate bond on me? Even though it's not needed. Even knowing it could drive us all to madness?"

"No, I won't force a mate bond on you."

Steven's outrage deserted him at her promise. The rant he'd about to launch into now entirely unnecessary.

"You won't?" Steven asked.

Jaclyn shook her head. "It's been pointed out to me that binding a husband's mind straight away was not always our custom. I think it's also a little hypocritical of me to say I'm going to ban the custom but still enforce it on you."

"Oh. Thank you. Is there a ceremony that I have to prepare for?" Steven asked, his mouth going dry. "I mean, in order for you to take me as a husband?"

Jaclyn chuckled and held out her hand to him. Steven stared at her fingertips for a moment. They were usually stroking his temple to gain his compliance. He reached out his own hand, and she tugged his arm and took a step towards the bedroom.

"No ceremony. Come, it's time for you to breed with me."

"That's all it takes? Just sex?"

"Normally I'd bond you first, but I just promised I wouldn't. I hope being my husband is not such a scary prospect for you anymore."

"I don't know what to think. I'm nervous but I already promised I'd do whatever you wanted."

"What I want is to breed with you. Then you will be my husband. I think perhaps delaying longer will just cause you more fear as all sorts of dire circumstances occur to you."

Steven smiled weakly as he followed Jaclyn into his bedroom. It seemed that perhaps Jaclyn knew him better than he thought she did. Now he wouldn't just be sleeping with the enemy, he was going to breed with them as well. A little traitorous part of his mind wasn't even alarmed at the prospect. Although he took it as a small victory that Jaclyn had agreed not to forge a mate bond with him. For now, he still had the privacy of his mind.

THIRTY-SEVEN

Allani looked at her fellow wives. "Alert me if any of our captors approach."

They all nodded and, with a small amount of shuffling, placed themselves in positions around her, effectively shielding her from view should the guards head down this way to check on them. She'd found it interesting those here had been so afraid they'd drugged the poor child. Yet they hadn't taken the same caution with her or her fellow wives. Granted, if those who held them scanned them with their othersight, they wouldn't glow with the veil like their warleader and his people did. Like Isabella and her brother did. Yet she had certain skills. Most Sylannians did, particularly those who were presented to be selected to breed with their husbands. Let alone those of them who were shown to men as prospective Firstwives. They excelled in mindgifts. Not surprising, considering it was a skill set her people seemed to favour and bred for. She may not be able to blast a hole in the cell's wall to free herself and her fellow wives, but she could use what skills she did have to help Damien. He may have been the one who'd brought them here and had them locked up but, he was also the one who'd shown them kindness when he didn't have to while they'd been on the road. She knew if the situation had been reversed, such kindness would not have been forthcoming. Damien, in particular, would have found himself in a much similar position. A captive. Although not harmed in the way this new warlord did but her people would never let a male like Damien run free. As her people saw things, he was far too valuable. Allani fancied even Jaclyn would give up her distaste and breed with such a specimen. Let alone when she encountered the warleader. Allani hoped she was alive and there to see Jaclyn's reaction to these people. Although, sadly, she doubted she would be.

Allani took a deep breath and sunk down into a trance. Normally, it was far easier for her to place her hands on the one she was trying to connect with, but she didn't have that luxury. Still, each day she got closer. She sent her mind out, questing towards Damien. It wasn't really that hard. His mind was alternately a beacon of pain, or lost in the drugs they fed him that shut down his ability to control the veil. She made her way to the courtyard and visualised herself walking across it to the man who lay slumped and chained in the centre. She wasn't sure exactly why it was the case that somehow projecting herself this way seemed to work better, but it did. So she wasn't about to question what worked. At least not right now, perhaps later when they were free, and she had time to contemplate the phenomena. Allani closed her eyes, feeling the faint breeze brush over her skin with a hint of warmth from the late afternoon sun before it disappeared behind the fortress and mountains. It wasn't real. She was still in the cell, but her mind was showing her what was there in this place.

Damien slumped on the ground, his mind shuttered and locked up by the drugs they fed him. Pain, misery, confusion and a hint of madness hung over him like its own visible cloud. She doubted even those born with little to no skill at all in the veil could approach him and not feel its effects. Yet beneath it all, there was something else that lurked. How these people didn't realise how dangerous Damien was, she didn't understand. At a forbidding rumble, she took in the dark thunderclouds that rolled across the sky. The flickering lightning that traced delicately through them. She shuddered, knowing they weren't real storm clouds, just as it wasn't really lightning. It was the veil. It was Damien. She feared she knew a secret they kept, perhaps even from themselves. A secret that her commander didn't even truly realise. The warleader, indeed all the Unwanted she'd set eyes on and Damien himself, were not like the rest of them. The drugs these people plied him with, thinking it kept them safe, were failing. It wasn't just the drugs and mistreatment that caused Damien's pain. It was the veil itself. She could see it. It ran through him. Changed him bit by bit, even if it wasn't in his conscious control. Soon the veil would claim him back, as it reforged him into its own creature. She shuddered again. It had been a relief to discover that most of the people in this domain were much like her own, born with a variety of strengths in the veil's use. It was only the Unwanted who were different.

Hearing a noise, her eyes narrowed as she recognised the man she'd seen in Isabella's mind. It was Aiden, the one who'd killed the Warlord, his own father, to take control. As a Sylannian, such a thing didn't shock her at all. It was how the Monarch House changed hands in her own land. Not content with his newfound power, he'd continued to force himself on Isabella, claiming her body as his own and trying to take her mind as well. The warlord was tormenting Damien, trying to get him, in his pain and confusion, to give himself up. Aiden thought he was an expert on mind control, and that the little bond he'd forged between him and Damien was enough. Her people knew the truth. It wasn't. In order for Aiden to own Damien's mind completely, Damien had to fully, willingly, submit to Aiden's control. It was why their men trained from birth to submit, to give their entire selves to the control of their wives. This was the little wrinkle Aiden had come unknowingly up against. While it was true Damien was an addict, it did not automatically make him weak of mind. She shuddered, hoping that drug they bound him and Isabella with never touched her lips. Even so, Aiden's assumptions were exactly what caused him to fail. Damien had not been raised to submit to another will, even if he wanted to give up to make the pain go away. His unconscious mind fought back against the one that was trying to invade his mind. Just like that little bond Aiden had forged in Damien's mind. Aiden worked hard to maintain it, constantly fostering it. Simply because Damien's body was busy trying to repair the damage and boot the interloper out.

Damien moaned, his breath catching in his throat as the muscles in his body contracted, his back arched as pain shot through him and a scream tore from his lips. She could see the damage to his body that his captors had taken a great deal of pleasure in inflicting on him. She'd seen on previous occasions they had dosed him both before and after such sessions. The drug held his mind in a fog and intensified everything he felt, including pain. She knelt beside him, reaching down, resting her fingers lightly on his temples. The mental touch, as light as it was, caused him to whimper. She heard the vile lies that Aiden whispered in Damien's head. They twisted and merged with his reality and nightmares, so he no longer comprehended which was which.

She glanced up at the one on the balcony, glaring furiously even though Aiden couldn't see or sense her. Concentrating, she pushed a small mental shield between Damien's mind and his tormentor.

Hush Damien, the foul creature who torments you lies. Isabella is alive. She soothed him as best she could without having her actual hands on him and bled away some of his agony.

The frustration coming from Aiden in waves from his position on the balcony caused Allani to grin. The warlord believed it was the tiscan interfering with his mind games, but was too afraid of his prisoner to stop the daily drugging, unless he had complete control.

Who? Damien asked.

Allani returned her attention to Damien and with a start saw his eyes were open and staring right at her. Or would be if she really had been physically standing here instead of back in her cell. Yet he seemed to know, to sense where this phantom presence of her was.

Don't fear, I mean you no harm. I'm Allani, you know me. She tried to keep her replies simple, knowing he was struggling to comprehend much of anything at this moment.

I, I don't remember... Damien whispered.

It is the drug and punishment they inflict on you, Allani said.

She knew the moment confusion chased away his moment of lucidity. As spasm after spasm wracked his body, he screamed again. The sight causing Aiden on the balcony satisfaction as he turned and opened the shutters. So that should those below look up, they would see both Aiden and Isabella, who'd just been escorted into his room. Even this minor detail was designed to torment Damien. Isabella would soon be undressed and in his bed under him as he satisfied his needs with her as he did every evening. Allani turned her attention back to Damien, taking as much of his pain away as she could. While trying to shelter his mind from the sights, sounds and emotions, from the activity up in the tower that Aiden did not even try to hide.

"Come here Isabella." Aiden ordered, his voice carried easily from the tower above down into the courtyard.

"Yes, master." Isabella's voice was soft, but her response still travelled down to the courtyard.

Allani sensed Aiden's spike of lust as his hand reached up and the flimsy, sheer garment they'd dressed Isabella in fell to the floor. Tears pricked her eyes as Isabella moaned as Aiden manipulated her emotions while he pawed Isabella's body. She sensed the resignation in Isabella not to fight back, but to give Aiden what he wanted. The man wasn't gentle with her. He enjoyed causing pain. She also sensed that brief spurt of longing for death that Isabella couldn't quite hide so she could escape the attentions Aiden forced on her.

"Oh, never fear, my pet. I'll make sure you are well cared for. You will not be permitted to take your own life. I'll not let you escape me by dying the way Michael's sister did." Aiden's laughter held a mocking edge to it, as Isabella's mental anguish only seemed to spur him on.

Then Allani's eyes widened as she realised what Isabella had done.

Oh well played Isabella. Manipulate him by his baser instincts, Allani whispered.

Allani glanced up to find Aiden had completely forgotten the sadistic games he'd intended to inflict on both Isabella and Damien this night. Instead, Aiden dragged Isabella onto the bed with him and she fell on top of him. While Isabella may exert some control over Aiden and what he did to her, Allani turned resolutely away. She didn't need to watch the display. The fact that Isabella considered this was the lesser evil didn't make it any better.

It wasn't long before sounds that could not be mistaken for anything else also filtered down. Turning away might stop her from seeing it, but didn't stop her from hearing the rhythmic creaking of the bed, accompanied by heavy breathing, moans and gasps. Closely followed by a spurt of satisfaction, of power and control as Isabella cried out before Aiden climaxed himself. Allani could sense Aiden's triumph that Isabella had also climaxed during sex. He seemed to have no idea that while he might manipulate Isabella; she was also manipulating him. If she could hear and sense it all, then Damien could as well. Although she doubted his drug addled mind could interpret what was happening above between his sister and Aiden. That Isabella was taking some measure of control over her current situation.

Allani stayed a little longer, sheltering Damien's mind from what was happening above. Knowing Isabella lived was important. Knowing his sister was Aiden's bed slave and being unable to help her or intervene wasn't. It would only torment him more, which was exactly Aiden's intent.

THIRTY-EIGHT

Michael rubbed his face as he paced. That much of the intelligence about what their enemy planned was coming from his brother gave him some concern. Although since Steven was quite literally sleeping with the enemy, it meant he was perfectly placed to overhear some of the Sylannian commander's plans. Although he had to admit circumstances had finally forced his brother to grow up.

While spending long days in the saddle, he'd been receiving and dealing with reports from Vallantia. The most astounding being the position Steven found himself in. At least they'd made good time on the road and, as predicted, they'd caught up not only with Taya and Harry's warbands, but the others as well. They'd promptly slowed down at that point as the other leaders expressed concern regarding the state their fighters would be in if they didn't. Their combined forces didn't exactly travel together, but leapfrogged each other. Some staying in better accommodations and camping areas in villages while others rough camped alongside the roads between villages. They took turns in staying in the better accommodations along the way to be fair to everyone. There'd been a push from some leaders of the other warbands for him and the Unwanted to take the accommodation in the town. They were deferring to him because he was leading them, but it was something he turned down. He didn't feel he was any better than any of the others, regardless of having the burden of being the warleader. Even if the role had a lot more pressure now that war had descended on them, in the form of the Sylannians and the Warlord was incapacitated.

He sighed and sat down at the table that Olivia and Nathanial were sitting at. Neither of them said a word. Nathanial just picked up a jug and poured him a drink and pushed the platter of meats, cheese and bread they'd been nibbling at closer to him.

"How's Steven?" Nathanial asked.

"Terrified, but coping better than I thought he would. Jaclyn has taken him as her second husband, but he's managed to avoided the mate bond so far."

"I can't believe I'm saying this, but I feel a little sorry for him," Olivia said. "Between finding out your mother is Sylannian and the commander of the enemy forces is your cousin who has now taken him as a husband, his entire world has imploded on him."

"I've added my mother to the list of issues I have to deal with."

Nathanial snorted. "It's unfortunate that list keeps getting longer."

"The report from Ben indicates Steven has been feeding all sorts of useful information to him."

"How are our operations in Vallantia going?"

"Between the efforts of Ben and Lukas, they've just freed another group of locals from under Sylannian rule. Once the fuss has died down, they'll send them on to safety at the Smith's estate. While Ben is sending through some great information, I keep coming up against the fact I have to get there first." Michael shrugged.

"We have to deal with the situation as we find it when we get there," Olivia said.

"At the current pace we'll be at the crossroad day after tomorrow, not that I want to add to the list but, we need to decide if we're going to divert to Yalleska or not," Nathanial said, taking a sip of his drink.

"I know..." Michael trailed off as he heard the mental equivalent of a knock to gain his attention a moment before Callan entered his awareness.

Michael?

Yes, Callan. We were just about to discuss the situation at Yalleska. What can you tell me?

Are you sitting down? Olivia and Nathanial as well?

Michael glanced at both Nathanial and Olivia, drawing them into the link so that Callan didn't have to exert himself further to include them in the conversation. None of them failed to miss the sadness and anger radiating from Callan.

I've linked them both in and yes, we're all sitting down. What's wrong? Michael asked.

There's no easy way to tell you this. The Warlord is dead, Callan said.

Michael nearly doubled over, as if he'd just received a physical blow.

How? Nathanial asked, giving him time to process what they'd just been told.

He was murdered, Callan said.

What? Who did this and how? He's supposed to be safe at the Stronghold in Yalleska, Michael snarled.

He was at the Stronghold. It will be easier to show you. If you'll permit. You'll need to brace yourselves. It's the memory of someone who was there and it's rough, Callan said.

Send it, Michael said.

Olivia grabbed his hand and, he saw the pain that he was sure she could see just as easily in him. They'd both seen the Warlord as a father. He'd insisted on treating them as if they were his own children. The connection between them and Callan strengthened when he drew more of the veil. He took a deep steadying breath as the memory that Callan sent hit him, and he was seeing through a woman's eyes. He stiffened as Damien burst into the room with Aiden right behind him. Damien's turmoil rolled over them and a woman called his name, explaining it wasn't what it looked like.

This is Isabella's memory. What was she doing there? Olivia commented absently.

Damien swayed and looked up at the Warlord. Confusion written on his face.

"Tiscan, why would he give me tiscan?" Damien whispered.

Aiden lunged with a blade, plunging it into the Warlord, whose eyes widened in pain and shock as he slumped to the ground.

Then Isabella gasped as Aiden threw himself at Damien, grappled with him and shoved the bloodied blade in his hand.

"Damien, what have you done?" Aiden yelled.

The guards crashed through the door, throwing themselves at Damien. Isabella ran forward to help Damien, but was hauled back by yet more guards.

"No please, he didn't do this it was..."

Pain exploded in her face and Aiden loomed in her vision. The awful sensation of Aiden's body pressing against hers flowed through to them and she asked why Aiden had killed his father, followed by Aiden's snarling reply.

My father wouldn't have the grace to die. I meant for Damien to kill him, but he resisted.

Michael stiffened at the words, buffering his mind against

the raw emotions that were contained in the memory as it rolled on with both Damien, then Isabella, being drugged with tiscan.

The memory cut off as Isabella slumped into unconsciousness.

Michael closed his eyes, feeling empty for a moment, his mind still trying to process what he'd seen.

Where are you? Nathanial asked.

Owen, the man who trained Damien, warned us that Aiden was sending teams out to locate and kill us. So, as a contingency, we left Yalleska. We're camped in the forest a few hours ride from the city. Callan sent through an image of their camp.

How did Owen know all this? What were he and Isabella doing in Yalleska? Michael asked.

He said Ranlith was sacked. They survived, and the Warlord took them with him back to Yalleska. He said Allani, the Sylannian prisoner, warned him. Allani is in the cells where Aiden throws Isabella every day when he's done with her.

What do you mean when he's done with her? Michael found his focus sharpen.

Aiden has forced Isabella into his bed by threatening Damien's life. Owen said everyone is saying he's collared both Damien and Isabella. She is now his bed slave.

I'll kill him. Michael's anger flared.

Silence settled for a moment, then Callen spoke again softly.

I'm sorry. I should have insisted on us staying with Damien in the Stronghold. He insisted he'd be fine. If I'd been there—

Then you'd be dead. Aiden would have known you'd be too dangerous to leave alive, Olivia said.

What are your orders? I, I don't want to leave Damien alone. He's hurting, lost in the tiscan they are drugging him with and in pain. They're torturing him. Even though the tiscan keeps Damien's abilities locked down, I can sense it through the veil.

Stay put where you are and stay safe. Do not go after Damien alone.

Yes, Warleader.

I'll get back to you with orders.

Michael cut the connection with Callan, wrapping his arm around Olivia as she leant into his shoulder, her pain and loss running as deep as his own.

Nathanial stood, turning to face the Unwanted, who all sat motionless, watching the three of them, knowing something was wrong but not what. Keeping it brief, Nathanial informed them of the report they'd received from Callan. Shock descended on everyone in the accommodation by the time he was done. Then Nathanial came back and sunk into his seat at the table.

"I know you need to mourn, but we have decisions that need to be made," Nathanial said.

"I know," Michael said, looking up at his friend.

"This changes things. For what it's worth, I want to spilt myself into two. I don't think we can afford to leave a traitor at our back. But admittedly, this whole thing of Damien and Isabella being collared and Isabella being forced to be Aiden's bed slave is something that I can't separate my past from," Nathanial said quietly.

"Strategically, as much as I want to turn us around and march on the Stronghold, I don't think we can afford the time. From the reports Ben has fed us, the Sylannians have already taken not only Vallantia but all the surrounding towns," Olivia said, reaching out to squeeze Nathanial's shoulder.

"We've been saving our energy. It wouldn't take us long to cover the distance between here and Yalleska by ourselves. The other warbands can keep going to Vallantia. I don't think we need the rest of them to take down Aiden," Nathanial said.

"We'd still have to get into the Stronghold. It's set up to withstand a siege." Olivia shook her head. "Aiden isn't the smartest at tactics, but Derick knows what he's doing."

Michael ducked his head. The image of the Warlord, his father dead on the floor, kept intruding on his attempts to think straight.

"Call a halt to all the warbands. They are to hold where they are. I want the leaders of the other warbands who are close enough here by tomorrow afternoon at the latest for a war conference. Tell them to bring whoever they need in order to advise them. I won't make this decision in isolation." Michael stood as Nathanial nodded. "Excuse me, I need some space."

Michael picked up his drink and downed the contents before turning and walking up the stairs to his room in the inn they'd taken over. He wrapped his personal mental shields around his mind, not wanting to inflict his emotions on anyone else. Particularly since right now he was having a hard time working out how he was feeling.

CHAPTER
THIRTY-NINE

Aiden walked out into the courtyard. He was in an extraordinary mood. In part because Isabella had finally capitulated to him. He took a certain measure of delight at her mortification when he'd finally managed to bring her to climax before he took his own. A lazy smile spread across his face. Her fear and pain when he tormented her was intoxicating. The Sylannian woman, though, she was a different matter entirely. She was a willing bed companion in all ways. He grinned as he walked across the courtyard. The moans of pleasure were not only hers when they were in bed together. Of course he'd worked out the brilliant thing was that there was no way Damien could know the cries begging him to take her were not those of his sister. Although he was certain she would be soon, Isabella was already biting her lip, trying to stop the moans from getting past her lips and not always succeeding. Last night she'd cried out her pleasure loud enough. He was certain Damien must have heard. It was time to continue with breaking his other slave.

His guards spread out around the courtyard and he strolled

across to Damien, who was a far cry from the confident member of the Unwanted he'd become. He was a pitiful sight. Drugged, chained and naked. He was currently slumped on the ground, body shivering. Probably because of the tiscan withdrawal rather than the cool morning air, since he'd ordered his people to delay his prisoner's morning dose so he could speak to him. He wanted Damien to understand every word he said to him.

"Haul him up," Aiden ordered.

A couple of his guards hurried forward and cranked the wheel that wound up the slack in the chains. It was really quite an ingenious contraption. Not that even his own father had come up with it. Apparently, it was a leftover from his grandfather, the warlord, before his father had killed the man. It was such a shame he'd never met his grandfather. He thought they'd have so much in common.

Hearing something a little more like a broken, pathetic whimper, he couldn't really call it a scream, Aiden turned his gaze back to his prisoner. Damien now hung, his arms pulled up and out by chains attached to each wrist, pulled up to their corresponding pylons. He'd been raised into the air, with his feet just off the ground, with his legs pulled out and down by the chains around his ankles. The chains pulled him taunt in four different directions. There was no give for movement at all. Damien's head hung, his chin against his chest as if he didn't have the energy to even lift it up. Aiden smiled and walked up the small wooden platform that a number of the guards wheeled into place for him. After all, he didn't want to have to crane his neck to look up at his prisoner. It would ruin the effect he wanted to present.

He reached around and grabbed Damien's hair, using it to yank his head back. Damien gasped, but little more.

"Good morning Damien. I'd ask how you are feeling, but I

think I can work that out for myself," Aiden said, smiling pleasantly.

"Aiden, please..." Comprehension flickered in Damien's eyes, even if pain and need dulled it.

"Don't worry, I'll give you your drugs soon."

"Please, no more, I can't." Damien swallowed, his voice rough and almost horse.

It was probably due to all the screaming he'd done while being flogged, or when his men engaged in inventive and entertaining ways to torture him. In some ways, those men could teach him a thing or two about how to be completely sadistic and break a person.

"I'm afraid you are much too dangerous. I can't afford not to give you your morning drugs. But I have news for you I'm sure you will enjoy," Aiden said, his eyes narrowing as he anticipated Damien's reaction. "Do you see the balcony up there on the tower?" Aiden hauled Damien's head up further and pointed to the balcony with his other hand. Relishing it as Damien gasped in pain.

"Yes," Damien whispered.

"You've probably heard a woman every morning, this morning in fact, calling my name and moaning rather prettily as we engage in sex. That woman is your sister." Aiden's eyes glittered as he stared at Damien.

"No."

Aiden laughed and got the distinct impression Damien would have lunged at him if his bindings allowed it.

"Oh yes. She warms my bed and takes a great deal of pleasure from our bed sport every day. Tell you what, I'll have the guards delay your morning dose and leave the shutters open on the balcony just so you can reassure yourself that Isabella enjoys her new life with me."

"Why?"

"Because she caught my eye and I can. It was an unexpected pleasure to find out she was still a virgin before I took her. I'm quite proud of how skilled she's become since she agreed to warm my bed. She's quite adept at pleasuring me now." Aiden taunted.

"Please, let her go. I'll do anything you want." Damien stared at him, agony and something else lurking in his eyes.

"Funny, my sweet Isabella begged and promised the same thing. It's why your daily beatings and floggings stopped. In return, Isabella willingly consented to give up her status as a free woman and become my bed slave. From what I can sense, she doesn't regret her decision. Isabella enjoys her new role immensely."

"No, you lie."

"Your sister wears a slave collar. She belongs to me. As such, I'm free to do anything with or to my property that I want. Now that the Isabella problem has been sorted out satisfactorily, I'm onto the next problem. I want your mind Damien, but you keep on fighting me. If you want Isabella to keep enjoying having sex with me, I'd suggest you cooperate and let me through your mind barriers. I can just as easily torture the girl instead, if that will help make your decision easier." Aiden kept his tone casual, as if they discussed the weather in a bar over an ale.

Aiden half turned, clicking his fingers impatiently at Tony, who hastened up to him and handed him a flask of tiscan. Hauling Damien's head just that bit further back, he tipped the flask, pouring it into his prisoner's mouth. Damien spluttered and tried to turn his head before his body betrayed him and he swallowed convulsively. Aiden stepped back and handed the now empty flask to Tony. He didn't have to wait long before Damien screamed in agony from the tiscan he'd just been given. It had been a double dose, just because it was a special occasion.

Damien's body wanted to convulse, but the only part of him that could move was his head. Aiden smiled, and he licked his lips as Damien threw his head back and screamed in agony again. It reduced to pathetic little ragged gasps as the spike of tiscan pain receded and he lost himself in what addicts called oblivion. A condition that all addicts craved and why they found it very hard to stay away from tiscan, despite the initial pain it caused them.

Aiden stepped forward and whispered in Damien's ear, knowing the words would haunt his mind. Tiscan was a double-edged sword. It gave ecstasy or pain, euphoric dreams or nightmares.

"It's alright I'll honour my pledge to your sister as long as she continues to please me. I won't have you beaten or flogged for now, but there are other sports that I'm sure my men have made you acquainted with. At the rate that Isabella is learning, I'm sure soon enough she won't care if you are flogged or not. I assure you I will take good care of her. I'm fostering an addiction to tiscan in her. What can I say? Like brother, like sister."

Aiden laughed and turned away from Damien, pleased he'd taken some time out of his day to pay this pleasant little visit to his prisoner. He walked back towards the small wooden door off to the side of the enclosed courtyard and paused, looking at the lineup of guards near the door. He'd tasked Derick with finding some of his more brutal guards who weren't all that fussed about if the individual was consenting or not.

"You may not beat or flog him. Otherwise, use and abuse him to amuse yourselves as much as you wish. However you wish." Aiden turned away then paused and said in an afterthought. "I want him alive and fully functional, so don't permanently harm or kill him."

The sense of predatory anticipation emanating from this small group of fighters made Aiden laugh. Aiden nodded at

Derick, who fell into step and accompanied him back inside the Stronghold just as that small group of guards turned to regard the prisoner.

FORTY

It was a slow process, but at some point, Damien passed from conscious but insensible to at least knowing his name. This development did have its drawbacks, being overwhelmingly sick, and shaking with uncontrollable tremors and convulsions among them. His entire body and mind screamed at him. One thing on the positive side, because they hadn't given him any food he wasn't throwing up. At the very least, this time, it was familiar. Damien recognised every one of his current symptoms. They had given him tiscan. Only the fact they'd chained him up out here in the courtyard told him he hadn't likely taken it by choice. Under the circumstances, that little detail wasn't as much of a relief as he thought it would be.

Various sources of pain assaulted him, making it hard for him to distinguish which one was worse. His back was on fire, a different type of pain from what he'd suffered before. Once more, he wished whoever held him would let him die. Of the potential people who might be responsible, the only ones he discounted were his squad mates. They at least would not need to chain him up and keep him drugged to contain him. Unfortunately, no poking and prodding at his memory turned up any reason for his current circumstances. While he found the terrible blankness of his mind disturbing, from previous experience, it was the effect of consuming massive doses of tiscan. Probably over an extended period. By the reaction in his body, he'd strayed into overdose territory again.

He lay on the cool stone, unable to control the trembling which ran through him. The numbness in his hip and shoulder told him he'd been in this position too long. Damien contemplated trying to sit up for a moment, then discarded the idea. Right now, the act would take far more effort than it was worth. A door opened and booted feet started toward him. He contemplated trying to twist to see if he recognised the person attached to the booted feet but decided it would hurt too much. Particularly since he'd find out soon enough. When whoever it was stopped behind him, he half expected a booted foot to connect with his back. Instead, hands grabbed him and he found himself hauled up into a sitting position. His shoulder pressed into the other man's, who braced and acted as a support. Even though the other person was careful of his back, he couldn't help the moan from the pain movement caused and he wasn't sure which was worse. The agony from his back or the need to throw up at the sudden motion.

Easy, they've been drugging you, the guard said.

What did I do?

Nothing. They set you up to take the fall for the Warlord's death.

As blank as his mind had been a moment before, the guard's words triggered the image of the dead man on the ground. Only this time he recognised the body being that of the Warlord.

Ah, so that image is real? I'm at the Stronghold?

You are, Aiden has seized control. I think, I hope the squad you brought with you has gone to inform the warleader.

The person who held him up lifted a flask to his lips, and he whimpered both from the sudden want for more, tempered by his knowledge that he really might die if they continued dosing him at this rate. He groaned as his stomach clenched, and then uncontrollable spasms ran throughout his body. The man who held him waited patiently.

Please, no more.

We've been giving you a diluted mixture. Drink it. It will hold your addiction at bay but not make you totally insensible.

Wait, you've done this before, or did I make that up? Who are you?

My name is Tony. I've been slowly reducing your tiscan intake for weeks. I'm the leader of one of the Warlord's personal warbands. Me and mine, we won't follow Aiden. Just survive, the warleader will come.

Damien accepted the reassurance, not that he had much choice. He swallowed the contents of the flask as his ally bid him to. It caused him to close his eyes and shudder as the liquid ran down his throat. His unexpected supporter had told the truth. It had tiscan in it, but not enough to sink him into that blissful escape. A part of his brain craved the oblivion that a good, potent dose would bring right now, but there was also the other part. A coolly logical side that whispered that it wasn't good for him and he couldn't help anyone while drowning in oblivion's embrace. The initial shaft of pain that consuming the drug caused barely registered as it competed with all his other aches and pains.

That should at least make you feel a little better once the pain has passed.

It's already passed. It's barely enough to hold withdrawal at bay. Thank you. Damien said then winced as pain shot through him. *Or I will when I get out of here and withdraw from this poison again. You must think I'm incredibly weak to keep falling back into this habit.*

No. I know what this drug does. My father and my brother were addicts. You managed what many never have. You've wrestled yourself free of its clutches more than once. That takes incredible strength. Remember, you did not do this to yourself. You didn't consume tiscan chasing oblivion. Aiden drugged you.

It suddenly made sense how Tony had the knowledge to care for a tiscan addict, even if he'd never been one himself. Or at least he figured this man had never suffered that particular affliction, because if he did, Damien doubted the flask containing the drug would have made it to him. Damien sighed with relief and relaxed as the pain faded. Washed away by tiscan to be replaced by a softer pleasure. Rather than a mind blasting euphoria that hit with a higher dosage, a part of him clamoured for. Right now he'd be more than happy to stay in this mind altered state forever.

What happened to my back?

You've been flogged by Aiden's orders. Tony hesitated before continuing. *He'll probably order it again, along with the rest of the torture his people inflict on you. He derives a great deal of pleasure from watching you scream. Reducing the tiscan you're on will probably help.*

How?

You're aware it amplifies pleasure. However, it also does the same to pain.

Damien couldn't bring himself to care about the prospect of being flogged again, although it was only because of the drug that saturated him. If there hadn't been so much that he wanted to know, he could have curled up and allowed the drug to carry him off. Other than the image of the Warlord dead on the floor, there was another image that flashed in his head that concerned him. Now that he knew who he was, he recognised the image of the woman that had been plaguing him. Damien stiffened as another partial memory hammered into his brain. Aiden's face loomed close as he crowed over having possession of Isabella.

What has Aiden done to *Isabella?*

As Tony stiffened, the hope he'd possessed that the memory had been a tiscan fuelled nightmare fled. Somehow, Isabella was here and in trouble, but even that knowledge wasn't enough to lift him from the haze of tiscan that fogged his mind.

Aiden has claimed her.

Those simple words caused him to try to sit up, but he managed little more than a slight shift in his position.

I'm going to kill him.

While he couldn't break the hold tiscan had on his mind and body right now, with the amount he'd consumed his body would burn through it fast. That would bring a different level of incapacity. However, unlike the drug, that was something he could push through and function regardless of how much it might hurt. A shudder run through his body as Tony eased him back down to the ground. The grip of the drug was already weakening. The guard had indeed given him far less than normal. Damien closed his eyes and opened his mind. The veil sat there, on the edges of his awareness. It wouldn't be long before it would flood back into him. The veil would only be held back for so long. He finally relaxed fully, allowing the drug to take him. The time to fight would come, but it wasn't right now.

CHAPTER
FORTY-ONE

Jaclyn ground her teeth as she listened to the report regarding the progress of the attack on Vallantia. It was hardly the fault of the daggerwife who was reporting the failure to her. Jaclyn took a steading breath, willing patience on herself.

"Show me the territory on the map," Jaclyn said, gesturing sharply towards the central table.

It was one of the benefits of taking the Rathadon Estate. They'd discovered extensive maps of not only the city and its surrounds but the entire domain. The daggerwife studied the maps on the table and walked around it to stand in front of the Vallantia city map. After a few moments of study, the daggerwife pointed to a corner of the city.

"This place."

Jaclyn frowned as she stared at the spot on the map. "What's so difficult about taking it?"

"We don't know Commander. We've sent three teams in, each larger than the one previous. None of them have returned alive." The daggerwife paused, her gaze sliding away as she flushed. "Now we're having trouble convincing anyone to go in there."

"Are they attacking our forces?"

"Not if we leave them alone. I can't even tell you if they're attacking the teams we've sent in there."

"They must be," Myra ground out. "How else do you all think daggerwife teams are disappearing?"

"There are locals in there. We can sense them, but that's all I can tell you. We haven't actually set eyes on any of them," the daggerwife said.

"Fetch Steven for me," Jaclyn ordered as she scowled down at the map.

"We can't expand from here until we secure the city," Ricardo said.

"I know," Jaclyn bit out.

The door opened as Arianne ushered Steven into the room. He stood hesitantly just inside the doorway until Jaclyn gestured for him to come to the table. Steven closed the distance between them, leaning briefly into her shoulder as she soothed him almost unconsciously. A shiver ran through her as he nuzzled against her neck and she forcibly drew her attention back to the array of maps. This new husband of hers was worming a way into her heart quicker than she'd ever given credit he could.

"You found the maps I see," Steven said as he studied the map and the markings that showed the extent of their war campaign. "You'll need to expand out further, much further. I think you really will want more territory between you and Michael when he gets here."

"Why is that?" Myra asked.

"It will give you... us more time to run."

Jaclyn tried to scowl, but gave up and snorted in amusement. "You said us. You've come to terms that you belong to me now?"

"I promised you that I was yours, that you didn't need to

force a control bond on me. As strange as this is for me, I've made my choice. You are my wife now," Steven said.

Jaclyn stared at Steven for a moment, sorely tempted to invade his privacy to see what he was really thinking, but keeping her bargain with him, she refrained. Instead, she leant forward and stroked the side of his face.

"This is strange territory for us both. I will say, the more I hear about this frighteningly competent cousin of mine, the more I'm looking forward to meeting him."

"That will be a novelty for him. It's not common for people to look forward to his arrival. Particularly when he's angry with them and I guarantee you he will not be happy," Steven said, his hand brushing against her abdomen, the light touch of his powers caressing her skin. "You didn't call me so we can breed, and I doubt your intent was to discuss my brother."

"What is this place?" Jaclyn asked, pointing down to the offending section of the map.

Steven peered at the place on the map that she pointed to. "Ah, that's the Burrow."

"Do your brother's forces reside within the Burrow?" Myra asked.

Jaclyn studied her fellow wife. It was a good point and an explanation she hadn't thought of.

"No. It's just the Burrow. All the disreputable types, the poor and destitute, reside in the Burrow. It's not really a safe place. Giving us some trouble, is it?"

"So the reports I'm receiving advise me."

"Not surprising. If the Warlord couldn't subdue the place and left it alone." Steven shrugged. "I can't imagine our daggerwives can."

"We'll see about that." Jaclyn gestured to Arianne. "Take Steven back to his rooms and arrange an escort for me."

"Yes, commander." Arianne held the door open and waited until Steven strolled out into the hallway before closing it.

STEVEN SAT DOWN and relaxed back into the cushions while he did his best to reinforce his mental shields as the daggerwife stared at him suspiciously. If he'd mated with Arianne already, he would have tried to flatter her, but unfortunately, he hadn't bred with her yet. Although he could be wrong about that detail. So many of the wives had already shared his bed, all with the intent of getting pregnant. As functional as the Sylannians seemed to view the process, he still didn't think it was wise to point out he wasn't sure if he'd had sex with this one or not. He wasn't sure it would go down well if he had, and he'd just forgotten. After what seemed like an eternity, his daggerwife finally turned and left him alone.

The door had no sooner shut than Steven jumped from the chair and ran to the window. The courtyard below was a hive of activity as horses were led into the courtyard and hordes of daggerwives streamed out of the estate. While he hadn't spent much time thinking about where his brother's agent in Vallantia must be based, he had a sinking feeling Ben and his team were in the Burrow. He'd never contemplated how absurd it was that the Warlord hadn't been able to clean out the Burrow. It was just one of those things that was. That only left him with one conclusion as to why his brother had left the Burrow alone.

Evan?

What's wrong?

If Ben is in the Burrow, warn him that Jaclyn with a team of my daggerwives are coming after him.

The Sylannians know Ben and his team are in the Burrow?

Not precisely, but it's the only area left they haven't managed to subdue. My firstwife is assembling our fighters to take with her into town as we speak.

So she could just be going to check the place out?

I doubt it. Jaclyn wants to expand further out from the territory that she's already taken. She doesn't want to do that until the city is secure.

As the silence stretched between them, Steven bit his lip as he watched the seething mass of Sylannians getting ready in the courtyard. He only hoped that Ben had the time to clear out of the Burrow before Jaclyn's forces got there.

Ben asked me to pass on his thanks, Evan said, a thread of concern threaded through his mind voice. *You're on first name basis with your cousin now?*

Jaclyn has taken me as a husband, so yes, you could say we're on a first name basis.

It's only been a couple of weeks.

It's nothing. Literally the only people I've been spending any time with are Jaclyn, Myra or Ricardo and whichever of the wives the underwives decide I need to breed with. They don't even allow me to visit with my parents. What did you expect would happen when you all told me to just fall in with their plans for me?

You're right, I'm sorry. It's just a shock. Be careful Steven, I'm sure it's difficult, but you said 'my daggerwives'. You call the Commander by name and referred to her as your firstwife. They're getting into your headspace, Evan said.

Steven mentally reviewed what he'd said to Evan and squeezed his eyes shut when he realised his friend was correct. He was beginning to think of Jaclyn and the daggerwives as his wives, rather than his enemy.

You don't need to apologise. You're right. It's difficult for me to play this game. Promise me you'll keep pointing out to me that the Sylannians are my enemies, not my friends. It's not an excuse, but I've never been good at separating enemies from friends. I spend so much time with only the company of my wives... the Sylannians. It's difficult. I fear the longer this goes on, the more I'm likely to forget who I am.

I promise, I'll remind you. We'll talk every day. Evan said, no condemnation in his tone, just understanding and support flowed through their connection. *Are any of the Sylannian's pregnant?*

I don't know but the underwives are happy with my performance so far. They say Jaclyn will come to my bed again to the exclusion of the other wives as soon as her next fertile period begins. Steven swallowed, unable to work out how he felt about everything that was happening. It seemed to him everything was moving so fast. *Forgive me Evan, I have to think of them as my wives. Or I don't think I'll be able to pull this whole charade off.*

As long as you're aware of it. Just be careful.

I'll try, Steven said, keeping to himself that he wasn't sure he wouldn't go too far.

When did you work it out? About the Burrow?

Just now when Jaclyn had me hauled into her rooms and then pointed to the place on the map demanding to know what it was. Honestly, if I hadn't been reduced to reading all those reports about Michael's conquests, I doubt it would have occurred to me.

How did reading old reports make you think about the Burrow?

I didn't realise just how many of the Warlord's conquests Michael was responsible for. He's my brother, but even I'm terrified of him. It just doesn't make sense the Burrow exists. Even Ben said Michael would never tolerate rebellion against the Warlord. So, that means Michael left it alone for a reason.

I can't believe it's taken you all this time to get around to reading up on your brother's exploits. His real ones, not just the stories people tell.

To be honest, I almost wish I still existed in the little fantasy world I created. Steven grumbled. *Nothing like traitors and invaders forcing me to grow up.*

I liked the old you. We had fun when we weren't engaging in rebellions and uprisings. We've been friends for a long time, but I think I like this you better.

JACLYN HADN'T SEEN anything like the mass that rose in front of her. This place the locals called the Burrow looked like a child had built it. A bunch of mismatched blocks and toys were all jammed together to form a confusing mess. Sasha, the firstwife of the sister house in charge of the Vallantia city campaign, was an uneasy presence next to her. The other wives under her command didn't appear any easier. This battle was already proving more problematic than their war with the trader clans had been. Inexplicably, they'd met resistance that appeared to be planned. It was infuriating that the raids that had been reported to her had been successful.

"Burn it to the ground," Jaclyn said, without taking her eyes off the eyesore to even look at Sasha.

"We could lose half of this section of the city if we do that," Sasha said.

"Then rebuilding it will give our newly collared workforce something else to do other than ferment rebellion," Myra said, her tone dripping with sweetness.

"Set the fire points around the whole mess. Don't give those within a chance to escape," Jaclyn said.

"Part of it backs onto a section of the river," Sasha said, her tone hesitant and flinching as if the objection was drawn out of her.

"Then put teams out on the river in boats," Ricardo said.

Jaclyn could hear the exasperation in Ricardo's tone. The representatives of the sister houses shifted, glances trading between themselves. Even though these houses had been with her during the conquest of the former home of the trader clans, they still didn't quite know how to take it when Ricardo spoke up. It was yet another visible point of difference between her house and others. Ricardo wasn't wrapped up in protective layers, out of sight from any but her own. Of all the bloodlines, it was only common for males of the Monarch House to be on public display. At least outside the upper-class circles. Samuel had made a decree after he took the throne that if he had to be present in formal court sessions as the king, then the males of the other houses had to be out as well. Only those of the upper class who regularly attended the court had to comply. Of all men present with the houses in attendance, only Ricardo exercised his free will. These houses, though, had limited exposure to the practice. None would ever loosen their control over their husbands.

Or so they think now. Myra said, tracking where Jaclyn's thoughts had been going through the bond they shared. *When you take the throne...*

It will be slow, generational change, but I won't allow the practice of binding our husband's minds so completely to continue.

"This is not open for debate. I want that whole place up in flames. Stop coming up with reasons you can't and do it now!" Jaclyn's anger flared.

Those in front of her flinched, then turned, issuing orders. Daggerwives scattered to do her bidding. Jaclyn's impatience rose, yet only the evidence they were complying with her orders caused her to hold her tongue. A group of collared workers trudged up carrying a barrel between them and tipped the contents onto a corner of the Burrow. Jaclyn wrinkled her nose as a sharp stench wafted over on the slight breeze that blew from the river. Jaclyn turned to Sasha.

"What is that?"

"It's a liquid, the locals call verdash oil. We found barrels of it stored here in the city. It's proven to be quite useful in clearing, even things that are difficult to burn as it's highly flammable," Sasha said, as she watched the progress of the work crews. "The fire will burn hotter and longer. Nothing inside that place will survive, not even in the huts built with non-combustible materials. It should get hot enough to kill those inside."

At the urging of the daggerwives, teams of the collared workers splashed the liquid they carried down the length of the Burrow. When they were done daggerwives with torches ran forward, lowering the flame to the sections of the buildings the liquid had been spilled on. Jaclyn rocked back as the fire roared to life, flames leaping up from the wooden huts. Heat from the fire radiated out and washed over her. Smoke billowed up into the sky and filled her lungs.

"Kill any that try to run and report to me when it's done," Jaclyn said.

Jaclyn turned her family around her, satisfied that by the end of the day, the city would belong to her. Tomorrow, she could further her plans and push out into new territory.

FORTY-TWO

Ben swore, then spun, yelling to their core group of fighters.

"The Sylannians have finally gotten sick of us and are coming to burn down the Burrow," Ben said.

Lukas went pale, but otherwise didn't question the information.

"Get everyone, as many as we can, down into the tunnels."

"There's too many we'll never..."

"We'll save even less if we just stand here arguing about it," Lukas said.

"I'll lead a group on the river escape," Ben said.

"You'll be exposed and in clear sight at this time of day."

"She's not here yet. The information is from Steven, relayed by Evan, the Sylannian Commander is mobilising from the Rathadon estate now. We have a little time if not much, besides you know the tunnel system better than me."

Lukas took several strides forward, closing the distance between them, and drew Ben into a rough embrace. "Stay safe, my friend. You didn't survive this long to die now."

"You as well. Michael will kill me if you die."

"What do you think he'd do to me if you died?" Lukas asked, snorting in amusement before he sobered. "You're more exposed. Take Tina with the fighting team. I have a bad feeling you'll need them."

"But you'll—"

"I need the time to get the remainder into the tunnels and out. Your friend Evan gave us that time, or more of it at least than we'd have if this place was already burning around us. Go, I'll see you at the Smith's place."

Ben nodded, sending a fervent plea out into the veil that they would both make it through to the safety of the Smith's residence. They'd formulated evacuation plans. One of the unfortunate things about being in an occupied city was it hadn't given them the luxury of practicing them, to work out the fail points. In his experience, that meant things would go wrong. They just had to trust they each had the skill, to work things out and come out the other side alive.

"You six get people mobilised and start getting them down into the tunnels and into the escape paths out of the city. Leave everything behind. Things can be replaced, people can't," Lukas said, then "You three with me, we'll cover Ben's escape on the river. They have the most dangerous escape route."

"Yes Lukas!" Those he'd nominated, hard men and women, all chorused before the six nominated to get people to the tunnels dashed out of the room.

"Tina, send out the alert. Get our group moving to the boats. There's no time to waste on packing. Everyone just needs to run." Ben raised his hand, gripping Lukas's shoulder. "I thank you for your help, but you need to get down into the tunnels yourself."

"There's a tunnel entrance near to our smuggler docks. We'll provide cover fire if necessary while you get going, then we'll get to the tunnels and join our group," Lukas said.

Ben conceded to his friend's knowledge of the Burrow and the various escape routes, and turned to run from the room. Calls were already ringing out with people streaming out from their huts and the warehouse areas they'd been using as sleeping areas. Each group heading to their evacuation mustering point. Ben gave thanks that while they hadn't had the luxury of practicing this evacuation, they had assigned each person a muster point for emergencies. There was no panic among those who crowded the winding paths through the Burrow. Others scaled the walls and took the rooftop pathways, some already disappearing down through the hatches to the underground tunnels.

"You two, take the high road," Lukas said, pointing to two of his team.

From the rooftop they'd have a good vantage point to cover as his group exited the locks into the open river. As they burst into the internal dock, Ben was relieved that people were already streaming into the waiting boats. Each had a cover affording some protection for the occupants from arrows that the enemy would undoubtedly send in their direction if they were spotted.

"Go, go, go! Get loaded onto the boats. We don't have time to spare." Ben shouted, twisting and guiding those behind that streamed into the docking area to the waiting boats.

Lukas and his partner ran forward to join those waiting by the doors. After what seemed like a lifetime, the flow of evacuees came to a stop.

"All accounted for Ben!" Tina said.

Ben waved at Lukas and leaped onto his assigned boat, moving forward to take his position with the fighters.

"Let's go, open the doors," Ben said.

Those on the oars started their strokes, while others helped to push them forward with small controlled bursts of the veil timed to the strokes of the oars. Those on the doors swung them open and jumped onto the boats as they drew alongside of them.

Lukas and his partner ran out onto platforms, drawing their bows ready to fire.

"Ware the enemy boats!" Lukas said, before he let loose with an arrow.

More flights of arrows joined the first, including flaming arrows from those above. As each of the flaming arrows hit their marks, the small globe of verdash oil exploded. The fire spread fast and hot, with the boats igniting in a roar of flames. Screams filled the air, bodies leaping into the water from the enemy boats. Ben's lips peeled back. They'd find no relief from the flames consuming them that way. Verdash oil couldn't be extinguished by water alone. The flames would continue to burn until the stuff was consumed.

We have free water in front of us. Go Lukas, get out of there.

Ben craned his neck to see his friend wave once before he disappeared into the darkness. Thick black smoke curled up from the Burrow. So much so it seemed the whole length of the Burrow had been set alight. Explosions rang out, with debris flying in all directions. Ben could only hope his friend and those taking the tunnel paths had time to get out.

FORTY-THREE

As Tony walked down the little used dark stone corridors with only the faint glow of the light stone, he disappeared into the bowels of the Stronghold. It was one of the more annoying things about the Stronghold, yet on this occasion it was also extremely helpful. There were so many remote little places hidden in this place. Not necessarily a secret, but few could say they knew this place like those of them who'd been the Warlord's personal warbands. They'd all spent considerable time within the confines of the walls, after all. More so than anyone else who rode with the Warlord. Sometimes certain conversations had to occur away from prying ears. Times like now.

He turned the corner and smiled to see a faint light coming from a disused storeroom ahead. Tony wondered if he should show a little caution. After all, that light might not be thrown by those he was expecting to meet up with. Then he discarded the idea. The only other people in residence were Aiden's warband, and they didn't stir themselves out of their comfortable surroundings for much. As for the staff who worked here, they had enough to do without coming down to areas that were currently unoccupied. Particularly with the extra demands that Aiden's people seemed to make. They strutted around, most of them not lifting so much as a finger to do much of anything. They'd even spread out, taking up previously unused rooms rather than the barracks, which they'd normally occupied when in residence. He hadn't thought it was possible for anyone to be lazier than some of the guard units that had been permanently based here. He'd been wrong.

Tony entered the room and smiled grimly at his counterparts, Con and Stef, who led the other two warbands that had previously ridden for the Warlord. Con raised one boot clad foot and pushed out a chair for him. The room didn't house much. A table, a hand full of chairs and a shelf on the wall that had some mugs and a couple of flasks. He sat down, and Stef pushed a mug of ale across the table to him. He picked it up and took an appreciative sip. Opening the flap of the bag he'd carried, he removed the two daggers and placed them in the middle of the table. One was still in pristine condition. The other was still sullied with the Warlord's blood.

"Spill Tony, what's this?" Con asked, his eyes drawn to the daggers in the middle of the table.

Tony pointed to the blade with the dried blood on it. "That is the dagger that Aiden said Damien used to kill the Warlord."

Stef and Con raised their eyes to his, then settling back on the blades again. Neither of them reached out to touch them, but he could see they were inspecting them.

"All right, I'll bite. The second dagger?" Stef asked.

"It's the dagger I removed from where it still sat in its sheath on Damien's weapons belt." Tony raised his gaze from the daggers to meet those of his opposite number.

Tension hit the room. He could feel it, like someone suddenly smothered him in a weighted blanket. Stef's hand hesitated, then picked up the blade, turning it carefully in her hand, then put it down and picked up the other one. A frown creased her forehead as her eyes tracked back up to hold his own.

"That one is one of the Unwanted's blades. The one that killed the Warlord is not," Stef said.

"So he picked up a different dagger on his way to the Warlord's rooms in an effort to throw off suspicion?" Con said.

"He didn't have time. He was under escort down in the cells after dropping off prisoners. The guards down in the dungeon passed him over to me. I escorted him until Aiden intercepted us and took over. Aiden's old rooms were just down from the Warlord's," Tony said.

"Could he have taken the Warlord's dagger?" Stef asked.

"No, the Warlord wasn't wearing his weapons belt. Aiden was wearing his weapons. He said he'd take Damien to the Warlord himself."

"Aiden did what?" Stef said.

"I know. It's out of character." Tony was aware his smile was at odds with the grimness in his eyes. "I objected, but Aiden insisted."

"Anything else?" Con asked.

"When I entered the room, Aiden was grappling with Damien on the ground. Aiden thrust that bloodied dagger in my hands and claimed Damien had killed the Warlord." Tony leant forward, placing his elbows on the table as he retold details that had been on repeat in his head. "I shoved it into my belt and restrained Damien. His eyes were glazed. He was insensible even before Aiden gave us a flask of tiscan to pour down his throat."

"Now that you mention it, why did Aiden have a flask of tiscan? I've never seen any sign he's an addict." Con frowned at that detail.

"He's a lot of things, most of them bad, but that isn't one of them as far as I know either," Stef said.

"How long between when you were with Damien and he was fine and when he was insensible?" Con asked.

"Moments. I'd barely gotten down the base of the stairs. Then there was Isabella."

"The girl? Damien's sister?" Con asked.

"She said it wasn't Damien. Aiden struck her and poured something down her throat, ordering us to throw her into the cells. I suspect the substance he used to restrain her was tiscan as well." Tony rubbed his temples with his fingertips, half hoping his two fellow leaders would tell him he was crazy.

"Wait, so Aiden walked into the Warlord's rooms with a known tiscan addict and two flasks of tiscan on him?" Stef said.

"That seems awfully prepared given what happened," Con said, a hard edge creeping into his tone.

"I thought so. Aiden's also ordered Isabella dosed with tiscan ever since."

"As well as hauling her up to his bed every night," Stef said.

The other leader sounded disgusted. Not that Tony blamed her, it was a circumstance he found personally repugnant as well. Silence hung in the small room. Tony eased back in his chair and allowed his two counterparts to consider the daggers and what they'd been told, along with what they'd already heard from their own channels. They'd be combining that information into their own personal experiences.

"Aiden killed his own father," Con said.

"What do you suggest?" Stef asked

"I'm not sure. Yet. As long as we all know what's happened," Tony said.

"We have the numbers," Con said.

"Except right now, most of our own people believe Aiden. We can't afford for anyone to hesitate."

"Our duty is clear. It is as it has always been, to the warlord," Stef said.

"Do any of us actually believe he'll be able to hold on to that title when the warleader finds out about this?" Tony's eyebrow rose as he waited for the other two to work through the situation. All three of them chuckled, although he noted he wasn't the only one with a faint trace of nervousness. He didn't doubt the warleader would find out and he would be extremely unhappy about many things, not just the death of the Warlord.

"More importantly, is he going to blame us for the Warlord's death?" Con said.

"I'm more worried about him blaming us for Damien being drugged, tortured and collard." Tony briefly closed his eyes before looking back at them. "I don't even want to think about how he's going to react to what Aiden is doing to Isabella."

Con licked his lips. "Surely the warleader wouldn't really expect us to intervene?"

Tony couldn't help but laugh bitterly. "Not only would the warleader expect us to act, but he definitely will blame us if we don't even try."

Con and Stef checked with each other, seeming to struggle with themselves before they sighed in unison.

"Alright. What are we going to do?" Stef asked.

"We can't be stupid about this. We might have more people, but Aiden is stronger in the veil than any of us here," Con said.

"Stronger than anyone here, except for one person," Tony said.

His fellow leaders frown at him.

"You don't mean Damien? He's incapable of anything at the moment with that drug they're dosing him with," Stef said.

"He's also a mess. Have you seen what they've done to him?" Con asked.

"You mean the drug he gets dosed with every morning and evening that my team now has the duty of administering?" Tony smiled, although he was aware it didn't hold even an iota of amusement in it.

"What have you done?" Con whispered, eyes widening.

"Diluted it. Bit by bit all week. He's not as out of it anymore as Aiden believes he is."

"Are you mad?" Stef paled. "If he goes off, he's not likely to recognise a friend from the enemy."

Tony shook his head. "Haven't you ever dealt with a tiscan addict before? Even for a high level addict, twice a day like that could kill him. We'd be in even more trouble."

"You were here. You didn't hear what everyone said about him. He's wild and loses control. Even the warleader apparently has trouble containing him," Con said.

"Even more reason to make sure he recognises someone who has been trying to help him from those who are trying to hurt him. Either way, it still interferes with his ability to touch the veil, but he's alive," Tony said.

"Even though he pleads for death," Con said.

"Only when those that torment him are at their worst. The rest of the time, he wants to live because Aiden has made sure he's very much aware Isabella is in trouble."

Stef rubbed her face. "Alright. What's done is done. What else?"

"I've already talked with every member of my warband and they agree to side against Aiden when the time comes. It's only a matter of time before the warleader gets here. We need, all of us, to be ready to take action when it happens."

Con shook his head. "The warleader will probably head for Vallantia to sort out the uprising from some merchant. It will be some time before he can draw his attention this way."

"There are members of the Unwanted far closer than Vallantia."

"What do you mean?" Con asked.

"Damien brought a fighting unit of the Unwanted with him and they're still out there somewhere. I'd lay odds that some-where is close and they've already sent word to the warleader." Tony frowned, staring at them both. "Whatever happens, we just need to be ready to act. We definitely don't want to be seen as being on Aiden's side in this mess."

The other two leaders looked at each other, then back at him, and nodded. In that, at least it seemed they were all in full accord with each other.

FORTY-FOUR

Michael lay back on his bed unable to sleep, then rolled his head on the pillow to stare across at the door, knowing that Olivia was on the other side, deciding on if she should interrupt him or not.

"Come in Olivia. You're always welcome," Michael said.

He didn't have to yell. Sound travelled well enough in this building. He hadn't been getting much sleep anyhow, and it seemed he wasn't the only one. Olivia came in, closing the door behind her. He'd been right. She'd been trying to rest since she wore a loose linen shirt that came down to mid-thigh on her. He shuffled over on the bed, making room, and held out his hand. A smile tinged with sadness touched her as she grabbed his hand and climbed up onto the bed. He waited until she got comfortable and wrapped his arms around her, pulling her closer against him.

Over the years, people often wondered about the relationship between them both. It was speculation the pair of them ignored. Some argued they couldn't possibly be a couple and work together as tightly as they did. Others were equally certain they must be together but couldn't work out how they didn't degenerate, at least occasionally, into a screaming match with each other. In the early years, he and Olivia had fallen into a relationship with each other. They'd been young when the Warlord had claimed their lives and it had seemed a natural enough thing to do. As the lives they lived didn't lend themselves to long term committed relationships, they'd settled into an easy friendship. Over the years, it grew into an enduring bond born from shared life experiences. In Olivia, no matter what, she would always be there for him as he would be for her. Other than Nathanial, there was no one else in the world either of them trusted that much. It was a simple thing they shared right now. Just the comfort of each other's company after losing a man that had been a father to them both.

"I didn't think it would hurt so much," Olivia said.

"This is a day I tried not to think about. Stupid given the life we all lead."

Michael waited as she turned, pressing into his chest. He wrapped his arm around her shoulders. He hadn't missed the tears in her eyes.

"He's always been there."

"I don't even know how to proceed," Michael said.

Olivia pushed away a little, brushing a tear from her eye. "I want to tear Aiden to pieces."

"You and me both."

"That might be a good place to start."

Michael took a deep breath, the silence stretching between them as they allowed themselves to drift into an uneasy sleep.

MICHAEL GRITTED his teeth as he gathered power and hurled it in a hammering blow before launching at his opponent. Nathanial staggered, but without showing a hint of concern, responded in kind, raising his sword to counter Michael's strike. It had been a night of disturbed sleep, alternating between a deep burning anger with pain and loss hitting him at unexpected moments. It had not been conducive to a good night's sleep. Olivia finally drifted down into a deep sleep, so he'd gotten up before his restlessness woke her up. He hadn't found pacing on the lower floor of the inn any more useful than staring at the ceiling in his room. Since being agitated and unable to concentrate wasn't conducive to holding a war conference in the afternoon, he'd settled on some training.

You always did better at working through issues when distracted by physical work, Nathanial said, grunting a little due to the impact of a blow from the veil which disbursed on his shields.

It's like my head is running in circles. Michael tried to lose himself in training.

Nathanial was correct. Somehow, the nature of it forced him to concentrate on his current task while the back part of his brain worked on the issues that confronted him. He was grateful Nathanial had obviously been awake when he'd tried to sneak out and came to the practice yard shortly after. Somehow, hitting the pells just didn't have the same impact and with Nathanial, he didn't have to hold back at all.

Perfectly understandable, Nathanial said as they traded another flurry of blows.

Michael kept his silence for a space of time, perfectly willing to lose himself in the flow of exchanging blows. There was a pattern to this exercise even if neither of them knew in advance which series of moves they'd be forced into next. Or what one of them might throw at the other. Michael almost started as hushed chatter seemed to burst that bubble around them both and impacted on his awareness. At some point, others had obviously decided to wander into the back courtyard and begun their own early morning exercises. With sweat rolling down his back, he finally withdrew, calling a halt to their practice session as he wiped his forehead. Michael took a few deep breaths, grateful to see Nathanial doing the same. They'd been at it longer than he'd anticipated.

Taya, with her shock of red hair restrained by a braid, leant on the side wall. Harry stood next to her with his arms crossed. He wondered when the other band leaders had arrived and how long they'd been there. The pair were excellent leaders for their warbands and superb tacticians. Michael was relieved they'd both shown up first, since they were among the most reliable of the warband leaders. He shouldn't have been surprised that they'd been close by, or that they'd shown up together. The pair of them, even though they led separate warbands, were often together and within proximity of each other.

"Are the others here?" Michael asked them.

"Not yet." Taya shook her head.

"I should go clean up before they all arrive." Michael went to turn to leave.

"Michael," Taya said.

He paused, the compassion in that one word rolled over him and almost undid him. He turned and Taya pulled him into her arms.

I'm sorry. He was much more to you than just the Warlord, Taya whispered.

Thank you. It was a complicated thing, Michael said.

Taya nodded and let him go, only to pull Olivia into her arms. He turned again as Harry walked over. Harry didn't say anything, simply placed his hand on Michael's shoulder and squeezed gently, support and determination flowing from him. Michael nodded his understanding but otherwise didn't comment.

"Go, my friend, get cleaned up. We'll greet the others when they get here," Harry said.

"Harry and I discussed this on the way here. We've a fair idea what the subject of the war conference will be. You have our full support, whichever direction you choose," Taya said.

"Just for the record. I don't think we can afford to leave that traitor at our backs and I won't accept him as warlord," Harry said.

Michael wasn't surprised they'd guessed what the choices were. They'd both been riding with the Warlord nearly as long as he and Olivia. While they didn't have many they'd consider as friends in the other warbands, these two would be among the few that he made an exception for. It wasn't the same as the friends he still had from when he was a child, but still there was that bond there. The shared experiences they all had, was something that couldn't be replicated outside their ranks.

FORTY-FIVE

Ben spared a moment to hope that Lukas and the group he'd led had made it out of the tunnels and city alive. When they'd come up with this emergency escape plan, they'd agreed to separate to give the best opportunity for some of them to survive. As a result, he led a mixed group composed of some of the hard-bitten crew that followed Lukas, along with some of the Rathadon's former house and city guards. Those were all the ones he could rely on. The rest of his group comprised about half the group of residents they'd rescued from the Sylannians. Ben was grateful they'd had time to at least get the former prisoners some sturdy boots to replace the light sandals they'd been wearing.

He'd led four groups from Vallantia to safety on this route during the occupation but wasn't certain it was still secure. It wouldn't have been his first pick of routes to use with this group, but their rushed exit via the river dictated this path. As far as he knew, they'd been undetected the previous times they'd come this way. Still, it made him nervous, particularly since he'd discovered the village he'd just skirted around was now occupied by Sylannians. Ben just hoped the enemy hadn't discovered signs they'd passed through this way previously.

Even though the last village was behind them, it was no time to drop his guard. Ben gazed into the distance at the tree-clad hills. All they needed to do was to cross the open rock-strewn hills and disappear into the trees. Preferably before the Sylannians in the nearby village woke up and discovered them. They just needed to get through to the other side of the forest clear of any pursuit, he'd call the Smith to arrange horses and carts to convey them all to the Smith's estate. If they had luck on their side, Lukas and the crew he led should have made it through already, since their path was shorter. Although it had its own difficulties. It was more out in the open once they came up from the tunnels. The Sylannians spread along the river rather than inland, which gave Lukas and the group be led the advantage. As it turned out, the enemy concentrated their forces along the river, which slowed Ben's flight from Vallantia. From a strategic point of view, it made sense. The Sylannians could get to their newly conquered villages and ferry their people, newly indentured workforce and supplies up and down the river.

We're clear Ben, now get moving and get yourself and those with you over here. The undertone of concern woven through Tina's voice belayed the gruff words.

"Let's get moving," Ben whispered, gesturing for his group to stand. "Remember, get to the trees and beyond."

Theirs was the last group to cross the open ground between them and the forest that ran up and over the hill. Only the fact that the area was also littered with rocks had saved it from being cleared and turned into farmland. These lands were fertile. Just one reason Vallantia thrived.

He had several reliable fighters spaced around this group. It was like they were trying to herd beasts that wanted to run off in different directions. Admittedly, he understood why some of them might think they'd be safer separating off from the group. The bigger group would draw any watching eyes easier than a single person. However, by removing themselves from the group, they also made themselves a target and away from the protection he and his fighters could give them. They'd only made it halfway across the open field when that hollering wail he'd been both expecting but dreading rang out from behind.

"All of you move. Get to the trees!" Ben ordered.

Ben spun to see a group of Sylannians break out from the small farming village they'd skirted around. He swore as he saw their pursuers were mounted. The Sylannians must have been rounding up the horses from wherever they could find them. It was unlikely they'd find any beasts in a village of that size, let alone in that number. Ben turned and jogged forward, knowing every step closer to the looming forest before he had to turn to engage those who pursued them, the better off he'd be. He left it to his team, who were waving the group past them to warn him when to turn. Although he was certain he'd be able to tell that point himself, given the enemy rode on horseback.

Finally, he drew even with the rest of his people and they turned with him and ran after the group they'd led. At least this group comprised some of the fitter and stronger members of those they'd rescued. Those who'd been injured and older had gone to safety in the first few groups. He noted some of those they'd rescued stayed included Jen, the woman he'd handed his dagger to in what seemed like an age ago.

"If you can fight, do so. Otherwise, don't be foolish. Run," Ben said.

Without a word, as those in grey fell back with them, his fighters passed spare blades back to them as they all turned to face the incoming threat. Jen crouched, adjusting her stance, the blade gripped in her hand that showed she knew her way around a fight. The quick orders she issued to two of her companions made Ben's eyebrows rise in astonishment, but as the first of the Sylannians fell upon them, he filed it away to ask about later. If there was a later.

As the horse was nearly upon him, Ben hurled his cloak at the horse's head. He stepped to the side and swung at the horse's legs. As the horse went down, Ben jumped aside. Before his enemy scrambled to their feet, he ran and plunged his sword through his attacker.

As another horse descended on him, Ben spun and grabbed the bridle of the horse and hacked at the rider with his sword. Luck was with him, as the rider's sword was in their other hand.

Air exploded from his lungs as he hit the ground. Ben's eyes widened as a pair of hooves plunged down towards his head. He rolled in the desperate hope he wouldn't get trampled by yet another rider. The air was heavy with the scent of horse, sweat and a haze of dust being kicked up from the fight. Ben scrambled to his feet to see two of his fighters take on the horse and rider that had nearly trampled him. Ben spun, his heart sinking as horses and fighters seemed to be everywhere around him in far more numbers than he remembered had been coming after them. Then he nearly wilted in relief as he realised that the others on horseback were their own people, defending them, not the Sylannians.

"Go, we've got this." A woman with the Smith's hammer and anvil emblazoned on her slate grey fighting leathers yelled.

Ben didn't waste time arguing with their rescuers, but simply turned and, getting his bearings, started running towards the safety of the tree line. A handful of his team came with him. He clenched his heart, knowing that by his best estimate, nearly half their number had fallen. He hoped that perhaps some others were down, injured but alive. Even though it was a slim hope. As Ben reached the trees, he kept running a little way in before finally stopping. Ben folded over and sucking in air sunk to his knees.

"Let's not do that again."

A flask appeared in front of him, and he grabbed it, pausing long enough to see the stopper had already been removed before swallowing mouthfuls of the water it contained. When he was done Ben passed the flask back to Lukas.

"I'll try. You won free," Ben said, not bothering to hide his relief.

"Obviously."

"You called for aid from the Smith?" Ben asked.

He twisted and looked back through the trees at those who still fought, although it didn't appear like they would be doing so for long. The tide of battle had well and truly swung the other way.

"I did. Some of my group weren't faring so well. The Smith sent a team with the carts in case of trouble." Lukas grinned as he regarded the fight. "Thankfully, they are a little more accomplished at fighting on horseback than the Sylannians."

Lukas held out his hand and Ben took it, allowing his friend to help pull him to his feet. Ben counted the heads of the survivors that had made it back here with him, grateful that more of them had made it to safety than he'd feared. His eyes settled on Jen, who'd issued quiet orders to her two companions earlier. She sat near another survivor, tying off a strip of cloth she'd ripped from the bottom of her own top to his upper arm.

"You're not a commoner," Ben said, appraising her with sharp eyes.

"I was on leave to see my family when Vallantia fell. They're farmers. These two are my brothers," Jen said.

"You're not of the former city guard, either."

"Personal guard detail to Speaker Rathadon and his lady," Jen said, her eyes narrowing. "Sorry I didn't speak up sooner, but I was trying to work out who you are. You aren't a simple barkeep."

Jen swung around as Lukas laughed. "Astute observation. If the worst had happened, and Michael learned we'd allowed Ben here to be killed or taken by the Sylannians, we might as well throw ourselves on the Sylannian's mercy before he gets here. They'll probably be more lenient on us."

"Michael...." Jen's eyes widened as she swallowed her gaze flicking between him and Lukas. "You mean the warleader?"

"None other and trust me when I tell you he is already extremely displeased about all of this, so getting on his bad side when it's avoidable is not recommended," Lukas said.

Ben threw an exasperated glare at Lukas, who was, unfortunately, immune to his filthy looks.

"Michael would be equally displeased if Lukas here ended up dead or captured as well, along with a couple of others."

"Yes, but there is a pecking order to this and of the little select group we have here, you are at the top of it." Lukas grinned unrepentantly.

"I've only ever heard the warleader's family call him by his name and even then, only rarely." Jen muttered almost to herself as she gave what could only be regarded as a warning to her brothers.

Ben gathered those muttered words had been for her brother's education, but he responded anyway. "Oh, there are a few others. Although I'll concede the bulk of them fill the ranks of the Unwanted."

Ben circled around the group that was left here, taking it that others had already been led off through the forest. It was still a good couple of days' trek to the other side, with nothing but hunting trails snaking through this patch of forest. Which was just as the Smith liked it. The Smith's ancestors had once numbered among the infamous Smith Lords in this region before the rise of the Rathadon's. These lands had been in the Smith's family for generations. Even in this day there weren't many who would cross the Smith, particularly since it was well known that he was aligned with the Rathadon's and, more particularly, the warleader. As those who'd come to their rescue rejoined them, Ben rounded up the rest of their group and, with the rescue party ranging in the forest around them, they continued on. He was determined to put as much distance as they could between themselves and the dead Sylannians in the hills behind them. It wouldn't take long for the birds of prey to alert anyone watching that something was wrong and investigate. That would lead their enemy into this forest after them.

Ben glanced around as he noted that his team had shuffled so that he was somehow towards the middle of the group. Somehow some of Lukas's people had done the same along with some extras that he guessed must be the Smith's people. Looking at Lukas, he threw another dry look in his friend's direction, who no doubt noticed, but continued to ignore him. All of them, including Lukas, seemed to overplay his importance in this little game. Yes, he ran this operation out of Vallantia in Michael's absence. However, that didn't really mean he was any more important than the rest of them.

FORTY-SIX

Michael came down the stairs, scanning the crowded room, spotting Olivia chatting with Taya over the far side. His bath had taken a little longer than he'd expected but reclining in the tub with the steam rising around him had been relaxing. No one disturbed him and for once he'd decided everyone could just wait. He couldn't remember the last time he'd allowed himself such a simple luxury. Even if it did make him feel guilty that he'd been wasting time given there was an invasion occurring in Vallantia, and Aiden had risen in open rebellion and killed the Warlord in Yalleska.

The time you took for yourself wouldn't have made a difference. The final band leader only just arrived, Nathanial said.

If anyone had disturbed you, they'd have me to deal with, Olivia said.

Indignation threaded through her words, and she threw an image of her holding someone's head under the water. The thought of it caused him to chuckle under his breath as he stepped off the bottom step and entered the common room. Which made the tension in the room decrease a notch. Her answering grin indicated she'd intended that as well. Between the Unwanted, who sat around the outside edge of the room and the other band leaders and their chosen advisers, the room was packed to bursting point.

The others made way for him as he walked through the room to take his place at the head of the row of tables that had been set up, all pushed together to form one long table. Olivia took the seat on one side, Nathanial on the other. Michael thanked those on cook duty who promptly appeared handing them kaf and platters of food that were placed at intervals down the table. They were all aware some of the people who'd ridden in would have been up long before dawn to get here, even for an afternoon conference. Michael took a grateful sip of his kaf, noting the small touch where the one who'd served him had taken the step to heat it for him as well.

"I want to thank you all for coming in. I know it was a shock, but as I indicated last night, I won't make this decision in isolation. You all have a stake in this game," Michael said.

"I'll say it straight. The Warlord could be a brutal, unforgiving man, but he kept us all alive and free," Shaun said. Michael nodded at the grizzled older band leader. Shaun had been a slave in Callenhain. Set free by the Warlord's actions and not so coincidently his own when they defeated Callenhain.

"Is it true that Aiden killed the Warlord? His own father?" One of the other leaders asked.

"How do we know this?"

As the amassed band leaders and their seconds talked over the top of each other, Nathanial held up his hand. There was instant silence from the room other than the creaking of the odd seat as people shifted.

"I can show you the memory that was sent to us by one of the Unwanted who was in town from completing escort duty. I'll warn you, it's an actual memory from someone who was there and witnessed the whole thing, so it packs an emotional punch."

Thank you. Even though I can't scrub it out of my head, I'd rather not relive the whole thing again, Michael said.

Me either, Olivia said.

I know I respected him. He helped pull me out of the hell that was my life and gave me a new one with purpose and a family for the first time. I respected him and was grateful to him, but I didn't love him as a parent figure, the way you two did. I can do this part, Nathanial said.

The others were waiting patiently, knowing the three of them were having a conversation they weren't party to. Nathanial received the consent of all the band leaders and their people, then one by one Nathanial drew them into a communication link with him rather than just broadcasting to everyone capable of mindspeach in the village. Regular people might need to know the Warlord was dead eventually, but they didn't need to actually live it. Which is what this memory was. It was so much worse than simply having someone tell you what happened.

Michael leant forward, his elbows on the table, looking down and waiting for the replay to finish. It was a complicated play of emotions, the spurts of fear they were subject to when Isabella had felt it. Although these men and women were experienced enough at such things to know that fear and loss were not their own, but that of the one whose memory they were reliving. He could tell what part of the memory they were up to by the emanations that were coming from them. In the end, he sensed many things from them, but it mostly settled down to shock and anger. There was a moment of stillness before they started reacting, one talking over the other.

"I never trusted that spineless little turd." Shaun grated, his expression fierce.

"To stab his father in the back that way," Harry said.

"That was your recruit that took the fall, but who was the girl?" Taya asked, keeping a cool head and cutting across the others.

"His little sister, Isabella," Nathanial said.

"Damien went there to deliver the prisoners, right?" Harry asked.

"His orders were to deliver the prisoners to the Stronghold, pass on my briefing to the Warlord, then he was meant to rejoin us in Vallantia," Michael said.

"He's the one who was only just getting over an addiction with tiscan if I remember correctly?" Taya said.

"Did I catch that right? Aiden tried to drug your man to get him to kill the Warlord in his confused state?" Shaun asked.

"Then when he backed off, Aiden committed the act himself. I'd have to see it again, not that I really want to, but it went so fast. I'm sure Aiden placed the blade in Damien's hand when he grappled with him," Taya said, her voice grim.

"Damien had only just gotten over a terrible lapse. It nearly killed him. I'll have to ask him, if he remembers, but it appears that way from what Isabella saw and felt," Michael said.

There was a brief silence around the room as everyone digested what they'd experienced. Michael could well understand the need to take a moment. While they'd technically known about the Warlord's death last night, witnessing it was another matter.

"So Warlord. What do you need from us?" Taya asked, breaking the silence.

Michael stilled and took a steadying breath. While he'd half been expecting it, it still shocked him that someone had actually called him that.

"If you'll accept my advice, Warlord, we need to deal with the treason in Yalleska. We can't go into battle with Sylanna with that unresolved," Harry said.

"I'd rather not take that title. There was one Warlord who dragged this entire region kicking and screaming into a better place, despite itself, and he's dead," Michael said.

"Well, you need a title and don't say warleader, it's not appropriate anymore, give that one to another. Olivia or Nathanial, if you wish," Shaun said.

"I'll not take it. As I argued with the Warlord when the Unwanted were formed. I ride with Michael," Olivia said.

"Same. If I wanted to lead another warband, I would have accepted the role long ago," Nathanial said.

The consternation on the faces of the other warband leaders was universal but didn't faze Michael at all.

"So, Your Majesty. Respectfully, I agree we should turn and deal with the traitor first. We can't leave him to fall on us from behind while we are battling with the Sylannians," Taya said.

Michael threw a filthy look at Taya. Of all the so-called titles they could give him, that wasn't one he wanted either. Taya, for her part, appeared entirely unrepentant.

"Fine. Commander, you'll report directly to me. Olivia and Nathanial are, as always, my right and left hand with right of command. Their voice is mine," Michael said, fixing each of the band leaders with his gaze in turn. "How about we deal with titles after the traitor and the war is done with?"

"Of course, Your Majesty," Harry said brightly, then turned to whisper in an overloud voice to Taya. "I wonder how we're meant to make him a king. Surely there must be a ceremony or something?"

"I would think so. Perhaps we can ask this commander of the Sylannians when we catch up with her? They have a king, so perhaps she'll have some advice," Taya said.

"All right, you two, enough. How about we stick with my name? It's worked every other time you wanted me for something." Michael growled.

They're letting off steam and reducing stress for everyone. Relax, Nathanial said.

"Of course Your... Michael." Taya's lips twitched, but otherwise, she kept her face impassive.

"One option is the rest of you continue to Vallantia. While I, along with the Unwanted, head to the Stronghold, deal with Aiden, then make it back to Vallantia. Once I get my hands around Aiden's neck, it shouldn't take long and, as you know, we can travel fast when we need to," Michael said.

The other leaders looked at each other and, he could tell, were equally unimpressed with the idea.

"With due respect, that is not a good idea. We need to show a united front," Taya said.

Michael glanced at her, then around the table, seeing they all agreed with her sentiment.

"What would you suggest?" Michael asked, leaning back in his chair.

Taya glanced at Harry, then back at him.

"I'd suggest we send a couple of warbands to Vallantia, as you planned. They can start setting up and conduct reconnaissance. The rest of us should travel with you. The Stronghold is a fortress and I'm certain Aiden would have ordered the gates closed as soon as he killed his father. He would have known you'd come after him," Taya said.

"You shouldn't face that fight alone," Harry said.

"It is not only your fight, but ours. Let us help," Shaun said.

Michael listened to them talk. All of them were unanimous in the opinion that the Unwanted shouldn't go by themselves, and this wasn't his fight alone. Eventually, he held his hand up, and they fell silent.

"Nathanial?"

"As much as in part it was my idea, Aiden taking Isabella and Damien as slaves press's some buttons. I really want to kill him.

Saying that, I'm not sure we should divert from dealing with the invasion."

Michael took a deep breath and nodded acceptance, then turned to Olivia.

"Your thoughts?"

"With the Sylannian invasion and the Warlord dead, we can't afford to lose you as well. I say we all deal with Aiden first, but you and I both know I have a soft spot for Damien, so I may not be thinking any straighter than Nathanial. I'm not in favour of only one or two warbands travelling ahead to Vallantia. With the numbers Sylanna has there, if discovered, they'll end up dead without reinforcements," Olivia said.

"For what it's worth, I agree with all but one point," Taya said.

"Which is?" Michael's eyebrow raised.

"With battle against Sylanna looming, we can't afford to lose any of you. The battle plan you came up with in Callenhain worked so well because we all worked together," Taya said.

The others all nodded their agreement, and Michael held up his hand again.

"As much as I don't think Aiden will have the backbone to ride out of the Stronghold to face me directly, if he does, we'd be caught between two opposing forces. I'll head to the Stronghold, but in concession to your concerns, Harry and Shaun, your warbands will ride with me." Michael said, cutting over the other leaders as they started clamouring for him to take more of them with him. "Taya, you'll act as commander and take the rest of our forces towards Vallantia."

"If you'll accept a suggestion, I'd recommend you go with Harry and Shaun and at least one other warband. Aiden has four full warbands at his disposal."

"He does, but I'm betting the three warbands that rode with the Warlord will side with me as soon as I get there."

"None of them liked Aiden," Olivia said.

"Which leaves us facing off against Aiden's warband with Derick at its head," Nathanial said.

"However, I do take your point. I'll take three warbands with me. If you'll use your best judgement and select the other team that will ride with us?" Michael glanced around the table. "Besides, I have a few tricks up my sleeve and a back door into the Stronghold if necessary that I'll wager Aiden knows nothing about."

"Colin?" Olivia asked.

"Colin. Even as old and disused as the door is, he'll get us access. He's only a day's ride from Callan's camp and will meet us there," Michael said.

"A backup plan is always useful, but I don't think we'll need it. I'll lay odds someone will get that gate open as soon as we show up," Olivia said.

"You know where the Smith's estate is?" Michael waited until Taya nodded. "Head there and set up a staging point. The Smith will be able to put you in touch with Ben and Lukas, who are both capable of reaching me and I'll pass orders through them if I need to."

"Any other concerns that need to be addressed now?" Nathanial asked.

Heavy silence settled around the table as everyone stared at him. If they were going to call him warlord or king, they'd best get used to the fact he'd no more tolerate rebellion than the Warlord had. He'd seek their opinions, but they would all do as he ordered.

FORTY-SEVEN

Liliana coughed as smoke filled her lungs. Her eyes flared open to see the grey smoke all around her. She broke off her morning meditation and hummed at her spidersilk, which under her guidance snaked up to cover her mouth. Liliana hauled herself to her feet using the central wooden beam that held up the roof. As the smoke became thicker and darker, she was about to call the alarm when a hollering battle cry shattered the early morning silence. The doors to her meditation chamber flung open and then her head daggerwife, Reyanna with her team burst in. Liliana gasped as the daggerwives surrounded her and hauled her back towards her bedroom. Liliana glanced back over her shoulder to see flames licking at the wooden walls outside and hastened her step.

"We need to get you out. We're under attack Primewife," Reyanna said.

"The Monarch House has found us?"

"I believe so Primewife."

"The children." Liliana tried to stop only to be physically picked up and carried by the daggerwives.

"Others are seeing to the safety of the children. My duty is to you."

"No. All of this is to protect Thomas and Carlos. They're Jaclyn's children, without them, it's all for nothing." Liliana's heart froze as even while the daggerwives broke down an internal wall to get to the next room, there was a stillness to them. "Put me down. What aren't you telling me?"

"We're cut off Primewife," Reyanna said, looking everywhere except her.

Liliana coughed, raising a hand to her mouth, looking around at the smoke seeping through the floorboards, walls and massing like a threatening storm cloud on the ceiling. She finally paid attention to the crack of splintering wood, then flinched as it was followed by a percussive explosion. Despite the early hour, heat radiated against her skin in all directions, as if she was standing in the middle of a cooking hearth. She lowered her mental barriers that she'd automatically slammed up when the attack started. Liliana staggered only to be steadied by the daggerwives. She held her hand up as an instinctual but ineffective shield between herself and the shrieks of terror, anger and pain that flooded her mind. The presence of minds, calling out into the void, there one moment, then gone the next, as if their light had been extinguished. Liliana's knees buckled, tears streaming down her face, as among the screams of terror and pain she identified some as children. Their minds were incoherent with panic, screaming for their mothers. Liliana screamed as she sucked in the veil and focused her power to blast into the ground below her.

FORTY-EIGHT

Steven sat back after breaking the mental connection with Evan, aware his breath was shallow and his throat was tight. Somehow, he'd held the hope that Michael and his warband were close by. That his brother would appear, as he always seemed to do and dig not only him but all of Vallantia out of the mess they were in. At least his warning about Jaclyn's attack on the Burrow had made it through on time. Evan had just confirmed Ben and his team had made it to safety. Even if his friend had wisely kept the details of where Ben had gone to ground to himself.

"What's happened? Who were you speaking to?" Myra asked as she strode across his bedroom towards his bed.

"Nothing, I'm fine," Steven said, but his heart sank as her expression hardened.

Steven shuddered as the ripple of a mental shield surrounded him, cutting him off from the miscellaneous mutterings of the residents of the estate waking up. Myra glared at the dagger-wives who stood duty on the door.

"Why weren't you shielding him?" Myra snapped.

As the language switched to Sylannian, Steven didn't understand the rapid-fire conversation that occurred between Myra and the guards. However, he did understand a reprimand when he heard it. Myra turned from the guards and closed the remaining distance between them. Steven shrunk back, but her hand connected with his temple, and he desperately tried not to think of Evan. It was unfortunate that as soon as he decided on a course of action, the only thing filling his mind was his friend. Myra's hand dropped, a satisfied expression on her face.

"We were just talking," Steven said.

"You are our husband now. I know you don't fully understand what that means, but we'll keep you safe, even from yourself. I think I need to have a conversation with this Evan that you're communicating with," Myra said.

"Please don't hurt Evan, he's my friend," Steven said, desperately trying to come up with something to divert Myra's attention. "I was just checking to make sure he was safe."

"You've been doing a lot more than that. It might explain why our enemy is constantly one step ahead of us." Myra switched her attention to the underwives as they appeared in the doorway. "Make sure you shield Steven's mind at all times. He's not permitted to speak with anyone without approval."

"I'm sorry Primewife. It never occurred to me that without the mate bond in place, he was susceptible," the underwife said, her expression troubled.

Steven shivered as silence enveloped his mind. While his mind shield may have helped keep his secrets, the Sylannian's shield effectively prevented him from mindspeaking anyone.

"Clear your mind of issues that are not yours to get involved in. Now that Jaclyn has taken you as a husband, you need to learn to leave all such decisions to your wives."

"I understand. It's a difficult thing to get used to."

"Your only concern should be breeding with your wives and

letting the underwives who care for you know what you'd like for your meals. Or to drink. Or if perhaps you'd like a massage."

"I was always urged to take more of an interest in the running of Vallantia."

"It must have been stressful for you to have that expectation forced on you," Myra said, her hand stroking his temple. "Leave the weighty decisions about the outside world to those more adept at understanding and dealing with them,"

As a wave of compulsion crashed into his mind, urging obedience, Steven bit his lip while he desperately held onto his mindshield.

"I'll behave and do whatever you want." Steven hated the tremor in his voice that gave away how afraid he was. "I won't disobey any of you again."

"Hush Steven," Myra said, her fingers brushing his temple again as this time she soothed away his fear. "Our ways are foreign to you, but you'll adjust in time. Now go, the underwives are waiting to assist you."

Steven allowed himself to be calmed, not that he would have much luck in pushing away Myra's influence. He'd been terrified Myra would attempt to gain control of his mind. Only the information from Michael that the Sylannians couldn't take control of him without his consent kept him on this side of panic. They could force the issue, but thankfully for him it appeared his wives didn't want to crush his mind all together. Steven climbed out of the bed before Myra could think there was more wrong and extract more from him than she already had. He sidestepped around her and then fled to the bathing room.

FORTY-NINE

Samuel stared at the glass of wine he held. Yet it was a pair of green eyes staring up at him from a child's face that he saw. As arms wrapped around him, Samuel jumped. Then, at a low chuckle and a brush of lips on his neck, he relaxed into Chelsie's embrace. Samuel pushed his current concern aside.

"Did you enjoy your visit with the children?" Chelsie asked.

Samuel hoped his smile didn't appear as forced as he feared it did. It was just as well Chelsie was behind him. "I couldn't remember the last occasion I paid them a visit, so I decided it was long overdue for me to spend time with them."

"The poor underwives were all in a state." A hint of rebuke was in Chelsie's voice. "You should send word to them so they can prepare."

"Ah, send my apologies. I didn't think me visiting the children would be an issue for anyone."

"Of course not. As you said, it's been sometime, and it's the first time some of those underwives had ever been in your presence. Some of them were understandably shocked."

The pair of green eyes flashed in his mind and he half turned to ask Chelsie to explain. "Chelsie, there are irregularities."

As he found himself captivated by her brown eyes and one of her hands rose up to stroke his temple, Samuel recognised his mistake immediately. His breath caught as his firstwife's mind surged forward through their bond, smothering him.

"I have news, husband," Chelsie said.

Samuel drew in a laboured breath, trying to hold on to himself. It was like he was twisting and turning, running desperately away from her all-encompassing presence. Even as he tried to escape, a web of interconnecting bonds flared as Chelsie asserted her control and it spread like a smothering blanket that enveloped him. His vision narrowed. In place of Chelsie's brown eyes, all he could see were windowless walls rising around him. They contracted, leaving him nowhere to run to or hide.

Samuel shrieked as his senses fled, and all that was left was darkness.

SAMUEL BLINKED and realised he was staring into Chelsie's eyes, her arms wrapped around him, with no notion of what happened.

"I'm sorry, what? I must have been distracted by something."

"Never mind, it happens to us all," Chelsie said, amusement shining through as her good mood washed over his mind. "I said I have news for you. Well, two pieces of excellent news, actually."

"News? Well, don't keep me guessing."

"I was waiting to tell you until the underwives assured me the child I carry is healthy and I will carry full term. Our breeding was successful. Soon we will have yet another son in the Monarch House."

Samuel's eyes widened as he turned in her arms. He lowered

one hand and brushed his fingers across her abdomen. With a small pulse of power, he sensed the glow of new life that gleamed to his othersight.

"How did you manage to hide this from me all these months?"

"It's not difficult to distract you husband and you'd be surprised what our silks can hide. Besides Fiona and the other wives conspired with me and helped to keep you entertained," Chelsie said, her eyes sparkling.

His gaze swept over his other wives in the room. "You will all ensure my firstwife is well cared for during this time. Nothing is to happen to this child."

A chorus of ascent followed his order, and he turned back to Chelsie

"It's an auspicious day since I've received word that the threat posed by your sister's children has been ended."

Samuel's eyes rose from her abdomen to stare at her. "They're dead?"

"Not just hers. All the children of Jaclyn's house have been dealt with."

Samuel sat bolt upright, pushing the hands aside of the wife who'd come forward and attempted to massage his shoulders. His eyes narrowed and a slow, vicious smile spread across his face.

"Finally." Samuel threw his head back and laughed

"I told you we'd find them," Chelsie said.

"I should never have doubted you." Samuel brushed a strand of hair back from her face, bathing in the presence of his first-wife. They were perfectly matched and he couldn't imagine Sylanna being in better hands than hers. "Now let's just hope the barbarian leaders follow through and deal with my little sister once and for all. After all, the threat will never be over until she is dead."

"Come, husband the firstwife should rest," the underwife said. As the underwife's hand touched his shoulder, he snarled and lashed out. Samuel flushed as his dagger plunged into his underwife. A wet splatter of blood sprayed on him as she sunk to the ground. Samuel licked his lips, and a salty, metallic flavour filled his mouth. Laughter near him drew his attention back to Chelsie, who leant into him, ignoring the blood as she kissed him. Samuel hummed, sending that small thread of power through both his own silks and hers, divesting them both of their clothing. As his firstwife pressed him back onto the cushions, the gurgling of the underwife distracted him. He met the dull eyes of the other woman, blood frothing from her mouth and spreading in a pool out towards him.

Chelsie's hand curved around his face and drew his eyes back to her as she lent in and kissed him. "Ignore her."

"Someone stop the moaning of that one and get rid of her," Samuel said

He paid no attention at all to the wives, who stepped forward to follow his orders. Their daggers flashed and the distracting noise from the underwife stopped. He laughed as they dragged her off, then devoted all his attention to Chelsie.

SAMUEL WOKE TO DARKNESS, the soft noise of Chelsie's slow breathing next to him, causing him to smile. Their breeding hadn't been that good since the first years of their union. He smiled as he remembered his firstwife was pregnant again and soon enough another male of the monarch blood would be born to his house. It was difficult to decide which was better. That another heir would soon grace the children's sanctuary or that the threat posed by Jaclyn's children had been dealt with. Samuel stretched, feeling content. Careful not to disturb Chelsie, he rose from the pillows they'd fallen asleep on. As he walked across to the washroom, delight bubbled up within him. Samuel couldn't even remember the last time he'd been this relaxed, with a sense that everything was as it should be with his world. His evening with Chelsie had been an unexpected bonus. It had been glorious. Samuel slid the door open and hummed softly as he stepped into the bathing room. The spiderweb silk strips patterned on the walls sprung to life, bathing the room in a soft blue glow.

He cupped his hands in a basin of water and splashed it on his face. As he dipped his hands back into the basin, he froze. Swirls of red patterned the water. Pain seared through his mind and he gasped, one hand grasping the edge of the bowl. His gaze rose to meet his own eyes in the mirror that stood affixed to the wall. Samuel's breath caught in his throat at the blood smeared down his face. Blood-soaked water trailed down his arms and chest to run through the dried smudged blood on his abdomen. He swallowed and stepped back, unable to take his eyes off his own reflection and evidence of the blood smeared all over him.

Samuel bit back a moan as rapid images flashed in his mind. He licked his lips as he made sense of the memories. His knife plunging into the woman behind him. The dying pain-filled eyes of one of his wives. Then his demand that someone get rid of her. The noise she'd been making while she'd been dying had distracted him from Chelsie. Neither of them had been in the mood to allow that to occur.

The threat posed by your sister's children has been ended.

Samuel squeezed his eyes shut, doubling up in pain as if he'd been struck as the echo of Chelsie's voice sounded in his head. Then he forced himself to stare at the man he saw in the mirror, barely recognising the person he'd become.

"What have I done?" Samuel whispered.

Hands shaking, he returned to the bowl. He splashed the water up to his face and tried to scrub the blood off. His breathing sounded harsh and ragged. A lump rose in his throat. Hands pulled at him, and with the touch, a sense of calm was imposed on him. Samuel turned his head to stare into the eyes of his wife, who pushed him to a larger tub, disposing of her silks as she joined him in the bath, and grabbing a sponge started to clean his skin. Samuel gazed up at the web like pattern of light on the ceiling. The memories of what he'd done were still there, but his emotions were suppressed. As he rested his head to one side, he caught sight of the sponge his wife used now stained with red as she washed the blood from him. Red tinged water washed off him and ran into the bath water. The blood spread. It tainted the water it encountered like an infection.

A part of him recognised he should be upset, yet he still felt remote, unable to escape his wife's whispering voice urging him to be calm.

Jaclyn, sister, where are you? You need to return to end this madness before we kill our people.

Samuel sent his desperate plea out in that tight little communication band they'd shared as children. He wasn't sure if she'd still hear him. She was a long way from home. Samuel gasped, knowing instantly when Chelsie woke and discovered him gone. Her presence dominated his mind, shunting aside his concerns even as he desperately tried to cling to the few memories he'd regained. Then she was there, sinking into the bath with him, her hands gripping his head. Chelsie's will rolled over him, urging him to forget.

CHAPTER
FIFTY

Evan was startled awake, as his cell door opened. It was something different. There was no need for their captors to open the cell doors to supply them with water and a bowl of slop. He swallowed as he took in the thick bands of maroon and cream woven through the woman's strange armour. This one was one of the commander's people. At least if he was correct about the colour coding. He suspected the thicker the maroon and cream, the higher ranking the person was. In the case of the usual attendants down here in the cells, the guards had only the thinnest threads of either colour to highlight the plain blue-grey uniforms they wore. Evan shifted uncomfortably as his captor just stood there. Looking at him.

"Your guards tell me they think you know the warleader," his captor said.

"Everyone knows the warleader," Evan said.

"He does. He's personally acquainted with the whole family," Peter said.

"On a first name basis with all the rank in this place. Probably in the pay of the Warlord as well," Constance said, a smirk curling her lips as she glowered at him.

Evan wanted to tell the Kastlers to shut up, but refrained because it wouldn't do him any good. He watched as the woman looked over at the Kastlers, then back at him, a faint smile on her lips. She turned and walked back towards the stone stairs that led up to the doors of the cells, saying something to the guards as she passed. He was just sagging with relief when two of the guards walked in. He stood, backing up against the wall, when one of them looped their strange silk around his neck. It slithered against his skin, causing him to shudder as it wound around itself, then solidified. The guard tugged on the end she still held and he stumbled forward.

He glanced at the Kastlers as they led him past them to see the nasty, satisfied expressions on their faces.

"I don't know why you're so pleased with yourselves. I'm getting out of this place, even if for only a little while. You're both still locked up down here," Evan said.

As the satisfied smiles faded from their faces, he nearly laughed. Except he really didn't feel like this was a victory. On the bright side, he really didn't know much. Then he paled.

Ben, are you there?

Evan swallowed, his nerves spiking, as he didn't receive an immediate reply.

Of course, I didn't expect to hear from you again so soon. What's wrong? Besides being locked up in the cells.

I think I'm about to be questioned. Not that I know much, and I know even less about Michael. I'm not the close acquaintance the Kastlers hinted at, but I know you.

Remind me to stick a sword through the Kastlers if Michael doesn't do it.

I have a bad feeling about this. They were looking for me before the Kastlers said anything. Just, I may not know exactly where you ran to after they hit the Burrow, but I can guess. I hope you have a back door out.

I have several, but don't worry about me. This place, well, let's just say it's much harder for the Sylannians to get to. Thanks for the warning. Are they questioning you down there in the cells?

No. They're taking me somewhere. I don't know where.

Spin it, particularly if it keeps you up in the estate where you can see what's going on. Find out how many people they have or anything useful.

What am I supposed to tell them?

I don't know. Make it up. They must know there is some sort of communication network. They obviously took out our sentries in the tributaries. Play on that and expand.

Oh. Of course.

Don't seem too eager to tell them things. Make them think they've tricked it out of you.

I'll try.

Also, find out what's happened to Speaker Rathadon and Lady Rathadon.

Any other minor thing you'd like me to do?

I don't think so but I'll think about it, that should do for now.

Are you sure? His tone was dry, but he couldn't help it.

I'll let you know If I think of anything else. Ben's reply was infuriatingly cheerful.

Evan drew his attention back to where he was being taken as his guards passed the line that held him to a couple of older women. As his guards turned and walked back to where they'd come from, he forced a smile as he realised the older women were inspecting him. He was pretty certain it was amusement he observed in their eyes as they traded comments before they herded him into the room off to one side. Evan paused on the edge of the room he'd been led into and started chuckling. It seemed one of his high-level captors might want to speak to him, but she obviously required that he take a bath first. There was a tub, it was full as well. The water was cold, of course. He sighed somewhat mournfully. Still, a cold bath was better than no bath right now. Evan's skin crawled. He could feel every little piece of his skin prickling. At the sight of the bath, he groaned, and resisted the sudden urge to start scratching. The older woman tied the lead that secured him to one of the wall fixtures. He'd never really paid much attention to the small rings that were affixed to walls in older houses. They were relics of the time when slaves had been the norm. He watched, fascinated, as the lead went from soft and pliable to hard. She was doing something with the veil, of that much he was certain. He guessed it was something the Sylannian had an affinity with. They went to stand by the door. He waited for a moment, but it became obvious they weren't going anywhere.

"Oh, so you're planning to just stand there and watch me bathe?" Evan said.

He was aware his smile was forced as the women just stood there their faces expressionless.

"Could you at least turn around?" Evan asked, twirling his hand around.

One woman huffed in impatience and gestured to the other, then they strode forward and before he knew it, they were stripping his clothes off.

"No wait, I can do it, it's just..."

He let out an indignant shriek as he was dumped unceremoniously into the tub. It was surprising how strong they were. Of course, he wasn't the most muscle bound male, but he didn't think he was that scrawny. He spluttered as he rose to the surface. The water wasn't just cold. It was freezing. The lips of one woman twitched, while the other laughed outright. Evan sniffed and drew in the veil, trying to channel it into the water, tepid would be better than cold. After a brief exchange in their own language, the women both reached forward. He flinched back, but then sighed in relief as the water warmed up. One woman gathered up his clothes and disappeared with them. He hoped fervently they'd bring him something else to wear. He didn't fancy parading around naked. Another undignified squeak left his throat as the woman grabbed his hand with one of hers and washed him down with the sponge in the other. He was definitely correct. The woman absolutely was trying not to laugh at him. When he tried to take the sponge, she simply pushed his hand away and continued to scrub him clean.

The door opened and the second woman came back in. At least he thought it was the same one that had left with his clothes. He was relieved she at least carried a shirt and trousers for him to wear. He didn't even care that they weren't his. Evan's eyes widened as she approached the other side of the tub and he groaned, mortified when she started washing his hair.

FIFTY-ONE

As the wind changed direction, it brought with it the fetid smell of rotting flesh. A screech of protest sounded as a giant bird of prey left its prize and took flight. Michael took in the remains of the deceased villager the bird had been feasting on. Michael's anger rose as he looked around the deserted village while his horse danced restively under him. Doors hung half off their hinges. A hide ball with bats lay discarded off to one side. A basket with the produce it had carried spread over the ground was nearby. Herd beasts bleated from the animal pens in the otherwise still village.

"Search the village," Olivia ordered.

"You lot find some shovels and get a trench dug to bury the bodies," Nathanial ordered.

"We're too far inland for this to have been Sylannians," Olivia said while dismounting from her horse.

"Callan said they'd been taking in fleeing villagers. I just thought he meant from Yalleska," Nathaniel said.

"He probably did. Whoever did this, they were thorough. I

don't think they left anyone to run," Michael said, keeping a hold of his temper.

"I should have trusted my instincts and killed Aiden long ago," Olivia said.

"You think he ordered this?"

"He killed his own father. Took Isabella as his bed slave. Drugged and imprisoned Damien. Who else would order such a thing?" Olivia said.

"This makes no sense."

"It does if he's taken some residents as slaves," Nathanial said, his voice flat and devoid of emotion. "He knows we're coming. He'll want to free up as many bodies as he can to fight on the walls of the Stronghold."

"Hopefully he won't think to use villagers as a human shield." Michael handed his reins over to a band member, who stood nearby and led the way over to the meeting hall.

"I'd like to say even Aiden wouldn't stoop to that kind of behaviour, but unfortunately I think he would," Olivia said.

Michael entered the meeting hall, relieved there were nothing more than a few overturned benches inside. As Michael grabbed one edge of a table that was toppled over on its side, Nathanial grabbed the other and they set it on its legs. Olivia dragged a couple of chairs over and they all sat.

"Just as well he doesn't know I have multiple ways into the Stronghold," Micheal said.

"Colin is on his way?" Nathanial asked.

"I spoke with him this morning. He'll be at Callan's location before we get there..." Michael took a swig from his water flask, acknowledging Harry as he walked in, pulling up his own chair to join them.

"Clean up here will only take a few hours," Harry said. "Are you sure you don't want me to be the distraction at the front gate?"

"Certain. If I can't get the gates open, I'll alert you to proceed with the backup plan. That's when Colin will open the tunnel beneath the Stronghold and you and your forces will gain access from below," Michael said.

Harry scowled. "But you'll be a fat target sitting outside the gate."

Nathanial snorted, then held up his hand in apology as Harry frowned at him.

"The gates will open. We won't be there long enough to be a target," Olivia said, her eyes glittering.

Harry turned his gaze around the three of them. "How?"

"Three of the Warlord's warbands are within those walls," Michael said.

"And?" Harry asked, a frown creasing his forehead as the silence lengthened between them all.

"I know them well enough to mindspeak to them alone. They'll do as I order," Michael said.

"I don't mean to be negative, but what if they don't?" Harry asked.

"One way or another, they will open the gates," Nathanial said.

"The only difference will be if they do so willingly or their minds are mush when I'm done forcing them to comply," Michael said, aware his tone was flat and cold.

Harry's eyes widened, and he swallowed. "You can do that?"

"I can," Michael said.

"If they don't open the Stronghold as ordered. They've aligned with Aiden." Olivia's eyes narrowed.

"In which case, they'll deserve their fate," Michael said.

Harry's face paled under his tan, but he didn't raise the topic again as they settled in to wait.

CHAPTER

FIFTY-TWO

A damp, earthy smell mixed with stale smoke filled her senses and clung to her body. Hemmed in, unable to move with the bodies pressed around her, Liliana clamped her jaw shut on the scream that threatened to escape. Layer upon layer of shields around her suggested at least some daggerwives who'd protected her also lived. Liliana twitched, her fingers sinking into the earth, and took shallow breaths, trying to remain calm.

"There's plenty of air, just breathe," Liliana whispered to herself.

Aware of the risk involved, Liliana reached out with her mind, relieved to encounter a dozen minds surrounding her. She sent her mind further. Tears trickled down her cheek to mix with the dirt as she encountered emptiness. Other than those around her, there was silence in the world above.

Liliana squirmed, buffeting the minds of the daggerwives until muffled groans indicated they were finally conscious.

"A moment Primewife, we'll dig ourselves out," Reyanna said, her voice subdued.

313

The heartbreak in the daggerwives around her as they too reached out and sensed what she had. The emptiness that surrounded them threatened to overwhelm her until, one after the other, their mind shields snapped into place. Liliana sensed their shift. Their job was to get her out and make sure that now their primewife had survived this attack, that she continued to do so.

The weight above her eased, and light filtered down to her as dirt shifted. Strong hands grasped her and she was hauled up out of the ground. Liliana brushed at the dirt that caked her as she took in the blackened forest. The smell of smoke was heavy in the air. Remnants of blackened stumps were all that remained. Some trees still smouldered, wisps of smoke curling up to hang there without a hint of a breeze to blow it away.

Liliana hummed to her silk, causing it to slither away from her mouth. Now that she was paying attention, some shapes she'd initially ignored thinking they were blackened stumps were the remains of their people. Liliana swallowed as her eyes burned with unshed tears. While she hadn't expected much from their attackers, the fact the bodies had been left where they fell showed no respect for those they killed.

"Check for signs of other survivors. For the remains of our fellow wives," Liliana said, brushing the tear from her face, "and the children. Consign their bodies to the sea as they deserve."

"Primewife, we need—"

Liliana gestured sharply, cutting Reyanna off. "No, we'd be dead by now if our attackers remained here on watch for us. We will do what is right."

Liliana watched as Reyanna ordered the search, and her team scattered. They began checking the blackened bodies and piling the remains to one side. Each scanning their surrounds, hoping against hope that others had done what they had, buried themselves under the ground until the fire passed.

FIFTY-THREE

Damien curled up on the ground, relief mingling with pain as the guards who'd come out to have their sport with him again ran inside to evade the coming storm. After Aiden had made it clear that he was a slave and the guards could use him any way they wished, it didn't take long for the depraved among the ranks to seek him out. Somehow, even though he hadn't been flogged again, what they did was worse. They came in groups to torment him, as if to bolster each other's courage. The guards brutalised him one after the other, then came up with quite inventive ways to torment and inflict pain on him. They didn't break any of his bones or leave so much as a cut on his skin. That didn't mean they didn't do their best to make sure his back, still ripped and bleeding from the floggings, didn't heal. It didn't break Aiden's rules after all, since they hadn't broken his skin. The damage had already been done.

They were so afraid, even though he was still chained up and drugged. His restraints were the only reason they dared to torment him. If they had any idea a group of their fellow guards had been progressively cutting down the potency on his daily tiscan dose, they'd be terrified. If Damien hadn't been certain he'd hurt more, he'd laugh. By Aiden's orders, they delayed his evening dose of tiscan until later. Just so, he was aware enough of a different type of torment. So he knew it was his sister in Aiden's bed. Yet every time he nearly tripped over the edge at the knowledge of the ordeal Isabella suffered just to keep him safe, Allani's mind was somehow between him and Aiden's sport. Little did Aiden know the delay, combined with the diluted dose, left him perilously close to withdrawal and far more aware than his captor would wish. Isabella was manipulating Aiden. She was far less the helpless bed slave than Aiden believed.

Isabella, don't worry about me, protect yourself. Damien sent his plea, but doubted she heard him. Even though he could sense far more now, the tiscan still hampered his abilities.

Pain lanced his back, fire shooting into him as if hundreds of spikes were being driven in through his skin. It took him a moment to realise it was simply the rain on his still healing back. The water mixed with the salt his torturers had rubbed into his open wounds again, causing yet another agony to mix in with all the others. He shuddered to think of the mess they'd made of it.

Hearing thunder rumble, he rolled onto his side; the movement causing his ripped and bleeding skin to scream at him. Tears streamed down his face, mixing in with the rain that fell from the sky. He'd long since lost the ability to feel ashamed. Besides that, right now, there was no one here. Ominous black clouds continued to boil up, as if it was being ripped from one place to another. The sky rumbled again and lightning struck all around, yet it didn't make him flinch. He welcomed it, willing it to strike him. Hoping it would force him into a transition attack and Nathanial's prediction that the drug wouldn't work on him any more would be true.

Damien fancied he saw silver-blue energy tracing its way through the black, boiling clouds. His sister cried out again from the open windows above, the sound intermingling with the storm. While the storm had given him a reprieve from the men who used his body or otherwise tortured him. The same wasn't the case for Isabella. Aiden wasn't bothered by the storm outside his bedroom. He was too busy easing his lust. Damien shuddered as he sensed the edges of Aiden's desire and extreme satisfaction exuding from the man. All of it centred on his possession of Isabella. When Aiden was done with her, all he sensed from Isabella was pain, mixed with fear and shame. Aiden was skilled at breaking people and rough in his pleasures. He had no doubt the man wasn't gentle in bed. Damien heard her weeping long after Aiden had slipped into sated slumber. It broke him that little bit more that she suffered, and he could do nothing to stop it. He was her big brother. He was meant to protect her, not the other way around.

Thunder and lightning pealed again, moving ever closer. This time, it gave him hope.

"Come on, I'm not scared of you," Damien whispered at the storm.

Thanks to the helpful guard reducing his drug dosage, he was at least comprehending things around him. Even if it didn't help him get free. The tiscan they gave him was still enough to block his ability to use the veil. At least he could feel the veil. He shuddered as cold washed over him and his skin prickled where it passed. Except the cold had nothing to do with the temperature. It was the veil. It was so close. He looked up at the sky again, his eyes widening as he finally realised the storm wasn't a natural storm. The turmoil above that seemed to swirl around his position was the veil.

"Oh. This is going to hurt," Damien whispered at it.

The pain the veil could inflict when it rushed back in to reclaim him put everything Aiden and his people tried to inflict to shame. Not that he'd ever feel inclined to point that out to them. It might cause them to get competitive. It was a different type of agony though, where the only escape was potentially down right deadly. For everyone else. So he'd been told. He regarded the chains that held him and, distracted for a moment, wondered if they'd hold him if he went out of his head the way he was prone to do. Damien started laughing, even though the action sent lancing agony through his body. Aiden obviously had a very short memory. Everything that had been done to him had been edging him closer and closer to a transition attack. For the first time in his life, he welcomed it.

"Powers help me. Take me. I'll never deny you again," Damien whispered the promise at that seething, angry mass of energy.

It wasn't sentient. It didn't think. It just was. Yet on the heels of his plea, thunder pealed over and over like waves crashing onto the rock wall, so much so the bedrock itself seemed to shudder and heave with the impact. Damien gasped, his body shuddering in reaction as the air all around him became infused with the veil. Moments later the sky turned to day, with the light charged energy cracking into him from all directions. His physical scream was lost in the peals of thunder that shook the ground and the veil, after a brief pause, rushed through him, burning through him.

FIFTY-FOUR

Michael took in the small but orderly field camp Callan had set up not far from Yalleska town. It was close enough that it sat in the shadow of the imposing mountain that the Stronghold perched on. Thankfully, the forest was big enough to shelter the three warbands he'd brought with him from any observation of those manning the Stronghold's walls. It had been an issue he'd talked about with the Warlord numerous times. While he'd been frustrated to be ignored at the time, now he was glad the Warlord had dismissed his concerns. Otherwise, the logistics of getting this far without Aiden being aware he was on his way would have been impossible. As it was, they'd diverted from the road that led to Yalleska when they were just out of range and travelled overland.

"Michael, I've never been so relieved to see all of you," Callan said.

Michael chuckled at the obvious relief washed all through Callan's tone. While Callan was eminently capable of a leadership role, he wasn't suited to the position and much preferred to be a second. A position he thrived in.

"Sorry it took us so long," Michael said.

"The others insisted we bring some of the other warbands with us." Olivia rolled her eyes.

Callan's eyes widened, and he craned his neck to see past them. "They're not all coming to this clearing, I hope. They won't all fit."

"No, just the one." Michael spared an exasperated glance at Harry.

"Well, we can't be too careful with your person, Your Majesty," Harry said, grinning irrepressibly.

Callan's eyes widened. "Dare I ask about the change in title?"

"Michael refused the title of warlord. So they're trying out others," Olivia said, her expression bland.

"Harry insisted on coming with us, too. Shaun's warband is further that way, on the other approach to Yalleska," Nathanial gestured in the general direction of Yalleska. "Kelsie has orders to loop around to the back."

"Hopefully we'll get this all sorted with minimal fighting and loss of forces we can't afford to lose in this idiocy," Olivia said.

"How are we planning that one?" Callan asked.

"I'll reach out to the leaders of the Warlord's warbands. I know them well enough after all these years to make the communication private. Particularly as close as we are. I doubt they are any happier with Aiden than I am, even if they don't know that Aiden was the one responsible for the Warlord's death. Pretty certain I can convince at least one of them to open the gates for us," Michael said.

Michael didn't feel the need to say either they open the gates for him willingly or he'd force them to. Just because he'd rather run someone through honestly with his sword, it didn't mean under the circumstances he wouldn't break another's mind to compel them if he had to. One way or another, someone inside the walls of the Stronghold would open those gates for his forces.

"I'll brief in your team. Everyone needs to rest up tonight. We'll make the attempt tomorrow. All going well, it's going to be a long day," Nathanial said.

Michael nodded permission and Nathanial walked off exchanging notes with Callan as they went over to the small escort team Damien had brought with him

"When did you get here?" Michael asked.

It might have been a long couple of days, but he hadn't missed the figure of Colin lurking in the shadows of the trees. Colin pushed off the tree he'd been leaning on and covering the short distance between them as they embraced.

"A few hours ago. I'm sorry," Colin said.

"Thanks," Michael said, then waved Harry over to join them. "You've met Harry before I take it?"

"He's dropped into my father's smithy a few times over the years," Colin said.

"The pair of you will stay put here until I give the signal. If I can't get someone to open the main gate, I want you to try the cave entrance."

"It's been a while since father sealed it but it shouldn't be an issue," Colin said.

"Why hasn't anyone ever mentioned a back door to the cells before?"

"It's not exactly a door," Michael said.

"More of a cave system. The cells were fashioned from the cave system under the Stronghold."

"Neither the Warlord nor I thought it wise to advertise that there was a back way into the Stronghold."

"Besides, there'd be no use in you knowing about it. It's not like you would have ever been able to use it."

"Why not?" Harry asked.

"Because you'd need my father, Adam, or me to unseal it for you," Colin said, then frowned. "Even if you don't need me to unseal the tunnel once you've settled this uprising, I might check and reinforce the seals. It's long overdue."

"Good idea," Michael said.

As he went to speak with Olivia, he froze as the veil erupted. Michael switched automatically to his othersight and saw a gaping rent in the air with the veil pouring through, forming dark masses like clouds all threaded through with bluish silver energy. The darkness boiled up and around the Stronghold. Opening his mind, he could sense the ripples of seething pain, madness and rage. He knew without understanding how, that the veil was echoing and multiplying what someone was going through. His mind raced, separating out the mental signatures he could sense.

It's Damien, Nathanial said.

It's not just Damien though? Olivia said.

He's sucked another into it as well? Nathanial said.

It's Isabella, Michael said, with absolute certainty that the brother and sister were both responsible for the disruption rippling through the veil.

I'd say Aiden is having a very bad day.

He could hear the satisfaction in Olivia's mental tone and he couldn't say that he disagreed with the sentiment.

"Everyone mount up!" Michael ordered.

"Plans have changed. We need to get to the Stronghold now," Olivia said.

Everyone sprang into action. Callan's group didn't even bother to pack up the small camp. Michael leapt back into the saddle and spurred his horse, taking the lead towards the town. The veil fuelled storm grew in intensity, with the leaves and branches of the trees thrashing in the wild swirling winds and stinging rain. The peels of thunder were deafening, with cracks heralding sheets of lightning across the otherwise dark sky. As they thundered through the town, he flung a shield up in front of them. Grateful because of the time and the storm, there was hardly anyone out on the streets. The few who braved the conditions had the sense to jump out of their way, since it was obvious they weren't about to stop.

Michael pulled his horse to a halt, the warbands stopping around him, somewhat surprised that Harry and his warband had kept up with him. Then, seeing the flow of the veil around them, he realised Nathanial and Callan had assisted. Everyone waited on him as Michael stared at the Stronghold. Lightning seemed to flicker and engaging in a dance in and through it. Elemental flames burst from the far tower. The one that had contained the Warlord's suite before his death. It was like a baleful whirling chaotic mass swirling around the place. The gates to the Stronghold that, according to Callan, had remained barred since the Warlord's death, other than to let search parties in and out, burst open and people streamed from the gates in a panic.

Michael shuddered as the fitful surging in the veil thrummed through him. He reinforced his mental shields as the minds intertwined with the chaos tried to suck him in. They sensed a source of more power and wanted to claim it for their own. Although he doubted the pair were doing so consciously, their minds obviously recognised his own, at least on some level. Even if only a primitive one.

"Isabella," Owen said softly, his eyes transfixed on the stronghold.

"When we get to Damien, stay behind us and whatever you do, don't draw your sword or pose any kind of threat to him," Michael said, wishing Owen hadn't been with them, but he understood why he'd come. Owen had been Damien's mentor, then Isabella's protector. Then he added as an afterthought. "Or Isabella, until we verify she's currently present in her own head."

Owen looked confused, but held back the questions he obviously wanted to ask and just nodded. As Michael lead the way through the open gates, Callan dropped back and shadowed Owen with a couple of the other band members. Satisfied, Michael reinforced his shield again as the anger in the veil clawed at him as they rode through the portcullis and into the chaos beyond. Michael was conscious of the fact that he was more than willing to be drawn into the destructive madness. However, he feared if he indulged in his anger right now far more people would die than necessary.

FIFTY-FIVE

Evan walked down the hallway. He knew his cheeks were still red. They'd bathed him, scraped the hair off his face with a razor, combed his unruly hair and tied it back. Any time he went to do something himself, they'd pushed his hands aside. They'd dressed him in the shirt and trousers they'd brought. It was like nothing he'd ever worn before. Evan realised these were made from the unadorned Sylannian spidersilk that the Kastlers had been trading people to get their hands on. His were plain, unadorned grey-blue with no other colour. Unlike every Sylannian he saw. They all had some sort of colour threaded through theirs. As they took him down the hallway, he spotted some of the house staff, noting they were all wearing clothing similar to what the women had dressed him in. All in the same nondescript grey-blue colour.

With a start, he realised his guards were taking him up to the upper floors. He was familiar with this level since it was where Steven's suite was located. As it turned out, he'd spent a fair bit of time over the years crashed out in one of the spare rooms just down the hallway. The Sylannians on this level all had the maroon and cream woven into their silks to varying degrees. Even those who stood guard.

Doors opened ahead of his arrival, or rather ahead of his guard's arrival. He was walking between them with the women holding the flexible end of the lead attached to the collar they'd put on him. So, in reality, he wasn't going anywhere except where they led him. As much as he wanted to. Guards were standing outside the door of Steven's suite. Although that didn't mean much, since there were guards stationed outside all the doors. Including the largest suite right down at the end that at one time had been the rooms used by Speaker Rathadon when he'd been the Rathadon warlord, prior to the Warlord conquering Vallantia. In recent times, it had been left waiting for when Michael paid a visit to his family, generally with his warband in toe. One detail of those guards outside the door to the warlord suite was they had thicker bands of maroon and cream. He took a stab that the Sylannian commander had taken them over.

The woman who had spoken with him briefly down in the cells turned and smiled, speaking to the guards who held him. He didn't understand what she said, but he understood an order when he heard it. The result was interesting given the collar around his neck unbound itself and his guards retreated and closed the doors. Not that they left him alone with this woman. There were guards lining the room, again like the ones who'd been down the end of the hall. He guessed these were higher ranked than those who normally worked down in the cells.

This sitting room had doors that connected through to the former warlord's suite. That, combined with the full set of maroon and cream clothing, told him while this person may not be the Sylannian commander. She was high ranking.

"Please, Evan, take a seat," she said.

"Thank you, I'm sorry. I must have missed your name," Evan said as he walked across and perched on the seat she'd indicated.

His stomach grumbled at him. While he'd been trying not to look at it, he couldn't help but notice the food that was laid out on the table between them. The woman smiled, although he didn't know if it was because of his stomach complaining or at his obvious attempt to find out her name.

"You didn't, but you may call me Myra. Please, you must be hungry. Help yourself." Myra gestured to the food ladened table.

He licked his lips, then remembered Ben's words to keep playing along with them. It wasn't like he'd be able to get any useful information if she got angry and just shoved him back in the cells. At a rumbling of his stomach again, he reached for some of the sliced sausage. It took more control than he cared to think of to place the sausage carefully on a plate before taking some cheese, fresh bread, and some fruit. Picking up the plate, his hand shook as his mouth watered. Not wanting to lose the food, he cradled the plate to his chest. With his hand shaking, he picked up some of the sausage and then took a bite. Evan closed his eyes as the savoury taste filled his mouth and deliberately chewed slowly. He'd heard if people who'd been starved ate too fast when reintroduced to food again, they'd make themselves sick trying to eat too much. When he was finished with that mouthful, his eyes darted up to meet Myra's before he hastily picked up a wedge of cheese and shoved it into his mouth. He noted Myra was eating as well, but not in the half starved manner he was. Evan threw dignity to the wind and applied himself to the food on his plate. He spied a flask, and he reached to pick it up. As his hand shook, Myra took the flask from him and poured the both of them a drink. Evan sighed happily as he discovered it was wine and not water. He didn't even know how long they had held him in the cells, being given nothing but water and a bowl of slop. Finally, he placed his plate carefully onto the table and reached out to snag some more food. He took a breath and sat back, aware she was watching him.

"Thank you."

"There is no need. I hope the underwives who helped you clean up treated you well?" Myra asked, her eyes sparkling.

Evan felt his face heat. "I'm not actually used to having people wash me. I've been doing that myself for my whole adult life."

"I hope you'll forgive us. Men are so rare in Sylanna," Myra said.

Evan's eyes widened. He was certain it was fond indulgence he sensed from her. She looked at him in much the same way as the underwives had when they gave him his bath.

"We're going to sit here and have a friendly chat, you and I. If you please me, I see no reason you need to go back down to be locked up in the dark," Myra said. "The underwives, in particular, will enjoy pampering you. You won't want for anything while in their care."

"I don't know what I can tell you. I'm not that important."

As he reached for another piece of cheese, her fingertips brushed his and he dropped it, feeling guilty as his face flushed again. Myra's smile simply broadened a little. He licked his lips as she deftly picked up the cheese and held it to his lips, her elegant eyebrow rising. Unable to help himself, he opened his lips and allowed her to feed him. He flushed again, thinking this probably wasn't what Ben had in mind when he'd said he should stall and string things along. It occurred to him that Ben would be much better at this game. After all, he had a partner and children.

"I won't hurt you, Evan, as long as you do as I ask. I think you underestimate how much you know," Myra said.

"If it was the Kastler's accusations that prompted this, I'm afraid I might disappoint you and I really don't want to. I don't know as much about Michael as they led you to believe." Evan grabbed a piece of fruit and bit into it. He couldn't help but close his eyes as the sweet juice of the fruit burst into his mouth. He would never overlook the value of these small pleasures again. "You're amused by me, aren't you?"

"Men, you're such strange, fragile creatures. Weak of mind, ruled by impulse and prey to your body's reactions." Myra's smile made him blush, which caused her to chuckle before she became serious again. "Many people rush to tell us things about this warleader of yours. Yet they, one and all, with the exception of his family, refer to him as the warleader. You call him by name."

Evan stared at her. She was correct in that little detail. While he mostly referred to Michael as the warleader, he was also one of the few who used his actual name. It wasn't something he'd intended to divulge, but since she seemed fascinated by him, he decided he should do his best to navigate through this dangerous path she led him on.

"People fear Michael, almost as much as they do the Warlord, so they use his title. I don't think he'd actually kill someone for calling him by his name, though."

"Did you have a pleasant chat with Michael this morning while you were passing on Steven's messages?"

Evan froze, then reached for a wedge of sweet fruit and jammed it into his mouth, his mind blank for a terrible moment.

"I... didn't speak with Michael."

"I plucked the detail from Steven's mind that you were an intermediary and passed on messages between him and Michael," Myra said.

"I was speaking with Steven. We're friends, but not Michael," Evan said, hoping Ben was as safe as he believed.

"Ah, who is this Ben that you just thought of now?"

Evan stared at Myra helplessly. "I don't know what you mean."

Myra eased back into her chair. Evan shivered as her power washed over him, then winced as she tested his mental shield. In this, at least he was a little better than Steven.

"Very well Evan, you have already told me something and proven you know far more than you admit," Myra said. "As a reward, you've earned yourself a room to yourself, a soft bed and food. This is but the first of many conversations we will have together."

"Ben's a common name. It could have been anyone." Evan clamped his mouth shut to stop himself from babbling.

He watched her as she stood and walked around to him, releasing a length of silk from her waist. She leant forward and slipped it around his neck. He couldn't help the shudder that ran through him, as it slithered against his skin until it formed a solid ring around his neck.

"There, none will bother you now," Myra said as she returned to her seat. "So if you haven't been speaking directly with your warleader, then it must be Ben who is in contact with him."

Evan took a sip of his wine, thinking furiously, but unfortunately his mind was blank. It was one thing for Ben to tell him to make things up. If he was honest with himself, he was a simple person. He'd never had to dissemble all that much, and he doubted his ability to be any good at it. This woman though, he had the sinking feeling she was much better at getting information out of people than he was at hiding the truth. Taking some of the bread, he used it to soak up some juices from the pan the sausage had been in, he moaned as he savoured the taste. It occurred to him this was one way to delay the inevitable, at least for a short time, and certainly gave him more time to think. She'd expect him to be hungry right now and focus more on the food than her and the questions she wanted to ask him. It was also a much safer thing to think about food and wine than playing this strange dance these women seemed to excel at.

FIFTY-SIX

Isabella lay staring up at the ceiling, barely even breathing as she listened for the telltale signs that would tell her Aiden was asleep. The use of his name, even if it was only in the sanctity of her mind, helped to safeguard that small flame of defiance that burned within. She refused to think of Aiden as her master. Even if that was the title that came effortlessly from her lips now. She didn't dare roll onto her side, at least not until she was sure he was asleep. If she disturbed him before then, she'd learned Aiden would continue to force himself on her.

As much as it killed a part of her, Isabella worked hard to make sure Aiden took his pleasure from her. No matter what he desired, she wanted him focused on her alone. She deliberately drew his attention away from thoughts of her brother or of the other young girls who were collared and now lived in the stable, awaiting his pleasure.

It was a contradiction. Aiden loved overpowering her at the most unexpected times. He took pleasure in the fear he caused. When she begged him to stop, it drove him into a greater frenzy. It was a constant battle within herself, but she used it all.

Isabella pushed Aiden's buttons so that the only person he could think of was her. This minor act of defiance that drew Aiden's attention and made her feel like she had some power also left her feeling helpless.

Warleader! Michael, please help us, Isabella called out into the void, even though the words were shackled by the drug her handlers plied on her.

She wrapped one hand around her waist, pressing her other hand against her mouth as she rolled onto her side, trying to stifle her sobs. Aiden would take too much delight in her crying. Then he'd be on top of her again, gloating over what he could do to her. Just to prove to her how powerless she was. Even though some of it was by her design, she'd feel powerless and somehow like this was all her fault. She turned her head and wept into her pillows.

The tiscan in her body was at a low ebb. Aiden liked her to be aware of every little detail of everything he did with her, to her, while they had sex. Nausea rose and sweat prickled Isabella's skin as heat raced through her. With a gasp, she eased herself off the bed, hand pressing against her mouth, and made her way to his washroom. Isabella eased the door closed, then flung herself to the washbowl and retched. Her body heaved, repeatedly, even when there was nothing left to come out. When the need to vomit passed, she lowered herself down onto the cool stones, pressing her forehead against the floor.

As the sense of wrongness faded, Isabella rolled onto her back, staring up at the ceiling. She tensed as images flashed and the rock ceiling above her faded. It was replaced by the vision of a storm swirling above, lightning cracking down, the wind howling. A gasp tore from her as a deep, burning desire for that power to draw closer hit her. Despite the tiscan that kept both her mind and her brother's caged, all of it sang to her senses.

Damien, Isabella whispered as she recognised it was her brother's desire that sang in her mind.

She rolled onto her knees and crawled to her feet, easing herself out of the small bathing room. Urgency thrummed through her. She had to get to the balcony where she could check if he was ok out there in the storm. With a darting glance over at Aiden to check that he still slept, Isabella half lurched towards the door that led to the balcony. She staggered as the shutters to the room slammed against the stone wall with such force they broke and shattered, sending splinters flying.

As cracking light flashed into the room, Isabella squeezed her eyes shut and raised her hand reflexively. She opened her eyes to see the world vibrating around her. Bolts struck around the room as if the lightning from the storm outside was now somehow inside. Isabella went to run but found she was transfixed on the spot. It wasn't just the room, the very air sparked and flared with flashes of power as the veil made itself increasingly felt. The room that stood around her flicked in and out of her sight. One moment she was in Aiden's bedroom, the next in the courtyard below with Damien. In her mind's eye, it was like multiple rents had appeared in the sky between where the veil normally resided and this place she lived. The veil boiled though, seething and looking for an outlet, echoing Damien as he battered at the mental restraints that held him.

Isabella reached out to Damien as she had back when they lived in Ranlith, trying to ease his pain by bleeding off some of the energy that hurt him. The moment their minds snapped together, in that familiar bond from her childhood, she knew it was a mistake. Multiple bolts of the light seemed to track around the room and slam into her one after the other. She flung her head back. Isabella wanted to scream, but nothing emerged to even give her that much release. The air from her lungs seemed to be sucked out. Pure agony ran through her from head to toe. It was so cold, yet it burnt through her, seeming to strip away the sickness she'd suffered ever since she'd woken up that first day in the dark alone in the cells of the Stronghold. Isabella panted, tears streaming down her face as the fire in her continued its job of searing her from the inside out.

Aware that the one who screamed with a pain, an agony similar to her own, was Damien, she went towards the balcony. Deep burning anger from Damien towards Aiden flared and pulsed through her, easily pushing aside what had the moment before been her goal. She paused and faced the bed. Somehow, Aiden still slept through the chaos that reined around him. Fire rose on her skin, flickering and running over her whole body and mind. It pushed away her fear and in its place anger rose. Yet it didn't hurt. Her skin didn't blister and blacken. Her lips stretched into a snarl as she stared at the man on the bed.

The fire in her wasn't hurting her, it was fixing her, but it would hurt him.

FIFTY-SEVEN

Jaclyn's eyebrows rose as the elation from Myra proceeded her entrance into the room. It bounced from daggerwife to daggerwife that lined the room as Myra entered the suite Jaclyn had taken over.

"What have you discovered?" Jaclyn asked, barely containing her excitement in response to what she sensed through the bonds they shared.

"Steven has been talking with his brother," Myra said.

"What! The warleader is here in Vallantia?" Ricardo asked.

"No, he—"

"Steven isn't a strong enough mindspeaker to communicate directly with his brother unless the warleader was here," Jaclyn said.

"There's another relay." Myra held her hand up to still their questions. "Steven was speaking to his friend, Evan, who was detained down in the cells. Evan was speaking to a man named Ben. I believe it is that man who has a direct connection to the warleader. Or so Evan thinks."

"He told you all this?"

"No, he was desperately trying not to think about it. Besides, I deliberately left him unshielded long enough for Evan to send out a call to the man. It is this Ben who is somewhere nearby."

Jaclyn spun to the daggerwives on the door. "Pass my orders to Sasha. She's to ensure no one gets in or out of Vallantia."

Myra held up her hand. "Wait, I don't believe Ben is still in Vallantia, but he can't be far. I believe Steven has been speaking not only with Evan, but with Ben. I'm uncertain which of them was acting as the intermediary with his brother, but I'm sure it was one of them."

"Do you suspect this Ben was the one in the Burrow?"

"It's hard to say, but if so, we may have driven him from the city, but we failed to kill him." Myra hesitated, then plunged on. "Unfortunately, I suspect it was Steven who tipped them off regarding our attack plans."

Jaclyn's eyes widened, then she turned a glare on the daggerwives who shifted uncomfortably.

"How was he able to communicate with anyone outside our circles in the first place?"

"I checked into that as well. When you took Steven as a husband, it appears everyone just assumed the mate bond would keep his mind safe from outside influence. We didn't exactly tell everyone that you have forgone the mate bond with Steven. I've dealt with the issue. He won't be speaking with Evan, Ben or his brother again," Myra said.

"It's understandable Steven still has some loyalty towards his friends and family, but I think it's time I had a chat with him," Jaclyn said.

"Now that we know it might come in useful..." Ricardo held up his hand in a warding gesture to fend off their twin glares. "Think about it. You may not have full access to his mind, but you could allow him to contact Evan or Ben or whoever in controlled circumstances. It would be better if he thinks it's just a slip up by the daggerwives and underwives. Those Steven has been communicating with might be strong enough to fully shield their minds, but we all know Steven isn't. We might just overhear enough of his conversation to piece together their plans."

"If you'd prefer rather than deliberately compromising Steven I can slip up in one of my conversations with Ben. It will be easy enough to arrange for his guards to be distracted and drop the shield they hold on his mind."

"That would be preferable." Jaclyn's anger fled as she contemplated the possibilities. "So I shouldn't take Steven to task for this betrayal?"

"Speak to your second husband. He'll be expecting it. Explain how significant this betrayal is, but allow him to crawl back into your good graces," Ricardo said.

"It is, in part, my fault. I should have realised the risk to Steven by not having a mate bond in his mind. I should have made sure the other wives continued to shield him."

"To be fair, we all missed it, and I suspect Steven has been speaking with Evan since we threw the man in the cells."

"You've removed this Evan from the cells?"

"I have and those I've detailed to care for Evan have strict instructions to shield him from outside contact at all times." Myra had a satisfied glint in her eyes. "I have a feeling Evan may prove just as useful, if not more so, than our husband in tracking down his fellow rebels."

"I'll leave the man in your capable hands. Now excuse me. I need to go and allow my second husband to. How did you phrase it?" Jaclyn paused, amusement chasing away the remnants of her anger. "To grovel his way back into my good graces."

FIFTY-EIGHT

Khaliun had never seen herself as a patient type, but somehow that seemed to be what she'd become. Yet another benefit she could chalk up to riding and fighting with the Unwanted. In her previous battle with her fellow clansmen for their doomed homeland, they'd spent the better part of years in what seemed like one continuous fight. Yet fighting alongside the Unwanted had been a hurry-up-and-wait affair. Michael planned his battles and left nothing to chance. At least not if he could help it. There was always the unexpected that could happen, but even that didn't cause the Warlord's warriors to stumble. Michael and his fighters rose to the occasion and overcame obstacles in their path. She'd learned far more from working with Michael and observing him and his trusted commanders than she'd ever dreamed possible.

"Do you need anything from us, leader Khaliun?" Vance said, his voice pitched for her ears alone.

Khaliun noted Vance didn't look strained at all, even though he'd been holding a protective shield on her this entire time.

Neither did he look concerned about the amassed tribesmen they faced. Not that the lack of fear surprised her in the slightest. If anything, her fellow tribesmen should keep in mind the display of force the Warlord and his people had put on in their first encounter. Most mistakenly seemed to believe that with only two of the Unwanted with her, they were less of a threat. They were wrong. She'd witnessed firsthand how much damage just one member of the warleader's fighters could dish out.

"There's been a dispute in the ranks of the leadership of the Kallith," Khaliun said, choosing her words with care. It would take far too long to explain to the Unwanted what had actually occurred.

"Worst-case scenario, we may have to leave in a hurry," Batu said.

"Even if this plays out well, we may have far more of the clan with us than we expected," Khaliun said.

"Including those of our people who are not fighters," Batu said.

"Understood," Vance said.

There was no panic or shock from the Unwanted in response to the information. Just a sense of heightened awareness. A readiness to respond to whatever came at them. A stillness that those familiar with their ways would understand could herald the calm before they unleashed a potential storm. Deadly to those in the opposing ranks.

At a shuffling of feet among the growing press of the clan around them, relief flooded Khaliun as Narantuya and Yangir appeared. They were in the midst of fighters from their clan who bristled with weapons, glaring at those who didn't move out of their path fast enough. Almost daring anyone to lay a hand on their co-leaders. Khaliun picked the moment they realised Erden was being restrained by other clan members. Satisfaction radiated from them.

Disregarding protocol, Khaliun threw her arms around Narantuya and Yangir, hugging the pair fiercely.

"You have no idea how happy we are to see you," Narantuya said.

"You know what's happened?" Yangir asked.

"Erden has gone rogue. How could any of you let this happen?"

Narantuya shook her head. "It was small things at first. They seemed reasonable."

"By the time it wasn't, it was too late."

Tuya, with Ulagan in step by her side appeared, both seemed serene in stark contrast to the circumstance.

"We had faith you would return. It seemed better not to make things worse."

"Although as events turned out and circumstances went from bad to worse, it was an error."

"We should have intervened earlier."

Orghana stepped forward, falling to her knees, placing her weapons on the ground in front of her.

"Before all those of the Kallith I declare, I failed in my duty as a leader of the clan to speak up for the good of all. I willingly step aside and will accept the punishment willed by the reckoning." Orghana prostrated herself on the ground.

At Khaliun's hand signal, two of the wolves stepped forward. One took possession of Orghana's weapons, the other stood guard over the now prostrate former leader of the Kallith. A scuffle broke out and in short order a group of men and women, representatives of most of the clans of the Kallith were stripped of their weapons and pushed onto the ground. Khaliun was relieved to see none bore wolf tattoos.

"What are these others accused of?"

With a little shuffling, one of the Crows stood in isolation, her face impassive.

"When former co-leader Orghana was confined to her quarters and under guard, they still took arms against their fellow Kallith. Even though it was clear Erden was acting alone. It flies in the face of the covenant."

"Are there any others who should face the reckoning?" Khaliun asked, surprised that her voice remained steady, without a hint of the heartache showing.

Never in her lifetime had she dreamed she would stand in such judgment over her fellow clansmen. Over former leaders of the Kallith.

"There are some more, but these were the leaders," the Crow said.

"Without fear, stand forward and let your voice be heard. Know you are safe, for this is the reckoning."

As the sun rose high in the sky and began to recede once more, throwing its last light across the plains, Khaliun stood and listened to the testimony of the tribe. There had been intimidation, fear and death. Even more shocking, since there shouldn't have been any threat here at all. The war against Sylanna was far from this new homeland. Khaliun's eyes were bleak as she stared at the row upon row of stones that stood in the failing light. Each engraved with a clan symbol of the death they represented. The stones cast their mournful shadows on the ground. Death markers for those who'd died. Not at the hands of their enemy, but the blades and fists of those who should have protected the ones who'd remained.

Khaliun walked in silence back into the camp, into the space before the meeting hut. The accused one and all were still prostrate on the ground. Of those on the ground only a handful had been bound and gagged, Erden among them when they'd tried to interrupt the reckoning.

"Is there anyone who would speak for any of the accused?"

Khaliun waited as the silence deepened, her heart sick before a man shuffled forward.

"Orghana didn't stand up as she should have but, there'd be a death stone for her if she had. She didn't commit any of the atrocities on her fellow clansmen." The man nodded and stepped back.

As a clanswoman with two children, all baring the wolf tattoos, stepped forward, Khaliun started as she recognised Delbee and her children.

Delbee gestured to three clansmen prostrate on the ground nearby. "These three were a part of Erden's followers, but they kept us safe. Allowing me and my children, as well as some others, to shelter hidden in their tents. There'd be more death markers if not for their actions."

Khaliun acknowledged Delbee's testimony and indicated the three Delbee had nominated should join Orghana on their knees to one side. She waited for a space of time and where none more stepped forward, Khaliun hardened her heart.

"As a leader of the Kallith I've considered the testimony of the tribe. Orghana." Khaliun waited until Orghana's head rose. "You took no part in the atrocities committed on behalf of Erden. Others of the Kallith speak up for you and urge leniency. However, your failure to speak up in opposition to your fellow leader shows you are not fit to be a leader of the clans. You will stand aside. Do you accept the judgement?"

"Yes. It is far more lenient than I deserve. I thank you for my life," Orghana said.

Two of the wolves assisted Orghana to her feet, and she moved to stand to one side. Khaliun faced the three who'd been nominated by Delbee.

"You three reportedly took action to protect your fellow clansmen. That action in the climate of the Kallith took courage. Do you have anything to say for yourselves?"

The Bears looked at each other before coming to a silent agreement and one of them spoke up.

"We didn't have the fighters to stand against Erden's crew, but what he and his followers were doing was wrong." The bear shook his head. "It wasn't courage, but we did what we could. Narantuya and Yangir were in seclusion. I don't know the right of it, but they are healers and we have so few. Throughout our history co-leaders have never been forced aside due to age like Ulagan and Tuya. When word passed via the cats to hold our hand until you and the wolves came home, in the absence of leadership, we did what we thought was right."

"Those of the Bears who remain, until this matter is decided, will you take these two as your temporary co-leaders?" Khaliun asked.

A chorus of approval rang out. Khaliun let out a long slow breath, then turned her attention to those of the accused who remained.

"Under the witness born by those of Kallith, even those of your own tribe, I find you guilty of trying to overturn the way of the clans. You sought to gain control for yourselves alone, to the detriment of others. You are no longer clan. You are no longer of the People." Khaliun paused as a muffled shriek sounded from Erden and he tried to surge upright only to be face planted back into the hard packed ground once more. "Yet banishment is not enough. As is the way of the clan, I sentence you as those generations before were for such a crime. Just as those who caused the last fracturing of the people were. You'll be stripped and tied to stakes at the outer edge of our territory for fourteen days and nights. No food, water or shelter will be provided to you. Any who try to aid you will share your punishment." Khaliun stared around the massed gathering of the clan. All right down to babes in arms, watched on. There wasn't even a flicker of descent to her ruling. Just an outpouring of relief that this nightmare was over.

She was grateful that so many of the non combatants survived. Yet heartbroken that those who'd spoken out and had some ability to fight back had been among those whose ashes were spread on the wind. Those whose death markers stood in silent testimony on the rolling hills. As warriors of the clan, if they were going to die in conflict, it should have been fighting an enemy. Not their own.

The sentenced were hauled up and dragged across the camp. Their muffled screams barely disturbed the silence as their former clansmen who watched on. Ropes bound the criminals and were tied to the back of horses. At her signal, the wolves spurred their mounts. Those tethered to the saddles took a few stumbling steps before they lost their footing. The bound crashed to the ground, rolling and tumbling behind the horses as they were dragged across the camp. As the wolves reached the outer perimeter of the camp, they reined in. They waited patiently as the rest of the clan made their way across to them, holding their mounts steady as the miscreants were untied from their saddles.

Cries from multiple voices broke the silence as those closest fell on their former tormentors, ripping their clothes from them. As Erden and his followers were stripped of their clothing, some dug holes while others hauled stakes. Four for each of their former clansmen. Screams rang out from the accused as other clansmen sliced through their skin and cut the clan and tribe tattoos from their bodies. When done, the flaps of skin were flung aside. The arms and legs of the bloody and beaten men and women no longer considered of the clan were stretched out as far as they could be and bound to the stakes without ceremony. Once done, one and all, they turned their back on the people who'd once been their own.

At a screeching cry from above, Khaliun raised her head to view the giant birds of prey as they flew in lazy circles above. As the old records advised, it hadn't taken long for them to be attracted by the blood. Last of all the Kallith, Khaliun turned her back on these men and women and walked slowly back to the camp. She was satisfied justice would be served. They wouldn't survive the night, let alone fourteen days and nights.

FIFTY-NINE

Due to the horses and carts the Smith had positioned at the edge of the forest, making this last leg to his estate was the easiest part of the entire journey. With a wave at the guards, Ben rode forward toward the manor house. He looked up at the place and smiled. It was ancient, older than even the Rathadon Estate, three stories high crafted in stone and far bigger than a regular person of seemingly modest means would ever own or live in. Still, this land was also the source of the fine metals the Smith used to craft his weapons and had been in the Smith's family for longer than records had been kept. There was even a small village. All who resided in it worked for the Smith in one capacity or another. There was, of course, a road that led to Vallantia, but so far the Slyannians hadn't ventured out this way, preferring to stick closer to the river. Given it gave them easier access back to their own homeland and supply chains, he could understand why they did so. It certainly aided their cause, making this an ideal base for all of them out of the way of direct observation of the invaders.

Ben rode into the courtyard out front and dismounted. One of the stable hands ran forward and took the reins of the horse.

"Smith's waiting for you both in the sitting room," the lad said.

"Thanks," Lukas said.

Ben didn't need directions. Despite the sprawling size of the manor house, Ben knew exactly where to go. He'd been here often enough or more accurately, he'd been here quite a bit when he'd been younger as guests of the twins and Michael, as well as off and on over the years since. Ben took the broad stone stairs at a jog and pushed open the doors. They swung open easily enough, but in times of threat, the Smith could seal them. If the Smith did that no one, other than the Smith or his sons, were likely to be able to get them open again. Although he had the sneaking suspicion Michael could if he chose to, but he'd never admitted as much. They might be long-time friends but there were things about not only his capabilities but those of the Unwanted as a whole that his friend kept secret.

Ben continued down the stone hallway and went into a room on his left. He smiled to see the Smith sitting in a big high-backed leather chair near the window. The room was opulent, with rugs on the floor, tapestries and paintings on the walls. It wasn't at all what one would have imagined of a man who was a smith. Until you remembered who he was in that context. Who his ancestors had been.

"Welcome Ben, Lukas. My people tell me you had a close call?" the Smith said.

Ben took one seat nearby that the Smith gestured to with Lukas sitting in the next one along.

"It was closer than I liked, but thanks to the guards you sent, I came out the other side," Ben said.

"I know you want to save everyone, Ben, but I think your

days of rescuing those captured by the Sylannian have come to an end," the Smith said.

Ben held up a hand. "As much as it kills me, I know you're right."

The Smith regarded him for a moment, then nodded. "You've done a good job. Iris and your children are here in the house up on the third level. I'm sure they will be relieved that these little rescue expeditions of yours will be stopping."

Ben grinned. "I'm certain you're right. Iris is going to scold me as soon as she hears."

"Which you will endure with good grace, I'm sure." The Smith made no effort to hide the smile on his face. "Have you had contact from Michael?"

"Yes, I've been in contact every day reporting on conditions here. He's at Yalleska and Colin has met up with him. Some of his warbands will start arriving here tomorrow."

"What's Michael doing at Yalleska?" The Smith asked.

"Ah, you wouldn't have heard the news yet. Aiden killed the Warlord and worse."

The Smith swore. "We're fighting against a Sylannian invasion and the only contribution Aiden can make is to kill the Warlord? What's the worse part?"

"He's drugged and tortured Damien and taken Damien's sister, Isabella, as a bed slave."

"That certainly warrants Michael's attention and Aiden's death."

"All of this is the worst possible timing, but Michael can't leave the traitor at his back."

"Understandable. I'd like to say I don't believe any of it, but unfortunately I do." The Smith shook his head. "Lukas, I trust I'm not going to have to ask the staff to count all the cutlery?" the Smith said.

"No sir, absolutely not. Your fine metals might be enticing if I thought I'd get away with it." Lukas frowned, tapping one finger on his lips, then sighed. "But you are the Smith, and I'm sure I'd find myself encased in the stuff if I tried."

The Smith laughed along with Lukas, but Ben noticed he didn't deny that was probably exactly what would occur. This was a standing joke between the pair. Lukas would never dream of stealing from the Smith. The man had been like a father to him when he'd discovered this boy his children had made friends with, not only lived on the streets, but ran and lived in the Burrow and had no family of his own. Lukas had been a frequent guest both at the Smith's workplace just out of Vallantia and here at his manor house. Lukas didn't have to be told where he'd be sleeping. He had a permanent room up on the third level. The same room he'd had, whenever he'd paid a visit, as a child. Ben stood to go and track down Iris then froze as his name was yelled across the veil.

Ben! Evan's mindvoice hollered at him.

I'm here. What's wrong? Are you safe?

I don't know that safe is the word I'd use, but I'm more comfortable than I was. They are keeping in under guard in a room on the upper floor.

To what purpose?

They're questioning me about Michael and you and well, trying to wring every piece of information out of me they can. I'm doing my best to feed them false information where I can. Myra already knows so much.

Who's Myra?

As close as I can work out, she's the Sylannian Commander's second in command. At least that's the easiest way I can describe it.

Have you had contact with Steven?

No. Until just now, they've had me shielded. There's a commotion down in the courtyard that has distracted my guards. It's a little convenient.

Ben drew more power. He threw it in the connection between him and Evan to secure it. At least from anyone weaker than he was.

Speak freely, but quickly. At this distance, I can't shield us both from being overheard for long. Convenient in what way?

I overheard Myra outside the door just after she left my room issuing orders for forces to be dispatched to Callenhain on the river. Supposedly to capture the Warlord who they believe is still there.

You don't believe it?

No. Before now she hasn't dropped her guard around me. This is the first time my guards have forgotten their duty to prevent me from speaking to anyone. Then Myra started talking about battle plans. That she did so close enough to my room I could hear her is unbelievable. Let alone when those two events coincide with each other. Still, I decided I should warn you just in case.

I agree it doesn't sound likely. Don't worry, I'll send a warning to those in Callenhain to be vigilant. I'm sorry Evan, I can't maintain this. I'll have to break contact.

It's alright. I didn't expect you to shield us. I don't think they'll kill me. Myra wanted me to reach out to you. Wait, can they track you because of this?

If they had that ability, I doubt I would have made it out of Vallantia. I'd probably be held captive in a room near you. Keep your mental shields up and stay safe.

Ben severed his contact with Evan and reached out blindly with one hand as he swayed on his feet. Strong hands on either side of him steadied him. Then a small pulse of strength passed to him from Lukas.

"Save your strength I'm fine, it's just draining holding a secure conversation over distance. Particularly when the other party isn't strong enough to hold up his end."

"Evan or Steven?" Lukas asked.

"Evan. He's fine, but they've been interrogating him. Give me a moment. I need to pass this on to Adam." Ben gritted his teeth and called out to his friend.

What's up? Adam said, then Ben could feel the frown and concern from Adam as his friend took over the bulk of the communication link between them. *You're exhausted. You won't do any of us any good if you collapse from overusing your abilities.*

I'm about to go to bed. It's just been a long couple of days, Ben said before filling Adam in on recent events and the information from Evan.

That was a close call, to close. I'm glad you and Lukas made it to my father's home in one piece. So, you believe Evan is compromised and they're feeding him false information? I'll pass it all on anyhow and stress that part. Now go and get some rest.

With that final injunction Adam closed the connection between them.

"Now that job is done, my apologies Smith but I need to find my bed and get some sleep."

"Go, before you fall flat on your face and I have to get my people to carry you upstairs to your bed," the Smith said.

Ben excused himself and went to find his rooms. As Lukas shadowed him up the stairs, Ben didn't know if he should feel offended or grateful. Then as he stumbled, and Lukas steadied him, Ben settled on grateful.

SIXTY

Aiden jolted awake, wondering for a moment what had woken him, then he saw her, his slave, standing in the centre of the bedroom, glowering at him. His irritation flared.

"Get back in bed, girl. I haven't given permission for you to get up." Aiden grinned and reached for her mind, only to freeze.

He grew cold, his eyes widening as he realised Isabella wasn't just glaring at him. Her eyes really were glowing, with the same power he'd seen in Michael's eyes when he'd been channelling excessive amounts of the veil. Wave after wave of fury rolled from her. Aiden scuttled out the far side of the bed as he realised she bore another startling similarity to Michael, who'd fallen into a similar state years ago. Michael had been a pure killer when he'd turned like this. Isabella snarled. Or what had been Isabella since this woman who stood in front of him bore only a superficial resemblance to the cowering girl he'd been taking to his bed. Flames danced down her whole body.

"Who's weak now?" Isabella said.

"I said…" Aiden tried to be firm with her but spoilt the whole thing with an undignified yelp as flames leapt up the walls around the entire room.

Finally, he gave up trying to appear unconcerned and turned to run for the door. He fumbled at the handle, wrenching it open as the thing behind him screeched.

"Now it's your turn to scream!"

As Aiden bolted down the hallway as fast as he could, he desperately raised his shields as an explosion of power occurred behind him. A blast of elemental fire racing down the hallway after him. Heat scorched his back. He turned his head as he ran to see a ball of seething energy closing in on him. As his shield buckled under the onslaught of pure energy, Aiden screamed as it engulfed him.

CHAPTER
SIXTY-ONE

Tony's eyes widened as the weather became wild. While that wasn't a strange circumstance here in the mountains around Yalleska, it was unusual for the traces of power to flicker from the stones themselves inside the Stronghold. Unlike many who dismissed the phenomenon, his warband had been around the Unwanted enough to know that this was the action of one of them. Although this was wild. There was only one person this current incoming mental storm could come from. As an explosion rang out, causing the building to shake and screaming started, he smiled grimly. Tony yelled the orders that all the warbands that previously held duty around their Warlord before Aiden's betrayal were waiting for. All of them tied a strip of cloth around one arm, a marker so they could recognise each other from those that supported and protected the new warlord, their enemy.

As they left the barracks at a run, they struck down their former companions. For the first time since the Warlord had run these halls dispatching any who opposed him, chaos reigned inside the walls of the Stronghold. Aiden's warband, under

Derick's command, had all been handpicked. Despite all appearances, the Warlord really had cared about what happened to his son. Unfortunately, all of Aiden's people became his. They supported their warlord above and before anyone else. Having seen what Aiden and his hand-picked people were doing, he and the other leaders of the other two warbands would fight them. They'd then throw themselves at the warleader's feet and take whatever punishment he deemed fit. One thing was certain, though. They would not stand for Aiden, being the new warlord.

Tony struck out at one of Aiden's people that fronted up to him. He flinched and ducked reflexively as another explosion made the building shudder. It was difficult to tell, but the last explosion had come from the warlord's tower. Which Aiden had claimed for his own, where he had the girl Isabella dragged to his bed each night. While the external explosion had likely been Damien, he'd lay odds the one above had been Isabella. Aiden had been a fool. It wasn't just Damien that was dangerous. Isabella might be younger than her brother, but any fool who'd ridden with the Unwanted could see her powers were developing and she'd likely end up as one of them.

Tony wrenched his attention back to the present problem and continued fighting. It was all he could do while he hoped the rest of the Unwanted who'd come with Damien to Yalleska would show up and hopefully be able to help Damien and his sister. One way or another, he was determined the Stronghold would be back in their hands, to hand over to the warleader when this fight was done.

CHAPTER

SIXTY-TWO

He lay in a small pool of calm while the chaos swirled around him. Elemental fire glimmered, flickering and dying, before it finally stuttered to life along his skin. He gasped, and the flames jumped higher before he moved and rolled onto his knees. Swaying, he pushed himself to his feet. He stared up at the sky, sucking in the veil from all around him. Fire now danced and leapt on his skin, although it didn't concern him. He saw the chain that ran from his wrist leading up to a ring on the pylon. Slowly, his head turned the other way, his head tilting up as he followed the chain on his other wrist, which led to the pylon on the other side. After he studied it, he allowed his head to sink to his chest. Somehow, he knew those who had possession of the keys to his bindings would come out to torment him again.

He knew this. Even though he knew very little else.

SIXTY-THREE

The power Isabella unleashed had turned the tapestries that had adorned the walls only moments before to ash. Even the stone walls were blackened. A crack trailed from where she'd stood towards where the door had been like a giant scar running across the floor. Where Aiden's fleeing form had been moments before, there was nothing. She paid no mind at all to the devastation in the room around her as a door opening, drew Isabella's attention.

She spun and ran to the balcony, staring down below where Damien still stood, chained between the pillars to see a pack of guards striding into the courtyard below. One of them was in the lead. A snarl formed on her lips as she heard the joking banter between those below.

"What's up? Afraid of a little storm?" A guard asked.

"Run," another said.

As Damien's head rose, Isabella could see the power that played around him. Isabella drew the grey place to her and jumped from the balcony to place herself in front of her brother. As the guard snorted in amusement, his hand unfastened his trousers. The smirk on his face dropped off as he turned back towards Damien and her. His eyes widened in shock.

"How, how did you get down here?" the guard asked.

"I jumped," Isabella said.

The air around her shivered as Damien drew in his power. Her own abilities flared in response and as the guard clutched at his pants and backed up. Emotion and power pulsed and echoed between her and Damien.

"You, you're not supposed to be down here."

"What? Not so eager now?" Isabella asked.

Flames flared to life all over her again as Damien screamed behind her. Pure rage rolled from him and power thrummed between them. The drug they'd used to control him was no longer hampering his ability to draw and use the veil.

At Damien's scream, the guard turned and ran cross the courtyard, back the way he'd come. Multiple shining bolts of energy cracked down, chasing the man back towards the door. Chips of stone from the paving exploded out and rained down on the courtyard after each strike. A metallic stench filled the air, along with dust motes that swirled and hung around the guards.

"They're not meant to be capable of doing this," a guard said.

"Someone should tell them that," another said.

As they scrambled for the door, Isabella snarled. The veil within her responded and flared to life, an echo of power leaping between her and Damien. As the men who'd been tormenting Damien reached the door, they skidded to a halt, as they fumbled at the door handle, bolts that resembled lightning shot from the clear blue sky striking the ground all around them. Isabella's power flared from her as she pushed that fire within her straight at the huddled men. For that moment, as they spun around, she saw the panic on their faces. They didn't even have time to scream as multiple bursts of energy consumed them. They had no hope of absorbing or controlling any of it. Isabella started laughing uncontrollably as tears streamed down her face. She knew exactly what that agony felt like. Damien did as well. It was like you were on fire and being incinerated from the inside out. Except unlike her brother and herself, those men had no ability to use or bleed off the energy. When everything settled in an eerie pool of calm, there was the smell of seared flesh which permeated the air and a pile of ash near the entry.

CHAPTER
SIXTY-FOUR

Every part of Allani's body felt like it was on fire. A smothering weight on top of her made it impossible to move. The fingers on her right hand twitched, free of whatever weighed down the rest of her. She breathed, then coughed as dust filled her lungs. With a groan, she heaved up, which caused some of what was on top of her to move. The slight reduction of the mass gave her added strength, and she writhed again, then rolled to one side and pushed herself up. A dull thump sounded next to her, and she turned, seeing one of her fellow wives motionless on the ground. As groans and the rustle of silk gave away that some of her fellow wives had also survived, relief surged through her.

Allani looked around the cell. Mesmerised by the motes of dust that hung in the air. She shook herself and swiped ineffectively at the dust on her silks. Then her hand stopped mid swipe, and she straightened as her gaze caught on the cell door half handing from its hinges.

"Thank you, Isabella," Allani said, her words a mere breath from her lips.

363

"First, the cell door is open," a daggerwife said.

"So I see, come let's see how far we can get from this place."

"Won't they kill us?"

"Somehow, I think those above have more to worry about than us right now. Besides, we won't survive long without food and water," Allani said.

Allani paused just inside the open cell door and peered into the darkness in the direction the guards normally came from. There wasn't even a hint of movement in that direction or any sign of light. Yet there was a stream of light from the other direction. Allani took a hesitant step before a hand restrained her and two of the daggerwives pushed past her.

"Wait, let us check," the daggerwife said, her voice sounding overloud in the silence of the dungeon even though she whispered. "Let's hope the light is coming from the outside."

As the daggerwives disappeared around the corner, Allani issued instructions to those that remained. Soon those of the wives who were able stood moving around the cell they'd been held in. Some aided their fellow wives to stand, tying strips of spare silk around injuries. Other survivors had their necks snapped to end their misery. There was no point in being sentimental regarding the fate of those too injured to walk on their own. After watching for a time to make sure her orders were obeyed, Allani turned away to watch for the scouts. A burst of excitement transmitted through the bonds they shared. Allani waited impatiently, about to demand answers, before the scouts appeared.

"There's an old section of the cave system back here. It was sealed, but some of the rocks have come loose. There's a big enough gap for us to squeeze through and there's light beyond."

"Let's go."

"But First, how do we know it leads to the outside?"

"We don't. Would you rather have your neck snapped so you don't have to find out?"

"No First."

Allani turned from her fellow wives, using her irritation at the timid nature of some of her wives to drive her forward.

"These barbarians have access to great power," the scout said.

"Their warleader and his people are the most powerful we've encountered, but I have a feeling that isn't what you were referring to."

"I couldn't work out how the cell we were kept in was fashioned. It was odd, but I dismissed it. Around the corner here, it's apparent this is a cave system. Yet feel the rock wall."

Allani reached out and trailed her hand on the rock wall, only to find it was perfectly smooth. Just as their prison had been.

"It's not a skill I've ever seen before, but it's like this place was fashioned by a master glassblower or woodcrafter only using rock." There was a hint of awe in the daggerwives tone.

"We should be grateful it's a power we haven't met," Allani said.

Allani paused as they reached what had been the end of the cave. Light streamed through a newly fashioned hole in the wall. Allani nodded, and the scout scampered through the hole before turning to assist her. Once on the other side, Allani could make out more details and saw what the scout had been referring to. This was definitely the continuation of a cave system, even if it didn't seem to be a cave at all on the other side. While the wall on the side she'd come from had been smooth, this side was raw and unfashioned.

It took longer than she liked for the remaining wives to crawl through the hole in the cave wall. Allani bit back her impatience as finally they were on their way again, with the scouts trotting ahead. All of them increased their pace as the growing light beckoned them forward. As light streamed into her eyes, Allani blinked and shivered in the cool air. The daggerwives ranged out, searching their immediate surrounds, but detected no other presence near them other than animal life. They had come out of the cave, surrounded by a tumble of rocks.

"First, up here," the scout said from a vantage point above the strewn boulders and rocks.

Allani climbed up, picking her way over the rocks being careful of her footing, then followed the pointing finger of the daggerwife. She'd only seen the Stronghold once, as they'd entered the huge stone fortress, but she had no doubt it was their former prison they were looking at. It loomed above their current position. As close as they were, she could hear screams and the sound of metal clashing with metal.

"We need to get off this mountain and away from the Stronghold before they finish fighting and discover we're gone," Allani said.

"Agreed. I don't know this land, but going in the opposite direction would seem to be a much better option unless we want to be locked up again."

Allani smiled shortly at the obvious statement but didn't comment as she led the way back towards their small group. Another of the scouts scrambled in their direction, stone skittering under their feet.

"There's a forest over this outcrop back this way." the scout gestured back the way they'd just come.

Allani snapped orders to her wives, and the scouts helped herd their fellow wives into action towards the promised cover of a forest.

SIXTY-FIVE

As far as fighting went, Michael had to admit they did very little of it. Particularly since most inhabitants of the Stronghold seemed to be intent on running in the opposite direction in a flat-out panic. Even the sight of their fighting leathers which glowed in response to not only the power they held but that which thrummed in the air, did little to abate the exodus. The only fighting they encountered was guard against guard. It was a mess since, except for his fighters, they all wore the same uniform. Michael skidded to a halt, raising his sword as a group of guards stepped out, blocking the hallway ahead. At a warning from Shallan, he spun to see another group coming up behind them and swore.

"Go, we've got this. Damien is being held in the punishment courtyard," Tony said.

To Michael's relief, Tony and his warband ran past them to take on the guards who'd blocked their path. Michael noted the armbands Tony's warband wore and realised it was how they were distinguishing themselves from those supporting Aiden. Michael ran, leading the way down a side hallway. He didn't need to ask directions to the punishment courtyard. He'd spent time in it when he'd been going through transition. Which meant he knew exactly where Damien was. The outpouring of power and that burning anger that was absent of any conscious control or focus was easy to pinpoint. Michael's eyes widened as a solid ball of energy blasted down the hallway.

Down! Shields up! Michael ordered. *Just let what gets through the shields roll over and through you.*

He threw up his protective shields, feeling the layer upon layer of the shields from each member of the Unwanted. The power washed over him, through him. Michael gasped as the level of the veil that pulsed through him burned and filled him to the edge of his capacity to contain. There was far more energy flowing around than he could ever hope to hold or channel. He checked on those around him, reassured to see they had all followed his advice. He reinforced his shield and followed his own advice, purposely leaving himself open so the power which overflowed and washed all over and through him wouldn't be trapped. The spiky nature of that ball of pure power told him the mind that had created it, intended that whoever encounter it would die. Finally, it was over. As he stood, Michael checked on each of his people and noted Nathanial was bent over Owen, who hadn't moved.

"He's alive, just. Although when he wakes, he's going to wish he wasn't," Nathanial said.

Nathanial pushed open a door a few paces down the hallway to reveal a storeroom before turning to the team. "You two, get Owen in here and stand watch over him."

As two of the Unwanted dragged the unconscious form of Owen into the storeroom, Michael took in the hallway the blast of energy had travelled down. It was now blackened. Shutters had been destroyed and everything on the walls had been disintegrated.

"He's furious," Olivia said.

"Or she is," Nathanial replied.

Michael refrained from comment but from what he sensed, that pulsing rage and pain was an intertwining of both Damien and Isabella. He pulled more of the veil and increased the layers of his mental shield and continued down the stark hallway at a run. It was difficult to determine which of the siblings had been responsible for that deadly ball of energy or if it was both of them. Although under the circumstances, it was hardly the fault of either of them. Finally, he reached the door, or rather the blackened stone frame where the door had once stood. Beyond the archway, he saw the internal courtyard where Tony said Damien was held. They'd used it in times gone past to punish those who'd displeased the Warlord since his rooms had a balcony looking down to where the prisoner was usually shackled. Michael stepped through the opening into the courtyard and raised his empty hands as not only Damien, but Isabella swung to towards the movement.

"The rest of you stay here and be careful not to present as a threat. Stop anyone else from coming in," Michael whispered.

Michael placed one foot carefully in front of the other as he walked into the courtyard. Nathanial and Olivia joined him, each showing just as much caution. All of them had their attention fixed on the brother and sister in the centre. Isabella tensed and tracked their movement. She stood in front of her brother in a protective stance. The veil jumped between the two, creating a strange echo of energy between them. He looked past Isabella to Damien, who stood chained behind Isabella.

Ah Damien, what have they done to you? Come on, come back from wherever in your brain you're hiding, Olivia said in a soothing whisper.

Michael tried to keep his mind calm. It wasn't helpful that he had to repress the desire to track down Aiden and kill him.

Damien stood naked. Obvious signs of abuse marked almost every section of his skin. Shackles bound each of his wrists and ankles, all of which bore the weeping wounds that showed they had suspended him between the pillars. His limbs pulled in four different directions more than once. They had sealed a slave collar around his neck, with yet more chains which led to each of the pillars. It showed how scared of Damien they'd been. Although, as present circumstances indicated, perhaps not scared enough.

Damien's head rose, and he glowered at them. There was no sign of recognition. Only a slight inrush of someone drawing the veil gave him warning just as he hit a solid barrier.

"Go away. I won't let you hurt him," Isabella said.

Michael drew his attention back to Isabella, his eyes widening at the evidence that while she was showing signs of having gone through a transition attack, unlike her brother, she was still somewhat in control. Like Damien, the only item she wore was a slave collar around her neck. He'd been hoping that piece of information had been incorrect. Unlike Damien, she displayed no signs of physical abuse, but that meant little. A wildness in her eyes and the spiky flares of emotion from her showed she was hurting and probably just as capable of incinerating any of them by mistake. Michael judged the only thing keeping her up and functioning was her desire to protect her brother.

Michael held his empty hands up. "I'm here to help Isabella."

"Even those who said they would help did nothing to stop him," Isabella said, eyes wild, swaying on her feet.

"You've met me Isabella, I'm Damien's warleader." Michael placed his hand on the emblem of the Unwanted on his chest. "He's badly hurt Isabella. Let me help you both."

Isabella's lips compressed into a thin line as she stared at him without a hint of recognition. She turned her head to check on

Damien before looking back at the three of them. Unfortunately, she didn't move so much as a muscle. Isabella clearly didn't trust him, although, given what she must have been through, he couldn't blame her.

The poor girl is traumatised. The only thing on Isabella's mind is the need to protect Damien, Nathanial said.

Damien might be chained up, but I don't think many people could get near him in his current state and live to tell anyone about it, Olivia said.

That power play between them is amazing, Nathanial said.

Michael switched his attention to the veil, watching as it rippled between the two in a way he hadn't seen before. It was as if Isabella was bleeding off the excess energy Damien channelled.

Please Damien, hear me. I'm here to help. Come on, come back to us, Olivia said.

The veil cracked around the courtyard. It was laced through with signatures that were both Damien and Isabella. Giving evidence that neither was feeling all that much like trusting anyone right now. Michael breathed a small sigh of relief that the deadly display didn't touch any of them. It was more in the nature of a warning.

You're hurting, I know, but so is Isabella. She needs you, Nathanial said.

Michael didn't take his eyes off Isabella. Of the two, he figured she was the most likely to kill them all if they made the wrong move. Which was an issue, since right now she was between him and Damien. It didn't help at all that her eyes didn't leave him. She focused on him with clear intent. Michael was sure it was because of all of them he was closest to Damien, however, that didn't fill him with confidence. Particularly since she still didn't seem to recognise any of them. He went to speak again, then stopped as Damien gasped, then groaned and sunk to the ground. Isabella swung around, frozen for a moment, then something broke in her, and the anger drained. Isabella dismissed their presence as she ran to her brother. Damien winced as Isabella flew into his arms, then his eyes raised to meet his.

Get these chains off me, Damien said.

Damien might be back in his head, but if Michael was any judge, not completely. Olivia and Nathanial shook their heads urging caution, both having more experience with someone in this situation than he did. Although he empathised more with Damien since he'd gone through the same thing himself. It was a careful juggling act to make sure Damien didn't slide back into operating on that protective automatic mode that didn't really recognise friend from enemy.

"Don't rush, he might just go into survival mode again, but come and help me get these chains off," Michael said.

Michael stepped forward, aware that Damien's gaze tracked their progress. Carefully, he knelt to one side and took one of Damien's wrists to examine the locking mechanism.

"The keys are probably in the ash piles by the door," Damien said.

Michael's eyes widened at the information and raised his gaze to look at the team. Damien usually only had flashes of memory after one of these events, but that was clearly something that had stuck in his mind. The team stilled over the other side of the courtyard, frozen. Then, one and all, they stared back at the piles of ash they'd just walked into and paled. He didn't have to order them to find the keys. They worked that part out for themselves. Without further comment, they turned, brushing their hands through the piles of ash, looking for the keys to the manacles that bound Damien.

SIXTY-SIX

Samuel rolled onto his side, trying not to disturb Fiona's sleeping form. A pair of green eyes of a child haunted him. Yet he had no memory of when or how he could have possibly come face to face with a barbarian child. They weren't commonly in his presence. Samuel supposed he should be grateful Fiona was in bed with him and not whoever it was all his wives were sleeping with to produce children. Samuel's eyes flared open, and he whispered into the darkness.

"I should be grateful my wife isn't sleeping with someone else?"

As preposterous as it sounded, as the words rolled through his head, something about them rang true. With his wives mostly asleep, except for the daggerwives who were on guard duty, it at least gave him some space to think. Samuel rolled out of bed and then with a soft tread, so as not to wake his primewife, he eased himself out the door. As the daggerwives on duty swung around, he raised his finger to his lips. They accepted his plea for silence, simply following him down to the hall as he went to his lounging room. Two of his daggerwives entered and checked the room while he waited patiently in the hallway. The practice amused him. How they thought anyone could get into his lounging room undetected he didn't know. The daggerwives indicated the room was clear and stood aside so he could enter. The door slid shut on its rails and a soft thump indicated they'd closed it to give him some privacy. His wives were getting used to his recent nocturnal explorations. For a wonder, these daggerwives who pulled the night duty had mentioned nothing to his firstwife or primewives. If the dagger-wives had, he was certain steps would have been taken to ensure one of them was with him. Samuel crossed to the window and hummed, sending out a vibrating call not meant for human ears. It didn't take long before hundreds of immature silk spiders scurried along their silken webs towards him. He closed his eyes, bathing in the soft glow their presence brought. A sense of peace washed over him. As a child, they'd always come to him when he'd called. It was a trait he shared with Jaclyn. Samuel crossed the room and sank into the lounge, folding his knees up to his chin and covering his face with his hands.

Samuel took a slow, deliberate breath, then uncoiled to rest back on the lounger staring up at the ceiling. It wasn't the peaked wooden roof he was seeing, but the threads of the veil. They crisscrossed each other, clumping into occasional knots. One of primewives was in the centre of those knots, maintaining control over the flow of information between them all. His primewives were all connected to him and each other. At its centre sat Chelsie, his firstwife. Each of the primewives had mind bonds with Chelsie. All the interconnecting mind bonds between them appeared like a giant spiderweb, but the primary mate bond ran between him and his firstwife. It was thick and solid. A connection that allowed not only Chelsie but all his senior wives to exert their control over him. It also allowed them to shield his mind from the trauma that would otherwise occur every time a wife who was bonded to him died.

Hints of red flickering in the blue drew his attention. He'd seen the like before in his mother's court, but never in his own house until recently. Worse than this. The lines of power in his mother's court had been the reverse. Almost fully red, with only hints of blue. Samuel wondered how long his house had left before the trace lines that bound them all turned from blue with only traces of flickering red to completely red with only hints of blue.

One bonus seemed to be he was coming back to himself more frequently. Samuel frowned, chewing absently at his lip. Before now he'd thought his wives had missed this piece of himself he'd walled away from them. Then evidence started to show that he'd been increasingly absent with frightening gaps of time between. It occurred to him that perhaps he hadn't been as clever as he believed he'd been. It made him wonder if the cause of his increased awareness of late could be credited to the fact that his wives were otherwise engaged and focused elsewhere. That combined with flickering red spikes in their bonds that heralded madness.

Samuel closed his eyes and allowed his mind to wander as it willed. A bowl of dye and the green-eyed child presented in his mind's eye. An echo of a conversation he'd had with Fiona whispered to him. Samuel was convinced Fiona had lied to him, although he had no idea why.

We must face the truth.

No husband, it will happen. We just need to keep trying.

Not a single child has been born in my house these past few years.

Samuel's eyes flared open at the echo of that conversation he'd had with his firstwife years before he'd taken the throne. With that remembered conversation, dredged up from the depths of his mind, was knowledge.

He was sterile.

Sharp pain speared into his brain, and Samuel gasped. Long forgotten memories slammed into his consciousness, as if something had triggered in his mind. Samuel lay as his body twitched. Fire surged through him, cleansing layer upon layer of lies his wives had woven in place. A false memory of who he'd been. Samuel lay panting as the avalanche of memories ceased and at its end his mind was startlingly clear. As if he'd had a reset. Rewound time itself to go back to his old familiar patterns. Now he remembered one of the other things he'd forgotten. A thing his wives had desperately tried to make him forget.

He shouldn't still be here on the throne.

Samuel had cleansed the Monarch House and the throne for two reasons. To save his people from a madness that could and would jump from one house to the next like an infection that spread through a body from a wound. The second reason was to ensure the only remaining chance his bloodline had of keeping the throne had the chance she deserved. Jaclyn. His sister had been born late to their mother, the queen, and the only one other than himself to survive. It was unfortunate that when the Monarch House started to fail, Jaclyn had been too young. Samuel finally remembered. It was he who'd sat with Jaclyn as a child, discussing politics, warfare, and tactics. He'd been the one who'd arranged for Jaclyn to escape the clutches of the underwives in order to be present when some of their sisters had been presented to Ricardo. Then, before he and his daggerwives cleansed the court, he'd sent Jaclyn running to Ricardo. Ricardo hadn't betrayed their friendship by saving Jaclyn from his daggerwives. Ricardo was loyal to the crown. To him. Ricardo had done exactly what his future king had requested of him. Ricardo accepted Jaclyn as his firstwife, even though she'd been too young when all these events had occurred. It gave her a chance to grow and prove herself. He and Chelsie had planned it all. Even down to a team of their most trustworthy daggerwives clearing Jaclyn's path as she fled the court.

Except Jaclyn had proven herself long ago. She was a celebrated commander and, more importantly, had birthed children. He'd forgotten until now that it wasn't him that had walled a section of his mind off before Chelsie had taken him as her husband. It had been his mother. The Queen had commanded that he be brought to her. All the other wives and even his father had been banished. His mother had spent hour after painstaking hour layering protections into his mind. A failsafe that would trigger in certain circumstances. In case of an emergency. One of those safety switches had just flipped. He was still king when he shouldn't be and Chelsie, along with all of his so called primewives and secondwives, had betrayed him. Worse. They'd betrayed themselves. His wives planned to usurp the Throne of a Thousand Islands.

"Did you discover what I'd done, Chelsie and take steps to remedy it?" Samuel whispered into the darkness as he rubbed his temples.

"Are you well husband?"

Samuel held out his hand, waiting. With a barely perceptible pause, one of the daggerwives by the door closed the distance between them. He wrapped his hand around hers and pulled her down on the lounge with him. She fit nicely into his shoulder. He hummed at her armour and it returned to its silken form around her. To her credit, she didn't display any shock at learning of his high level ability to command spidersilk keyed to another.

"What is your name?" Samuel asked.

"Ellith, my king."

"And you?" Samuel asked.

"I'm Beth."

"I've seen you both before. Your team seems to be permanently assigned to night duty." Samuel caught Ellith's hesitation before she finally answered.

"I'm a daughter from one of the lesser houses, but I out fought my fellow daggerwives to earn my right to protect you," Ellith said, then nodded at Beth. "We all did."

"You haven't told any of my senior wives about my nighttime ventures?"

"Even a husband needs time to himself. It's our job to protect our husbands, not smother them."

"Is this how it is in the lesser houses?" Samuel could hear the wistful note in his voice.

"Yes husband. Forgive my intrusion, I sensed you wanted solitude, but I also sensed pain."

"Are you loyal to me, Ellith?"

"Always. I am yours to command. You are my husband and king."

"I am surrounded, always, yet isolated from everyone. It's hard for me to tell sometimes if those around me are loyal to me or just my firstwife." Samuel brushed her silk from her shoulder. "I want you."

"I'm honoured husband, but it's not my fertile time," Ellith said.

"I know, but even a husband needs some things just for himself rather than duty." Samuel brushed his lips against her neck. "You will not mention our liaison to anyone. Not even my firstwife."

"As you will, husband."

"Not the liaison we have this night, or the ones that follow. You'll take over night duty on my person from now until I say otherwise," Samuel said as he divested them both of their silks.

"Yes, husband."

Samuel glanced at the daggerwife who stood by the door. Ellith's partner for the night. "Beth, wait outside, with the rest of your team. No one is to enter. I hardly think Ellith and I need an audience."

"Your will, my king." Beth's face was impassive as she stepped outside, closing the door quietly behind her.

Samuel rolled to his knees and pulled Ellith down in front of him. Guilt assailed him. Then he shoved it aside. He had little time to act and the continuance of the line of the Monarch House was more important. All of his wives would die.

He'd just make sure that some of them, starting with Ellith and her team, died while fighting on the right side.

CHAPTER
SIXTY-SEVEN

Michael watched on with distaste as Colin studied the slave collar that bound Damien and Isabella. Colin spared him a glance.

"These are the work of the local smith. I'm surprised the man had enough ability to craft them. Could you send someone to fetch him?" Colin asked.

"Go, take a team with you and bring the local smith to us," Olivia ordered.

Gavrel selected a couple of his teammates to accompany him and left the room.

"Is it just my imagination or do those collars look new?" Nathanial asked.

"It's not your imagination," Colin said.

Damien's eyes narrowed at that, but otherwise didn't move from where he sat on a chair near the low cot where Isabella had fallen into an exhausted sleep.

"Unless he's run from town, he'll be here soon enough. Can you get that thing off?"

"Of course. Damien, hold still." Colin's hand paused, hovering just above the slave collar as Damien flinched. "It's alright, this won't hurt."

Damien took a shaky breath before he nodded, fixing his gaze on the far wall of the room.

Michael opened his awareness, and it wasn't long before he could sense that deep throbbing beat emanating from Colin as he rested his fingers on the collar. While Michael could hear and understand its beat, Colin was a master. The collar spoke of being fashioned, being infused with the veil, and the time it was given its purpose. The local smith had imprinted the memory into the collar when it had been fashioned, so the metal would always know its purpose and couldn't be turned from its function by another person. Unless that person also had an affinity. Michael could hear the deep rumbling beat, but unlike Colin, he didn't possess enough power over metal to fashion such a thing or release it. Or at least not quickly. Michael heard the beat, like a hand hitting a drum that Colin sent to the collar. It intermingled with the song of the collar until its song changed to mimic Colin's. Then the locking mechanism sprung open and Colin opened the latch. Colin handed the collar to Nathanial, who stood nearby.

"Thank you. Can you remove Isabella's collar now?" Damien asked.

"Of course. Will you wake her? I don't want to frighten her."

Damien nodded and urged Isabella awake with a gentle mental prod. Isabella gasped, sitting up to stare around wildly before she spotted Damien and leant into his arms as she shook.

"Shh, you're safe now. It's over. This is Colin. He's a friend," Damien said, his eyes flicking over to Colin.

"You came with Michael to rescue us?" Isabella said.

"You did an exceptional job of saving yourself," Michael said, sending a wave of reassurance at the girl as she blushed, "but he did."

"Colin wants to remove the collar. Just hold still, he practiced on mine first. It doesn't hurt a bit," Damien said.

Isabella's eyes were full as she looked at Colin, then nodded, although her hands clutched Damien harder as Colin came near. It broke Michael's heart to feel the surge of fear from her as Colin's fingers brushed the side of her neck when he touched the collar she wore. It wasn't long before the collars lock cycled just as Colin willed it to. Being careful not to make contact with Isabella's neck, Colin gently removed it. Nathanial reached out and took the collar from Colin, keeping possession of both. They were too open for misuse by others to leave them lying around as they were. Even for the short period between now and when Colin would destroy the things.

As the door to the room opened, Michael stared unerringly at the man who was ushered in under guard. His senses told him this man had to be the local smith. While the local smith's abilities were much greater than his own meagre affinity, they were much less than Colin's. Michael thanked Gavrel and those who'd escorted the local smith and they retreated a step back while staying close enough to restrain the man. The local smith scanned the room, the colour draining from his face as he caught sight of the collars in Nathanial's hands. Then, as the local smith caught sight of Colin, he gasped and stepped back, only to have the hands of the guard behind him clamp onto his arm.

"Perhaps you'd care to explain these?" Nathanial asked, holding up the two slave collars.

"It was a special job for Aiden. I couldn't refuse—"

"Was this before or after Aiden stabbed the Warlord?" Michael asked.

"Before, but—"

"Then you could and should have refused," Nathanial said, his voice cold. "In fact, it was your duty to report the request to the Warlord."

Michael swung around in time to see a dagger fly into Damien's hand as he pulled it to himself. It was over in an instant as Damien lunged, his veil strengthened arm plunging the blade into the local smith's chest. The local smith's hands grasped ineffectually at the blade. Michael could feel the pulsing of his abilities as, even though it was too late, he still tried to repel and unmake the blade.

"That blade was forged by the Smith himself, the likes of you could never fashion its unmaking," Michael said.

Damien wrenched the blade out and shoved the man away, allowing him to slump to the floor. Damien watched the expanding pool of blood flow onto the floor. When it was done Damien held out the bloody dagger to the guard on the door.

"Thanks," Damien said.

The guard swallowed before he hesitantly retrieved his blade. "No problems."

"Well, I can cross the job of stripping the smith of his abilities off my list of chores," Colin said, his voice dispassionate as he contemplated the now dead local smith.

Michael sighed. "I judge his skills as a smith, as limited as they were, are no loss. It's just as well we brought you with us."

Colin shook his head. "You have the skill enough to open the collars, even if you couldn't destroy them without my help."

"Get a detail here to remove the body and clean the mess up," Nathanial said to the guards still by the door.

The guards seemed only too grateful to have a task and muttered hasty acknowledgment of the orders before retreating.

⌇

Colin held out his hand and grimaced at the slave collars that Nathanial handed him.

"Can't say as I blame Damien for killing the local smith. I don't think I'd be pleased if someone tried to put one of these filthy things around my neck either,"

Michael snorted and held up his hand. "Sorry, as if anyone who tried to collar you would come out of the experience in one piece."

"Granted, it would be problematic for them, particularly when every scrap of metal on them was reduced to a useless lump. Besides, you're the one to talk. They'd be dead if they tried it with you as well." Colin absently inspected the collars in his hand. "Shoddy workmanship," Colin said.

"Thank you for your aid in removing them. Damien was just a little agitated, figured he might calm down a lot quicker once we got those things off him and his sister." Michael shrugged off the accomplishment.

"You would have gotten them off without my help. You're much stronger than you think," Colin said. "There are some smiths who wouldn't have had the ability to unlock these things."

"Huh. Not compared to your father, you, your brother or Jenna I'm not."

"That's hardly a fair comparison." Colin glanced up from his inspection of the collars. "It's a shame that the pathetic excuse of a smith died before I could find out if he fashioned more of them."

"I should have thought before I asked for the man to be brought into the same room as Damien and Isabella."

"Never mind, I can't sense anymore here in the Stronghold, but I'll check more thoroughly here and at the smithy, just to be thorough before we leave."

"We have time. There are a few details I need to clean up here before we head towards Vallantia but you're not to go alone. I'll send a team with you," Michael said, glancing towards Nathanial, who nodded.

Michael watched, fascinated even though he'd seen it before, as Colin almost negligently sent a deep beat that increased in tempo into the slave collars. The surface of the collar undulated, and strands of the veil separated from the metal. It wasn't a flashy display, but just like that. Between one moment and the next, the collars were now dead, with no more strength to them than normal metal. Colin had made it look easy, for him it was, but he'd expanded a great deal of energy into the things to unmake them. Colin stood, taking the collars to the cold fireplace on the far wall, and placed them inside. Then the beat Colin streamed to the collars increased, becoming a complicated rhythm as his power poured into the metal collars. For a time, nothing seemed to happen. Then the metal became fluid, the collar melting and pooling before becoming a solid lump.

"It's a pity making blades, and the like isn't as simple as unmaking things," Michael said.

Colin snorted in amusement. "Then the blades true smiths crafted wouldn't be as valuable. When we manipulate the ore, the blades start as it becomes something else. It remembers the form we bid it to hold. It's much easier to manipulate true smith crafted metal into a different form than to make it in the first place."

"For you, it's easy," Michael said.

"Well yes. Regular people can fashion blades, but..."

"The blades made by a normal person have only a superficial resemblance to those crafted by those with your skill."

At a rap on the door, Michael turned as it opened and Shallan entered.

"Sorry to disturb you but you said to come to you if we found something unusual," Shallan said.

"What is it?"

"There's a door still intact in the Warlord's old suite. It's barred and locked from the other side. We could break it down but—"

"It's unusual and you're right. I did tell you to come and get me." Michael glanced at Colin. "Care to come and help with the door? I'm sure you can deal with the lock easily enough."

"Of course," Colin said.

MICHAEL STEELED himself as he walked up the stairs that led to what had been the Warlord's and then Aiden's bedroom. Members of his warband mixed with some from the other warbands stood duty while others still scoured the Stronghold for the rest of Aiden's warband. He acknowledged the guards on duty at what had been a door to the suite before walking into the rooms. Michael's eyes were drawn to the one door that stood intact in the otherwise blackened room.

"There are people on the other side, but they aren't responding to our orders for them to open the door," Gavrel said.

Nathanial frowned, taking one step forward. "There are a handful of people within, but all I sense is fear."

"Could you get rid of the lock and bar?" Michael asked.

"Easily," Colin said as he stepped forward and used his abilities on the door. "The late and unlamented smith had a hand in reinforcing this as well."

"What was this room?" Nathanial asked, a hint of suspicion in his tone.

Michael spared Nathanial a glance but couldn't think of anything he could say that would lessen the anger bubbling inside of his friend. It was, after all, an anger he shared and since

Aiden was already dead, they couldn't even get the satisfaction of killing the man.

"They used to call it the stable, it housed—"

Nathanial held up his hand, his expression bleak. "I know what the term means. I used to be kept in one. Surely Aiden didn't have time to enslave anyone else? I mean, besides Isabella and Damien?"

At the clatter of metal striking the stone floor, followed by the muffled thunk of a bolt sliding back, Michael returned his attention back to the door. He nodded at Gavrel, who pushed the door open, then entered, with Shallan and the rest of the team following behind.

Michael shook his head at Colin. "You stay here."

Michael only waited long enough for Colin's acknowledgement before he followed Nathanial down the long hallway the doorway revealed. As shrieks sounded from the room beyond the hallway, Michael broke into a trot, then skidded to a halt as he entered the room. Nathanial started swearing, white hot rage boiling from him before his mind barriers slammed up, cutting off the emotion.

Olivia, if you've finished settling Isabella and Damien into rooms, we could do with a little help. Bring a few more of our female fighters and some cloaks or blankets or something.

What's... never mind I'm on my way, Olivia said.

Michael placed his hand on Nathanial's shoulder and moved past him, sending out steady waves of reassurance to the young girls huddled in the corner of a small sitting room. All the girls were naked like Isabella had been. Although instead of slave collars they all had chains around their necks held in place by padlocks. The other end of their bindings were attached to metal loops on the wall.

"P, please don't kill us!" A dark-haired girl sobbed, holding her hands up.

"We'll do whatever you want."

"I won't be bad…"

"It's alright I'm here to set you free," Michael said.

"Only the handlers have the keys," the dark-haired girl said.

Nathanial stiffened. "Where are the handlers?"

The girls all stared up at Nathanial, fear rolling from them in waves. None of them said anything, but a furtive glance down the hallway lined with doors told Michael the answer, regardless.

"Clear the rest of the rooms. Bring the handlers here alive," Michael snapped.

Gavrel and several of his team went down the hallway. Doors slammed open and calls that the rooms were clear rang out as they systematically searched room after room. Michael half turned as Olivia entered, leading some of the female fighters from their ranks, radiating a pool of calm. Although he sensed that underneath the calm was a similar burning anger at the pitiful sight that the rest of them felt.

The fighters Olivia brought with her stepped around him, each of them wrapping a girl in the cloaks they'd brought with them. Olivia inspected the chains, her eyes meeting his before she called over her shoulder.

"Colin, we could use your help once more," Olivia said.

Colin walked into the room, his eyes on the huddled girls, instantly taking in the chains. He raised his hands and knelt down on one knee next to the closest one.

"Easy. I won't hurt you. I'm just going to get these chains off you," Colin said, waiting until the girl, half hiding behind the fighter's shoulder, nodded. Colin easily manipulated the locks, each one opening in turn. The fighters made quick work of divesting their charges of the chains once the locks opened. At a shriek down the other end of the hallway, Michael throttled down his anger as two older women were dragged into the room. The girls shrank back as the older women appeared.

"It wasn't our fault. We had to do as the warlord bid or we'd be dead." One of the older women pleaded.

"Enough." Michael snapped. "Lock them up. I'll deal with them later."

Gavrel and his team reacted promptly, dragging the now weeping women who protested their innocence out of the room.

"You, you're the warleader," the dark-haired girl said.

"I am, but don't be afraid. You have nothing to fear from me or the Unwanted," Michael said.

"Is Isabella alright? She was with our master when the fighting started."

"She will be fine. Isabella is resting now under our healer's care."

"Isabella said she'd do her best to make sure our master focused on her and forgot about us. Our master didn't call us to his bed, just her every night. I'd like to thank her."

"I'll see to it. You're all safe now, and you don't belong to anyone. Aiden, the man who ordered this done to you, is gone. You are all under my protection," Michael said.

"Get the girls to more comfortable rooms and stay with them for now. See if you can find out what villages they've come from." Olivia ordered.

"As soon as we've ascertained their home villages, send squads out to locate their parents and escort them here to the Stronghold," Michael said.

Michael stood on the raised platform in the great hall. He stopped himself from shifting from foot to foot by sheer willpower alone. Many of the residents of the Stronghold that had served the Warlord crammed into the room. His fighting forces lined the walls.

"The last time we stood up here, we were children," Olivia said.

"Were we children? No child commits the acts we did," Michael said.

Isabella stood off to one side of the platform, with Damien on one side of her and Kesha on the other. Unconditional support coming from both of them. Although every member of the Unwanted had volunteered, it was Gavrel and Shallan stood guard nearby. Michael noted the rest of the team Damien had led was nearby. All seemed determined to protect not only Damien, but if he was any judge of their sentiment, they'd adopted Isabella as their little sister.

"It was a different world back then. Far more brutal than the life Isabella led growing up," Olivia said.

The doors at the other end of the hall swung open and Aiden's bed slave handlers, Ella and Cait, shuffled down the length of the hall between their guards. Shocked whispers ran the length of the hall from the onlookers raced as the handlers walked past with their heads bowed, looking neither left nor right. They wore chains binding their ankles, preventing them from even taking a normal step, let alone running. Their wrists bore manacles with a chain leading from the central solid block to a belt around their waist, down to the bindings on their ankles. They could stand, but not stretch. The handlers, with their guards, finally made it the length of the hall. They stumbled to a halt as the guard pulled them up short a couple of lengths from the raised dais Michael and his party stood on.

"Do you have anything to say to excuse your actions before I pass judgement on you?" Michael asked, his voice loud enough to carry around the great hall.

"Please, I'm not to blame. I did my best to care for the girl," Ella said desperation written on her face.

Ella took a half step forward, hand raised up towards

Isabella. Isabella took an involuntary step back, hand raised as if to ward off a blow. Damien moved, shielding Isabella from view, and glowered down at the handlers. The guard behind Ella hauled her up short, then forced the prisoner down to her knees. A gasp of pain wrung from Ella as her knees hit the stone floor.

"You struck not only Isabella but the other children you held in the stable. All the girls have given their accounts you doused them in cold water, then used a hard scrubbing brush and laundry soap for bathing. You drugged Isabella with tiscan, even though you were aware it made her feel sick. The pair of you only provided her with meagre portions of food, even though the kitchens staff told me they were ordered to give you as much and whatever you required. You denied all the girls even the comfort of a blanket as cover while they slept. You call what you did care?" Nathanial said, his eyes beginning to glow as his anger boiled up.

"You may not have been able to free Isabella or the others, however, it was you who dictated their daily living conditions and treatment while in the stable—" Michael said.

"No! The warlord—"

"It is true Aiden ordered Isabella enslaved and dosed with tiscan. It was Aiden who ordered his warband out to procure more people to enslave. However, it was you who dictated how Isabella was treated when she wasn't with him," Michael said.

"There is much you could have done to make her life a little easier between those moments. Yet you relished the control and power your position of authority gave you over Isabella and the other captives," Olivia said.

"I'm advised even the prisoners and guards down in the cells showed more care and compassion towards Isabella than you did." Michael took in all those gathered to hear his judgement.

"Please—" Cait begged.

"If you'd shown even a hint of compassion, your fate would

be different. As it is, you'll spend your life paying off the debt you owe for your role in the emergence of slavery in the domain. Take them both to the cells," Michael ordered.

"No, please, I did what I had to." Ella sobbed and tried to no avail to twist out of the hands of her guards.

Michael regarded the screaming women as the guards dragged them away, unable to feel even a hint of empathy.

SIXTY-EIGHT

Liliana sat in the boat as they powered along the tributaries. She was empty inside, as if she'd shed every last tear she was capable of. The daggerwives around her had pushed their mourning aside and replaced it with icy determination. Even though they didn't share the mental bonds like normal houses did, she could sense the deadly intent that radiated from them. If she'd been capable of feeling sympathy for anyone, she could almost pity anyone they encountered. Not that they'd seen anyone this last week since they'd fled up the rivers towards the barbarian city their firstwife had already taken over. Liliana couldn't bring herself to contemplate the idea that Jaclyn and their entire house might already be dead. That they were the last survivors of their house. Although if Jaclyn and their husband were lost. They had no house.

Reyanna cast a worried frown in her direction. Liliana didn't react, she never did, and the daggerwives had no idea she was aware of their scrutiny. It was just the void that wrapped around her that seemed to keep emotions at arm's distance now. The daggerwives were worried about her. She was aware of that as well, but it didn't make any difference.

Liliana blinked and was drawn from her isolation as she realised the boat she was riding in had come to a halt. They'd pulled in close to land on a small island with the branches from the trees obscuring them. Reyanna was in the middle of a whispered conversation at the front of the boat.

"What's wrong?" Liliana asked as she rose from the pile of cushions she'd been seated on to walk forward.

The daggerwives parted, closing around her as she passed through their ranks to join Reyanna.

"Nothing Primewife. We're just being cautious. We're near Vallantia and there is a fleet docked there." Reyanna said, speaking with care as she pointed off in the distance.

"I would expect so. Jaclyn's forces would have already secured the enemy city by now."

"I've sent out some scouts to check. We don't have any recent reports on how the war effort here is going."

Liliana's focus sharpened, the ache inside receding. "Granted, there are a few of the barbarian boats moored, but the vast majority are Sylannian."

"I just want to make sure our firstwife's forces are in charge here and she didn't end up changing her plans to attack elsewhere."

"Very well," Liliana said, realising there was no point in pushing the issue. It's not like she could really fault Reyanna for her caution after recent events. After all, she didn't really want to end up in barbarian hands because she demanded they dock before the scouts' reports confirmed it was Jaclyn in charge of the city. Even if she thought it unlikely. Jaclyn wouldn't have given up on this target for a smaller centre further down the river.

The array of boats jumped into sharp focus as she opened her senses. The multitude of colours of all the sister houses out on the water gave testimony to the sheer size of the fleet that was docked or anchored.

"I'll let you know when our scouts return," Reyanna said.

"I understand your caution, but I'd rather not sit out here longer than we need to."

"It shouldn't take long to make sure Primewife, we'll dock as soon as the scouts bring back confirmation that it is safe to do so."

Liliana signalled her agreement and then allowed her under-wives to guide her back and install her in the small cabin she'd taken over. The underwives fussed over her, piling up the pillows and tempting her with a tray containing a selection of bite-size pieces of food. Her hand slipped down onto her abdomen as she grabbed a small pastry filled with meat and vegetables. A curl of steam rose from it as the underwife holding the tray promptly heated it for her, just before she popped it into her mouth.

"Will I give birth on this boat, do you think?" Liliana asked. This child of hers was alive simply because she hadn't given birth yet.

"I don't know Primewife, but hopefully not. We'll be on our way soon enough. You are overdue, but the boy will be born when he is ready to. Either way, rest assured, we will all care for you and the child."

In another time, the statement would have caused Liliana to shudder. Except for luck, she and her unborn child would have died in the devastating fire that had ripped through their tempo-rary home. Liliana settled back while the underwives made her comfortable.

CHAPTER
SIXTY-NINE

It was a subtle change. But it was one he'd become accustomed to waiting for. The wife he'd just mated with had fallen into a deep sleep. Tarkhan waited, monitoring as her mind slipped deeper into sleep. If they discovered he was exploring his new world while they slept, they'd place further restrictions on him. As it was, he'd been the perfect 'warrior bed slave' for them. At least on the surface. He exercised as they bid him, to maintain the physic the wives enjoyed and engaged in vigorous bed sport with them. Ate the food they told him to and slept when they ordered him to. He gave them no sign of any resistance to their will. As far as his keepers and the king's wives that he mated with were concerned, he was thoroughly under their control. He'd been doing his best to portray the perfect, willing slave.

Tarkhan's eyes opened to darkness. Other than the soft breath of the woman who slept curled into him, her hand resting lightly on his chest, everything was silent. Even the whispering of his keepers, urging him to comply, was at a low ebb. It always was when he was performing the only duty he had now. His keepers expected the wife he was breeding with to maintain control of him. He'd learned Chelsie was not the only wife he'd been breeding with to fall pregnant, although she had been the first. If the wives he'd successfully mated with carried to term and gave birth to a child, let alone a boy child, their station within the Monarch House would rise. When the babies they bred with him were born they would be passed off as being the child of the king. Not the progeny of a bed slave from a conquered people. He'd learned even the fact that he was here was a closely guarded secret. Which in turn made him wonder if the king even knew his wives were deceiving him. He might die if the king learnt of his existence, but then again, hopefully, so would those who'd imprisoned him.

Tarkhan expanded his awareness, sending his mind out from this place they kept him. Somehow the confinement and restrictions he was under helped him grow stronger with his mind gifts. It made him wonder if it was due to having no other outlet. The only freedom he had was these explorations of the mind. He flitted over his immediate location, pausing just a half breath to check on the muddy glow of the woman next to him. Her mind was deep within the clutches of exhausted sleep. Tarkhan fled outward. He'd explored this place. There were only a few of them here, leaving him to suspect they were fellow breeding stock like him. He'd already explored down. Unlike the level he was on, down was inhabited by so many people. Even the muted glow they gave off while sleeping formed a solid mass in his mind's eye. Tarkhan threw his othersight out. It still shocked him he was high in the vast, interwoven branches of giant trees. Below, far below, thrived and hummed with a life of its own. The muddy glow of life-forces coalesced into a whole, which suggested a massive population. Where he was, in the upper canopy, it was sparsely populated. The section he was imprisoned in was off to one side, with a dead patch separating him from a collection of glowing life. A great many people, yet not as many as those below. He suspected this was where the king and his wives resided, while the mass below was the serving class.

If anyone could call an end to this current existence he was forced to live, it was the king. While it seemed strange to pin his hopes on a king whose minions had invaded his homeland and taken him captive, it was his only hope.

Strands of the veil glowed. They formed an intricate pattern connecting those that lived here. It had taken him time to be able to see it. To narrow his field of vision, blocking out the other more prevalent sources. Then again, it wasn't as if he had much else to occupy his mind. At least once he'd slept off the sleep of the exhausted from years of war and the much newer stress of being taken by the Sylannians. After that, even with the few tasks they allowed him, time had become monotonous. The spiderweb tracery of the veil seemed to connect all the Sylannians who lived here. He took care not to touch it for fear it would send vibrations along the strands. It might give away his explorations. His mind flashed along the strands, jumping over the fitfully glowing embers of the Sylannians the threads connected. It both horrified and fascinated him. All of them were connected to each other. Except for the handful of life-forces that stood separate from all the other people that lived here. Each member of the small, select group showed signs of being stronger in the veil than many here. While he couldn't tell if those individuals were male or female, he suspected they were males consigned to serve like him. Tarkhan decided against attempting to communicate with them until he had more details about his fellow captives. His experience with Chono had taught him that not all those taken by the Sylannians were unhappy with the direction of their new lives.

Tarkhan's mind raced along the interlinked veil pathways, leaping effortlessly over the women. His goal was the shining mass at the centre, with thick bands linking them all together. It was like a giant spider sitting in the centre of a web. A spider that had spawned babies that spread out to fill the web. At the centre of this bright mass was where he guessed the Sylannian king would sit. While he knew he lay in his bed with a Sylannian asleep next to him, it was like he was suddenly there, looking down on where the king and his wives lived. As he sharpened his focus, narrowing down the bright mass separated into individual beings. Triumph surged through him at the achievement. On every other night he'd tried this experiment, he'd failed to separate the individuals from the collective. As he flitted around, studying one sleeping person after the other, he came to a halt. This one he recognised it was Chelsie, and she wasn't alone.

Who are you?

Tarkhan froze as a strong male voice demanded his attention and the figure of a male wearing a flowing robe coalesced in front of him. Tarkhan gasped as the man seemed to stare straight at him.

Tarkhan stilled, withdrawing into himself as a suffocating presence moved closer. Red sparks flickered within the shadowy figure of the man he belatedly realised was the king. A pressure came to bore down on his mind with such intensity Tarkhan flinched back. A flash of anger not his own washed over him and Tarkhan finally fled back to his own body. Tarkhan didn't need to look back the way he'd come to be aware the other pursued him. His eyes flashed open as he stared up into the darkness. Tarkhan shifted carefully, trying not to disturb the woman he slept with while he checked his surroundings. Relief hit him as he saw no sign of the man he'd encountered and determined he wouldn't try that particular trick again.

CHAPTER

SEVENTY

The firm hands of the underwives gripped Liliana's arm. One on each side as they supported her against slipping as she walked, or rather waddled, down the docking boards to the stone pier. Much to her frustration, this child of hers stubbornly refused to be born. The first kindling of interest sparked inside her as she took in the sight of this strange city Jaclyn had conquered. Her daggerwives formed around her, hands on daggers ready to kill anyone if they strayed too close.

"What is this place called again?" Liliana asked, taking her gaze off the row of stone buildings that lined the dock long enough to regard Sasha, the firstwife Jaclyn had left in charge of keeping order.

"This is Vallantia Primewife Liliana," Sasha said as she gestured off to one side. "I've had a carriage brought. It will make your journey to the estate firstwife Jaclyn has taken over as her home base easier."

"My daggerwives?"

"I've called for horses." Relief crossed Sasha's face at the

403

percussive sound of horse's hooves as they struck the cobbles from the far end of the dock. "Here they come now."

Liliana waved a hand in dismissal to the woman and walked over to the horse-drawn carriage. One of the collared pulled open the door as she approached and the underwives assisted her up the steps and followed her inside as she settled on a surprisingly comfortable seat. Liliana brushed her fingers over the smooth leather.

"This place has many riches," the underwife said.

"So it seems. I have a feeling we'll be far more comfortable in this barbarian land than we were while conquering the traders," Liliana said.

Liliana eased back into the seat, staring out at the stone buildings that came and left her field of view out of the carriage window. Like the traders, everything was on ground level except some of the buildings, which went for multiple stories. Ladders on the external walls of the buildings leading to entrance ways on upper stories. Stone buildings gave way to some that were a mixture of stone and wood, where the bustle of people increased. Daggerwives shouted warning and the collared sprawled on the cobbled street when they didn't move out of her path soon enough.

"These people will learn their place soon enough," the underwife said, sniffing in disdain.

While Liliana agreed with the underwife, she didn't feel the need to say so. It was something Jaclyn's house was adept at doing after their experience in the former homeland of the traders. As the buildings they rode past changed, Liliana wondered if among them were the estate Jaclyn had taken over. In this section, there were enormous buildings with gardens and fences surrounding them. Yet they continued on and out of tall gates, the rumble of the carriage changing as the road they travelled on went from cobbled streets to a wide, hard baked dirt road. As dappled light replaced the burning sunlight, Liliana sighed and lent forward. Giant trees stood on either side of the carriage, forming a forest.

"At least they haven't cut down all the trees," Liliana said.

"Obviously ground dwellers, though," the underwife said.

Liliana switched to her othersight drinking in the sight of the forest. The veil swirled around the trees and shrubs, but there was no sign these trees had been protected and encouraged to grow like they did in Sylanna.

"This forest is entirely wild. I can't see any trace that anyone has helped it grow."

"Impressive in its own right, I guess, but it doesn't match the beauty of our forests back home."

Liliana heard the grudging approval in the underwives tone. Many found it difficult to give credit to any other people other than their own.

"Nevertheless, at first glance, this land has much to give Sylanna. For one, these trees will be perfect for expanding our courts."

The underwife's eyes widened as she leant forward, hands on the window to peer out at the forest. "Oh! I see your point. Our foresters won't have to clear any more of our own trees for building materials. We can have these cut down and our builders can use them instead."

Liliana settled back for the ride, although she doubted wherever they were going was far. Jaclyn's base wouldn't be too far from the city. No sooner had she closed her eyes as the carriage rumbled along the road than the echo of horses' hooves clattered over stone. The light dimmed as a shadow passed over them and the wheels of the carriage rumbled over cobblestones. Liliana opened her eyes to see stone walls on either side of the carriage for a moment before they passed through what appeared to be a tunnel, and then light burst into the cabin again when they exited on the other side. As they pulled up and the door was promptly opened by daggerwives wearing Jaclyn's crimson and cream marking, Liliana held out her hand and the underwives assisted her down the steps. Liliana stared up at the gigantic multiple story stone building that dominated the grounds. It had large arched windows and, at the top, what looked like vantage points for guards to station in each corner. There was a stone wall that disappeared from view behind the building, and Liliana assumed it surrounded the building and grounds. Stone steps gave access to the top where daggerwives patrolled the walls. Manicured gardens with shrubs, trees and flowers adorned the grounds. A faint floral scent from a nearby flower bed caused her to smile.

"This way Primewife, Jaclyn has been alerted of your arrival," a daggerwife said.

An undertone of worry rippled through the daggerwives that she was here, but obviously the children were missing. She ignored the unasked question from the daggerwives and gestured for them to lead the way. Each step she took drew her closer to a conversation she'd been dreading since the Monarch House had attacked their refuge.

"Have you ever seen it's like?" Reyanna asked.

"No, I hate to admit it, but it's an imposing sight," Liliana said.

Liliana walked up the stone steps and through the double wooden doors that swung open for her. As she walked inside, the temperature dropped noticeably. Her party was ushered upstairs to the upper floors, then shown into an opulent room down the end of the hallway.

As doors on the other side of the room opened and Jaclyn appeared, her face expressionless, Liliana's lip trembled, then to her horror she started to sob. Not wanting to see the heartbreak in Jaclyn's face, Liliana shook her head and covered her face.

Then Jaclyn was there, pulling her into her arms, with Myra on the other side. Liliana didn't say a word, but the events that occurred rolled out of her, communicated through the bonds they shared.

"I'm sorry—" Liliana gasped as pain radiated from her lower back around to the front as her abdomen contracted.

They were the only words she managed before the under-wives descended on her. For once, Liliana was glad they were here to care for her.

CHAPTER

SEVENTY-ONE

Damien surged up, struggling with the weight of his bindings. His breath coming in short breaths. Eyes wide, he swung around, scrambling back until he hit the wall. Then he finally took in his surroundings and stopped wrestling with the blankets. As his memory came back to him, he slumped back onto the mattress. After taking one last long, slow breath, Damien rolled onto his side, taking in the details of woven rugs on the floor and the tapestries on the walls. There was a leather couch with comfortable plump cushions, with two single chairs, on either side. They formed a half circle with a low wooden table in the centre. There was even a round dining table, with high-backed wooden chairs ringing it. Although he had the sneaking suspicion it had never been used for that function. Somehow, he hadn't noticed any of it the previous night. Olivia had brought him here, to her rooms in the Stronghold when he'd confessed he was afraid to sleep. She'd chased away his fear and kept the nightmares at bay that had woken him screaming from his bed.

Olivia had told him to stay in bed as long as he needed. No

one expected anything of him today or anytime soon until Kesha had cleared him. Finally, he rolled over and hauled himself out of the bed. He ran his hand down the loose linen shirt and comfortable soft pants someone had found for him to wear. Damien went through an open a doorway and spied a small collection of clothing on hangers that seemed lost in the closet. He smiled faintly. That those above his station would own that many clothes they needed a room the same size as his bedroom had been back home in Ranlith was astonishing. On a shelf to one side, he spied a uniform, cleaned and folded with his weapons on a rack nearby. Damien trailed his fingers over what he gathered was his uniform, seeing the spark of blue energy flare in the metal embedded in it. He guessed someone had located them for him and handed them off to Olivia. Seeing another open doorway at the end of the clothing room, he walked through it and into the next one. He stopped in his tracks. It was a private bathing room complete with a sit down tub that had been fashioned from stone. There was even a smaller stone wash basin on a pedestal, made in the same way as the bath. Damien glanced over his shoulder, then smiled and flipped the tap with a small thrust of power while he stripped off his clothes. With a second burst of energy, he stepped down into the tub as the steam curled invitingly from the water. He eased back down and relaxed back, closing his eyes with a sigh.

As a hand grasped his shoulder, he gasped and sprung up, water going everywhere. His hands rose, power springing to life, dancing over his fingers and licking up his arms. Then they spluttered out, and he dropped his hands as he realised the hand that had touched his shoulder had been Nathanial's.

"Easy. Kesha wants to see you, so I said I'd fetch you. I found you asleep. I was afraid you'd drown in the tub," Nathanial said.

Damien closed his eyes again, taking in deep breaths, trying to dampen down the instant panic it had caused to wake up with another person's hands on him. At least hands that weren't Olivia's since he'd been perfectly calm in her presence and slept peacefully with her, soothing him into sleep.

"Sorry, didn't mean to overreact," Damien said.

Finally, he opened his eyes to see Nathanial was holding out a drying sheet to him. Damien took it, not even caring that his hand shook as he did so. It was a little late to try to pretend he hadn't been scared.

"It's alright. You're safe now." Nathanial kept his eyes steady on his own. "There's no shame. It takes time to recover from abuse. No one thinks less of you."

Damien swallowed. He was certain Olivia wouldn't have divulged what he'd shared with her last night. However, since Nathanial had his own history, his reactions probably made it easy for Nathanial to understand what must have occurred.

"I guess the other warbands that were here told everyone what happened," Damien said as he busied himself putting the towel to good effect. He contemplated his uniform in the wardrobe, then pulled on the comfortable clothing he'd been wearing when he woke.

"That you were tortured was obvious when we found you. The members of the warbands in residence have already reported details of their own actions and the abuse you suffered while Aiden had you chained and drugged in the punishment courtyard." There wasn't even a hint of condemnation in Nathanial's voice or expression as he spoke. "When you're ready to talk, no pressure, but I'm here."

Damien swallowed and nodded, his hand brushing the fine fabric of the garments that had been left for him. "I take it these mean I'm a non-combatant until you all say otherwise?"

"They do. You are free to rest wherever you want but we'd prefer it for now, if you stay on this floor." Nathanial led the way from the bathing room and back across the outer rooms. "This floor houses these rooms, which are Olivia's, and at the other end of the hall are Michael's. There's only one other slightly smaller suite up here which I'm in. There's also a common sitting room that the three suites open onto. No one comes up here without permission, and we have guards stationed at the foot of the stairs down below. If you decide to wander about the stronghold, take guards with you."

Damien swallowed again and nodded acceptance. It wasn't like the restrictions were hard or unexpected. If anything, they were more relaxed than the last time he'd been drugged and chained up. Then he'd been restricted to the room they'd put him in with at least one of them keeping watch over him. At least this time he could go for a walk on the grounds, even if it was under guard and they'd prefer he didn't.

"I wasn't even contemplating being adventurous. I was only thinking of crashing on the couch, or perhaps in that sitting room you mentioned." Damien's eyebrows rose as he regarded Nathanial. "Now that I think about it, I'm surprised you all left me alone."

"We're just in Michael's rooms, war planning. Olivia knew the moment you woke."

Damien didn't even bother to get shoes, particularly since he'd just been expressly told to stay put up here on this floor. Nathanial walked with him out into a large open room with an assortment of lounging chairs and tables around it. He eyed the arched windows, resisting the urge to go and sit on the cushions on the window seats and stare down at the grounds below. Nathanial led him to doors on the far side and, without even a perfunctory knock, opened it and gestured for him to enter.

Damien's mood lightened as soon as he saw Olivia, Michael, and Kesha sitting in chairs, much like the ones that had been in Olivia's rooms. It gave him a little pause to think of these rooms being empty most of the time while its occupants rode out in the

Warlords Domain. He swallowed, remembering the Warlord and now Aiden was dead. So this entire realm was Michael's now. Olivia held out her hand to him and, without hesitation, he took it and sank down on the long couch to rest back in Olivia's arms. The underlying current of tension that he hadn't realised he was feeling bled from him. Physically speaking, he felt better than he had for a long time, even if he was exhausted. Of course, it might have something to do with the fact he'd slept soundly, for the first time since he'd found himself chained up in the courtyard of the Stronghold. That and Kesha had already spent hours the day before helping his body to heal from the physical effects of the torture he'd been subjected to. Mentally, his recovery would take a little longer.

"Thank you for your healing efforts, Kesha. I'm sorry I didn't have the presence of mind to thank you yesterday," Damien said, although truthfully, the events from the day before were a blur.

"You were injured, sick, worried about your sister and deeply traumatised. Under such circumstances, I do not expect more than you can give. No healer does." Kesha stood and sat on the couch next to him, her hands rising to rest on his temples.

Damien appreciated that she sat in front of him, rather than approaching him from behind as she normally would. As her power rippled over his body, the swelling dissipated and the aches he'd barely noticed anymore diminished. Then his terrors from when he'd woken, the fear of being bound, of being touched, faded into the background. Not gone, she'd explained to him before they were issues he'd have to work through. She could help give him the breathing space to confront them, but the work would be his. Kesha's power just gave him the space to breathe, to make it through the days, without being a terrified wreck. As Kesha withdrew, Damien sat for a moment, allowing the healing to settle on his mind and body before he finally opened his eyes.

"Thank you. I think I'd be a mess, again, without your help," Damien said.

He'd have to face what he'd been through eventually, but for now Damien was content to rest, free of pain, fear, and anger. Even if just for a space of time. Instead, he decided to tackle a subject that didn't make his stomach tie itself in knots or push him into a panic.

"So, do we think that was my last transition?" Damien asked.

"It's a little hard to tell," Michael said.

"If you have another one, we'll know it wasn't." Nathanial answered with a crooked grin on his face.

"That's not particularly helpful," Damien said dryly.

"I know. Not craving tiscan is a good sign." Nathanial shrugged.

Damien blinked, then turned his attention inside. Nathanial had been correct. He couldn't detect even a trace of longing or need for tiscan. Last time if he'd even started thinking about consuming the drug, he'd be doubled over with pain, his whole body in knots with his head screaming at him to consume again. Now, there was nothing.

"Although that could have just been the amount of power you channelled blasting through your system," Michael said.

"One way to find out. Kesha, do you have a vial of tiscan in your bag?" Damien gazed over to where she'd been quietly curled up in the corner of an oversized high backed upholstered chair.

"Yes, of course," Kesha said.

"Can you get it for me?"

Kesha looked uncertainly at Michael, who shrugged and nodded. Kesha stood and disappeared out the entrance.

"Are you sure you want to try this?" Nathanial asked.

"Better to know now than find out the next time someone tries to drug and chain me up." Damien grimaced.

"Let's try not to do that again," Olivia said with a pulse of support flowing to him, her personal shield strengthened just a notch more around them both.

"I admit I'm getting sick of that one myself," Damien said.

Despite everything he was amused, and with the work Kesha had done along with Olivia's protective power wrapped around him, he felt safe and content. Kesha came back into the room with a small vial in her hand.

"I'll get some water so we can dilute this. We don't want you to overdose."

Damien chuckled, feeling him relax Olivia relaxed her shield, and he held out his hand.

"Kesha, I don't care how strong you think that stuff is. It will not cause me to overdose." It amused him she was afraid that tiny little vial would be too much for him.

"Damien, it's highly concentrated. Patients only have the smallest amounts."

"I'm an addict, Kesha, or if Nathanial's theory is correct, was. That will barely hit the sides and be just enough to send me seeking more if my last transition didn't resolve this little issue."

Kesha hesitated clearly worried.

"He's right Kesha," Nathanial said as he shrugged. "Besides, you are a healer and standing right here so you can intervene if he discovers the stuff still affects him."

Kesha frowned and came around the table, sitting on Damien's other side. She handed him the vial. As she bit her lip, he smiled reassuringly and removed the stopper. Damien sniffed and admitted she was correct. It was strong, but he'd had the equivalent and a lot more of it than was in this little vial. On the positive side, the smell of it didn't immediately drive him into a frenzy for the stuff. He brought the vial to his lips and sculled the contents in one hit.

Kesha gasped, her hand reaching out. "Damien, no."

Damien closed his eyes briefly, then grinned as he opened

them to find everyone staring at him intently. Of them all, only Kesha appeared concerned.

"Nothing, no pain, not even a little spike of pleasure, and I don't need more," Damien said.

Kesha's eyes widened as she stared at him intently. He could see she'd been using her powers to observe him.

"You're like them now," Kesha said.

"Pardon?"

"I suspected it yesterday, but I was also using my healing abilities on you. Now I'm not. You heal like they do. Your body, your powers, however you are doing it, you're tracking down the poison, the tiscan, and neutralising it just like a healer could do for you."

"Well, if a healer can do this, it's not that unusual." Damien shrugged it off.

"As a healer, I can't heal myself. No healer can. Only others," Kesha said.

Damien digested that for a bit, then something else she said finally triggered in his brain.

"Wait, what do you mean I heal like they do?" Damien transferred his gaze to Michael, his eyebrow rising. "Was there something else you haven't been telling me?"

"Well, we didn't know if you'd develop that particular ability," Olivia said, pulling him back against her.

"We heal most things quite well." Nathanial shrugged.

"You're not just harder to drug now, you're harder to kill," Michael added.

"Just don't let someone stab you in the heart or something equally stupid," Nathanial said. "Not that any of us have tested that one, but I don't think even we would heal from that."

Damien regarded them while he was thinking through the idea that he could heal himself. The knowledge that they were all different from regular people wasn't new, but he was only just starting to come to terms with how different he was. How different they all were.

"Is that the explanation for the age thing?" Damien asked.

"Age thing?" Nathanial asked.

"Why Michael doesn't appear old enough to have been born before the fall of Vallantia? Why Olivia doesn't seem old enough to have been that child who was thrown out the gates at the fall of Callenhain and you saying you are older than you look and have been in the Unwanted almost as long as them?" Damien asked.

Damien was aware his tone was dry as all three looked at each other, then back at him.

"We think so," Nathanial said.

"We don't exactly know ourselves. It's only become apparent to us recently," Michael said.

"It's not like we've discovered anyone else to ask," Olivia said, her hand stroking his temple.

"Most of the ones who might be like us are, well, us or seem to be the ones trying to kill us. So sitting down for a quiet chat and comparing notes is hardly in question," Michael said.

"Did you know this little detail?" Damien asked.

Kesha blushed and bit her lip, nodding. "I saw Nathanial healing from an injury back in Callenhain. That combined with the, we're older than we look thing, it makes some sense. I think it's because of the self healing ability."

Damien groaned, then sensing the instant concern from them all, couldn't help the chuckle that escaped his lips. "Sorry, I'm fine. The implication of this conversation makes my head hurt."

CHAPTER
SEVENTY-TWO

Khaliun was empty as she stared across the campfire at those who'd once been her fellow leaders. Beyond them, young and old alike, the clan members massed. It was as if all the tragedy of everything that had happened settled on her. Along with a deep sense of sole responsibility. She was surrounded by people, but she'd never been so alone in her life. She wished that Tarkhan, her former co-leader, was here to share this burden.

"I failed you all," Orghana said, her voice only a whisper, but it carried in the stillness of the camp.

"You weren't the only one who failed our people."

"We never imagined by stepping aside the way we did, by not standing up and speaking out, it would come to a reckoning."

"What do we do now?" A voice called from the gathered clansmen. "There is no other tribe to turn to that will take us in."

As the silence stretched again, Khaliun looked up to find she was the focus of the attention of all that remained of the People.

"Right now? I don't know but this isn't the first time the People have had to change because of a reckoning."

"The ways we've followed for generations were not those of our ancestors. They were adopted after the first reckoning," the lore keeper said, her head held high as she took in the crowd.

"What will you do, leader Khaliun?"

"I will return to the warleader's side and fight with his forces. The truth is, if Sylanna wins this fight, there will be nowhere safe left to run and hide."

"Where Khaliun goes, the wolves will follow," Batu said, then shrugged. "Decisions about how we continue, if at all, can wait until after the war."

"I came back to gather more fighters. If any seek to come with me, they are free to petition."

"What will those of us who can't fight do?"

"The Warlord issued orders that any could seek safety in his stronghold. Any who seeks to come with us when we leave will be welcome. Wolves or not, I'll petition the Warlord for sanctuary on your behalf," Khaliun said.

"I warrant the Warlord will allow it. Particularly if the warleader asks on your behalf. It will count in your favour if those of you who can, take on some of the tasks, like cooking and hunting. Many of those who sort sanctuary in the Stronghold did so because they'd struggle to care for themselves or others," Vance said.

"Each of you have until the end of this night to make your decisions and pack if you need to. I'll be at the edge of the village at dawn to ride out if you wish to come with me. If you don't, know if I survive this war I'll be back if only to check on you all."

Khaliun rose smoothly to her feet, bowing her head in acknowledgement to all those present, then she turned and walked from the gathering. As the light from the campfire lost its hold and she walked into the darkness where none could see, a tear traced down her cheek. Khaliun took a shaky breath, then locked down her grief and the overwhelming sense of loss. In the end, they had done to themselves what the Sylannians had started.

The People were no more.

K HALIUN RODE her horse at a slow walk towards the outer edge of the camp. The wolves and the team of Unwanted in ranks around her. Khaliun gazed around the camp as she rode through. Even this early, with the dawn just breaking, there were signs of the transportable huts being pulled down and loaded onto pack animals.

As hard as she tried, she couldn't feel anything for this place. She felt more of a sense of anticipation over rejoining the Unwanted and the other warbands than loss at the idea of leaving New Home. She snorted in amusement at the mental tag of this place. New Home. Even those who had lived here all this time while she'd been away fighting hadn't come up with a name.

"We're nomads again. At least for a time," Batu said.

The comment made her feel uncountably better. A reminder that in the old times, they'd had no permanent bases. The People back then had been nomadic.

"Perhaps this is not such a bad thing," Khaliun said.

"This place, this home, will still be here if we survive this war."

"You're right, and we'll be better positioned to sort out who we should be after this is done."

For herself, Khaliun would lead the wolves as long as they wanted her and fight with their allies against the Sylannians. All so those who'd formally been the Kallith would be safe. So that one day this place would have a name, a real name.

She reined in as she saw a line of their people, with more

coming out from between the tents. Cold washed over her as the Unwanted who rode with them raised their shields, expanding them to encompass their small group.

"Easy, they won't attack us. That isn't why they're here," Khaliun said.

"I seek your leave to ride with the Wolf warriors."

"Do your leaders give you leave?"

"No, I have no leaders. I was a Crow. My leader broke faith, and the tribe has fractured. I would still act for the good of all our people that remain, rather than go my own path alone."

"The Wolves still stand, alone of all the tribes of the Kallith. Should you choose our path, you are welcome to ride as a wolf warrior. As a leader of the Wolves, I pledge to act where your leaders have failed."

The new member of the Wolves thumped his chest and rode to one side. Clan member after clan member rode forward. By the time she was done accepting the new pledges, all the former members of the Kallith and their former leaders were mustered up behind her.

Khaliun signalled the riders around her and spurred her horse forward. It was a fracturing of the clans that would change how they lived with the balance of power and responsibility now resting with her. She knew it, yet she didn't for a moment regret it. She would deal with the consequences of this day and the best path forward for their people if they all survived.

SEVENTY-THREE

Isabella froze in the hallway, looking up at the stairs, her mind screaming at her as the very walls seemed to close in on her. She stumbled as the guard jerked on the chain attached to her slave collar, the feel of it around her neck. She shuddered and squeezed her eyes shut, hand reaching out to steady herself against the wall. Her other hand rose, fingers brushing her neck to reassure herself she wasn't wearing the collar anymore.

"It's not real, it's not now. He's gone," Isabella whispered to herself.

Her breathing was harsh to her ears. She opened her eyes, looking around, relieved to see the hallway around her was empty. There was no guard escorting her down this corridor anymore.

"It's over."

Taking a deep shuddering breath, she pushed down the fear the memory had brought with it and stepped up onto the first stair. Tears sprung in her eyes and she wiped them away.

"No, I won't let you control me in death!"

She sniffed, then walked steadily up to the top. Pausing as she reached the landing, she stared at the door that stood on the other side. It wasn't the same door, the one that had been opened, time and time again as she'd been escorted to him, had been blown apart and reduced to ash. Scars from the impossible fire that had raced around this room marked everything, including the stone walls. Leaving an enduring testament to what had occurred here. The shutters on the windows, allowing the filtered light into the room, were new. They'd replaced those, too. She walked up to the doors with a determined step, hand reaching out, then paused, not even bothering to wipe away the tears. There wasn't anyone to see right now, anyway. Not wanting to touch the door, she drew the veil and shoved them open with a burst of power.

Swallowing, she walked slowly, one hesitant step after another, into this room she'd been in so many times. They'd been diligently repairing the damage that had been done, but like the room outside, it still bore the damage of the fight that had occurred. As she caught sight of the balcony, her skin prickled as his heavy breath brushed against her neck, his hand on her breast and whispered words in her head.

You're mine Isa, you belong to me now.

She closed her eyes against what was only a memory, but somehow the phantom hands that caressed her skin and the voice in her head felt real. She sunk to her knees, hand pressed to her mouth as she sobbed. It was her own memory haunting her. She knew it, but it didn't help. It was like he was right here with her now, forcing himself on her.

That same feeling of hopelessness welled in her as it had when she had lain there and let him take her. Knowing this man who possessed her, taken her as his bed slave, would torture Damien if she fought back.

Isabella didn't flinch as a hand touched her shoulder. She'd known it was Damien the moment he came up the stairs and into the room. He knelt down beside her and gathered her into his arms. She fought back the tears until he spoke.

"No need to try to hide how you're feeling. Cry as much as you need." Damien's voice was low and soothing. "You were brave and strong when you needed to be. You did your best to protect the children, Aiden enslaved. I'm the eldest, but you defended me. I knew it was you, even when I was out of my head. It's over now. He's gone other than in our nightmares, but those will pass too. It's all right to cry and scream at the unfairness in the world."

She buried her face in his shoulder and wept. He didn't say anything more, just wrapped his arms around her, all the while sending a steady mixture of comfort, love and protection. Eventually her sobbing reduced to little hiccupping breaths, and she realised that protection she perceived wasn't just an emotion. Damien had thrown up a shield around them. A bubble that kept everyone out unless they were stronger than he was and could force their way through it. She'd heard even in the ranks of the Unwanted there were only three that were his equivalent. It reassured her just a little.

"I'm sorry. It's stupid of me." Isabella raised her hand and wiped her eyes.

"You're not stupid. You've been through a great deal," Damien said.

He kissed the top of her head, as if she was still that little girl in the village who'd fallen over and skinned her knee. Her big brother had shown up and somehow made it all better. That memory made her smile. She couldn't resist but share it with him, which caused him to chuckle.

"I'd forgotten that. It was so long ago I'm surprised you remember," Damien said.

"If only the injuries now were so easily mended," Isabella whispered.

"You will, just give yourself time. In the meantime between now and then, it's ok to feel however you feel."

She sniffed again, content to soak up the comfort and protection he was still sending her.

"You're not crying and carrying on, after what he did to you," Isabella said, looking up at him.

Damien smiled sadly and shook his head. "He was feeding me tiscan, enough of it that I'm surprised I didn't overdose. Between that poison and the resulting transition attack it played with my memory, on this occasion, it is a distinct advantage."

"But I saw, he made me watch. You were conscious and screaming in agony as the metal tips on the whip they used ripped up the skin on your back. He punished you because of me. Because I flinched when he touched me."

"His actions aren't your fault. Nothing you did made Aiden and his people torture me. He didn't need an excuse, he enjoyed inflicting pain. Aiden inserted his little connection into my mind long ago, just so he could own me. To try to turn me into his creature. You saved me from that and woke up my mind. You stopped me from killing the Warlord."

Isabella smiled and drew away, sitting up. There was much he wasn't telling her. She could see the shadows in her brother's eyes.

"Even if you had killed the Warlord, it wouldn't have been your fault. Aiden drugged you and was trying to manipulate your mind."

"I know, but I think if I'd allowed him to push me to that, I would have been lost to him. The fact that I wasn't is because of you." Damien stood and held out his hand to her. "You saved me Isabella, let me be the shelter you need now."

Isabella grasped his hand and allowed him to help her to her feet. She looked around this room. This place, which had been the location where what had remained of the innocent child within her, had been destroyed. That piece of her she didn't realise was still there after the invasion of Ranlith and death of their parents. She turned, allowing Damien to guide her out of this room, determined she was never coming back.

CHAPTER

SEVENTY-FOUR

Allani stretched as she came out of her makeshift shelter. While the camp they'd made for themselves in a small clearing in the forest was far from luxurious it was much better than the cells where they'd been held captive. The daggerwives had ranged out their first day, and they'd discovered no sign of any barbarian settlements. They'd also kept an eye on what had been happening in the Stronghold and the battle, for the most part, seemed to be finished. While there had been much traffic between the Stronghold and the village below it, none had come further up the mountain it was perched on let alone to the other side.

"First!"

Allani frowned at the daggerwife who came pounding up to her.

"What is it?"

"We've found a barbarian man."

"A dead one now, I hope."

"He's unconscious but alive."

"We can't touch him First, there's a shield fashioned around him as he sleeps."

Allani sighed as the daggerwives stood moving from foot to foot, with a wildness to their eyes as they waited for her reply. Both had seemed to be level headed, but she wondered if everything they'd been through had started to play on their minds.

She sent of soothing pulse to the pair. "Show me."

They turned and led the way through the forest back towards where the stronghold stood. Allani was about to question the pair as the forest thinned and they came to an abrupt halt. The platitudes she'd been about to utter died on her lips. A man lay unconscious on the ground. A barbarian surrounded by what her othersight told her was a shield of power. It flickered as if about to extinguish itself. While this barbarian was grubby, his clothes blackened and hair singed thanks to Isabella's memories, she recognised him.

"Set up a campsite. Make sure no sign of us can be seen from the village or the stronghold," Allani said, then knelt near the head of the man, content to wait.

As the shimmering barrier flickered out, Allani's hands snapped out and latched onto either side of the head of the man. A ragged gasp was all he had time for as his back arched as she punched her way through his mental shields. His groggy mind, still shrouded in sleep, had no time to muster a defence as she battered away and seized control of his mind. As she worked through the layers of the man's conscious mind, Allani set a deep, binding compulsion, making it impossible for him to even think of escape or disobedience. The addled state of his mind allowed Allani to gain control in a much faster fashion than normal. Even so, as she sat back on her heels, the sky told her hours had passed by while she fought for control of the man's mind. Allani took a deep breath, weary enough that she allowed the daggerwives to assist her to her feet.

"We're taking this as our husband First?" The scout said, staring down at the man Allani had just bound to her will.

"This will be our ticket back into Sylanna and Jaclyn's good graces when she takes the throne."

The daggerwives blinked at her. "He's worth that much?"

"His power level isn't like the barbarian warleader but he's stronger than most in Sylanna. With such an abundance of aptitude for the veil, we'll be welcomed with open arms." Allani stretched, then regarded her prize. "I'm much stronger and more skilled than you. You won't escape my control, so the sooner you stop trying Aiden, the happier you'll be."

Allani snapped her fingers and her daggerwives clustered around her newly bonded mate, assisting him to his feet. Aiden stared around himself in confusion but followed along behind her, compelled into obedience.

SEVENTY-FIVE

Samuel's eyes flared open as the presence that had brushed over his mind fled. It was the touch of a stranger. A consciousness that was undoubtedly male. He flung his senses out after the fleeting trace of the other. Samuel was conscious of his hands gripping the windowsill as his mind raced to follow the other to where the strange male lived. Samuel hoped he found the male's hiding spot before Fiona woke up in his bed in the next room. She'd come seeking him if she woke and found him gone. Then he halted. Far closer than he'd have suspected. Samuel's jaw clenched. They'd dared to put this male up here in the high court, which was his home and sanctuary. Then Samuel gasped as he sensed there wasn't just one foreign male.

Samuel pushed down his surge of anger. He'd known these men must exist from the moment he'd seen the bowl of dye. From the moment the green eyes of a child that was meant to be his stared into his own. Then his memories had returned to him. Recollections that reminded him he was sterile. Yet there were children in the Monarch House. Hundreds of them. Which meant his wives had found men somewhere to breed with and they were keeping them nearby.

It turned out that barbarian men dreamed in their language. So it answered that burning question for him. Chelsie and his other wives had found a source of men outside Sylanna. That didn't mean they weren't Sylannian males by their heritage. Purges for the monarch house weren't always as all-encompassing as the one he'd conducted. Other than Jaclyn, he, along with his daggerwives, had made certain none others survived. At the time, they hadn't wanted any of his other siblings to get any ideas about overthrowing the line of the Monarch and becoming the first of their own line. In the past, if some of the children fled not only the court but survived to escape Sylanna completely, they'd been allowed to run. As long as they and their progeny never came back. Samuel eased the door of his sitting room open.

"Come with me. Quietly, we do not want to disturb anyone," Samuel said, gesturing to both Ellith and Beth to accompany him.

Not that they would have allowed him to wander off by himself anyway, but this way, it made him feel like he had some form of control over his life. Samuel doubted many would believe how little say he really had. Even over the running of the kingdom.

"Forgive me Samuel, but where are we going?" Ellith asked.

"I'm going to see the men my wives are using in their attempt to wrest control of the Monarch House."

"The men husband?" Ellith asked, genuine shock colouring her tone.

"You'll see. They're not far. After all, it would be noted if my firstwife kept paying regular visits to the lower levels of the palace," Samuel said.

Samuel ignored the incredulous outburst of emotion from Ellith and Beth. They would see soon enough. He led the way through little used passageways that wound their way through the Monarch House. He knew them as only one who was born to the house could do so. It was a regular game to escape the clutches of the underwives and explore the palace when he'd been a child. Coincidently, it was also how the purge had been conducted with remarkable success. Yet another reason to eradicate any and all siblings since most of them would know the passages as well as he did and could use them to their advantage if the notion had occurred to them.

Samuel paused, cocking his head to one side to listen to the whispering voice he could hear. Not that he was using his ears to hear them, but he found it fascinating that the body generally mimicked habits as if he was. Unless the person trained themselves not to give away, they were utilising their mind abilities.

"One of my wives is in here. She is a traitor. Kill her immediately and dispose of the body, but do not harm the man," Samuel said, waiting until he got tense nods from both his daggerwives, then added as an afterthought. "But do not let him raise the alarm."

"What if the wife raises the alarm first?"

"Make sure she doesn't. At least you'll have the benefit of surprise to aid you."

Samuel concentrated on the locking mechanism and the bolt snicked back. He went to pull the panel obscuring the secondary entrance aside, only for Ellith to ease past him and do it herself. He followed his daggerwives into what proved to be the outer rooms. This might be a prison for the male his wives kept here, but at least it was a comfortable one. As much as he tried to feel outraged at the males that were breeding with his wives, he found he couldn't. If he'd discovered they'd been pure bred Sylannian males, it would be treason, and he'd have them all summarily killed. Yet these men, if their dreams were anything to go by, were captives from another land. They were as much victims of the deceit and treachery of his wives as he was. If not more.

Ellith slid the inner door aside and with Beth close on her heel ran on light feet into the room. There was little more than a gasp before he entered to see Ellith's blade slicing with deadly accuracy across the throat of his traitor wife. Samuel watched dispassionately as blood sprayed and the struggles of his mortally wounded wife grew weaker. He recognised this wife. She was one of his secondwives who had reportedly born a girl child to him. Samuel felt like he'd been punched in the stomach. It was one thing for him to suspect his wives were conspiring against him. It was another thing to know it.

Samuel hummed softly at the silk wall, which threw off a cheery blue glow in response, then turned his attention to the male. From the tattoos that adorned the man's face, he was a former resident of the trader lands. One with rank. If his memory served him correctly, although no matter how much he prodded, he couldn't dredge up the details of what the swirling patterns meant. The clansmen's eyes were wide, his breathing coming in short gasps as he lay on the bed, now splattered with blood, next to the woman he'd undoubtedly bred with before slipping into stated slumber. As the man seemed to understand he wasn't about to be killed, at least not right away, he stilled. Samuel was glad he'd taken the time early on in the war to strip the language of the trader clans from one of their collared. He remembered thinking it had been a waste of his time and certainly not worth the headache the procedure had cost him. After all, when would one of their newly conquered and collared servers get anywhere near him. As it turned out, he'd been wrong.

"Who are you?" Samuel asked.

"Tarkhan, I was a co-leader of the wolf tribe of the Kallith," Tarkhan said.

Samuel frowned. Something about the Kallith and wolves

seemed familiar. When the memory came back, Samuel only just stopped himself from stepping back. If his sister was correct, this man was dangerous.

"One of the wolf warriors from the missing Kallith clan. However did you end up here in my court and in a bed breeding with my wives?" Samuel asked, smiling pleasantly at the immediate spurt of fear he sensed from Tarkhan.

"I was captured trying to free some of the members of the Hallaran Clan." Tarkhan licked his lips. "You're Samuel. The Sylannian king."

"At least you know my name," Samuel said, his tone dry. Then he sighed. This circumstance was not Tarkhan's fault. Unfortunately, he couldn't just blame his firstwife either. There were a great many wives involved in pulling this off successfully. Every single one of those wives should have come to him and reported the treason. Yet not a single one had done so. "How long have you been here?"

"I don't know. Until recently, I had no reliable way to track time. They only moved me here a few weeks ago. Before that, the place I was confined to had no windows. It's been months? I think?" Tarkhan said, confusion evident in his tone and expression.

"How many of my wives have you..." Samuel paused, rubbing his face in aggravation. "Never mind, I doubt you'd know the answer to that either."

Samuel signalled to Beth to let Tarkhan up. After a slight hesitation, Beth withdrew her blade and stepped back. Although she was still in place between him and this man.

"I'm sorry, husband," Ellith said.

"For what?"

"I, I didn't quite believe you, I thought..."

"I was paranoid? I can hardly blame you. After all these years under Chelsie's control, I can't trust my memories either.

Dispose of the body and get this room and Tarkhan cleaned up."

"Yes Samuel. I can sense six other life-forces in this wing. Some of them are dreaming in a language other than Sylannian."

"Have you met any of the other men here?" Samuel asked.

"No. I've only interacted with my keepers and your wives. My keeper told me there were others. That if I behaved I might get to interact with some of them, eventually."

Samuel nodded, then turned his attention back to Ellith. "At a guess, that means there are at least three other men. Leave them for now, get your team to clean up."

Ellith nodded, then issued hushed orders to the daggerwife team who sprung into action. Samuel was grateful most of the blood ended up on the sheets and not all over the room. Two of his wives bundled up the dead body and disappeared back the way they'd come with her.

"I'm sorry. What are you going to do to me?"

"It's not your fault. None of this is. Don't mention I was here. Bury it in your mind. My wives will only discover this meeting if you let them into your head. If they catch an image of blood and a dead body, hopefully they'll think it was from the war, not from my actions tonight. Don't give my wives an excuse to kill you. Obey them." Samuel snorted in amusement as panic a flashed on the other man's face. "Yes, even to breeding with my wives. If it helps, I haven't even met most of them, let alone bred with them. Some of them will never breed with me, and I certainly don't even remember all of their names."

Samuel gestured to his daggerwives, who descended on Tarkhan and left the man to their care. It was time, more than time, for him to get back to his own place before one of his senior wives woke up and noticed he was missing.

"Was this wise, my king?"

"Probably not, but I had to see it for myself."

"So all of them?"

"All what?"

"All the secondwives, your primewives, and your firstwife. All the senior wives have betrayed you?"

"All of them."

Unaccountably, a wave of support came from Ellith with traces of unwavering support for him and anger towards his senior wives. Now he had an even bigger mess to clean up than he had originally. For himself, he'd been prepared to die. He just had to wait until Jaclyn got here. Yet somehow he now felt responsible for the foreign men his wives had imprisoned and used. He had to try to save them. How he was going to achieve any of it without the bulk of his wives finding out about it was another thing entirely.

SEVENTY-SIX

Giant silk spiders spun their webs. They were like giant nets layered down through the levels of the monarch trees. Samuel hummed, sending thanks to them, and the nearby silk spiders paused in their work, a vibration roughly translating as happiness transmitted back to him. A door slid behind him and he turned as Ellith and her daggerwife team entered. Ellith's face was grave as she closed the distance between them and sank to her knees, her forehead resting on the floor.

"My king, I petition you for a favour," Ellith said.

"What do you need, Ellith?" Samuel asked, frowning at the formality.

"Take me as your bloodwife."

Samuel froze. "Ellith, no. You don't want to be my bloodwife. It will kill you."

"Every daggerwife is aware she might die protecting her husband. As your bloodwife, I can stand between you and the firstwife."

"The Monarch House hasn't had bloodwives since the era of

the Dancing Daggers. My ancestor wiped out half our population before he and his bloodwives died."

"You won't commit such atrocities but with us as your blood-wives, we can stop the firstwife doing so. We can keep you alive and send word for Jaclyn to return."

"We?" Samuel asked, taking in the solemn faces of the daggerwives who ringed the room.

Each of the daggerwives sunk to her knees in front of him, heads bowed.

"Take us to start with and we'll gather more of our fellow wives who are loyal to the Monarch House."

"You do realise I won't come out of this alive, Ellith?"

Ellith reached up and grabbed his hand. "I know. I can't believe your mother, the Queen would scar your mind the way she did. You were a boy."

"Such protections have always been placed in the minds of the males born with the blood of the Monarch House. The old records suggest it's what triggered the Dancing Daggers."

Ellith tugged on his hand, and Samuel knelt in front of her. "Let me help you defend the Throne of a Thousand Islands. Without us, I fear the firstwife will seize the throne. Then she'll send the sister houses to kill Jaclyn. Take me as your bloodwife. It is the only way."

Samuel leant forward and kissed Ellith on the forehead. "I'm sorry Ellith, forgive me for what I do."

"There is nothing to forgive. I observed inconsistencies in how the senior wives behaved that concerned me, but I dismissed them. I told myself I was jealous of their positions." Tears welled in Ellith's eyes. "As a daggerwife, my job is to defend you against all attacks. I failed. I would rather die performing my duty to protect you than fall in ignorance to the blades of traitors."

Samuel placed his hands on either side of Ellith's head. At the sense of calmness and resolve which emanated from her, Samuel settled. Before he could instruct Ellith, her shield dropped, leaving her mind open. Samuel was relieved he could sense nothing but willingness and acceptance from Ellith.

There was no subtly in creating a bloodwife. As he swarmed into Ellith's mind, her eyes barely had time to widen before he seized control of her vocal codes. The scream died on her lips and bounced off the mental shield he wrapped around them both. Then, without caring for any damage he might do to her mind, he bored a one-way control bond into her mind. When he was done the store of the veil within him refilled, flowing from Ellith. Just as he was bursting with energy, his new bloodwife slumped into his arms. At his gesture, two of his daggerwives carried Ellith off to one of the lounges to rest.

Samuel drew his attention to Beth, who took her place in front of him. As soon as Beth dropped her shields, Samuel took over her mind. This time, it was even easier since his power had just been expanded. He didn't even have to think of drawing Ellith's power to aid him in capturing Beth's mind. It flowed into him naturally through the one-way bond he'd just created with her. Ellith had no power to stop him anymore, even if she wanted to. With each bloodwife he created, he would grow stronger. Once they'd recovered, the mind shields of his bloodwives would protect him. Not even his firstwife could harm him without first killing all of his bloodwives.

"It's one reason bloodwives were banned. Bloodwives protect a husband's mind but interfere in the firstwife's control," Ellith said.

Yet another benefit of bloodwives. They were of one mind. So Ellith knew what he was thinking. His bloodwives would fight and react without him having to consciously exert control over them. Samuel didn't even feel drained this time as Beth was taken aside to recover and he gripped the head of the next daggerwife to kneel in front of him. It was going to be a long night, but he had no concern that his senior wives would notice his fatigue and investigate. Soon he would have not only the natural energy stores his own body produced but that of an entire daggerwife team.

CHAPTER
SEVENTY-SEVEN

Michael strode out into the inner courtyard, his focus on Derick, who stood, hands bound behind his back with two of the Unwanted keeping watch over him. A surprisingly short line of others knelt, their arms bound, each with a guard stationed behind them. They were all that was left of what had started as a full warband. Regardless, he was still aware of the faces that peered down from every window that faced this courtyard, from the battlements and towers. Even the courtyard itself was packed with onlookers, and not all of them were his fighting forces. In one corner, a group of villagers who had walked up from Yalleska town stood watching. Next to them, others brought from nearby villages by his forces to be reunited with their children stood witness to the events about to play out.

"Do you think there's anyone in the Stronghold who hasn't turned out to witness this?" Olivia asked.

"Doubtful," Nathanial said.

Michael spared them a glance. "Then they'll soon learn what will happen to them if they turn traitor."

"They already know that part. I think they are waiting to see if you'll do this yourself, or just command someone else to do it," Olivia said.

Michael came to a halt, drawing his sword, ignoring the tense expectations of the spectators.

"You can't do this. I was just doing my duty," Derick said, glancing around at those who watched an air of desperation about him.

"Your duty was to the warlord. You betrayed that trust and turned traitor," Michael said.

"Aiden—"

"Is already dead and if he wasn't, I'd meet out the same justice to him." As a memory surged in Derick's mind, Michael seized control.

Derick uttered a strangled gasp as he attempted to push Michael out of his mind. Michael tightened his control watching as he forced Derick to relive that moment when chaos descended onto the Stronghold. Percussive explosions rang out down the halls, followed by screaming, smoke and the thump of booted feet as people fled down the hallway. Derick pushed people aside as he ran in the opposite direction towards the warlord's private rooms. As he made the top of the stairs, he skidded to a halt. Aiden sprinted towards him, a giant fireball baring down on him. Aiden's head turned as he ran, and he screamed, raising his hands ineffectually as the fireball fuelled by the veil and fury enveloped him. Panic filled Derick's mind as he spun and fled back the way he'd come. As the heat intensified, Derick wrenched open a door and then dived over to the window. Derick fumbled with the catch before giving up and smashing it. The door cracked then burst into flames moments before fire leapt into the room. He climbed out the window and scrambled along the ledge. Derick yelped as fire roared out of the window and singed the soles of his boots.

Satisfied Michael released his prisoner's mind.

Derick's face was pale, and he surged forward. "Who are you to—"

Michael's blade plunged into Derick. He grabbed the man with his other hand, closing the distance between them.

"You, all of you," Michael said, his eyes sweeping over those kneeling nearby, "answer to me. I think you forgot who I am. It was me by the Warlord's side all these years. Me who helped conquer these lands. I may have never wanted it, but on the Warlord's death, all his lands became mine," Michael said, his voice carrying across the courtyard to all those who watched. "Even if you were afraid the Warlord wouldn't believe your testimony against his son, you could have sent word to me. I could have prevented all of this."

Michael withdrew his blade, and he shoved Derick away from him. As the body fell back, Michael swung his sword in an arc, a blue glimmer running down the sword's length as he channelled the veil, slicing through Derick's neck. He glanced up at those who stood on duty behind the other members of Aiden's warband.

"Kill them." Michael snapped.

Blades flashed with brutal efficiency and bodies slumped to the ground as life fled the condemned. Michael turned slowly, surveying those who watched on.

"Is there anyone here who'd care to step forward and dispute my claim?" Michael yelled. His eyes glittered as there was a universal step back from those who watched on. When there was no response, he turned to the single line of band leaders. "Make sure my warbands are ready to ride in the morning. I have a war to fight."

With that order Michael returned to the keep, Tony and a number of his warband following in their self appointed duty to act as protection detail. Numerous eyes followed his progress as he disappeared. As the doors closed behind him, noise erupted outside as everyone started talking at once as if they'd been frightened any noise at all in his presence would draw attention from him that no one wanted. He climbed the stairs to the upper floors two at a time, barely pausing on the first floor before ascending to the next. Even though he'd barely spent much time here over the years, he'd had the same suite of rooms assigned to him from the first time the Warlord had brought him here.

Michael led the way into his rooms. His guards took station outside his door with Olivia and Nathanial following him inside. The pair sat in a couple of the chairs near the window, content to sit quietly while he went into the small wash closet to clean his face and hands.

"How's Damien?" Michael asked as he walked back into the room and collapsed back onto a long couch.

"Recovering," Olivia hesitated, her eyes shadowed, "he's not ready for active duty yet."

"I wasn't thinking of pushing him, more concerned if he'll be ready to ride tomorrow. I don't like to leave him here after what's happened to him," Michael said.

"He'll be able to ride. Between his own natural healing abilities and Kesha, his back along with his other physical injuries have healed. I've got him in with me. He's afraid to go to sleep if he's by himself," Olivia said.

"I don't blame him."

"Kesha tells me Isabella is determined to ride out with us when we leave. Kesha has offered to take charge of her," Nathanial said.

"I wouldn't ask Isabella to stay here either, particularly after what Aiden did to her." Michael grimaced, running his hand through his hair. "We'll head to the Smith's estate to meet up with the rest of our forces. Isabella can remain there when we ride out, as can Damien if he's not cleared by then."

"I'll detail some of Tony's people to act as a guard detail for both of them," Olivia said.

Michael groaned. "I'm not sure exactly how that happened. I just had a guard detail following me around. Go away doesn't seem to aid in getting rid of them."

"Go away didn't work for the Warlord either." Nathanial grinned. "It's your own fault. You're the one who threatened dire things would befall them if they let him order them away."

"If it helps, they're following the pair of us around as well," Olivia said, not quite able to hide her exasperation.

"You know after that little display out there you have no chance of reverting back to what you were?" Nathanial said.

"I only realised I'd laid claim to the domain after the words came out of my mouth," Michael grumbled, throwing a filthy glare in their direction. "Why didn't either of you stop me?"

"Either warlord," Olivia held up her hand, "or king, pick your title before they do it for you, but get used to the idea. You are the ruler of this entire realm."

Michael groaned dramatically and buried his face in his hands.

"King sounds so pretentious."

He couldn't even bring himself to be annoyed as his friends' laughter followed his muttered complaint.

SEVENTY-EIGHT

Damien walked down the corridor between Olivia's and Michael's suites. Two guards positioned outside Michael's rooms were a new development since the execution when Michael had also laid claim to the domain. The guards forestalled Damien having to ask if he could see Michael by opening the doors for him. It surprised him a little. Damien guessed they must have orders to give him access. Damien thanked the guards as he entered. As he expected, he found Michael, Olivia and Nathanial relaxing in leather chairs off to one side of the outer sitting room.

Olivia held out a hand to him and he took it, allowing her to pull him down onto the couch next to her. He sighed as a wash of comfort and peace enfolded around him. Other than his sister and sessions with Kesha, he hadn't mixed with anyone other than these three. He'd been content to mostly keep to himself in Olivia's rooms, grateful Michael was taking a few days to clean things up here at the Stronghold. That at least gave him some time to sort himself out, with Kesha's help. There was no way he wanted to risk Michael deciding he wasn't well enough to ride out with them all.

"Sorry," Damien said.

"For what?" Michael asked.

"That I couldn't bring myself to watch justice being served out to Aiden's men." Flickering images appeared in his mind of the time he'd spent chained in the punishment courtyard. He wished, not for the first time, that the entire episode had been wiped from his memory. "Isabella and I killed some of the guards who came to play the other day but that warband, they were a brutal lot."

"I was aware some of them had some despicable habits. I rejected them from the Unwanted even though some were strong enough, but I had no idea they weren't being kept in line."

"I fear what we will find out about their excesses. It's hard to believe they didn't indulge themselves over the years." Olivia shook her head. "I wish someone had come to us."

"It was Aiden's warband, the Warlords son. Why would anyone have believed that anything would be done about him and his men?" Nathanial asked.

"I fear the Warlord's reputation did us all a disservice in that regard," Michael said.

"Olivia tells me you've given permission for Isabella to accompany us when we leave, at least as far as the Smith's estate. Thank you, I don't think I could bring myself to stay here after what happened, let alone Isabella," Damien said.

"I expect not. She'll be safe with the Smith." Michael paused, and the brush of his power wash over Damien. "I'll reserve my decision regarding if you will ride with us once we leave the Smith's for the battlefront or if you need to stay behind for a time."

Damien wanted to protest, but knew it wouldn't do him any

good. Olivia's fingers brushed his temples, and he allowed her to calm his agitation.

"Fair enough. I've had sessions with Kesha, but it's only been a couple of days." Damien did his best not to let his disappointment show. After all, it was something he expected. "My back has mended. Kesha tells me she didn't really need to do much to help. I levelled up a little during that last transition attack."

"Kesha tells me you're cleared to ride tomorrow. Feel up to it?" Michael asked.

"I can ride and, to be honest, I'll be glad to get out of here. I know Isabella will be as well." Damien half turned before he stopped. "I almost forgot to tell you. Isabella wants to speak with you. She says it's important, but she won't tell me what it's about. She was too nervous to come here to your rooms."

"I'll go drop in on her now," Michael said.

"Thank you. If you'll excuse me, I'll go and pack. Not that I have much."

At Michael's nod, Damien left them all to their plans. There was no way he was admitting he was still feeling a little lethargic after recent events. It might cause Michael to go back on his word and tell him he had to stay here instead of riding out with them.

SEVENTY-NINE

Michael rapped on the door and waited. He smiled as a gentle touch of the veil brushed over him as Isabella checked who was knocking. The door swung open, and Isabella stared up at him before backing up a couple of steps. Michael glanced over, relieved to see Kesha sitting on a chair near the window. He waved his hand for her to stay as she half rose from her seat.

"I'm sorry to intrude Isabella but your brother said that you wanted to talk to me?" Michael said.

"Yes, please come in." Isabella wiped her hands on her trousers, then retreated to sit on a chair near Kesha. She gestured to a vacant seat opposite her own.

Michael closed the door and crossed the room to sink into the indicated chair. He sent a soothing pulse at Isabella and was rewarded as she relaxed incrementally.

"I've approved your request to ride out with the warband when we leave tomorrow."

"Thank you. I couldn't stay here. Not after what happened." Isabella shuddered and turned her head to gaze out the window.

"I don't know how to tell you, but you have the right to know what he did."

"You don't have to confide in me. You're already speaking with Kesha and I'm aware you've been talking with Damien as well."

Isabella's eyes were full as she turned her gaze back to meet his. "No, not about what Aiden did to me. It's about your sister, Nera."

Despite his best efforts Michael stiffened. He increased his mental shield but otherwise tried not to let his shock show. "What about Nera? She died a long time ago."

"I know. Aiden gloated about what he did to Nera. He said I was like her."

Michael's heart twisted. "The Warlord allowed Nera to stay here in the stronghold. She wasn't a fighter like me."

Silence stretched between them as Isabella looked down at her hands, which were gripped tightly in her lap. Kesha's hand rose, her fingers resting lightly on Isabella's shoulder, reassurance flowing between them. Isabella's face was pale as she looked back up at him.

"Nera didn't kill herself."

Despite his control, Michael gasped as Isabella flung her memory at him. Aiden's gloating presence filled his mind. The conversation, complete with Aiden's lust rolled over him. He squeezed his eyes shut for a moment, processing the nightmare his sister's last moments had been. It was bad enough when he believed Nera had taken her own life. This was so much worse.

"If I had Aiden in my hands right now, I'd condemn him to torment for the rest of his life for what he's done. A quick death seems like an easy out." Michael shook himself, struggling to regain control of his emotions. "Thank you for telling me and for dealing with Aiden. I fear I would have become no better than Aiden if his fate was left to me."

"No, you would never be Aiden." Isabella hesitated. "Are we sure he's dead?"

"As far as I can be. I ripped this memory from Derick before I executed the man." Michael shared the moment Derick had seen Aiden being consumed by the fireball Isabella had let loose. Although he carefully edited out the guard's flash of terror. Isabella had her own horrors to deal with without him adding to them. He noted when Isabella relaxed back in her chair, some of the tension she held dissipating.

"The other girls that Aiden took as bed slaves, I've visited them, and Kesha has been treating them as well, but what will happen to them?"

"I've left orders for their care and summoned another healer. She should arrive before nightfall and Kesha will brief her. For those whose parents didn't survive, their long-term care until they come of age will be provided in my name."

"Thank you. It felt wrong to just turn my back and abandon them after all that happened."

"Is there anything else you'd like to know?" Michael asked.

"Not that I can think of."

"You'll be riding in company with Damien and Kesha tomorrow. I've assigned Damien's team, and another team drawn from Tony's warband to the protection detail of the three of you." Isabella's eyes widened at the mention of a protection detail. Although Michael sensed he'd deflected any objection she might have to the precaution by including Kesha and her brother. Michael stood and walked to the door, pausing before he left. "You're welcome to join us for dinner tonight in my sitting room. It's just simple fare with no fuss."

"I didn't have any plans other than to pack. That would be nice if you don't think I'll be in the way."

"Not at all. Damien will be there, and Kesha as well." Michael waved farewell to the women and closed the door behind him.

Michael kept his grief over learning his sister's fate carefully behind his mental shields. Aiden was gone and there was nothing more he could do to avenge Nera's death. He couldn't help Nera, but he could help save many innocent people in this realm who would otherwise die in this war if he didn't join the battlefield. Michael's shoulders straightened as he strode down the hallway. He had a war to fight.

Tarkhan sensed the storm of emotion before his keeper came into his room. That in itself was unusual. On every other occasion she'd come into this room, she'd shown no emotion at all. At least, none that he could sense. He was certain she had feelings. She'd just kept her emotions firmly behind her shields.

"Where's Lana?" The Keeper demanded.

"Who?" Tarkhan asked, concentrating on keeping his mental barrier firmly in place. He was unsettled, but if his keeper sensed it, he hoped she dismissed it thinking it was in reaction to her state of mind. Not the fact he'd had a late-night visit in the king's person who'd killed Lana without blinking.

"The wife you were breeding with last night." The Keeper's eyes flashed in annoyance.

"I don't know. She's not here," Tarkhan said, rather proud of himself that both statements he'd just made were true. It was one of those interesting facts about being able to sense people's thoughts and emotions. If she caught anything, he hoped she'd hear the truth behind his words. Rather than get suspicious and dig for what he was hiding.

"No one can find her," the keeper said.

"Not all the women you have me breed with are terribly talkative. They certainly don't confide all their plans to me."

The keeper's eyes widened, outrage coming from her in waves. Then, as suddenly as her annoyance had peaked, it fled, and she threw her head back and laughed. Tarkhan breathed a sigh of relief. For a moment, he'd wondered if his keeper was about to punish him.

"I'm sorry Tarkhan. You're right. I don't know why I even entertained the idea you might have something to do with Lana's disappearance. You may have been a warrior in your previous life, but your conduct has been exemplary of late."

"I've worked out that it makes my life a little easier when I do as I'm told. Besides, you don't even allow me to possess eating implements, let alone weapons."

Tarkhan didn't think it prudent to mention he didn't particularly need a weapon to kill someone. He may not be as proficient as some warriors at unarmed combat, but he had learned the skill and other forms of combat. He couldn't have been a wolf warrior without a broad fighting skill set, let alone the co-leader. The most debilitating thing he'd faced that kept him off balance and unable to even think straight, let alone fight, was the constant mental manipulation. Most days his mind was assaulted, dominated by the will of the keeper or one of the others that surrounded him every waking moment he had. They were never far away. The new thing was memories of his mother and father, their dishonour and death. It was a certainty that his keeper was conditioning him to separate his feeling of being of the clans and feeling a kinship with Sylannians instead. Tarkhan paused, preventing his eyes from widening through sheer willpower alone. For the first time since the Sylannians had captured him, there wasn't a continuous flow of compulsion urging him to calm acceptance.

Something had changed. Not only was that all pervasive whispering absent, but there was also far less random mental chatter than he'd become accustomed to. A sense of agitation vibrated through the air.

EIGHTY-ONE

Michael sat easily in his saddle, not betraying even a hint of his frustration at their slow pace. It at least allowed him to communicate with everyone he needed to while they rode.

"How's Ben? Everything still going to plan?" Olivia asked.

Olivia's knowledge of exactly who he had been speaking to didn't surprise Michael at all.

"More rested than he has been. Adam made it back to his father's estate a few days ago. Adam and Lukas are combining to give Ben a strength boost."

"It worked? I know I suggested it was worth a try, but I'm still shocked," Nathanial said.

"It does. Between the three of them, they have a vastly boosted reach. They tell me our forces have settled in and Taya will have a briefing for us when we get there."

"Your brother and Evan?" Olivia asked, concern colouring her tone. "I don't like either of them, but from all reports, they've both risked their lives to help and pass on what information they could."

"Nothing, and even with the extra strength, Ben can't get through to either of them. I vetoed the idea that Ben and Adam could lead a team back through the tunnels of my family estate." Michael shook his head, deliberately pushing his concern aside.

"If they're dead, then getting ourselves killed just to find out wouldn't do any good," Nathanial said.

"If they're alive but cut off as Ben suspects, then we'll get to them soon enough," Olivia said, sending a wave of reassurance to him.

The three of them settled into an easy silence until one of the outriders rode up, making those around him tense.

"There are riders, a lot of them, coming from the high road," the outrider said.

"There's not much out that way," Olivia said.

"Just a few small, scattered villages," Nathanial said.

Michael was about to call the alert when a scout called back.

It looks like the clans that settled in the heights, lots and lots of them. Hold on, a couple of ours are with them.

Michael acknowledged the message as Nathanial passed the information back, and the tension in the warbands decreased. As they came around a bend in the road they were following, he saw a mass of riders where the roads intersected.

"Khaliun, it seems like you've got the bulk of your people with you," Michael said.

"I have all that remains of what was Kallith clan with me," Khaliun said, her face clouding, eyes refusing to meet his own. "I'll explain later."

"When you're ready," Michael said, knowing better than to push an issue, Khaliun wasn't ready to discuss.

With little effort, the two groups merged, and they continued on their way together. Michael signalled to the others and spurred his horse on. They wouldn't reach their destination by sitting around on the side of the road chatting.

"There's far more of them than I expected," Olivia said.

"I know. She also has the healers, Narantua and Yangir with her, but also children and those who don't have the markings of the fighter," Michael said.

"Bringing their non-fighters and children with them towards possible danger, that's unusual, right?" Nathanial asked.

"Kallith clan's healer died of old age at their oasis during the war. It surprises me they've come even if they wouldn't normally be strong enough to put into seclusion. The children, those clearly not fighters, yes that's unusual. By custom, they'd normally keep their vulnerable as far away from trouble as they could."

"They could stay back at the Smith's estate while the fighting units go forward to the battle lines. Fall back with our own people if it proves necessary?" Olivia asked.

"If needed, it shouldn't be that much more hassle than moving our own non-combatants. Probably easier. The Kallith has practiced packing up and moving in face of an invasion more than our own. I'm more concerned about the why."

"It feels like they've faced death. They mourn but have a fierce resolve," Nathanial said as he scanned the ranks of the Kallith.

"Disagreements of the clan leaders that can't be resolved can lead to what they call a fracturing of the clan. If that has occurred, the Kallith Clan is no more. With no more functional clans to turn to, the People are no more." Michael said, recalling knowledge of the People's traditions that were not his own but a product of sharing way too much when he and Khaliun linked minds to learn each other's language.

"Just what you need, another problem to solve," Nathanial said, his tone bright and cheery.

Michael threw a disgusted glance at Nathanial, then rolled his eyes, but refused to take the bait and whine about why it was his problem. If anything, if his guess proved to be correct and the Kallith clan had fractured, then they were his problem. Even more so than they had been to start with.

EIGHTY-TWO

Tarkhan calmed his mind and breathing with effort. It wouldn't do for this woman he'd just bred with, or his keepers, to sense his agitation. He'd kept it buried deep down inside himself since his keeper had revealed his heritage. Or at least what she believed his heritage to be. Now that he wasn't subject to the constant compulsions, he could think clearly for the first time since his capture. That allowed him the clarity to examine the memories he had of his mother and compare them to the ones they'd shown him.

They didn't match.

The mother they showed him had bare skin without a single tattoo, not even the clan tattoo everyone bore. It was unheard of. In the memories the keeper had shown him, he remembered little about his mother or his father. Other than what he'd been told his whole life, they both died when he was a child for some infraction against Kallith Clan. No one ever shared with him what they'd done. It was taboo to speak of things. By clan belief, they'd paid their debt with their lives.

Yet what Tarkhan remembered about his parents when his

keeper wasn't here was different. One point of difference was the mother in his memories had clan tattoos. He'd only been a child, but his parents hadn't died in shame. The leaders of the tribe had sat him down and explained to him that his parents had been killed while returning from a trading mission. A freak storm had hit the caravan. A deluge of rain caused the road they'd been travelling on to collapse. Everyone in the trade contingent, including his parents, had tumbled down the side of the mountain to their death.

It was frustrating that he had emotions tied to both sets of events, and the more he picked at the memories, it stirred up greater confusion. Yet he suspected the keeper had concocted this whole thing. He just couldn't work out why.

He wanted to hate Samuel for the invasion the king ordered on the People. Yet if the keeper was to be believed, it seemed they were related. So the Sylannians were his people too. Tarkhan squeezed his eyes shut before he took a steadying breath. He didn't understand the politics behind what was happening to him, but there was perhaps one man who could unravel the knots tied in the web he was caught in.

Samuel?

Tarkhan held his breath and waited. Not daring to call again in case the hundreds of wives that stood between him and the king overheard his call.

Tarkhan? I told you not to contact me like this. It's dangerous, you could have found yourself talking with the other me. I'm fairly certain that version of me would have no hesitation in ordering your death.

Tarkhan caught the image of Samuel standing by the open windows of his bedroom suite, looking out over the canopy of his island home. As Samuel faced his bed, Tarkhan caught the image of the wife Samuel was with that night sleeping soundly in a mess of silks and pillows.

I'm sorry, I know what they told me the other day is important, I just don't understand the politics at play but I fear what this means for us both even if I don't know why.

Samuel's attention shifted. *What did they tell you? Show me.*

The order in Samuel's tone was unmistakable. Even though in his other life Tarkhan might have rebelled at complying, now he replayed the entire memory. He literally threw it at the king. Both of them, the childhood the keeper had shown him with the stark contrast to the one he remembered when his keeper wasn't with him. Then, as an afterthought, he threw in the moment he'd discovered he could control the spidersilk, which his keepers seemed to think was critically important. The silence stretched between them as Samuel stood frozen. Then the king's focus sharpened and Tarkhan sensed the king's presence as if the man was looming over him.

So, they want you to believe you are my cousin. Do you really not understand?

Tarkhan swallowed. *No. The whole thing is making my head space a jumbled mess. I was not born into this world. I am adrift, desperately trying to keep my head above water.*

The silence stretched between them again and Tarkhan waited, accepting the king's regard, as the man weighed up his response.

My firstwife is pregnant with a child, from her breeding with you. So she told me.

Your life, my life, will be safe until she gives birth. If the son she bears is born healthy and whole, our days will be numbered.

You mean she'll have us both killed? Why? I don't understand.

Because through the child she has a legitimate claim to the throne, for the good of Sylanna, in trust for her child. Or so she will convince everyone. The confusion in your mind is because of the keeper layering another version of your life over your original memories. Eventually, you will forget who you were and believe the version of you they have implanted in your memory is the only one that exists.

Chelsie will try to not only deny Jaclyn the throne, but attempt once more to eradicate the threat she poses during the purge she will initiate.

Tarkhan mulled over what Samuel told him.

But what of all the children she's had with you? If she was going to kill you, why hasn't she done so already? Besides, she slept with you as well. The child might be yours.

There's no chance the child was conceived while my firstwife was breeding with me. I'm sterile. We took the throne, for the good of Sylanna, to preserve it until Jaclyn grew of age. Chelsie supported what we did back then. We should have stood aside years ago.

But, there are children, your children in the monarch house. I remember the keeper telling me so.

They did to me what they are trying to do to you, except it was easier for my wives to achieve since I am mind bonded to them. I'd forgotten it was impossible for me to have children for the longest time. Chelsie imprinted another version of events on my mind and made me forget. When I finally remembered, I didn't know where the children might have come from. Except that you, someone like you, must exist. So, rather foolishly, I went looking for you.

I'm sorry.

This was not your doing. Try to hold on to the memories, the real ones of your mother and father. Of who you were. They will find it much more difficult to erase the real you because they haven't mind bonded you yet. Do everything they command of you. Breed with my wives. Anything you need to do in order to live, do it. Give Jaclyn time, she will come. Then prostrate yourself at Jaclyn's feet and beg your new queen to save your life.

Jaclyn? Your sister? Won't she save you too?

It is impossible now. My fate is sealed, yours is not. Remember, comply with everything my wives demand of you and beg for Jaclyn's mercy when she comes. Tell her everything. It is your only hope.

What do you think your sister will do with me?

I don't know for certain, but she will not be unkind and you will have a much better life with her than with my wives.

Jaclyn will not free me? Even if I beg her for mercy?

No. You can control the spidersilk. That means you are a male child with Sylannian heritage who survived the purge. Potentially even the heritage my wives are trying to impress on you, but which they find they have no proof of. Now that you have been reclaimed, your place is here. You've already proven you are fertile, siring both male and female children on my wives. Your role in this life is to breed for the good of Sylanna. Accept it. Go to Jaclyn's bed and breed with her willingly, if she asks it of you. Or with whoever she tells you to. Jaclyn will ensure you are looked after for the rest of your life. You will never be a wolf warrior of the Kallith again. That life is over. For Jaclyn to take you into her household is the best you can hope for. Samuel hesitated before continuing. *For what it is worth, I'm sorry. This is not a life you ever could have foreseen.*

Tarkhan expelled a pent-up breath as the king's presence faded, the man's words sinking in. He didn't understand these people. No matter how he tried to prevent it, the dual images of his mother flashed in his mind. The pure blood Sylannian woman and the woman of the clans. Yet even he had to admit he could see signs in her that could be said to be characteristic of a Sylannian. There was also the issue that no one else back home could learn the trick of commanding the spidersilk. No matter how hard they listened or how hard they tried. He didn't believe the keeper's version of who his mother had been, yet it seemed an inescapable fact that she'd had Sylannian blood. The more he learned about Sylannian culture, the more it horrified him.

The night Samuel had appeared in his room and the dagger-wife had brutally murdered the woman in his bed, one of Samuel's wives, Tarkhan had to admit to himself he'd been terrified. He also wasn't stupid. The daggerwife had clearly killed the woman in his bed on the king's orders. Samuel had ordered the death of his own wife without waiting to hear her side of the story. Still, if he had to pick a side in this war, he found himself mixed up in, he'd pick Samuel. If anything, he was feeling a little sorry for the king. At least Tarkhan had grown up free. Made his own choices and regardless of how they'd turned out, they'd been his moments. His choices. At least before the war had interrupted everything and turned his world upside down. Although he'd only met the king in person briefly under difficult circumstances but unlike the king, he'd actually had the chance to explore and enjoy all life offered. Much more so than the king, or any Sylannian born male, ever had.

Prior to him being brought here, he'd always assumed the Sylannians saw him, all the People, as lesser. So it had confused him why Chelsie, the king's firstwife, had bred with him so persistently. After Samuel's explanation, he understood. Chelsie intended to overthrow the Sylannian royal family and supplant it with her own son. To start her own dynasty, and she was planning on using him to do it. Yet on the birth of that child he would become surplus to requirement.

As the woman next to him stirred, Tarkhan pushed his thoughts aside. He would follow Samuel's advice. He would be the perfect Sylannian male and give them everything they wanted from him. At least on the surface. As Samuel had advised, he'd bury his emotions deep in his mind. Tarkhan surprised even himself with his desire to live. They played a game with him. Perhaps it was time for the wolf warrior of the Kallith to start playing his own game. As the woman's eyes opened and focused on him, he pushed his own pulse of playful delight at her to be rewarded by her chuckle.

"Want to try that again before my keepers drag you from my bed?" Tarkhan asked.

EIGHTY-THREE

Michael dismounted, looking up at the ancient house. Unlike many where you could see the faint trace work of power from a long-dead master, this one was overlayed with new power. It glowed. At least it did for anyone who had the talent to check for it. Michael grinned as Adam crossed the yard and embraced his long-time friend.

"Only a fool would try to take this place," Nathanial said as he gazed up at the house.

"Unless you were a Rathadon warlord," Olivia said.

"Granted, it was a rather terrifying Rathadon who went on to become the first Rathadon warlord, but he never took the residence. He didn't have to. Michael's ancestor and his fellow slaves didn't have a scrap of metal on them when they attacked our ancestor, the Smith Lord. They took him captive when he was on the road between the mines and his house," Colin said absently as he greeted his brother.

"Then ensured the loyalty of our house by taking the former Smith Lord's daughter as his wife and allowing our forefather to keep status, including the residence," Adam said.

"Which makes us family if a little bit removed," Colin said.

Nathanial and Olivia traded looks between him and the twins, astonishment radiating from them. Michael had almost forgotten they didn't know all the family history. In his mind, they'd all been together so long, they were family. A slow smile spread across his face, and he shrugged.

"They're right."

"The more I learn about your ancestors, the more I understand how they rose to prominence," Nathanial said.

"They weren't just brutes who happened to be insanely strong with the veil. Trust me, they would have given the Warlord pause," Michael said.

"By all accounts, Michael's ancestors had brains as well, which made them even more terrifying," Adam said.

Michael spotted Harry dismounting with his warband off to one side.

"Harry." Michael called out, waiting until the warband leader closed the distance between them. "Consult with the Smith's staff and bed down the warbands around the back. Then find Taya. I'll want a briefing before nightfall with a full war planning session tomorrow morning."

"Yes, your Majesty," Harry said, then turned, issuing instructions to his seconds as he went back to the gathered fighters.

Michael sighed. He'd mistakenly thought if he ignored the title, it would go away. At Olivia's open amusement, Michael rolled his eyes, then thanked the staff member who ran forward, taking the reins off him.

"Gavrel bed the Unwanted down..." Olivia glanced at the twins

"Second floor, as usual," Adam said. "The staff aired out those rooms, anticipating your arrival the other day. Back entrance is open."

"Usual wing Gavrel. Damien and Isabella will be with us on

the third floor. So if you could detail someone to take care of their gear?" Olivia asked.

Michael waited long enough for Damien to join them as he guided his sister between the ranks of milling fighters in their direction.

"Who lives here?" Isabella asked.

"The Smith, don't worry, you'll like him. He's Colin's father and Adam, there is Colin's twin," Damien said.

Michael smiled faintly at the hint of awe that seeped from Isabella's shield as she stared up at the house. As soon as the brother and sister had joined them, Michael crossed the open cobbled courtyard towards the house and then went up the stairs. Just as his hand reached out, the doors opened as if of their own volition. Of course, they could all open doors. It was just a different application of power. In the case of those with the affinity for metal, it was like it called to them. He raised his eyebrows at the twins.

Adam shook his head. "Father."

They were no sooner through the doors than the Smith appeared, coming into the hallway from the sitting room. Michael held back to give the Smith a chance to greet Colin, but it seemed the man had different ideas as the Smith turned to him.

"Come here, boy." The Smith pulled him into a hug and whispered. "I'm sorry about the Warlord."

"No, you're not," Michael said.

"No, I'm not, but I am sorry for you all the same. I know what he meant to you." The Smith pushed him back and looked at him. "He could be a cruel and unforgiving man, but he did more to pull this domain together than any other. Despite everything he was, the fear people had of him, the common folk ended up living free lives in relative peace. More so than any other period in our history."

The Smith turned and greeted both Olivia and Nathanial as well before leading them all into the sitting room.

~

DAMIEN HUNG BACK as the others greeted two other men at the far end of the room. As one of the men turned his head, Damien's eyes widened in shock. While he didn't remember much about the kidnapping in Callenhain, he recognised that man as being confined in the basement with both him and Kesha. Olivia noticed his hesitation and grinned, waving him over to join them.

"I don't think you've been officially introduced, but I believe you've met Lukas in that mess in Callenhain," Olivia said.

Damien nodded at Lukas, who grinned at him.

"Remind me to give you some lessons on how to pick locks when we all have some time," Lukas said.

A chuckle escaped Damien's mouth, and he grinned at Lukas. "Thanks. It might be useful since people keep insisting on chaining me up."

Olivia clapped the solid-looking man next to her on the shoulder. "This is Ben."

Ben nodded a greeting at him.

"Rooms have been prepared for you all on the upper floor," The Smith said, then glanced past him. "This would be your sister that I've heard so much about Damien?"

Damien turned and reached out a hand to Isabella, who'd hung back near the door. With a barely perceptible pause, Isabella crossed the distance between them and smiled uncertainly at everyone.

"This is Isabella."

Isabella greeted everyone in turn as they introduced themselves.

"You'll want to rest after the ride today I'm sure, but while I'm told you'll be staying with me here, I'll still have some protective gear altered to fit you just in case," the Smith said.

"Thank you," Isabella said.

"Come Isabella, let's leave them all to catch up and talk war and go find our rooms," Kesha said, taking Isabella in hand and guiding her back towards the door they'd entered.

Damien sent a brief pulse of reassurance at Isabella as she hesitated and twisted around to stare back at him.

"Go, get some rest. I'll be doing the same shortly. I promise you I won't be going anywhere for the evening except to soak in a bath and then to bed."

After a brief hesitation, Isabella nodded and allowed Kesha to lead her out of the room.

"You'll stick to the estate and immediate grounds until Kesha fully clears you," Michael said, holding Damien's gaze until he nodded. "No training either."

"Of course." Damien took in the luxury of the room with the scattered chairs adorned with plump cushions, plush rugs on the floors and hangings on the walls and shrugged. "I don't think staying here is going to be uncomfortable."

He didn't have to pretend to be at ease since he was more than confident that Kesha would clear him. The low level exhaustion that had plagued him like a hangover after his excessive use of the veil in the Stronghold had lifted. Damien judged the fatigue he had now was only what everyone felt after a hard day's ride. If anything, he was feeling much better than he ever had.

Adam entered the room, his face lighting up with a smile as he greeted everyone before he passed a bundle of clothes to Damien, complete with a pair of soft house shoes.

"Take these. I figured you could use a few changes of clothes. These are somewhat tight on me but will be loose and comfortable on you. Besides, if you aren't in your uniform, you'll be less likely to forget you are convalescing."

"Thank you, but I'm sure my regular clothes will be fine." Damien tried to hand the clothes back, only for Adam to grin at him and shake his head.

"Honestly Damien, take them. It's not like Adam's going to miss them. He might be my twin, but he's a clothes horse. He has a wardrobe that would make anyone who had to attend a function at the Rathadon or Strafford estates giddy with envy," Colin said.

"Who said the only ones who should be well dressed are those who frequent the high estates of the Straffords or Rathadons?" Adam asked, his eyebrows rising.

"Make that the Rathadon estate functions. Callenhains fashion sense is terrible," Olivia said, then she brushed Damien's arm. "Go, I know you're tired. I'll be up soon."

Damien ducked his head, then excused himself. He'd almost felt obliged to say he was fine. He had been moments before, but now that they'd stopped, exhaustion was weighing him down. While he might be better than he had been in a long time, he still didn't have his stamina back. All he wanted was to get clean and crawl into a comfortable bed. It seemed for the first time in his life, after being chained up in a cold, hard courtyard, prey to the elements and the abuse of those who held him, he now had a thing to be clean and comfortable.

EIGHTY-FOUR

Steven turned expectantly to face the door. He could sense it was Jaclyn who approached even before the door opened. His heart ached as she closed the distance between them. For all that the wives shielded his mind, the devastating mourning the house had sunk into had still filtered through. It had taken a couple of days, but finally the underwives had told him the events that had occurred. The fate that had met the children of the house had shocked him to his core. He wrapped his arms around Jaclyn and tried to comfort her as best he could.

Jaclyn kissed him lightly, not even attempting to hide the loss that weighed on her heart and gestured to the Sylannian who'd come into his room with her. It had taken him some time to work out the patterns on the silks of the Sylannians, but even though he'd never met or seen this wife, by the markings on her silks, she was one of his primewives just like Myra. He hadn't even known there was another primewife.

"Steven, this is Primewife Liliana. It will be some months before the underwives declare her fit so she can breed with you but she will ensure you are cared for during my absence," Jaclyn said.

Liliana approached him. Her hand rose and stroked his temple. The gentle brush of her power over him caused him to gasp as he gazed into her eyes.

"We will have plenty of time to get to know each other before I come to your bed, husband," Liliana said.

Steven swallowed, his mouth suddenly dry. "I look forward to spending time with you Liliana." Steven blushed as he realised he faintly regretted that Liliana wouldn't be in his bed tonight and she'd caught his desire. Then he recalled Jaclyn's words and Steven swung around to Jaclyn. "You're leaving?"

"I am. I will take several new villages into my territory. From the maps and details on them, they are small and it shouldn't take me long."

Steven felt guilty that all he'd been thinking about was breeding with Liliana when Jaclyn was talking about progressing with her war campaign in his homeland.

"You'll try not to kill too many of my people? Please? The villages surrounding Vallantia are farming villages. They and the people who live there are no threat to us."

Jaclyn smiled faintly at his use of the word 'us'. It confused Steven that he now meant it, yet Vallantia and the people here were his people to protect as much as possible.

"The land and the people are valuable. As long as they don't fight back, the locals will be collared and then put to work. Their lives won't change as much as you imagine, husband. By contrast, you have faced more upheaval than they will."

"It might help my guilty conscious to think so, but I'm not sure that's true."

"I wouldn't lie to you. The only difference to those who live in the farming villages is they will owe their allegiance to me instead of the Warlord. They will number among the collared, of course, but that can't be helped."

"They'll be slaves."

"We don't use that word but, yes. They'll be slaves. It is our way, but fear not. That isn't a fate that will ever await you."

Steven had no choice but to relax as a pulse of comfort flooded his mind from Liliana. He'd forgotten her fingers still rested on his temple.

"Come, it's time we got to know each other," Liliana said and grabbing his hand she led him over to one of the lounging couches.

"All going well, I won't be gone long, so don't fret Steven. I'll leave you in Liliana's capable hands. Do your best to follow her instructions and treat everything she says as if it was coming from me," Jaclyn said.

"Yes Jaclyn," Steven whispered. Dread filled him as she walked towards the door. "Jaclyn, please, you don't need to do this. I was a fool most of my life, but if you go up against Michael, you'll lose. Even after all of this, he'll understand your situation—"

"Hush husband. You'll see everything will work out. This isn't the first time we've conquered another land," Liliana said, her fingers stroking his temple and with them reassurance flowed into him.

As the door closed and Jaclyn disappeared from view, Steven had the sinking feeling he'd never see her again.

EIGHTY-FIVE

As Nathanial gazed pointedly back towards the manor house, Michael glanced over his shoulder to see Ben, the twins, and Lukas weaving their way through the milling fighters of the massed warbands. All four of them dressed and armed for a fight. The fact they were each leading a horse as well caused his eyes to narrow.

"Where do you four think you're going?" Michael asked.

"Fairly certain you already know that part," Lukas said.

"We can argue about it first if it makes you happy, though," Ben said.

"You know we're only ensuring the forest here is clear of enemy forces to ensure the estate is secure. Then we'll be back to plan the next stage," Michael said.

"We know but since Ben and I are part of the reason the Sylannians are in the forest we decided to come and help kill them off," Lukas said.

Michael realised his jaw was clenched and made an effort to relax. "Why is it of late everyone keeps arguing with me?"

"You're not the warleader anymore," Adam said.

"It's what happens when you become the supreme leader," Colin said.

"Now that's a title that has a ring to it," Adam said.

"Why thank you, I thought so," Colin said.

"All right, you two," Michael grumbled.

The twins, for their part, just stood there to all appearances in wide-eyed innocence, which made him chuckle under his breath. He shook his head as the brothers shared identical triumphant grins with each other. Then held out their hands to Ben and Lukas, who laughed and handed over a handful of coins to each from their belt pouches.

"We told you we could make him laugh," Colin said.

"You doubted the twin's abilities?" Olivia's eyebrows rose.

"That was foolish," Nathanial said.

"Enough, mission successful."

"Yes, all mighty one..." Ben ducked, laughing as Michael took a swipe in his direction, landing solidly on his shoulder.

"You four are going to insist on coming with us, aren't you?" Michael asked.

"We are, but as I said, we can argue about it if you want," Ben said.

Nathanial and Olivia traded glances with each other, then turned their attention back at the group of friends. He could sense them appraising the four of them. Finally, they both shrugged.

"Realistically, the four of them have been unofficial members of the Unwanted for a long time, even if others didn't know it," Olivia said.

"They were the first recruited into our little group," Nathanial said.

"They've been doing well in our absence. If you didn't think they were capable, you wouldn't have been confiding in them or relying on them all these years." Olivia reasoned.

Michael nodded, then turned back to look at his friends, assessing each of them in turn.

"You two trouble makers ride with Nathanial, Lukas, stick on Olivia and Ben. You are with me." Michael ordered.

All four nodded. Michael decided to ignore the satisfaction coming from them. After all, Olivia and Nathanial were correct. These four friends of his had always been in his confidence, even before there was an Unwanted. The Warlord had known about them but left them in position. Although it had taken some fast talking. It was when his idea of the communication relay and the information network had been born. Somehow, the Warlord had agreed with him it might be useful. Of course, then he'd had to scramble to turn the half-baked idea into a reality. These four had been the core of it and ran the network, expanding it beyond what even his fast talking had envisioned.

He patted his horse on the side of the neck, then swung up into his saddle. At that unspoken order, everyone hastened to mount their horses. At a glance from Nathanial directing his attention over to Taya where she waited, Michael clamped his mouth closed on any other objections.

"Stay safe, all of you," Michael said.

Without another word, he urged his horse into a walk over towards where Harry, with his warband, waited. Ben and the smaller team of the Unwanted that would ride with him followed. Olivia and Nathanial split up and moved over to the warbands they'd been assigned to. They had smaller groups assigned to each of the other bands, although the three of them would pull the bulk of the fighting.

"When you're ready, Taya," Michael said.

Taya smiled faintly then straightening scanning the massed fighters. Each of them had been briefed on their tasks. All that remained was for them to kick off. Taya held up her hand and called the order for them to ride out. Michael spurred his horse along with Harry and his warband as they rode towards the trees at the top of the hill. As the warband shuffled around him, Michael clamped his mouth shut against an objection. It was a recent phenomenon that occurred no matter who he rode with. The warband seemed to shuffle around him, so that he rode in towards the centre of their ranks. By preference he led, he'd never been the one to sink back into the protective folds of fighters around him. Michael was gaining an appreciation of why the Warlord would grumble.

As they drew closer to the tree line, they pulled to a halt and dismounted. From here for the next stage, they would be on foot. The forest was too thick to fight in from horseback. He handed his reins off to one of the stable hands who'd ridden with them this far as he raced forward to grab them and led it off. There was no milling about or waiting Michael reached out, checking on each of the members of the Unwanted who'd ridden with him first as they took their own positions scattered within the ranks of Harry's warband. Michael drew his secondary sword, much shorter and more useful for fighting at close quarters. As it would be if any of their enemy got close to him. Besides that, it was far more effective a weapon to use here in the forest than when he was fighting out in the open. He raised his protective shields, then expanded them like a bubble to encompass those around him. The other Unwanted did likewise. Their shields overlapped as they expanded so they covered the entire warband.

"Remember, don't get drawn away from the group. The Unwanted can't protect us effectively if we aren't close enough to them," Harry said.

It only took a rudimentary scan with his othersight to dismiss the life signs of the animals, small or otherwise, to locate their first group of enemies. Bigger prey stood out in his mind's eye with a much bigger glowing mass. It appeared like the intelligence gathered by the scouts Taya had sent out prior to his arrival was correct. Pockets of Sylannians riddled this forest.

First cluster off to the left, Michael said.

Along with the words, Michael sent a burst to the scouts in front of their group so they could see what he'd seen. They acknowledged what he'd sent to them silently and altered the direction they led the group in. The lead scout held up their hand, calling for caution. Everyone set eyes on Harry, who, with a few quick gestures, set their own fighting band in motion. At sounds of fighting off to their far left, the enemy they were about to engage spun in that direction.

Attack! Harry ordered.

Their forces ran forward, falling on their enemy from behind. While many of the Sylannians turned to face them, drawing their blades as they did so. It was near on impossible to run up on them in a forest without them knowing about it. Some did not, and those fell without having a chance to draw their weapons. Once they'd closed in on the Sylannian fighting group, Michael kept himself focused. He couldn't afford to get lost in battle. In this, his job wasn't just to use his powers to fight and protect himself, but those who fought nearest to him. They in turn had to trust that his mental shields and thrusts shunting the enemy aside at need would be there to assist them while they fought as well.

Michael pulled the veil into himself as he ran through the trees. Not only from around himself but the trees, ground and the very air in his vicinity. This way, he'd be at full power if he needed it. If he or the Unwanted he led waited to draw in extra power when they needed it, they risk a rupture in the veil. If that happened, they'd probably lose control and, while it would undoubtedly be effective, he'd rather have conscious control of the events that unfolded. They'd found the Sylannians were scattered throughout this forest like an infestation, and they'd been battling them this way, hit and run for the last week. It had taken concerted effort and searching, but their scouts had finally located the camp where the Sylannians had been coming from. A clearing deep in the heart of this forest.

They should be just up ahead, Shallan said.

Michael concentrated some more and switched to his other-sight and saw the tell-tale signs of people ahead. Lots of people, far more than the groups they'd been battling all week.

I see it. Is everyone in position? Michael asked.

We're in position on the other side, Taya said.

Taya is meant to be commander, remember? Olivia said.

You hated it when the Warlord did that to you, Nathanial said.

All right, all right. Michael heard the half grumble in his tone and grinned. *When you're ready, Taya.*

Michael sensed the surge of shock from Taya. It took a moment; he gathered she was still coming to terms with him throwing the control over to her. The warband around him stilled, all of them waiting for the order to go. While they'd been fighting all week, their groups had been fighting as separate units until now.

Let's get this done. Remember your positions and move in, Taya ordered.

Michael barely paid attention to the affirmations from the other leaders as he drew in the veil and ran with the warband around him. With his senses hyper aware, he could see their units converging in on the Sylannian camp from all directions. The Sylannians had nowhere to run. Nowhere to hide. He sensed the moment the Sylannians became aware of their presence. As his ranks broke through the trees and fell on the enemy's camp, Michael blocked out all concerns except his own part and that of the people he led. By the time the Sylannians realised they were surrounded and under attack, it was too late for them to flee as his warbands all converged on this camp from all directions.

With all the Unwanted drawing and using their power, it came from everywhere at once, making it impossible to pinpoint a location. They came from all directions since once again, instead of fighting as a unit, the Unwanted had split into their small teams to support the other warbands that rode with them in this battle. Michael channelled more power into his shields, expanding them to help protect those around him.

Although it went against his instinct, he was at the rear of his own group as they fought. It made it easier for him to see and protect the members of the warband around him. Seeing Harry misstep and stumble on the uneven ground and one of the Sylannians instantly launched a flurry of strikes, Michael hauled in more power and shunted it at the attacker. The enemy was flung back into an unbroken line of other Sylannians who tumbled back in a mass of limbs.

"Watch it Harry, if you keep trying to get yourself killed this early on, I'll get very angry with you," Michael said.

Michael lunged forward as another group of the enemy ran forward screaming their hollering cries as their blades flashed.

"Thanks, I'll try my best not to do that," Harry said.

"Don't worry about Michael. He gets testy during a fight," Ben said.

"Huh!"

Michael ignored the efforts of the others to keep him behind their own lines and kept his focus on trying to keep those who fought around him alive. He suddenly had an appreciation for how the Warlord must have felt during battle. Being smothered by the layers of people around him as if he was incompetent on the battlefield was irritating.

Get used to it, my friend, Ben said.

What if I don't want to get used to it?

That's not how this works. You're the natural successor of the Warlord and all your people care about you.

As a Sylannian charge threatened to break their defensive line, Michael sent a burst of power at them. Michael staggered as they came to a halt, twisting around to see only a few fights were still ongoing. He sucked in air, grateful that everyone else with him did so as well.

Fighting this way is harder, Olivia said.

Much harder, Nathanial said.

So it's not just me? Michael said.

No, we're going to have to come up with something else, Olivia said.

I don't like it, but you're right. We've done too many days like this. If we keep it up, we're all going to collapse, Michael said.

Michael refrained from pointing out this was only the beginning. It was a fact that all of them were well aware of. While they'd all known this style of fighting would be draining for them, he didn't think they'd realised how exhausting it would be. Somehow, protecting not only himself but an entire warband at the same time was far harder than just looking after his own personal shields.

EIGHTY-SIX

Michael rested back in his chair, staring up at the roof, allowing the conversation to flow around him. He didn't even try to pretend that fatigue wasn't catching up with him. Which was a bad sign. If that deep, bone aching exhaustion was creeping up on him, it was that much worse for the rest of the Unwanted. It wasn't arrogance. It was a simple truth that he was the strongest of them. While this battle against Sylanna was going well, it was too drawn out for the Unwanted to keep up this pace. Unlike the decisive win in Callenhain, this fight was slow, which was the enemy of all his people but of the Unwanted in particular. The sheer level of energy they'd been channelling day after day was adding up. Where the Unwanted came into their own were those short, sharp, decisive blows that drove a wedge into the opposing forces, allowing the other warbands to finish the job.

Unfortunately, where the seemingly endless wall of Sylannians faltered and cracked, other blades replaced those of the fallen. It was that niggling little thing he'd known about their fighting style that hadn't quite surfaced before he'd seen it in play at this level. They were stronger in the veil and better fighters overall, but the Sylannians outnumbered them. This group they faced was not nearly as incompetent as those they'd faced in Callenhain to make the advantage of their greater numbers negligible.

"The Unwanted are our biggest asset, but we need to rest your people, more than we are. That includes you, I know you can't keep this up," Taya said.

"You won't do any of us any good if you all get yourself killed," Harry said.

"I don't think you'll have to worry about that. It's more likely they'll just collapse and sink into unconsciousness until they've healed or whatever it is their bodies do when that happens," Kesha said.

Michael realised there was that brief pause in the conversation, and they were finally speaking to him rather than about him and the Unwanted. He removed his feet from the table and adjusted his position, so he was looking at Taya. He rolled his head to catch Olivia's eyes, who he admitted didn't look any brighter than he felt, but she shrugged.

"She's right," Olivia said.

"How do you know this?" Taya's eyes widened as she stared at Kesha.

"Sorry, I didn't realise they didn't know." Kesha blushed. Michael shook his head and waved permission for her to go on. Kesha bit her lip before gazing back at those arrayed around the table. "I've been riding with the Unwanted for long enough. I've seen it. More than once. I imagine it was a hard thing to hide from the rest of you, but impossible to keep me from finding out, eventually."

"When the Warlord took the field in battle, he always had two full warbands with him," Michael said.

Taya frowned. "The third stayed in Yalleska. They all rotated.

I'm aware of the arrangements the Warlord had in place for his protection details."

"The task of the second warband wasn't to defend and protect the Warlord in battle. It was to protect and hide the Unwanted's flaw, even from our own people. To hide what you've only just become aware of recently," Nathanial said.

"It was carefully managed, but on those rare occasions we pushed ourselves, we'd sleep off our exhaustion hidden within the ranks of that second warband," Michael admitted.

"So that whole sleeping in later than the rest of us, then catching up during the day, wasn't just showing off?" Harry traded an exasperated look with Taya.

"We can obviously function earlier if we have to, but by preference we'll sleep in." Olivia grinned at them.

"Why didn't you just admit it when we were on the road to get here?" Taya asked.

"Habit?" Michael couldn't help the fact that his lips twitched at the consternation that radiated around the table.

"But doesn't that mean you're using more of your powers just to ride that way? That's how you catch up right, you're using your powers?" Taya asked.

"The distance we were covering each day while on the ride here? No. We'd need to push ourselves and our horses a little more than that to be negatively impacted." Olivia snorted in amusement.

"We didn't have to feed that much energy to our horses to catch up with the rest of you. The extra sleep is more beneficial." The ripple of amusement from Nathaniel echoed Olivia's.

"I think it's beyond their control. Their bodies draw in the veil constantly, even in sleep. It seems to be a natural rhythm for them," Kesha said.

"What do you mean?" Harry asked.

"Think about how tiring it is for the rest of us to draw in the veil and use it for simple things. Then imagine your body does that automatically, all the time, even while you sleep. Except they channel more power even when they sleep than the rest of us do on purpose," Kesha said.

"So you might all be formidable but there is a trade-off." Taya mused, her eyes narrowing.

Michael could see she was thinking things through as she gazed at them all.

"We even knew. It was right there in front of us on those occasions where we all fought together. All those gripes about the Unwanted being lazy. Everyone else had to keep going with all the camp duties while the Unwanted were still lying around in camp." Harry laughed.

"We needed, I needed to know this, but I can see why the Warlord was careful to hide this little wrinkle," Taya said.

"If those we face learned this." Harry paled a little.

"We'd do damage to them, a lot, but yes, they'd just keep throwing bodies at us and we would go down," Michael said.

Kesha's eyebrows rose and she bit her lip as she waited. Michael shrugged.

"They wouldn't have a choice. I've seen it. Up in the Heights, they collapsed at the end of the battle. The Kallith had to haul them all out. It scared me. I didn't know what was wrong with them and my healing powers couldn't reach them. Then the Warlord showed up and explained it was normal. They go into a protective state, almost like hibernation. They won't wake until the veil is ready to release them."

"You speak of the veil like it's a sentient thing healer," Taya said.

Kesha frowned at Taya. "It isn't, I don't think, but they are, and the interaction between them and the veil is incomparable to how the rest of us function."

"We can't keep trying to fight on their terms. We need to fight on ours," Harry said.

"You appointed me commander of this little conflict," Taya said, her gaze unwavering as she stared at him.

"I did, at the urging of the rest of you, for me to take overall command while you take on the actual running of the fighting part," Michael said.

"Then it's time we actually functioned that way. You and the Unwanted need to rest up before you collapse on us." The order in Taya's voice was unmistakable.

"We do. We will. We're about to change things up," Michael said.

Nathanial pushed himself up from the chair he'd been lounging in and approached the map hanging on the wall. Then pointed to a clearing on the other side of the forest they were fighting in the last couple of weeks, clearing out the Sylannian incursion.

"Now that our scouts have confirmed we've cleaned out this area of the forest, we want you to take the warbands forward and set up your command post here," Nathanial said.

Taya frowned. "How precisely will that help you all rest?"

"It will take you all the better part of a week to move everyone forward and set up camp." Olivia said, shrugging. "We'll stay here and join you once you've established the camp and your forward command."

"As we explained, the Unwanted can travel fast when we need to and it doesn't take anywhere near the energy to travel that way, as fighting does."

"It will take us a day to reach your position. Two, if we take it easy," Michael said.

"That's more than enough time for us to recuperate."

Taya stood and joined Nathanial at the map and pointed to several locations on the map. "I can send our forward scout teams to assess the villages here, here and here," Taya said, pointing to each village in turn.

Ben cleared his throat. "They're occupied by the Sylannians. Or they were, unless that is where the enemy forces in the forest were from."

"Given the reports I received from the sheer number of fighting forces they were shipping into Vallantia before we had to vacate, I'd say those villages are still occupied. Our enemy would have just sent new troops," Lukas said.

Taya and Harry considered Ben and Lukas. Michael could see them weighing their words. All either of them had been told was that the pair were associates of his.

"I'd trust the assessment of the situation from Lukas and Ben more than I would others," Michael said.

"They were both helping to free the citizens of Vallantia from the Sylannians and sending them here to safety until recently. They know the lay of the land between Vallantia and here more than any of us," the Smith said.

"Do you both think you could spare me some time to brief me on the enemy forces in each village between here and Vallantia? At least as you last knew it," Taya asked.

Ben and Lukas simply indicated agreement with the request.

"Won't that leave those here at risk if we all leave?" Shaun asked.

"I'm more than capable of defending my estate," the Smith said, the bedrock rumbling as he spoke.

"This house and land have been in my family and its protections reinforced generation after generation since the era of the Smith Lords. You needn't fear for those who remain here," Colin said.

"Besides, they'll be behind our lines. We've no intelligence to suggest the Sylannians have got a foothold behind our position," Olivia said.

"You'll leave a small contingent here to assist, and those who've been badly injured on the battle front will be sent here," Nathanial said.

"We'll systematically clean out the Sylannians. Push them back to Vallantia," Michael said, his eyes glittering. "Then we'll finish them."

"I don't doubt you, Michael, but that's an enormous task," Harry said.

"It is, but once we get to Vallantia, we have an advantage they don't and are unlikely to be able to counter."

"You?" Taya said.

"That wasn't the advantage Michael was thinking of. By all reports, the Sylannian Commander and those close to her are strong in the veil," Nathanial said.

"Power negates power. I remember," Harry said.

"So, what is this secret weapon?" Taya asked, one eyebrow rising.

"Vallantia and the Rathadon Estate are settled on bedrock. It dates back to the Smith Lords. The blood of whom runs through the veins of the Smith and his sons. We have three equivalent in strength to the Smith Lords of old. I've never seen any sign of the ability in the Sylannians," Michael said.

"Vallantia and the Rathadon estate have their own defences of old, just as my estate does. I've been calling to the stone to wake it up ever since Michael made the request when the Sylannians invaded," the Smith said and gestured to his son's. "We can activate them."

Michael ignored the curious stares of his warband leaders. While it was well known the Smith was the strongest of his kind and whispered he was the equivalent of the legends, that his sons had equal ability, was not. The same dangerous light shone in the eyes of the Smith and his son's. For the first time in generations, they'd been given permission to utilise the gift they'd been born with to its full capacity.

CHAPTER

EIGHTY-SEVEN

Tarkhan shook his head as the underwife offered him another slice of fruit.

"I'm done, thank you, although another kaf would be appreciated," Tarkhan said.

The underwife gestured to another of her companions, who stepped forward and refilled the mug she held. Then she raised it to his lips, and he sipped appreciatively. He'd long since gotten over the embarrassment of being fed like he was a child. His keepers still wouldn't allow him to hold so much as a mug or plate, let alone eating implements. They kept firm control of the trays of food and flasks of drink throughout all his meals. Not even trying to refuse food in protest had worked. His keeper had subjected him to a barrage of mental prodding, and he'd given in to her promptings to eat and drink so quickly it had been embarrassing. The Sylannians wouldn't allow him to harm himself, not even the simple act of refusing to be fed. Although at least his keeper asked him what foods and drink he'd prefer. He'd wistfully asked for kaf from his homeland and been astonished when it had appeared as a choice with his breakfast every morning.

499

When he'd taken the last sip of the kaf, the underwife, raised her eyebrow at him.

"More?"

"No, I'm done, thank you," Tarkhan said and waited until the underwife who'd fed him and the others holding the array of food and drink selections left the room. Then he stood and walked over to the drinking fountain and took a couple of sips of drinking water. He loved his morning kaf, but he did like to clean his mouth after, as the residue would turn bitter. The water fountain was the best he could do.

The remaining underwives moved around his living space, tidying and putting everything back in its place. The last one paused by the door that led to the outside garden and hummed. A snicking sounded occurred as the bolt slid back and she, along with the others, left his sitting room. Even though his life had settled to predictable routine with a few exceptions, it took him a few moments to process the slight deviation to the morning routine. The underwife had unlocked the garden door.

Tarkhan took a step, then paused, glancing around, but no one appeared to scold him. One slow step after the other, he reached the door. He reached out with his hand hovering above the latch. Then leant his head against the wall.

"I can do this. I've spent my entire adult life going where I willed." Tarkhan muttered to himself.

Taking a deep breath, he pulled the door open and stood, staring out into an oasis filled with sunshine, burbling water, birds chirping, insects buzzing and lush green leaves from the trees and bushes with the bursts of colours from the flowering plants. Tarkhan took a couple of hesitant steps out, his eyes drinking in the garden. While he'd seen such things before, he'd never spent long in such places. The home of the Kallith had been a rather barren place and even the new homeland, while green and lush was nothing when compared to this. Although he conceded the nearby jungle that had separated them from the closest of the Warlord's villages probably was. He just hadn't spent much time in the forest. Besides, he'd been locked in barren rooms for what seemed like a lifetime, so this was a luxury. One he didn't want to be taken away.

He chuckled as his cynicism rose. Of course, there was a double edge to every concession the Sylannians made for him. He would give them almost anything they wanted, if only so they wouldn't take this new treat away from him. Tarkhan allowed his anger to fade and instead enjoyed the moment. Good moments these days were few and far between. If he was honest, they'd been rare for years now, even before the Sylannians captured him. Tarkhan wandered around the garden, stopping at the edge of the bathing pool. Amusement hit him that he still wasn't allowed eating implements, but it didn't occur to them all the things he could use to kill himself or others in this garden. The cool morning breeze ruffled his hair, and he ran his fingers along one of the broad leaves of the shrub nearest him. The fringes on the leaves tickled his fingers. As he wandered down a winding pathway, a shower of water bathed him as he brushed past the plants, disturbing the collection of early morning dew on the leaves. Tarkhan took a deep breath, smelling the moisture in the air mixed with the soil and the sweet scent of the enormous purple flowers on the plants around him.

A door slid open, closely followed by others, disturbing the early morning solitude.

"Ah, we wondered how long it would be before the Keepers allowed you to join our number." A melodic voice, threaded with amusement, spoke from behind him. "I'm Altan."

Tarkhan turned to see a tall man with dust coloured hair and startling green eyes. The silken pants and top he wore did nothing to disguise his clan origins. Altan's tattoos gave away he'd been an artisan from one of the lake clans.

A gasp made Tarkhan focus on the second man who'd just walked out his own door.

"I'm Chengiz. You were a leader, a warrior of the Kallith," Chengiz said.

Tarkhan nodded. "I was, I'm Tarkhan."

"So the war is over?" Altan asked.

"I don't know. At the end, only the Kallith survived to flee to another land, but the homeland of the People is lost. As you can see, I've ended up here, so I have no idea what's happened since I was captured."

"How in the powers did they manage that one?" Another man said, taking the sting out of his words with a friendly grin. "My name is Bilguun."

"We returned to attempt to free some of the Hallaran Clan. Things went wrong, and I ended up here," Tarkhan said.

The words didn't even hurt anymore. He seemed to have come to terms with his loss and capture. Not even his current status seemed to cause him any sense of loss or embarrassment anymore. It was like his old life was that lived by another man. As Altan gestured to an empty chair, Tarkhan walked over and joined the other men. Thankfully, other than filling them in on the war and how the Kallith had escaped, the others expected little from him. Instead, each took turns in telling their own stories. After all this time being apart from others of the People, he lost himself in the conversations. Tarkhan didn't miss the hint of deference to his rank, or rather former rank, that had crept into the tone and body language of the other men as they talked.

"Tarkhan, come I only have a little time to breed before I have to be back," a voice called from behind him.

Altan shot up to his feet, and the others followed as they all started backing up towards their doors.

"That's Fiona. She's one of the primewives. Try not to displease her. She's important in this world," Altan said.

Tarkhan nodded his understanding, and with a wave at the other men, he walked towards Fiona. He'd bred with her before, but it had been some time. Although the information that this one had a higher rank than some of the wives he'd bred with had occurred to him, it was useful to have it confirmed. He'd just been judging Fiona had rank from the amount of crimson and cream threaded through her robes.

In a snap decision, Tarkhan reached out and grabbed Fiona's hand, swooping her up into his arms. Fiona let out a startled squeak and had no time but to struggle briefly in his arms as he plunged them both into the cool waters of one of the nearby pools. As they came up for air, Tarkhan heard Fiona's spluttering laughter as her indignation gave way to amusement.

"Tarkhan!" Fiona said, her will washing over his mind, then receded to be replaced with bubbling amusement before she waved back his Keeper and the underwives as they surged into the garden from his rooms. "It's alright, he's not trying anything sinister. He's just feeling playful."

Tarkhan got the distinct impression that Fiona was pleased, and she believed his actions were showing he was getting used to his new life. He chuckled as he stared deliberately into Fiona's eyes.

"Sex is more than a chore in order to produce a baby," Tarkhan said, pushing Fiona up against the wall of the pool, brushing her wet hair from her face then with a hint of command in his tone he spoke to the men he could sense were still congregated at the chairs they'd been sitting at. Equal waves of astonishment and horror emanating from them. "Go."

Fiona's lip twitched as the other men beat a hasty retreat from the garden without even a hint of protest.

"Not that I'm objecting to the results, warrior, but how did you manage to have the other men follow your orders after such a short period among them?"

"I was a warrior and leader of the Kallith. Even after all the time they've been here, their first response was to obey. Even if it occurs to them later that they don't have to do as I tell them anymore." Tarkhan said, then tugged at her silk. "Come, let me show you what you've been missing out on all these years."

With a hum, Fiona disrobed herself and him at the same time. Tarkhan moved them over to the shallow end of the wading pool and set about ensuring Fiona didn't just see breeding with him as a duty. The other captives had been correct. These women now controlled every facet of his life. One way to ensure his safety was to make sure they didn't see him as inter-changeable with any of their other captives. Rather than just going through the motions and performing the duty they required of him, now, he'd do his best to make them desire him above any other.

EIGHTY-EIGHT

Damien lay back on one of the long couches, his head on one of the plush pillows in the sitting room as Michael and the others rehashed their battle plan. He took it as a good sign he wasn't excluded from these sessions, even if he wasn't actively participating right now. While the bulk of the fighting forces other than a few small teams had moved out under Taya's leadership yesterday, he was more relieved than he should be that the Unwanted would be here another week. Michael had already made it clear he'd be left behind here at the Smith's residence if Kesha didn't think he was ready to face battle. It had been bad enough being left behind when the Unwanted and the others had fought the Sylannian forces in the forest. So he'd been doing his utmost, working with Kesha so she'd have no hesitation in clearing him before the Unwanted left to join the rest of the forces.

Damien allowed the conversation to flow over him. Not that he wasn't interested in the conversation or plans they were making. He was aware of what they were talking about, but he was distracted. There was just something that was on the edge of his mind. An idea that was proving to be frustratingly elusive. For some reason, he kept going from considering the battle plan Michael had suggested back to his fragmented memories of the courtyard in the Stronghold where he'd been held. Olivia's hand rested on his shoulder and he realised she was picking up the directions his thoughts had kept being dragged to. He closed his eyes again as two images flickered through his mind. Isabella was on a balcony above where he was held. Then Isabella was down in the courtyard with him, and he'd came back to himself as she bled excess veil from him. It was a particular skill she'd always had. Damien's eyes flared open, his breath freezing in his throat as he sat abruptly upright.

"Damien?"

"I might have a suggestion, but there's something I need to check." Damien heard the uncertainty in his voice but pushed it aside and ploughed on. "Do you mind if I ask Isabella to come here?"

"Of course not, if you think it will help." Michael frowned, staring at him. "This has something to do with what happened to you in the Stronghold?"

Damien paused long enough to put in a silent call to Isabella before answering. "Sort of. It's that and the fighting technique we've been working on. I just don't remember what happened in the Stronghold too well. It could be nothing," Damien said, pushing his sudden unease aside. "When you walked into the courtyard where you found me, was Isabella there?"

"Yes, Isabella was there in the courtyard. She was protecting you. Standing between me and you, then she seemed to draw the excess power from you, which helped you come back," Michael said.

Damien shook his head. "No, I mean, did you see her standing there in front of me when you first entered?" Damien stared intently at Michael who frowned and sat back in his chair.

"Well." Michael paused, a frown creasing his forehead. "She must have been."

"Did you see her when you entered?" Damien persisted.

"I believe so. I turned to warn the others to stay back and when I looked back, she was there." Michael glanced at Olivia and Nathanial, who both nodded in confirmation. "There was a bit going on at the time."

Damien could feel the others were all gazing at him. He didn't respond to them yet. He glanced over at the door unsurprised as Isabella walked in. She closed the door, stopping and looking at them all, swallowing.

"You needed something?" Isabella asked.

Her eyes held his own, like she thought if she ignored the others in the room, then they wouldn't actually exist. While she'd come a long way in her sessions with Kesha, she was extremely hesitant about intruding on their meetings. She tried not to be a burden and get in the way, as if she was fearful that they'd send her away.

"I did. Isabella, that last day in the Stronghold." Damien saw a shadow in her eyes, one he was certain was mirrored in his own. "You were up in the tower." Damien swallowed, not wanting to cause her pain, but went on. "In Aiden's rooms."

Isabella breathed in a shaky breath and nodded. "He rolled over and went to sleep, like he usually did. I was about to be sick so went to the bathroom. I didn't want to wake him. Kesha said I'll never be an addict to the stuff. I'm allergic to it."

"Then I flipped out, down below."

The others in the room were staring intently, their gazes transferring between him and Isabella.

"I felt it, the power arched through me. It was agony. I wasn't quite thinking straight. I just released it and set everything on fire, but I don't really understand how I did it. Stone isn't meant to burn," Isabella said, her voice quiet.

"Then you were down in the courtyard, defending me and bleeding off the excess veil." Damien hesitated, looking up to see her nod. "Isabella, how did you get from the top of the tower down to the courtyard?"

Isabella's eyes widened as she stared at him. "I..."

She stopped and reached out abruptly and grabbed his hand and then she pulled them both into the grey place. Damien sighed with relief as the veil seemed to thrum all around him. He realised the grey place was the veil. The place where the veil lived. Now the cold didn't send shivers through him. It was comforting. He could wrap it around himself and hide from the world, feeling perfectly safe and content.

It's like my interaction with the veil has changed, Damien said.

It feels safe here, like no one can touch you or hurt you.

Or if they tried, the veil itself would protect us.

Isabella grinned at him. *Could you imagine the mayhem if the veil really could think for itself?* Isabella's hand covered her mouth as she giggled.

He smiled, happy to see that she could laugh at the absurdities in the world. It had killed a part of him inside to think that his little sister, who could laugh and enjoy life, had disappeared forever because of Aiden.

So, show me. How did you get from the top of the tower down to the courtyard where I was held?

Damien expanded his awareness, paying particular attention to Isabella and what she was doing. His eyes widened as she walked, a path appearing in front of her feet as she did so. In her mind, he could see she was thinking of the garden outside the house where she walked every day with Kesha. They had gone only a few steps before she stopped and pulled them back from the grey world. Damien gasped as he stood in the garden. He looked around, then back towards the house. While it had been only moments, a couple of steps, they had travelled a fair distance from the house. A lot further than a couple of steps. He pulled them both back into the grey place.

All right, humour me.

Of course.

So you just think about where you want to go, then start walking and you end up there?

Sort of. It has to be somewhere I know well, or I can see even if it is in the distance. I haven't really experimented much.

Damien frowned, then thinned the veil, staring around him. He smiled, seeing a jagged rocky outcrop in the distance towards the mountains.

Be ready to intervene if I mess this up.

Damien sensed Isabella's pride that he'd asked for her help. He reached out and grabbed Isabella's hand again and turned to look at the outcrop in the distance, then focused on where he wanted to go. The veil shift around them as he focused and started to walk. Fascinated, he could see the real world shift around them. For each step, they travelled further than a horse could gallop. Then the grey thickened around them and between one moment and the next, only a handful of steps later, in what should have taken an hour or so for a horse to gallop, he pulled them out. The outcrop he'd focused on appeared in front of them. He turned to comment when he became aware of movement around them. Without thinking, he threw up his shield, thrusting out with a strike of power. He sent their attacker reeling as he dragged them both back into the grey place. Even though they were in the grey, he pushed Isabella behind him, wishing he had his weapons and fighting leathers. Then took a deep breath as he recognised the unadorned grey and black uniforms of fighters from the other warbands. He swore softly and, gesturing for Isabella to stay put, he dispelled the grey from around him as those who'd been on lookout duty scrambled to their feet, facing off towards him.

"Easy, I'm sorry. I didn't know you were out here keeping watch," Damien said.

The perimeter guards look at each other, then back at him, their swords lowering as recognition hit them.

"You're not meant to leave the confines of the estate and garden area unescorted, let alone be out here," one guard said.

Damien's face heated. He'd been aware the Unwanted had been briefed that he was confined to the estate and obviously Tony's warband knew since if he wanted to walk outside in the gardens, they were tasked to go with him. However, Damien hadn't realised everyone in the combined warbands had been briefed.

"Was that your sister you brought out here?" The other guard frowned at him.

Damien was positive about the disapproving tone this time. There was a definite protective streak running through everyone when it came to Isabella. It was like they all held themselves personally responsible for what Aiden had done to her.

"It was..."

Isabella appeared next to him as she pushed the veil away. "Don't blame him. It was my fault we were trying something new and I couldn't fully explain. I'm sorry, we didn't know you were out here."

"We have orders. We'll have to take you back to the house," the guard said.

Damien sighed as he remembered he was still wearing a set of the lounging clothes that kept appearing in his room on a daily basis. Along with socks, but no boots. He wasn't meant to be out here, by Michael's orders, but he'd totally forgotten about it as they'd experimented with this new ability Isabella had discovered.

Olivia, a little help?

Where did you both go?

Damien could hear the concern colouring her mental voice. In all honesty, if he'd realised what they were actually going to do, he would have said something. It was just in his excitement he'd forgotten all about the orders to stay put in the house or the gardens. Even in the garden he was only allowed out with a guard detail following him around. Somehow, the new ability had driven that restriction right out of his head.

We're fine, I'm fine. Isabella has discovered a new ability, I'll explain, but I'm afraid I startled the perimeter guards out by that rocky outcrop.

How in the powers did you get all the way out there?

Can you or Michael please just tell them it's fine? I promise we'll come straight back.

Damien waited, his eyes flicking over to the guards, and he raised his hands a little, trying to smile reassuringly. He could hear the senior most guard's mental dialogue as he tried to work out if he and Isabella were a risk to themselves. The other seemed to be more concerned about how they were meant to get them both back to the manor house if they didn't want to go.

Hold there, we'll send someone out to collect them both.

Damien groaned as Michael spoke to the guards. He'd heard the exchange on purpose. He grinned at them as they turned their gaze to him and, with a sigh, sat down on a boulder to wait. Isabella bit her lip then sunk down beside him.

CHAPTER

EIGHTY-NINE

Nathanial reigned in his horse and his lips twitched despite his determination to appear disapproving. Damien sat on a boulder with his sister perched on another nearby under the careful watch of the guards. There was a distinct air of embarrassment and chagrin coming from the siblings. Although he also sensed excitement from Damien as well.

Nathanial nodded to the guard detail. "Thanks for keeping an eye on them."

"No problems."

"Not even sure how they got out here, but, well, we were looking for people coming the other way."

"It's fine." Nathanial reassured them, then turned his attention back to Damien and Isabella. "All right, you two, mount up and let's get back to the house. Oh, and you might want to put these on for the ride back."

Nathanial kept his face neutral as he held out Damien's boots to him. Damien looked down at his feet and sighed before standing and reaching out to grab the boots. Damien muttered

513

what he thought was thanks before returning to sit on the boulder and drag the shoes on. When Damien was done, he walked over to the horses that members of Tony's warband had brought with them. Damien paused, assisting Isabella to mount, making sure her stirrups were the correct length before he mounted his own.

"Don't worry, he's not angry. Even if he is trying very hard not to allow his amusement to show," Damien said.

Nathanial ignored the comment and turned his horse back towards the estate house. Damien was partially correct. After he'd gotten over his initial shock of the pair disappearing like they had and reappearing so far away, it wasn't anger he was feeling. Damien's contriteness when he'd advised them of the minor issue he was having with the sentries, had swung him over to amusement. It also prompted a burning curiosity about how the pair of them had gotten where they'd ended up in such a short time. Both Michael and Olivia were in accord. Although all of them had felt that moment of panic when the pair had disappeared. Isabella appeared so downcast. He relented.

"Your brother is correct Isabella, neither of you is in trouble but an explanation can wait until we get back." Nathanial then frowned at the pair. "Although whatever you did, don't do it again until you get permission. You, in particular Damien, haven't been fully cleared to go anywhere. Even if it is a formality by now, you aren't exactly dressed for it and, what's worse, you aren't armed."

"I know, I'm sorry. It just totally slipped my mind until we nearly got skewered by the sentries," Damien said.

Nathanial shook his head as Damien's face flushed red. Tony's men maintained their silence as they followed dutifully along behind, not even giving away a hint of anger or amusement. Then again, they were used to overhearing conversations they weren't meant to be a party to and acting accordingly. Since they hadn't been on Damien when he pulled his disappearing act, they didn't feel at fault for that either.

They rode the rest of the way in silence, although Nathanial had to admit it was a lovely day for a ride. Even if it hadn't been a planned one and not something he generally did as a pastime when he was relaxing. When they rode into the courtyard, he dismounted and turned, waiting for the pair before leading the way back into the house and the sitting room where they'd been before Damien and Isabella had gone on their entirely unexpected excursion. He refrained from comment as those assigned to protection detail followed along behind. As he opened the doors to the sitting room he stood aside and gestured for Damien and Isabella to enter. Then as the guards started to follow, Nathanial adroitly stepped into their path.

"Thank you, we've got it from here," Nathanial said.

He stood in the doorway and stared at them as they were about to argue. Then, wisely, they thought the better of it and positioned themselves on either side of the door. Nathanial closed the door behind him and turning saw the pair standing in front of Michael and Olivia.

"Don't you ever frighten me like that again," Olivia said.

There was no doubt about the fact that the scolding tone was directed at Damien, who held up his hand.

"I'm sorry, I didn't mean to."

"It was my fault Olivia, I'm the one who dragged us both away," Isabella said.

"Sit down the pair of you and stop apologising. After we removed our hearts from our throats, I'm sure the prevailing emotions out of us all were equal doses of incredulity with curiosity," Michael said.

Damien half grinned and sat down on the long chair he'd taken up residence in prior to his experiment. He took a moment to pull his boots off and placed them to one side before he stretched out again, although this time he remained sitting rather than laying down.

"Spill, now. What in the powers did you do? How did you end up all the way out there?" Nathanial asked.

Nathanial sat down, staring at them both. Damien grinned back at him, excitement shining from his eyes.

"I needed to check first, it's why I asked for Isabella since my memory could have been painting a picture of something that just didn't occur." Damien turned to Michael. "It's the grey place. Isabella discovered it can be used not only to hide but to travel from one place to another. To me, it was almost instantaneous, but I don't know what it was like on this end?"

"It was quick. You disappeared from here and called for help all the way out there at the sentry post a moment later," Olivia said.

"I'll need to practice, with your permission, of course," Damien added hastily, raising his hands defensively against their glares. "But I think I have an idea, more an embellishment on the battle plan, if you'll hear me out."

Nathanial looked at Michael and shrugged. He could tell they were all intrigued and a little excited about this new ability, even if they were all trying not to show it.

"Go on, you've managed to capture my attention," Michael said.

"As I said, I'll want to practice a few more times, but I think we can use this ability of ours to our advantage." Damien frowned, as if he was still thinking through whatever it was that had occurred to him. "When we return to the battle, what if we use this ability to jump around, hit them from different places? So far from each other, it will seem impossible. But acting together in a big group, make it obvious it is us."

Nathanial flicked his gaze to both Olivia and Michael before nodding. "Go on."

"Then, when we're sure they've noticed, we split in two. Isabella could stay here if she agrees and help jump the pair of you and half the Unwanted around to continue the attacks at this end. While Isabella's group is drawing their attention, I can jump Michael and half the Unwanted to the Rathadon estate to go after the Sylannian commander. If she's certain we're all over this way, she's never going to expect us to hit her there." Damien stopped, looking from one to the other of them, waiting for a response.

There was calculation in Michael's eyes as a smile slowly spread across his lips. It was an expression that was echoed on Olivia's face as well.

"That might just work. Kesha will have to clear you as being medically fit then, and only then, can you experiment with this travel in the grey space." Michael nodded. "I would, however, have to insist you go armed and I'd still prefer you to go with one of us as well."

"Your fighting leathers are also recommended."

"Wearing your boots might be a good start as well, after you've been cleared, of course." Nathanial chuckled and kept his expression carefully bland as Damien threw him a filthy look. "Just saying. It's not like you don't have priors for running off without any of them."

"I get it. I should have explained what I was thinking first and cleared the second jump with you all first," Damien said.

Nathanial grinned as Isabella bit her bottom lip, staring from one to the other of them as if she was still trying to work out if everything really was fine. He was about to reassure her when she settled for a hesitant smile.

CHAPTER
NINETY

Damien walked out into the training courtyard. He checked the facilities and was suitably impressed as he had been by the entire estate. Of course he shouldn't be surprised that the Smith had a good training ground set up given his line of work. As the Unwanted trained at these grounds, perfectly at ease as if on home ground, he wondered how many times they'd done so in the past. He grinned. It was a strange feeling being back in his fighting leathers after being in soft lounging clothes this entire time until Kesha finally pronounced he was ready to resume partial duties. She'd approved training, but not actually going into battle.

"Decided to join us, Damien?" Gavrel joked.

"What can I say? I slept in."

"I'll bet," Gavrel said.

"Are you meant to be here?" Shallan asked.

"I have permission," Damien said, holding his hands up, glancing over to where Olivia stood talking with Michael and Nathanial.

While he'd realised the whole warband was perfectly aware

he'd been sleeping in Olivia's room since the events in the Stronghold, this kind of banter was new. After all, it was his teammates that delivered his bags to wherever he was sleeping at every stop they'd made along the road. Likewise, when they'd arrived here. Shallan had even given him directions to Olivia's rooms that first night they'd stayed here at the Smith's estate. Damien's face warmed and he ducked his head, not sure quite how to respond.

"That's enough out of the both of you," Olivia said. Despite her words, she was clearly amused.

"We are all frankly relieved you took the lead," Gavrel said.

"It's not like Damien would have without prompting," Shallan said.

"Do you seriously want to spend the next few evenings on night shift guard duty?" Olivia asked, her eyebrows rising.

The others merely grinned at her, but the warning had the desired effect, and they all turned back to their drills.

They all think that you and I... Damien trailed off, flustered.

I know, don't worry about it. They don't need to know about your nightmares.

It doesn't worry you? Damien asked.

Not in the slightest. Besides, the more we denied it, the more everyone would believe we were in a relationship. When you are ready, tell them as much or as little as you choose. Or not, it's up to you, Olivia said.

Olivia guided him across the training grounds towards where Nathanial and Michael stood, and Damien pushed his concern aside. If Olivia wasn't concerned about what the others might think, then he certainly shouldn't be. Besides, what he sensed coming from his squad mates was relief that he was back here among them all. Even if it was just for training. They'd been concerned about the treatment he'd received, of which they'd heard rumours from

Tony's warband, and it had left them wondering if Aiden had broken him completely. As he drew up to the group, Nathanial turned from the conversation he'd been having with Michael and slapped him on the shoulder, then passed his weapons belt to him. Damien accepted it and strapped the belt around his waist.

"Ready to train?" Nathanial asked. "So what's this new fighting technique you were so excited to try?"

"More than ready. I don't think this new fighting technique I want to try is really new."

"What do you mean?"

"I think we've been doing it all along, but on an instinctive level," Damien said.

"So spit it out, what is it?" Nathanial said.

Damien went to respond when his attention was caught by the sight of Isabella walking with Kesha further out on the grounds and even though both women were trailed by a couple of Tony's warband he frowned.

Michael looked over to see what attracted his attention and shook his head. "Don't worry, we have people out, not just the two on duty with them today. They are both perfectly safe."

"She's been through so much. I worry." Damien ducked his head.

"Don't. As Michael said, we have people out and as you know, Kesha is a very good mind healer if people want to work on their issues," Nathanial said.

"Isabella trusts her and Kesha will help," Michael said.

Damien took a breath and turned his attention back to their training. He trusted all of them. So he also trusted that Isabella was safe. Even if she was out there, quite a distance from the manor house.

"All right, what is this thing we've all been doing that we didn't know we were doing?" Michael asked.

"So the other day Isabella and I proved we can travel through the grey space," Damien said.

"I remember," Michael said, his tone dry.

"Well, I think we've been using it when we fight," Damien said.

Nathanial's eyes widen. "Wait, we've what?"

"Do you ever remember wondering how you crossed the intervening space between one spot and another?" Damien asked, unable to contain his excitement over his idea. "Or how an opponent's blade possibly missed you, since it was right on target?"

Michael, Nathanial, and Olivia appeared shocked, but nodded slowly.

"Yes, many times," Michael said.

"I think we've all been slipping in and out of the grey space automatically as we fight," Damien said.

"That's not such a safe thing if we aren't doing it on purpose," Olivia said.

"It's just a theory. I could be wrong, but I think it should work. Thus the practice, if you'll indulge me, Michael?" Damien said.

Olivia and Nathanial moved to one side of the training ring. Damien's face heated as he realised he had an audience with the undivided attention of the ranks of the Unwanted watching on. A wave of reassurance washed over him from Olivia and he drew his attention back to Michael.

"I'm willing to experiment. So you have the lead. Where do we start?" Michael asked.

"Let's start with basic drills, loosen up and go from there," Damien said, withdrawing his blade and flipping it up to signal he was ready.

Damien found himself grinning in anticipation, a far cry from the person who used to dread these moments. Michael withdrew his blade and in a move that replicated Damien's, he flipped it up in front of his face before moving into the guard position.

As the training session progressed, Damien found his worries faded away, lost in the rhythm of their sword play. As they cycled through the last of the warm-up drills, he called a halt.

"This is where it gets interesting. I want you to do a lunge, straight for my heart," Damien said, then held his free hand up as Michael went to protest. "Don't worry, I'll slip into the grey. Your sword won't connect."

"When you're ready," Michael said.

As Damien nodded, Michael reacted instantly and lunged forward, his blade heading right for its target. Just before the blade struck, Damien pulled himself into the grey. He shivered as Michael's sword plunged through the air where he'd been moments before, then stepped to one side and reappeared. Michael spun, resetting himself, looking at Damien warily.

"Can we do that again? I want to watch with my othersight as well," Michael asked.

Damien simply nodded and reset his position. Once again, Michael waited until Damien showed he was ready before he lunged, his sword thrust out right on target. More assured now that he'd done it once, Damien drew his power and wrapped the grey around himself for the barest moment before pushing it aside. Michael blinked and stepped back, his blade dropping to a defensive position.

"We've all been doing that without realising it?" Olivia asked from where she stood on the sidelines.

"It's hard to say, but I think so. It would explain so many instances where I just put the oddity aside," Damien said as an air of excitement hummed around the practice ground. "Ready to try, or do you want to see another demonstration?"

"No, I think I've got that one. Let's try. After all, if I make a mistake, Kesha isn't too far away," Michael said.

Laughter spluttered around those watching at Michael's comment as they both reset. This time Damien waited until Michael indicated he was ready before he lunged at his opponent. Just before his blade was about to strike, cold wafted over him and Michael disappeared. Damien stepped back and reset his position as Michael reappeared a moment later.

"Can we try that one more time?" Michael asked. "Except this time, get ready for a counterattack and let the fight flow."

Damien's excitement mounted, and he nodded in agreement.

"How about we play watcher for this one?" Nathanial said as he and Olivia obviously heard their exchange and drew closer.

He and Michael traded equally exasperated expressions, but nodded to the request. Nathanial and Olivia took positions on either side. It showed how concerned they were that they thought they needed the pair of them to watch over this training session. It wasn't like he and Michael hadn't exchanged blows in the past with no need of anyone to supervise.

Damien waited until their self assigned spotters signalled they were ready, then he and Michael both reset. Damien flipped his blade and receiving the response from Michael, he immediately lunged. Michael drew the veil to him, entered the grey. This time, as Michael reappeared back in the real world again, his blade was striking towards Damien. Despite an audible gasp from onlookers, Damien responded, blocking his opponent's weapon, then responded in kind. They went off the scheduled training lessons and drew the veil, stepping in and out of the grey space as they fought. Except this time it was on purpose. Their battle with each other flowed as they experimented with their formations and how to best integrate that with their fighting style.

"Hold!"

It was one word called by two voices that brought instant attention. Damien stilled and found his blade a hairsbreadth from Michael's throat. He chuckled as he realised Michael's blade was in a similar position against his own. He stepped back, flipping his blade in front of his face, only to see Michael mirror the move on the other side. Both of them were panting as they let go of the veil and returned to normal time.

Damien took in his teammates who stood in a ring around them as applause rang out around the training grounds. He'd forgotten everyone was watching the experiment.

"I hope someone was paying attention to all of that because you all need to respond like that," Michael said.

Damien grinned at the universal groan that issued from the throats of those who'd been watching the display. He took a deep breath, realising, despite his nervousness at returning to training, Kesha was correct. He was ready to participate in life again.

CHAPTER

NINETY-ONE

Michael eased back into his saddle as they rode, grateful to be on the move again. There was an air of anticipation among the Unwanted, they'd all been briefed on what details they would be in and what was expected of them. Since they'd all worked in their smaller teams before, none seemed to show any concern at that part of their role. They were a little hesitant about the fact that their leadership would spearhead their own attack without them. He could feel they were torn but trusted his judgement and there wasn't even a hint of rebelliousness from any of them. Not that he'd expected any, but there was always a first time.

As Damien glanced over his shoulder, Michael followed his gaze to see Isabella.

Isabella is fine. Stop fussing, Olivia said.

She's right where I ordered her to be. In the middle of those assigned to protect her, towards the centre of the warband, Michael said.

I know involving Isabella was my idea, but she's never been to war, Damien said.

527

Isabella has been diligently practicing her shields and strikes every day. She's much better with that already than her blade work, Olivia said.

Thank you for giving the order for her to ride with her protection detail and follow their instructions, Damien said.

I thought it might save arguments, Michael said.

If anyone else had tried it, she'd get stubborn, and we'd find her riding up here.

I have no doubt, Michael said.

It's just as well the Smith altered a set of fighting leathers to fit her, Olivia said.

That relieves me to no end. Although I'd be more relieved if she'd stayed back at the Smith's residence, Damien muttered.

Michael was amused, despite a part of him agreeing with Damien. There was a part of him that wished she were safely back there as well.

You came up with the addition to the battle plan. If it's going to work, we need Isabella and her skills as well, Olivia said.

At least she's right where we can see her, and that crew is excellent at what they do. They've trained specifically to act as a protection detail, Nathanial said, as he rode forward to join them.

Tony is unlikely to allow anyone near her or Kesha. He still feels he somehow failed the Warlord even though he wasn't assigned to be on his door that day or on the Warlord when he went down at Callenhain, Michael said.

Assigning Tony and some of his people to Isabella's protection detail averted the only serious objection I could foresee to the plan. There was no way Tony was going to allow you to run off without them, Olivia said.

I know, he assigned himself, and his men to protection detail around us, Michael muttered. *I'd hoped he would have gotten over it by now.*

Would you stop following me around doesn't work either. Just so you know, Damien muttered.

Michael couldn't help himself and laughed outright at the consternation that Damien's mind voice contained. It seems he wasn't the only one who wasn't sure how to take the self appointed guards. While he'd always had people at his back. It was different when those people were Olivia and Nathanial or, at the most, a protection detail from the Unwanted. Having another entire warband ride in and start filling that role and clarifying that was their only role. Specifically, one of the warbands who'd been trained to protect the Warlord was a little disconcerting. Although he had to admit Tony and his warband were competent at what they did and he got on with them reasonably well. As he had with most of those who'd been assigned directly to the Warlord.

Ah, so that wasn't just me, they ignored. I thought I was losing my touch, Nathanial said.

Michael snorted in amusement, then drew his attention back to what they were doing. They were getting close to the area where they had to start paying more attention, as they weren't far from their own fighting lines and the towns that were currently in contention. Taya and the combined warbands were camping out with their headquarters well behind their own lines. Their people would fight to regain a village, then search the countryside to make sure they had missed none of the enemy before pushing their line forward. Not that they held an actual physical line. As it turned out, it didn't prove to be necessary since the Sylannians clumped together and didn't seem to go anywhere alone.

We've just passed the outer sentry post for the current headquarters, Shallan said.

Michael sent a small pulse in acknowledgement of the information, but otherwise didn't comment. He spotted the sentry as they rode up immediately. He gathered the man was out in the open, knowing it was them that were incoming. The man stood a little stiffer as they rode past his location, but otherwise didn't move.

It was a relief as they rounded the bend to see tents sprawling out over the land in front of them. There were several warbands combined here at this location, and they were rotating through the various duties. These here in camp, other than those on guard and lookout and other assigned duties, were obviously stood down to rest up. It was important for them as well. Even if they didn't use their powers as much as the Unwanted did in battle, they still used them more than the average person did. It also didn't take as much use of the veil to tire them out. That was one circumstance he expected the influx of the Unwanted to help them would resolve.

Heads turned as they rode in, and he was relieved to sense the mood in the camp was upbeat. It was one of the tell-tale signs of how the fighting was going. It told him his band leaders hadn't been sending back reports telling him one thing regarding how well the fighting effort was going, when it was actually the opposite.

Michael's eyes widened, and he groaned. His band leaders. It was such a small thing, but meant a whole different mindset.

Is everything alright? Olivia asked.

Yes. I think the others treating me like their leader in replacement of the Warlord is rubbing off.

In what way?

I just thought of them as my band leaders, with them being subor-dinate to me, Michael muttered.

Olivia's laughter filled his head, and he sighed.

Get used to it, my friend. You are now the leader of the whole domain. You have been since the Warlord fell in battle and transferred leadership to you.

Can't it just go back to the way it was before the Warlord? He asked pensively.

A feudal world? Where the various Warlords fought for supremacy? Where owning people was the right of the rich and powerful?

Where life was actually worse for the common person if people cared to look back on how many died in those conflicts? Nathanial said.

Alright. It was a stupid wish. I'm just not really sure why I'm the one who has to take on that mantle.

If you didn't want it, you shouldn't have done such a superb job. Besides, you already laid claim to the whole domain at the Stronghold, Olivia said.

Take heart. You have until the end of this war before much is going to change, Nathanial said.

Just be aware, by refusing the title of warlord, they are going to keep calling you your majesty. It might have started as a joke, but the form of address seems to be catching.

You should start turning your mind to how you are going to govern the domain because it is going to be you.

It's something that every leader of every warband agrees with. They follow you now, as they did the Warlord. They never would have followed Aiden or anyone else who thinks they can fill a power vacuum.

Michael sighed again, wanting to protest, but unfortunately he was afraid Olivia and Nathanial were right. Despite what some believed, he hadn't actually done anything he'd done all these years with the goal of becoming the next warlord. He'd just wanted to keep his people safe. It was just unfortunate that his definition of 'his people' had kept expanding to include people spread all over the domain. When he thought about his people, it didn't just mean the members of the Unwanted or the communication network or even the people of Vallantia. It had started to encompass all those of the domain, particularly those who couldn't fight for themselves. That was his job. To do his best to protect them all. Or to do as Olivia had done and appoint an overseer to watch over the ruling family to make sure they did their jobs in her absence. Michael pushed such thoughts aside and dismounted as they drew up to the command tent.

He gestured for Olivia and Nathanial to follow him, then, on an afterthought, waved Damien over to accompany them as well. Damien appeared surprised, but complied. Increasingly, he was ending up in their circle and his responsibilities had been increasing. He wasn't just a team member who was strong in the veil. He was shaping into being an excellent leader amongst them, and it was time to step him up to the next level.

Apart from Damien learning all the bits and pieces he needed to be a leader in the Unwanted, it also showed the others it was exactly what he was. Not that Michael expected any in the Unwanted would push back. They all knew or had guessed already. However, it was also a signal to the other leaders and members of the other warbands that he now regarded Damien as a part of his own leadership team for the Unwanted.

"Your Majesty," the guard on duty at the command tent said.

Michael ignored the form of address as he stepped into the command tent, restricting himself to a simple nod of thanks to the guard who opened the tent flap for him. Taya and Harry both looked up from the map table they'd been looking at as he entered and greeted them. He saw the moment they spotted Damien, although, to their credit, they took his addition in their stride. As Michael glanced around the command tent, he smiled. It was a lot more comfortable than he'd imagined it would be. It was one of the benefits of actually fighting this way now that the enemy had engaged with them. They had tents, carts, supply chains, and workers from other villages came in to assist where they could. On the negative side, it meant they were far less mobile. Although in the type of battle they were in, they didn't really need as much mobility. If they did, smaller units could spear off from their main fighting force.

"Commander, how's is the fighting going?" Michael asked.

"Your Majesty, we've been expecting you. We have a meal prepared. If you approve we can discuss where things are at while we eat," Taya said, a twinkle in her eye. "Sorry I couldn't resist."

Michael glanced over to the table, noting an extra camp chair had appeared and those on duty to serve them tonight were hastily putting another setting on the table.

"The rest of the Unwanted?" Michael asked.

"There is food waiting for them in one of the meal tents. I've assigned others to show them to where they can set up tonight and a brief tour of the camp so they know where to find things," Taya said.

"We were informed by the sentries that the size of your warband has increased, so we've prepared extra space and accommodations," Harry said.

"Khaliun managed to settle the Kallith at the Smith's with a list of instructions and people nominated to act in a liaison role with the Smith. The best warriors from the group she brought with her from the Heights have joined ranks with the wolves to fight with us," Michael said.

The smile on Taya's face at that news was genuine, although he suspected she'd already been informed of this detail. The members of the clans were distinct due in the most part to the tattoos they bore. "They are more than welcome to our ranks, and we can certainly use their help."

"The members they left with us have proven themselves to be invaluable," Harry said.

"Tony and his warband also joined us and are quite insistent about maintaining Michael's protection detail," Nathanial said blandly.

"Excellent, I don't have to assign anyone else to the duty. Tony's band was the best of the three," Taya said, her lips twitching in amusement.

"Which also explains why a couple of them have taken up post outside the command tent as well." Harry added.

"Very well, some food while we talk would be appreciated," Michael said choosing to ignore the banter between them and at a gesture from Taya to proceed her, he walked over to the table.

He went to sit at the side when one of Taya's people pulled out the seat at the head of the table. He sighed, knowing he was meant to sit there. Feeling both Olivia and Nathanial willing him to behave himself, he thanked the man and took the seat they'd assigned him.

You are the leader of the domain now, Michael. Stop fighting it. You'll only get frustrated, Olivia advised.

Olivia and Nathanial took the seats to either side of him and Damien, with only a slight hesitation, took the seat next to Olivia when one of the others, obviously assigned to serve them, pulled out the chair. Michael decided this was going to be an extremely long meal, then he cheered up at the prospect of dropping his bombshell on them. He smiled and reached forward to grab the goblet of wine that had been poured for him and sipped. Olivia glanced at him suspiciously, but his grin only widened, and he ignored her.

NINETY-TWO

Chelsie sipped the cool glass of juice as her finger tapped on the hand rest. While Samuel was currently engaged with one of the daggerwives, she didn't have to think about putting up a front. Not that he was hard to divert. He was just a male, after all.

"I don't think it's enough to just kill Jaclyn's children. The way she seems to breed, despite being tied up in war, she'll just have more," Fiona said.

Chelsie drew her attention over to the pacing primewife. Fiona had been in her confidence from the start.

"What more can we do that we haven't already done?"

"Let me lead some of our sister houses against Jaclyn and her forces," Fiona said, scowling as she kept pacing. "If I time it right, we can catch her between the barbarian forces and ours."

"It has merit, but I can see a couple of flaws straight away."

Fiona stopped dead in her tracks. "Like what?"

"If you succeed, then what's stopping the barbarian from killing you?"

"Unlike Jaclyn, I will not make the mistake of leading from

the front. I'll stay long enough to make sure she's dead, then return home."

"Leaving the sister houses behind you to cover your retreat?"

"Of course. They'll likely die," Fiona shrugged, "but what else are they useful for if not to sacrifice themselves for the good of Sylanna? You said a few problems. What else?"

"Our husband will notice your absence."

"I've just finished my breeding cycle with Samuel, so he won't be expecting me in his bed for another month. We already have sister houses in position in case of need. I'll sail out tonight and take command of them. Then I'll go to Vallantia. Our forces will just walk right in. Who would dare to stop us? As soon as it's confirmed Jaclyn is dead, I'll return." Fiona smirked, her eyes sparkling. "I'm sure you and the other wives can divert Samuel's attention for a few months. Although I doubt I'll need that long to dispose of our rival."

Chelsie sipped her juice while she considered the proposal. She had to admit it had merit, and making sure her rival ended up dead filled her with anticipation.

"Are you sure? It could be dangerous. We can always order someone less important to fall on their daggers for us."

"Oh, they will, I assure you. However, if we want to ensure this is done correctly, this time one of us needs to be there. Of the two of us, you are too important, besides you're pregnant and Samuel will definitely notice if you go missing. If anything, that causes me some concern. What if you go into labour while I'm away?"

Chelsie waved her hand. "I have Samuel well in hand. My other births went smoothly so I imagine the other wives will manage during my brief absence. As soon as my son is born the underwives will have the care of him. I won't be gone from our husband's side too long. If he does notice he hasn't seen you around, I can tell him you're pregnant and have withdrawn to the care of the underwives due to feeling poorly."

"Then I can conveniently have lost the child when I get back." Fiona poured herself a glass of spice wine from the decanter on the sideboard, then sent the barest thread of power into it. As the glass frosted in response, she joined Chelsie on the lounge.

"It just might work."

The door opened, giving entrance to a messenger. Chelsie's eyes were drawn to the sealed letter the messenger held out to her. Chelsie accepted the message and waved the woman off, waiting until she had left before Chelsie glanced at the seal, then opened it, scanning the contents.

"Well?"

"It's from Jaclyn. Our husband's sister advises the war is going well and they have full control of the barbarian capital of Vallantia. The commander is now expanding our hold on the land."

"So Jaclyn is once again thriving while commanding our attack forces during an invasion. Her children might be dead, but she has Ricardo with her and being at war didn't stop her breeding successfully last time."

Chelsie gritted her teeth. Her husband's sister was always the constant problem that just didn't have the curtesy to go away.

"Do it. Go to the barbarian lands and take whatever forces you need. Throw the sister houses against Jaclyn's forces, but this time make sure she dies," Chelsie said, her gaze rising to meet Fiona's to see a fierceness and determination that matched her own.

NINETY-THREE

Michael allowed the arguments to run around the command tent. Sitting back, he sipped his wine as they argued. Olivia, Nathanial, and Damien kept quiet beside him, although he could tell both Olivia and Nathanial were highly suspicious that he kept his peace. So far.

"Enough," Michael snapped.

They all turned to look at him, startled, as if they'd forgotten his presence.

"Sorry Michael…" Harry began.

"I wasn't asking for your opinions on the plan or your approval or alternatives. You're the ones who decided I get to be in charge of this mess, so you'll all do as you've been ordered to do," Michael said.

"We're just…."

"Fine, I accept it. I am your king, and this is now the kingdom of Vallantia. Make no mistake this is my kingdom. I am no more just a figurehead than the Warlord was. It is something you should have considered before you made your choice. As I said to those who were with me at the Stronghold in Yalleska. You will obey."

The softness of his tone was in stark contrast to his words. "That's the thing about the title you've all chosen and insist on using. Kings have ultimate authority just the same as Warlords do."

Michael allowed them to see the hint of the feared Rathadon scion of old. The young man who'd done his utmost to prove his worth to the Warlord. That part of him might have been partially hidden over the years behind who he was now, yet the monster still lurked just below the surface of who he was. He went from leader to leader around the table, holding their gaze until they conceded to him. He could see most of them recognise he was perfectly willing to enforce his orders and silence settled around the table as they all waited for their orders.

"There will be teams of the Unwanted left with you. They will have their orders from me and be assigned to some of the battle groups to assist. The bulk, as Michael has said, will ride with our attack groups," Olivia said calmly as she spoke into the stillness.

"As you know, the teams we leave with you can communicate with us and will do so if there is a need," Nathanial said.

"You've all done well so far in setting up and I'm pleased to see the first couple of strikes against the Sylannians by my forces have gone well." Michael found he was more at ease now that he'd dropped the pretence. Olivia and Nathaniel had been correct in their council. Despite his protests, it was unlikely he would have accepted anyone else. They were his band leaders who led his troops. This was now his realm.

"Now that you will have the added benefit of some of the Unwanted riding with you, we'll appoint an appropriate member to liaise with you on their capabilities."

"Although you should all be well aware of what they can do and how they can assist after Callenhain." Nathanial added smoothly.

Michael could feel the mental change in the other band leaders as they realised he'd stopped fighting them on him inheriting this whole mess and the domain. He glanced around the table as the stunned silence still held them and stood. Olivia, Nathanial and Damien stood as well, moments after he had, with the other band leaders scrambling to their feet as he turned and walked from the tent. He didn't even object as the people Tony had detailed to remain at the tent formed up around him. It was kind of useful since he didn't know which tent he was meant to be going to, and clearly they did.

It would have spoilt his exit if he'd had to stop and ask for directions.

Michael looked up as the tent flap was pushed aside by one of his guards as Nathanial and Olivia, who were trailed a little uncertainly by Damien, entered his tent. He'd given up getting irritated by the guards on station outside his tent or anywhere else he happened to be and just advised them who was to gain admission to his tent without having to request permission every time. He grinned and waved them all in. Turned out the tent they'd put up for him was larger than he expected as well.

"Well, that went about as well as I expected," Nathanial said with a laugh.

"So did I manage to channel the Warlord?" Michael asked.

"No. I think you managed something much more terrifying. You channelled the spirit of the Rathadon warlords of old," Olivia said.

"You channelled you from your early years. That youngest son of a warlord doing his utmost to survive. They finally remembered who you are," Nathanial said.

"Why do I think you enjoyed that far too much?" Olivia asked.

"If they are going to put me up on a pedestal, then they can just accept it when I overrule them and give them orders. But yes, I loved dropping my plan on them a little too much." Michael waved them all to sit down.

"We could tell," Nathanial said, slumping into one of the camp chairs.

"Besides, I finally worked out it was getting exhausting fighting what all of you are determined I am. It was distracting me from my job, which is protecting our people. Right now, that means I need to eliminate the threat that the Sylannians pose."

"Which is you at your best," Nathanial said then his eyebrows rose. "The kingdom of Vallantia? You couldn't come up with a more original name?"

"Give me a break, I didn't even think about a name so that's what came out."

Michael shook his head and determined to ignore Nathanial's laughter. He glanced at Damien as he hesitated, clearly wondering if they were still in work mode or just relaxing mode.

"This is a more casual affair Damien, sit. Our people made sure all your gear was in the same tent with Olivia?" Michael asked.

"They did." Damien said, keeping his gaze level on Michael.

"Kesha cleared you to ride and fight with us, but she briefed me fully. If your nightmares return, I expect you'll let me know," Michael said, the order in his voice clear.

"Of course. Even if I didn't admit I was having difficulties, I imagine Olivia would advise you anyway."

"We can change the plan if we have to. You can jump us in, then stay back with a guard detail or jump back out as Isabella will do," Nathanial said.

"I know what Kesha has told me, along with Olivia's and

Nathanial's opinions. I'd like to hear your own. Do you think you're recovered enough to fight with us? There is no shame if you need a little more time. We'll work it out," Michael said.

Nathanial poured a round of drinks from a collection that sat on a small table to one side of the tent and passed them out.

"Honestly, I'll be fine," Damien said, then screwed his face up. "I haven't had one of those nightmares since just before Kesha cleared me to train again. She tells me I might still have some, particularly if circumstances trigger a memory, but they shouldn't be as bad as they were. I think now what I feel is more mental exhaustion rather than physical. I'm still getting used to this whole leadership thing and me being one of the people deciding and passing back orders. Instead of just kicking back and doing as I'm told," Damien said.

"It gets easier with time," Nathanial said, grinning at him. "Besides that, you led the team in Callenhain, or had you forgotten that already?"

"Huh, I was still following the orders and instructions of all three of you, and you know it."

"Except when you deviated and followed your own judgement with great successes. If you hadn't wanted the extra responsibility, that was the wrong move," Michael said, grinning at Damien.

"Physically speaking, I actually feel better than I have since… Well, I've never been better. Which surprises even me," Damien admitted.

"I'd say given your recovery and the self-healing of your physical injuries without Kesha's intervention combined with you, feeling physically fit means you've gone through your final transition."

Damian had a hint of relief in his sigh. Not that Michael blamed him. Going through that transition period hadn't been fun for any of them, even if some of them were impacted more than others.

"Is not feeling the effects of alcohol as much as I used to a part of that, or am I just imagining it?" Damien asked, taking a sip and looking up at him.

"We think it's because of that self healing thing that Kesha mentioned," Nathanial said.

"It seems our bodies heal that as well, cleaning it out of our system almost as quickly as we consume it," Michael said.

Damien sighed, this time a little regretfully, then grinned when he found the others were all looking at him.

"So what you're telling me is I shouldn't expect to get a buzz from anything anymore." Damien contemplated his glass, then shrugged. "Given the way I reacted to tiscan, that isn't such a terrible condition to be in."

"Trust us, there are more good things than bad. You can still feel the stuff. You just won't get drunk and certainly never end up with a hangover in the morning. At least not from substance abuse," Nathanial said.

"The way you're feeling now is about as close as we get. Sheer exhaustion from the overuse of our powers," Olivia said.

Michael paused, assessing Damien for himself, then finally asked what he had to.

"You're much better at shielding than you used to be. We're all capable of hiding what we feel if we want, even from Kesha. How are you really coping now? Being tortured, suffering the metal and physical abuse Aiden ordered inflicted on you, is no simple thing."

Damien swallowed but met Michael's eyes and they were clear. "I was a mess at first. You all know that you were there. Kesha has helped me with the nightmares I was suffering. I didn't even need Olivia's urging to go to her for help. I didn't need her to heal my physical body. It seems to heal itself now, but she's helped with my mental state."

"She can achieve a great deal when her patient will admit they have a problem," Nathanial said.

"I'm aware enough to know if someone tries to drug and chain me up again, I won't cope with that so well. It won't go so well for anyone who tries that again. Particularly since it seems the drug won't be terribly effective." Damien's eyes narrowed. "I know I can fight back, even against that now."

"Let's just do our best to make sure that never happens again. Understand that if I stop you from going into certain situations, it isn't because I don't trust you, it's because I think there could be things that will bring back those nightmares for you. I do the same for Nathanial and Olivia."

"Like the cells at the Rathadon Estate. We don't know what we'll find there or even if the Sylannians have made use of them, but it will probably be my team that will descend to find out. Not yours," Nathanial said quietly.

"Yet when I was taken in Callenhain that time, you came after me as well. I don't remember much but the front end was a pleasure house of the worst kind," Damien said, his eyes shadowed.

"It was a long time ago, but regardless, I would never leave you in such a place and not even try to help. Besides, Olivia took the pleasure house side. I searched and cleared the basement. Michael enforces the same rules on all of us," Nathanial said.

Michael watched Damien's reaction and was pleased to see he took the news calmly, without the spike of hurt feelings.

"I was trying to avoid thoughts of how the prisoners may be treated. I'll be honest enough to admit if I see people strung up with signs they've been tortured, I may not take it so well," Damian said, a shudder in his otherwise too calm voice.

Michael nodded. "Fair enough. I think we'd all be astonished if you did take such things well."

"We have enough strength and will have enough to do in this attack of ours that it is a task I can and will assign to another."

Michael watched Damien carefully, satisfied that what he sensed from Damien was more relief that he'd admitted there were things he would have an issue with going forward and wasn't going to be automatically left behind out of harm's way. Michael also had more confidence that if Damien encountered something he was having difficulties with, he'd say so. Not just bottle it up and end up falling apart, as many people did.

"So we're still planning to do the big flashy attack, to send your message to the Sylannian commander?" Damien asked.

"That's the plan. Everything is in place. Taya was just waiting for us to arrive, so the attack will probably be the day after tomorrow."

Michael watched as Damien relaxed and the conversation turned to more banter between them. Olivia noted his observation and nodded. She'd monitor Damien's mental state, but at least now he wasn't as concerned about the most recent addition to his command team. Damien, regardless of if he knew it or not, had come a long way from the recruit he'd pulled out of Ranlith.

NINETY-FOUR

Michael sat on his horse. It was odd to be waiting while their forces had already engaged with the massed fighters of the Sylannians. The idea was for a decisive blow from this battle. One that would help to demoralise their enemy.

There were far more Sylannians than he'd thought the enemy could get into place in the time they had. Still, it was what they'd planned for. They'd hoped their enemy would draw substantial numbers of their people here to face them. The idea was, after all, to make it obvious that the Unwanted had returned to the battlefront. Hopefully, to the point, word would go back to the Sylannian commander. Of course, they couldn't help but embellish. Just a little. They'd added the fighters of the clans, split into two groups on either side of the Unwanted. He could feel the bristling energy coming from them. They were ready for a fight. The Sylannians had taken one homeland. They weren't about to allow themselves to be driven from another. At least not without a fight. The gritty determination was filtered with a desire for payback. The new fighters Khaliun had brought with her had been filled in on the complete defeat of the Sylannian fighting force in Callenhain and were spoiling to see a little retribution dished out.

While those of them here fought this group, other individual warbands would be retaking several of the smaller villages. If they pulled this off, it would be a decisive victory and herald a morale-crushing defeat for the Sylannian forces. One that would undoubtedly grab the attention of the Sylannian commander. Once they took the villages and surrounding farmland, the main body of their fighting force would move their line increasingly closer to Vallantia. Or that was the plan.

When you're ready, Michael, Taya said.

Time to make an entrance. Let's put on a show people, Michael said.

Michael spurred his horse forward, cold washed over him as all the Unwanted sucked in energy from all around. He, along with Olivia, Nathanial and Damien rode in the centre and as they crested the hill to ride down on the enemy, they all drew even more energy. The skies rumbled ominously in an otherwise blue sky. Their regular forces peeled aside as they thundered down on those below. As the fighters of Kallith loosed flights of arrows, they arced through the sky, unerringly striking the front ranks of the Sylannians. Michael watched, waiting for that precise moment the arrows were about to hit.

Now!

It was all he had to say. The Unwanted collectively drew in even more power and the winds picked up. Dark rents appeared in the sky, with peals of deafening thunder rolling out. The darkness spread as the boiling clouds shrouded the sun. Its warming yellow glow being replaced by an eerie blue glow as light raced through fissures in the blackness. It was as if the surrounding space held its collective breath before forked cracks of lightning struck the ground within the enemy ranks. Right at the same time, the arrows from the Kallith felled the first ranks of Sylannians. Along with Olivia, Nathanial and Damien, he collected that energy the ranks of the Unwanted had collectively drawn and slammed it into the Sylannians. The Kallith riders let loose another volley of arrows, then peeled off to ride back the way they'd come. Between the arrows, and the wave of pure energy they'd sent at the Sylannian ranks, the enemy toppled. Michael's senses were alive, alerting him to the precise moment Taya and the rest of the warbands rode up in behind his own ranks.

Shields up, Michael ordered.

The air in front of them shimmered as their shields reinforced. His order had more been a warning than because any of them were riding in without them already. Michael drew his sword and lashed out as they hit the fragmented line of the Sylannians. As his horse reared and took out the head of an attacker that rose in front of him, he thrust out with a blast of power.

We've got this, Unwanted, retreat! Taya ordered.

Michael didn't stop to second guess, riding in behind his own ranks as they were, Taya had a better view of the whole fight than he did right now, immersed in the middle of it as he was. Striking with his sword one more time as he reined in his horse to wheel around, he reinforced the muscles down his arm as the sword made contact with an opponent. As if a shroud had been removed, the screams and the clash of blades surrounding him were deafening, tiny droplets of red sprayed in the air, then his horse reared and lashed out again. He felt and heard the hooves connect as they turned and rode back out. Now that he was facing back towards their own lines, he could see they'd speared a good way into the ranks of the Sylannians.

Form up, let's get out of here, Michael ordered.

Not that it was really necessary since those he could see had heard Taya's order and were already riding out. All of them had been briefed. They were just here to make a splashy impact. Not to fight the battle out. Besides that, for this plan to work, word had to get back to the Sylannian commander. For that to happen, these Sylannians they faced had to live.

Or at least some of them did.

NINETY-FIVE

Steven stared absently over the canopy, past Vallantia and off in the distance, wondering what Jaclyn was doing. He bit his lip, admitting to himself that he hoped she wasn't facing off against Michael in battle. She'd die.

"Fool." Steven wrenched his gaze aside from the general direction Jaclyn's forces should be and swore softly to himself.

Movement on the open grassland between the edge of the forest and the estate drew his attention. Steven frowned, taking a half step towards the window, resting his hand against the glass as he peered out at the Sylannians who appeared to be running across the open space between the edge of the forest towards the estate. It wasn't just a single patrol. He'd been with the Sylannians long enough that he recognised the size of the groups they normally travelled in. Besides. These particular Sylannians were running. Jaclyn's forces tended to arrive on horseback.

Liliana? Steven called.

What's wrong? Liliana said, her mind voice laced with concern as she picked up his agitation.

Are we expecting company from Sylanna?

Are we... no. Why?

There seems to be a whole swarm of Sylannians running in this direction. I could be wrong, but I don't think they're friendly. They have their blades out and everything. It's just a suggestion, but the guards at the gate might want to close them.

Steven watched in morbid fascination as what looked like an attack force descended on his family estate. It wasn't the first time. In fact, it seemed to be the favourite pastime of every one of late. Although it was the first time he'd been awake and watching it. To his surprise, Liliana seemed to take his word for it, and the gates slammed shut.

What seemed like hordes of daggerwives swarmed out from not only the barracks but the house itself and took to the walls. Steven was aware the force that approached their walls vastly outnumbered them. Jaclyn had taken the bulk of her fighting forces with her leaving one security detail behind. Steven jumped as his doors slammed open and daggerwives rushed into his room. Before he knew it, they'd bundled him up and herded him out of the room. Reyanna hummed and Steven gave an indignant squark as the silks he wore hardened. It was a decidedly odd feeling as the silken garments solidified into a protective shell encasing his body. Steven raised his arm, flexing it, noting the shell was both firm yet oddly flexible.

"Come Steven, you can experiment later," Reyanna said.

"What's happening?"

"We're under attack."

"I gathered that. By who? Those forces are not my brothers."

"By the look of the silks, it's the king's wives." Liliana said, as her group merged seamlessly with his own.

"Isn't that unusual?"

"Extremely. The Monarch House hasn't actively gone to war in generations. I'll give you a history lesson later. Now we need to get out of here," Liliana said.

"They're coming to finish what they started?" Steven asked.

Liliana grabbed his arm, hauling him along with her. "In far greater numbers than we have here."

"I was hoping I'd been wrong about my assessment of their numbers and ours."

Steven shuddered at the thought of the enemy catching up with them. Then he skidded to a halt or would have if the wives weren't dragging him along with them. He believed the forces from the Monarch House that descended on them were his enemy, but not Jaclyn and her house.

"What is it Steven?" Liliana asked as they hit the lower floors and ran towards the rear of the estate house.

"I thought of the Monarch House forces as the enemy," Steven said, a little breathless as they ran.

"They are," Liliana said.

"I know, but I don't think of you as being the enemy anymore."

"You haven't done so for some time. We can discuss it later if you like, but right now we don't exactly have much time," Liliana said.

As if Liliana's words had been the harbinger of the assault, screams rang out.

Steven twisted as the daggerwives ushered him out a back entrance and they ran towards the postern gate.

"That sounded like it was coming from within the castle."

"It is. They're already inside. I checked for outsiders as soon as you gave warning of the attack. Their foolishness of launching their external attack too soon and your warning of it may just have saved our lives," Liliana said.

Horses were being led, one by one, out of the open gate. While Steven was glad to see them, he was a little concerned that they were leaving the estate while they were under attack.

"How did they manage that?"

"Just walked in, I presume. No one would have challenged them. The ones inside the house are wearing the royal crimson and cream, just like the ones outside the gate."

Steven's emotions were jumbled as he mounted the horse that one of the daggerwives held for him. Steven's eyes widened, and he went to dismount, only to be prevented.

"Evan and my parents are still in there."

"We don't have time, Steven," Liliana said, gesturing to the daggerwives around them. "Let's go now before we're spotted."

Steven stared desperately back at his home as his group thundered away from the castle. Guilt weighed him down, even though under the circumstances there wasn't anything he could have done. Except to think of his friend before he ran. After all, Evan had been captured because instead of running for his life ahead of the Sylannian invasion, he'd come to wake Steven up.

CHAPTER
NINETY-SIX

As splinters sprayed over him, Evan raised his hand to shield his face, ducking reflexively. Dust particles rose in the room and a space appeared where the solid wooden doors had stood moments before. Evan's eyes widened as Sylannians poured into the room. Then he was flat on his back with a blade pressed against his throat.

"Um, hello..." Evan said.

It occurred to him he was getting a little sick of ending up in this position and he really wished Sylannians would find an original method of introducing themselves. Evan shivered as the collar around his neck vibrated, then stilled.

"Who are you?" the Sylannian said.

"No one, no one at all," Evan said.

"Then why would you wear Jaclyn's collar?"

"It's Myra, the primewife, who collared me. I've never met Jaclyn. Well, except that first day when she took the estate, and she had me thrown in the cells," Evan said, then mentally kicked himself. He really had to learn not to give up so much information to the enemy.

"So Primewife Myra obviously decided you have value, since she went to the effort of taking you out of the cells and placed Jaclyn's collar around your neck. If you're no one, why would she do such a thing?"

"I'm friends with Steven and he's Jaclyn's husband now, or one of them at least…" Evan said, trailing off as the woman on top of him appeared outraged.

The blade lifted from his throat as the woman stood issuing rapid fire instructions to those with her. The Sylannians hauled him unceremoniously to his feet and dragged him out into the hallway and down the stairs. His captors shoved him into Speaker Rathadon's rooms and he found himself on his knees towards the centre of the room. Evan didn't dare look to either Lady Rathadon or Speaker Rathadon. He froze under the glare of the Sylannian.

"You're not with the other group who invaded, are you?" Evan asked brightly.

"Evan, be quiet," Lady Rathadon said, then she spoke to the Sylannians in their smooth flowing language.

The imperious looking Sylannian swung her head to stare at Lady Rathadon. Her eyes widened just a fraction before her blade flashed out. Lady Rathadon dropped and rolled. As she came up to her feet, her hand slammed into the abdomen of the Sylannian guarding her, who doubled over and gasped of pain. Metal rang as the blade the Sylannian had carried clattered on the stone floor. Lady Rathadon snatched up the blade and blocked another attack.

Evan yelped as a hand grabbed him until he realised it was Speaker Rathadon. The Speaker tugged at his shirt and they scrambled back as the enemy seemed to forget his existence as they surrounded Lady Rathadon. Blood sprayed as multiple blades plunged into Lady Rathadon.

"No!" Evan yelled.

Evan caught sight of her through the ring of the enemy as she swayed on her feet. Impossibly, a smile was on her face, as one hand pressed ineffectively against one of her wounds.

"My son may have let you and your king live if you'd left this land and never returned. You think you've won Fiona, but you haven't." Lady Rathadon coughed, blood splattering from her mouth, yet satisfaction and triumph filled her tone. "He may not like me, but I'm still his mother and for this one act, he'll kill your whole family line."

"Silence!" Fiona screamed in rage as her blade swung once more, striking across Lady Rathadon's neck.

Lady Rathadon's knees buckled, then she slumped to the floor, an impossible seeming amount of blood pooling around her from her injuries. Evan flinched as Speaker Rathadon screamed, as if mortally wounded. Evan barely had time to catch Steven's father before he collapsed unconscious. He stared down at the unconscious Speaker a moment longer, then lowered him gently down to the floor.

"Who is her son?" Fiona said, as she paced towards him, her eyes glittering with rage.

Evan swallowed, taking in the blood sprayed on the woman's face and hands and the damp patches on her maroon clothes. With a start, he realised the blood didn't all belong to Lady Rathadon. Despite the odds, it seemed as if Lady Rathadon had at least managed to injure Fiona during the brief fight.

"Which one?"

Pain filled the side of his face as her hand slapped him, and Evan toppled onto his side. Hands grabbed his arms and hauled him to his feet.

"There's more than one?" Fiona asked.

Evan nodded. "Steven and Michael, but neither of them are here."

"Where are they?"

"Well, Steven was here, but I guess Jaclyn's people got him out before you broke in. Jaclyn took him as a husband, you see. Something about him having royal Sylannian blood because of his mother," Steven said before it occurred to him that he probably shouldn't have mentioned that part. His gaze slid over to the dead body of Lady Rathadon before returning to his questioner.

"You lie!"

"No, Steven was certain about that part. He was terrified about the idea of having one wife, let alone when he found out he had hundreds..."

Fiona spun, words streaming from her mouth. Evan didn't understand a word of it, but he was fairly certain they weren't pleasant or polite words. Finally, Fiona turned back to him, her eyes glittering. Evan had the rather unpleasant impression that perhaps she wasn't quite of a sound mind.

"Where is the other one, this Michael?"

"I don't know. Maybe a good place to start looking will be wherever Jaclyn and her forces are fighting."

"Why would he be there? Did she take him as a husband as well?"

Evan clapped a hand over his mouth, which unfortunately did little to hide his laughter. As Fiona's eyes narrowed and she took a step towards him, Evan's humour evaporated and he held up his hand.

"No, Michael would never accept that, and I doubt anyone would be able to force him to. You'll probably find Michael riding at the head of the warbands."

"Michael is the Warlord?"

"No, Michael is the warleader."

"Take him to the cells and someone find out where in this barbaric land Jaclyn is hiding. I want her head and that of her barbarian husband on spikes," Fiona said, her voice threaded with malice.

"The old man Primewife?" One of the Sylannians standing guard on him asked.

"His mind is likely gone. He was mate bonded to the lost daughter of the Monarch House for a long time. Kill him," Fiona said.

Before Evan could protest, hands took hold of him in an iron grip and started hauling him away. As a blade flashed and blood sprayed, Evan called out in denial as he was dragged from the room.

EVAN NEVER THOUGHT he'd be grateful to be locked up in the cells again, and yet he was. Somehow, it seemed far safer locked up in the cell than it would be up in the house. Evan waited until the doors clanged shut, cutting off the sight of the enemy who'd proven to be far more brutal than the previous lot, then slumped to the ground, curling into a ball. He paid no attention to the tears that tracked down his cheeks.

"What's wrong with you?" Peter Kastler demanded.

"They killed the Speaker and Lady Rathadon."

"They killed Constance as well. She was just trying to negotiate our release, and they killed her."

"These are worse than Jaclyn's forces."

"How do you figure that?"

Evan just shook his head and ignored Peter. There was no value in getting into an argument with the man. Evan squeezed his eyes shut and tried to settle his mind. The screams that filtered into his mind didn't make it an easy proposition. Evan's eyes flared open, and he pushed himself up from the floor. From the moment he and Steven had been discovered talking with each other, the Sylannians had maintained a shield around his mind, effectively preventing him from calling out to anyone. Now it was gone.

Steven? Evan waited, then sighed. He hoped the lack of contact meant Steven was still shielded or just too far away. *Ben?*

What's gone wrong?

How did you know something has gone wrong?

I can feel the grief in your mindvoice. What's happened? Steven?

The Sylannians got him out before the attack. I think.

What are you talking about? We haven't attacked the estate.

Another group of Sylannians did. They aren't like Commander Jaclyn. They killed... Evan paused as tears welled up in his eyes and his throat restricted. *Michael needs to know the one in charge of this new lot, Fiona. She killed Speaker and Lady Rathadon.*

Why?

I couldn't understand the argument they were having, Lady Rathadon and Fiona. It was in Sylannian, but then the Lady Rathadon attacked them first. She fought better than I could have, but there were too many of them. They surrounded her. So much blood...

Easy Evan, just breathe.

Evan took a moment before he resolutely pushed his grief down and swiped at the tears with the back of one hand.

I think she did it on purpose. She knew she'd die.

Why would Lady Rathadon do that?

She, Lady Rathadon, told Fiona that Michael might have allowed them all to live for the invasion alone but for killing her, he would avenge her death. That Michael would destroy Fiona and her king for what they'd done.

Powers, all right, tell me the rest of it. What happened to Speaker Rathadon?

He was in agony when Lady Rathadon died, then he was unconscious. They said he'd been connected to Lady Rathadon too long for him to survive her death. As they dragged me away, I saw their knives plunge into him. Over and over, he was unconscious. He couldn't fight back...

Evan swallowed the bile that rose in his throat, aware he'd unwittingly shared the complete nightmare with Ben. Somehow, the shared horror over the event he could sense coming from Ben made him feel a little better.

You're not weak or a failure. None of this was your fault and if you'd tried to fight, you'd be dead. Don't give them cause to kill you. I need to go and pass this on to Michael, but if you need anything at all, call me. I might not be able to help directly, but I can listen.

Thank you Ben. I don't think I'll come out of this... just say goodbye to Steven for me. Make sure Michael knows none of this is Steven's fault. Lady Rathadon manoeuvred events so Jaclyn would take him as a husband. Steven's done what he's had to.

You can tell Steven yourself when we get you out of there. Ease your mind. Michael is already aware that Jaclyn has taken Steven as a husband. In fact, Michael gave Steven some of the same advice I'm going to give you. Do what you need to do. Just stay alive until we're in a position to help you.

Evan had the uncanny feeling as if the other man was standing right next to him and squeezing his shoulder in support.

I'll try. Evan whispered as the presence faded, leaving him alone in the nightmare's company that replayed in his head. Over and over again he saw Lady Rathadon's death, followed by the Speaker while he was being dragged away.

NINETY-SEVEN

Olivia waited, leaning on her horse with the Unwanted around her and the other fighting bands when everyone's focus shifted, Olivia tracked what grabbed their attention and spotted Isabella walking through the gathered fighters. Men from Tony's warband trailed behind her. If the pair who trailed the girl were annoyed at being tasked to protect Isabella rather than travelling with Michael, it didn't show. If anything, some of them appeared to be fiercely protective of the girl. They felt a sense of responsibility and blamed themselves, a little unfairly, she thought, for failing to protect her from Aiden. As it had turned out, Isabella did not need protection now that she came into her powers. Isabella had kept her head and not only dealt with Aiden herself, but then protected Damien until help arrived.

"Ready?"

Isabella looked down at the ground before looking back up again. "As I'll ever be."

"You'll be fine." Olivia reassured the girl and stepped forward, checking that Isabella had her fighting leathers on correctly. "We've practiced this. Once you jump us to the drop off point, you'll stay with your guards. We won't let anything happen to you."

"Damien would kill us if we did." One of the others muttered.

Olivia spared a moment to stare at the offending team member who raised his hands palm up, looking totally unrepentant. Of course, he was correct, but that didn't mean he had to voice their likely fate if anything happened to Isabella.

"I would as well." Isabella said, a fierce note in her voice.

"You would what?" Olivia asked.

"If anyone tries to hurt Damien again. I'll kill them. I might not know how to like the rest of you, but as Aiden found out, I don't need to know the how," Isabella said, a breath of the veil dancing in her eyes.

"I don't doubt you would. We all would. However, if anything goes wrong, jump into the grey and go back to the Smith's estate."

"I will, I promise."

Olivia smiled at the girl's earnestness. She was so calm and mature some moments before reverting to the young woman she'd been at others. Right now, thankfully, it was the quiet, responsible Isabella who stood in front of her. Olivia guided Isabella to her horse, taking a moment to stare at Isabella's guards who nodded at her, their expressions grave. They didn't need any orders to be issued to them, they'd already been briefed. Their only part in this was to ensure Isabella's safety. It was one of the few concerns she had with this plan. While it was true that Isabella had proven herself capable against Aiden, and in defending her brother. She'd also reacted on pure instinct alone, and her brief exposure to fighting was more of a liability than an asset. It was something Olivia vowed to remedy when she had time. If she had anything to do with it, Isabella would learn how to defend herself with her powers and with weapons.

Olivia rubbed her horse on the neck as it leant into her. "Come on now, we have work to do, you and I." Olivia smiled as her horse snorted again. She sometimes wondered if their beasts understood far more than they gave them credit for. She pushed such idle thoughts aside and mounted, then nodded at Isabella who took a deep breath.

Everyone, stay calm and focused on the person in front of you.

Olivia's eyebrows rose. All hints of the nervous young woman had totally disappeared from Isabella's mindvoice. Instead, her voice was strong and calm. That woman who'd spoken screamed of self assurance and competence. It gave a peek into the woman she would become, even if the girl didn't believe it herself. Waves of cold smashed over her, crashing out over their entire group. In this Isabella was much like her brother had been. Extreme raw talent. She groaned to herself. They'd just gone through all this with Damien. It made her wonder what they'd done so wrong that the powers served up another one.

They were wrenched into the grey with a suddenness that was startling despite the warning prior to it happening. Olivia craned her neck, glancing around their group, relieved to see they all appeared to be present. She leant forward and rubbed her horse's neck, although she had to admit the beast didn't seem concerned in the slightest. It walked forward along with the rest. Given she'd practiced this manoeuvre with Isabella picking the target from her mind a few times now, she shouldn't have been surprised. Yet she was. They'd no sooner entered the place where the veil resided than they'd appeared on the other side exactly where they were meant to. Where Isabella had directed them too on the crossroad that led to an occupied village. They'd worked out during the practice sessions that Isabella and Damien could take the reference point from just about anyone to take them to a place, as long as that person was familiar with the location. Not just somewhere they personally knew. As the cold dispelled, Olivia scanned the area one more time.

"Isabella, stay put with your guard detail. Everyone else, let's go. You know the drill."

Olivia didn't wait for the acknowledgement. Isabella and her guards would stay right where they'd been told to. Isabella had performed her job. Now it was the time for the Unwanted to do theirs.

The inrush of the veil gave away that the Unwanted had drawn the veil to them to obscure themselves from casual observation as they travelled the relatively short distance to the village. The thinnest of layers of the veil surrounding them and a gentle push emanating from their group, encouraging any who might stumble on them to forget what they'd seen and go elsewhere. They weren't invisible, just extremely hard for anyone to focus on. Olivia waited until the warband flowed around her so she had a protective layer around her.

Stay alert, I'll range ahead.

Her horse was well used to keeping up with its herd mates and paid no mind at all as she sent her consciousness out ranging ahead. She trusted those around her to pick up threats that may be closer to hand while she was looking for the outer perimeter guards. While they'd spent the last few days preparing for this fight, she wasn't willing to leave even that small detail to chance. While human nature was basically lazy and fell into habit. It didn't mean that just because the guards had been in certain positions the previous nights, that they were in the same positions tonight. Her mind raced ahead, fleeting past trees, ignoring the soft little sparks of the animals. A huge glow of life mass caused her to backtrack and double check. As she focused in on what had tugged at her attention, a distinct shape took form in her mind. A gigantic tree cat on the prowl. It was early for the beast to be up and on the move. It caused her to wonder what had drawn its attention and what it stalked in these early morning hours.

It shouldn't come near us as big as our group is, but be warned, there's a tree cat on the prowl between us and the sentry post off to our left.

Olivia sensed the acknowledgement of the warband around her and an uptick in the level of alertness from them all. She drew her focus back to her current job. Wisps of the veil had appeared, weaving their thin strands through everything. Thin traces sparkling through the trees heralding that the dawn wasn't far off. The perfect time to attack was fast approaching. The hours before dawn, just as the sentries were at their lowest ebb. As a muddy red glow came into focus, Olivia's eyes narrowed.

The sentry post to our left remains unchanged.

Olivia didn't allow the departure of her own riders tasked with taking out the enemy sentries to distract her. Instead, she sent her mind racing over the forest, looping around the village. It didn't take long before she spied the second sentry post with the muted, nearly indistinguishable glow of the sentries inside.

The sentries at the entrance of the village are exactly where we expected them to be. Currently, they are asleep. If you play it right, they might never wake.

Olivia caught the amused response as the second group went off towards their targets. Not completely satisfied, even though they'd hit the outer perimeter of the village where they'd dismount soon, she sped forward over the village. There was a stuttering, almost fitful, massed glow towards the centre of the village, where the villagers were being kept in a cage constructed of wood. The second sign of life, showing many people all in close proximity, was at the town meeting hall where the bulk of the Sylannians slept. Only a few of the huts had survived the attack to take it over and a cursory scan told Olivia they were all empty. She felt a tug on her awareness, knowing it was time to withdraw, but briefly checked on the final sentry post and those keeping watch over the water on the jetty. Satisfied, she fled back to herself. Olivia lent forward and patted the neck of her horse as she noticed they'd stopped just out of town. She dismounted and passed the reins off, her eyes scanning over the various members of the warband before focusing on the small group to her left.

"As expected, your targets are on the jetty. Kill most of them but remember at least one needs to escape to report us being here to their commander. Then get to the villagers." Olivia paused as they nodded, then looked over at the rest of the team. "Give me a moment I'll make sure the three other assault teams are in position at their targets."

"We'll do our best," Vance, who had the lead of the jetty team, said.

We're in position, Olivia reached out connecting effortlessly with Michael and registered when Nathanial and Damien joined their conversation.

My team as well. Nothing unexpected here, Damien said.

My team is just about to ride over the hill and commence our attack on our target. A thunder of hooves and an image of a grassy slope accompanied Nathanial's words.

Good work everyone. Don't forget this is only going to confuse our enemy about our location if someone from each of our villages escapes to report that the Unwanted attacked them. Attack your targets when ready, Michael said.

Olivia drew her attention back to her team. "Let's go."

With her othersight overlaying her night vision, she could see well enough as could the rest of those with her. She'd often mused it must be a strange thing for people to be incapable to see things around them clearly just because it was dark. Of course, she could put up light easily enough, but in this case it was not only unnecessary, it could also give away their presence.

She'd rather the first warning their enemy had occurred while she was slitting their throats.

As they reached the outer limits of the village, she paused, quickly scanning the quiet village. A stillness that was about to be disrupted. She focused in on those who stood on the jetty. Satisfied they still stood with their back to the village and consequently to her entire warband, she drew her long dagger and jogged lightly through the village towards where the Sylannians slept. While she'd seen all this when she'd used her othersight to scout ahead, it was a habit to make sure everything really was as she'd seen it in her mind. Not that she didn't trust her abilities, more that she didn't know what abilities others might have. If she could use her sight to check places in the distance, then it was within the realm of possibility that another could cause it to appear different from the prying mental eyes of a spy. As she reached the hall, Olivia paused, waiting with the rest of her team.

We're in position near the Jetty, Vance said.

Go. Olivia ordered.

Olivia wrapped her power around her and nodded to those nearest the doors. Without hesitation, they pulled the double doors open and Olivia wasted no time in running into the room. She was grateful that these village meeting halls all tended to be built the same way. Just an open room with little else in it, except for a few chairs. Of course, this one was filled with improvised cots with Sylannians sleeping in them. She sprinted further into the room, heading to the rear, knowing her team followed her in. There was no point in having a team with her if she was going to stop in the doorway, preventing their entrance. She reached the far end of the room before the first scream sounded as some invaders woke, even if it was only briefly as they died under the blades of her team shortly after waking. As a Sylannian near her reared out of the cot, Olivia struck across the enemy's throat. Not all their opponents died straight away. It was feeling more than sound that made her dive to one side as multiple blades came for her from behind. She swore. It meant at least one of her own had gone down, but she didn't have time to check. She turned to face the threat, thrusting out with her shield as blades came, striking at her again.

We've secured the prisoners.

Good, get them out.

Olivia twisted to one side and struck back at her opponent. Pain lanced down her side, giving away someone had managed to get through not only her guard while she was distracted but through her shields as well. Thrusting out with her power, she pushed the other person she'd been fighting aside, satisfied to see her opponent stagger back and take out another of their companions.

Olivia turned, wincing as her side protested the move. Her blade rose reflexively to deflect another strike from the enemy who'd successfully penetrated her defences. Olivia drew her second blade, her othersight bringing the room alive with the swirling power all around her. While it wasn't as useful in these settings, there were too many of them all drawing power in a confined spot. It was enough to show her the one she faced was far stronger in her abilities with the veil than her companions. Olivia's eyes narrowed as she realised that was how her shields had been defeated. A drop of blood splashed onto her hand, her own, not her opponents, and she knew she had to finish this battle fast. She might heal better than most, but it wouldn't stop her from bleeding out.

As her opponent focused on the blood, she flushed with triumph and renewed her attack. Olivia ignored her side and slammed her shield into her enemy. The Sylannian staggered and Olivia lunged forward with a lightning fast series of strikes.

Olivia, down!

She didn't know why one of her team had yelled the warning, but she trusted them implicitly. Olivia dove for the floor, her vision blurring and darkening around the edges as her side protested. She rolled onto her uninjured side, looking up to see several members of her team press forward, stepping over her to take out the opponents who'd been going for her back. As a blade struck down from the momentarily forgotten attacker, she raised her booted foot and slammed it repeatedly into the enemy. Power flared around the Sylannian's blade and heat sliced down her leg as her opponent struck. Her attacker staggered and went down as Olivia slammed into her opponent's knee. Olivia rolled up and hurled herself on top of her attacker, drawing on the veil she used it to help her pin her enemy to the floor. Olivia sucked in more power and her whole body flared. The flame and sword on her blade flickered with the veil being fed through it as she plunged the weapon down towards the enemy's heart. There was a slight resistance as Olivia encountered the Sylannians body armour before her power flared once more and her blade sliced through it. The smell of burning flesh assaulted her nose as her blade seared through the woman's flesh. The enemy's scream cut short as Olivia's blade thrust into the woman's heart.

Olivia checked for another threat, but only observed a handful of the enemy being engaged by her team. As they fell, she rolled over onto her back and closed her eyes, sucking in air as she let go of one of her blades to press her hand against her side.

NINETY-EIGHT

Jaclyn rode through the forest, for once grateful she'd spent so many years in the trader lands and learnt how to ride. After a fashion, at least. It still galled her that not only did those of the clans outride her and her people. It appeared the barbarians did as well. Not only did they know how to fight while on the creatures, but they were experts at fighting people who were on them. At least if all their losses of late were anything to go by. She still preferred fighting on foot but to get from one place to another, if the river wasn't an option, she had to admit horses made the journey easier.

"First, there is no need for you to be out here. You should retreat to a place of safety," Sasha said.

"There is every reason for me to be out here. I need to see what is happening myself to make the best decisions for not only our house but our people." Jaclyn kept her tone neutral with effort. After all, it was the woman's job to protect her.

Jaclyn kept her exasperation to herself. Or at least tried to. She glanced across at Myra and they shared a smile. It was the difference between being one who had actual responsibility and one whose job was to follow orders. It was also extremely likely the pair of them didn't behave as most of their peers would. None of the elite in their world would normally take more risk than they were forced to. Staying back in the safety of the Rathadon estate, the way she had, while others died for her and their king, was more the norm than the rarity. No one had thought anything of it. Yet the reports she'd been receiving had been concerning. She'd learnt to see things for herself and take a lead in battle, even if it put her and her family at risk. It was a major reason they'd succeeded in the trader lands, because she led.

"This plan of attack was ours. Of course we want to be here," Myra said.

"Of course Primewife, but these people, they are not the clans."

Jaclyn frowned, looking over at Sasha. "What do you mean?"

"They are much better at fighting First even without their warleader." Sasha looked like she wanted to be having any conversation other than this one, but continued on. "With their warleader and the ones who ride with him, joining their other forces in battle. Well, they are different First, abnormally strong."

"They shouldn't be able to do what they do," another wife whispered.

Jaclyn understood what the daggerwives meant but didn't acknowledge it.

"I still don't understand how they got here so fast. They were all the way over the other side. The diversion we arranged should have kept them occupied for much longer," Myra said.

"It gave us some lead time." Jaclyn didn't add that she feared it wasn't enough.

With Myra, she didn't have to. They were both of one accord in this. Although hearing these who'd been up close and battled the barbarians come to the same conclusion she had helped in the decision, she had to make. This was one of the last checks she had to make before making that call. She'd have no one say she ran away without good cause.

It was impossible for her to hide her innermost thoughts from Myra any more than her fellow wife could hide from her. Their minds were too intertwined with the mate bond they shared with Ricardo. No matter how hard they tried to distance themselves from each other over the years, it was impossible. If this was the case with them, she shuddered to think what it must be like for regular family units with hundreds of wives all holding mate bonds with their husband. With their innermost thoughts, bleeding into each other's minds.

You know we can't go back unless you take the Monarch House, Myra said.

I know.

Jaclyn glanced over at Myra, seeing the compassion in her eyes, before turning to look straight ahead. Before that battle occurred, she needed to push the weakness in her heart aside. That small part of her, the young girl who remembered her brother and that he'd taken the time and the risk of saving her life before he took down their mother's house and took the throne for himself. Jaclyn shook herself and drew her attention back to the current battle.

"There were no problems taking your assigned villages?" Jaclyn asked.

"None First. When the barbarian fighting units aren't around, their habitations fall easily enough," the daggerwife said.

"No problems with getting through this forest?"

"We've taken steps to avoid the large estate on the other side," Sasha said.

Jaclyn smiled at the hesitation she heard. "But?"

"There are signs the barbarians cleaned out some of our fighting forces that made it into the forest," the daggerwife said.

"We've had losses here already?" Myra asked.

"Why wasn't I informed?"

"I don't know First. I think the sister house involved went off on their own for some reason. We didn't realise they'd gone missing at all. Until we found the bodies." Sasha said.

Jaclyn's lips pressed together. Those with her here should have known better than to go it alone. They won by fighting together against a common enemy. Not by going off to find their own glory. Instead, they found their death. She barely stopped herself from sighing in relief as her group rode into their camp. Their tents spread out through the trees, bright splashes of colour in the predominant green, brown and tan of the forest. She frowned.

"I hope you've scouted the area for signs of the enemy camp. If they've wiped out sister houses in the forest, it's likely they're around here somewhere," Myra said.

"Of course Primewife Myra. Our scouts have checked. There are hills around our current forward camp and more forest land. Even from the top of the hills, there's no sign of our camp, not even smoke from the cooking fires."

Jaclyn dismounted, turning as one of the daggerwives ran forward and took the reins of the horse she'd been riding and led it away. The others scuttled around, daggerwives forming around her, while some went into the tent to clear it before they allowed her to enter. Not that it was conceivable that anyone else would be in it, but she hadn't survived this long by taking stupid risks. With the maroon and cream spiderweb pattern, no one else would dare to take it over. Unless, of course, there was someone here that was aligned with her brother's wives, but she was fairly certain someone would have noticed if anyone else had gone in there before her arrival.

NINETY-NINE

Kesha stood growling under her breath and paced. While she understood why she'd been left behind, it didn't mean she had to like it. Regardless of how much sense it seemed to make on the surface. All it had taken was for the Unwanted to get busy running their raids and some patients who were too injured to stay at the forward camp. The leadership who remained decided it would be better if she remained with her patients here at the Smith's estate. Well behind the lines of their camp, let alone the enemy. It didn't matter how much she'd argued with them. They all seemed to disregard the fact she'd been riding with the Unwanted for over a year. It was funny how this was the first time anyone had decided it was too dangerous. If someone had told the person she'd been back then that she would be displeased that the Unwanted had left her behind, she would have doubted their sanity.

She was taking a break in the garden behind the healing hall. Not that anyone in the hall currently needed her help. Narantuya and Yangir, the Kallith healers, took over the day-to-day care of the patients. Others with healing had been arriving at the

Smith's to assist as soon as word went out their forces had engaged the Sylannians. As she looked up she stopped mid-turn. Kesha's eyes widened as Isabella appeared in the middle of the garden and started running towards the house. Kesha shrieked in protest as arrows rained down towards the girl and guards started running from the house, drawing their swords. She stood transfixed as Isabella looked up, her lips pressing in a thin line and the arrows seemed to bounce off something Kesha couldn't see. Power flared in Isabella's eyes, just as she'd seen in the members of the Unwanted when they were drawing a great deal of the veil. It was the only warning there was before the guards charging towards her went flying. Kesha heard yelling and calls from deep within the house that they were under attack and groaned. How they didn't recognise the uniform that Isabella wore was that of an Unwanted she didn't know. She turned and started running towards the door when she heard a deep bellow that was unmistakably the Smith.

"Stop you fools. She's one of the Unwanted."

Kesha almost wilted with relief, except she could feel Isabella's urgency. Kesha gasped as Isabella was suddenly in front of her. Isabella's eyes were still glowing with unreleased power. The other woman reached out and grabbed Kesha's hand.

"You must come. Olivia needs you."

Before Kesha could respond, a deep aching cold slammed into her. She doubled over in pain, then shivered as the cold seemed to be pushed away. Her breath caught as, other than the fact she could feel Isabella's hand grasping her own, she couldn't see anything. A deep, impenetrable grey enveloped her.

Sorry Kesha, stay calm, you're safe. We're nearly there, Isabella said.

Kesha swallowed, trying to follow the instructions she'd been given. If this was how they were all travelling around, she wanted no part of it. Kesha shuddered, squeezing her eyes shut against the nothingness. It made her want to shriek in absolute horror. Then, after what had seemed a lifetime, they stepped out, back into a world she recognised. Although they were nowhere near the Smith's estate. Row upon row of tents, along with the uniforms worn by the warbands, told her she was now at the camp. She stumbled into a run because Isabella had broken into a run and dragged her along with her. She could see the startled glances from those in uniform as they passed by. Their calls asking what was wrong went unanswered as Isabella continued steadfastly through the camp. Kesha was gasping for breath before Isabella drew to a halt and propelled her towards a tent. She had the moment to recognise those who stood on guard around it were members of the Unwanted before she was pushed inside.

"Isabella what...." Kesha stopped as her eyes adjusted to the sudden dimness inside. Olivia's unconscious form came into focus where she lay on a cot to one side of the tent. Those surrounding the unconscious woman turned, their eyes widening in shock at her entrance. "Get out of my way. Isabella, get me two of the Unwanted in here. I might need their power." Kesha didn't care that her tone was harsh as she shoved her way between them and fell to her knees at Olivia's side.

"The healer needs a couple of you to help. In case she needs more power."

Kesha ignored everyone and started undoing all the fastenings on Olivia's uniform. She was about to growl at whoever pushed beside her, then realised it was Shallan, who immediately went to work stripping Olivia of her fighting leathers. The process was completed far faster than she could have done herself.

"Thank you." Kesha sucked in her breath as the wadded fabric, soaked with blood the leathers had held that in place, fell away revealing the deep knife wound that had plunged into Olivia's abdomen.

She placed her hands on the open wound and closed her eyes, allowing her consciousness to flow into the other woman. She ignored the strident orders for everyone to clear out, although a part of her mind was amused to identify Isabella as the one giving orders. She sensed the others retreat, except for Isabella and the two members of the Unwanted who knelt by her side, leaving her security and that of her patient to others, she dismissed everything and sunk deep into her healing trance. She allowed her energy to flow, aiding the efforts of Olivia's own body to heal. Even for one as powerful as Olivia, the wound was dangerous, and she'd lost far too much blood. Kesha pulsed her own healing over the deep cuts and internal organs, willing the flesh to knit back together just that bit faster. There were some parts of the body that, when struck or pierced, meant death. She was certain if the person concerned hadn't been a member of the Unwanted, that person so injured would already be dead.

As it was, she made a mental note to advise Isabella she'd chosen correctly in jumping through that horrible cold greyness to fetch her to her patient, rather than the other way around. She hated to think what the impact a second journey through that bone aching cold would have on the open injuries that Olivia had. Kesha's awareness ran through her patient's body, grateful there was only one injury she could find that she needed her help with. She was just feeling her energy fading on her when a flow of power streamed into her from another. Kesha relaxed, recognising the pureness of the veil as coming from a member of the Unwanted and put it to good use. It was different, stronger, but she could use it anyway, even if she couldn't store or keep any of the excess they might feed her for long. Kesha did one more sweep of Olivia's body, assuring herself this was the only thing that needed her attention, as bad as it was, then drew her attention back to knitting the ripped, bleeding flesh. She'd already mended the internal organs that would lead to death if untreated. Now it was time to close up the wound, one small piece at a time. Slowly withdrawing as she did so until she reached the skin on the surface. She sunk back, sighing, allowing the strong supporting hands that steadied her to ease her back onto a pile of cushions.

"On my orders, don't let anyone near her, let alone try to move her," Kesha said.

Her job was done for now. She could afford to slip into an exhausted sleep, just for a short period of time. Kesha set a mental trigger so her awareness would alert her when her patient woke up. She didn't have to worry about the Unwanted, they would follow her orders in this regard. When it came to healing, they trusted her far more than they would anyone else in the camp. Add to that, with Olivia's safety, they'd not allow the possibility of anyone hurting her. Kesha rolled over to her side. A blanket was drawn over her and she allowed sleep to drag her into its depths.

CHAPTER
ONE HUNDRED

Steven closed his eyes and took a deep breath. In this moment, he could convince himself that he was free and walking in the gardens of his family estate. Which, oddly enough, is where he'd rather be. Instead of in his wife's war camp, surrounded by those who were the enemy of his people. Much to his surprise, they hadn't travelled too far away from Vallantia when they'd fled his family estate. They were only a couple of days' ride from the city of his birth. Part of him wished they were further away from the newly arrived forces of the king. Except now they were in an unenviable position. Stuck between his brother's massed warbands and the Sylannian king's fighting forces. Both those opposing forces wanted Jaclyn dead. It was unfortunate that now he wasn't certain he wanted Jaclyn or any of his wives to die.

If he called out to his brother, Steven knew Michael would do his best to make sure he lived. At least until Michael inevitably worked out, he was a traitor. Steven had to admit, if only to himself, despite his best efforts, he cared for the fate of these women. So now he wasn't convinced Michael wouldn't have him

583

strung up as well. He also wasn't entirely sure he didn't deserve such a fate.

"Come, husband, it's best you return inside."

"Just a little bit longer?"

Arianne shook her head. "It's not safe."

"Ricardo gets to wander around more," Steven said, grumbling under his breath.

"Ricardo is far more capable of defending himself from attackers. I've practised blade work with you. With all due respect, husband, you're just as likely to cut yourself and do the enemy's work for them."

Steven spluttered indignantly, then sighed. He'd like to be offended, but unfortunately, Arianne was correct. It had taken him a lifetime to come to the conclusion that he was incompetent with the sword. Or more recently, as he'd discovered, he was even worse with the long daggers his wives favoured.

"Very well."

Steven closed the small distance between where he'd been standing to enter Jaclyn's command tent. The thing was the largest he'd ever seen. It was even segmented inside with separate rooms, one of which was his. As far as tents and camping went, the Sylannians, or at least Jaclyn, didn't believe in roughing it. There were collapsible chairs, tables, cushions, and plush beds. His bed was even more comfortable than the one he'd slept in back home. Despite his apprehension, it didn't even take long to pack everything up and move. Although he didn't know why he'd been concerned about that little detail. It wasn't as if he was expected to pack anything. Not even his own things, what there were of them. The thousands of wives that surround him did all that.

Steven strolled across the thick carpets and through the silken divide, then fell back onto the mound of pillows and cushions that made up his bed. One duty he hadn't been exempt from, much to his shock under the circumstances, was his sole duty these days. To breed with one of his wives. The Sylannians seemed to throw themselves at the duty with an almost fanatical obsession. Then again, as few boys as the Sylannian's birthed, he guessed they'd die out as a people altogether if they didn't. They more than made up for that with the birth rate of girls, which explained why there were so many of them. At the whisper of silk, Steven rolled over lazily to check on who'd entered. Jaclyn stalked into the room, a scowl firmly in place.

"Bad news?"

"Your brother's position is proving hard to locate with any certainty." Jaclyn scowled. "He shouldn't be able to move around as much as he reportedly is, but the firstwives of the sister houses all swear they've faced off against him, and lost, in wildly different locations."

"Shouldn't we be concentrating on your brother's wives and their forces?"

"I know where they are," Jaclyn said, a growl of impatience in her voice.

"If you can't find Michael and his warbands, then surely it's better to deal with the Monarch House forces? From what I've heard, they are much closer to us," Steven said.

"How do you know the location of the king's forces?"

Steven mentally kicked himself that he'd given away more than he'd intended to.

"I've been with you all long enough to pick up some words. Add to that the echo of what people are thinking. I kind of pieced it together. Besides, we aren't that far from Vallantia."

"Well, the Monarch House fighters don't know our precise location just yet. As it turns out, while I may not know where the warleader is, I'm told we've found his command camp."

Steven weighed his words, then sighed. It wouldn't matter

how he phrased it. Jaclyn wasn't going to like it, but he had to try.

"Let me try to speak with him."

"I know the warleader is your brother, but he is also the leader of the enemy, and I won't allow you to be at risk. Even from him," Jaclyn said, stroking his temple with gentle fingers.

Steven took it as a positive sign that at least his wife wasn't angry with him.

"We're running out of options though. Aren't we?" Steven swallowed, then rushed on. "With the Monarch House on one side, they may not have found us yet, but they must know we're not too far away. Then Michael, on the other. I'm not the best tactician, but we're not in a good position."

"Hush husband. Leave such decisions to me. It's not your fault. No wonder you're stressed being in the middle of my war camp. You'll see. I'll win this war, then deal with the Monarch House. Once I'm on the throne, you'll be safe in the heart of my court."

Steven battled with himself for a moment, then let the issue go. He was certain Jaclyn was aware of the situation they were in, even if she wouldn't admit it to him. He'd just have to try again tomorrow. If they had a tomorrow.

"I trust your abilities to find some way out of this, even if I can't see how," Steven said, then raised his hand to cup Jaclyn's face and sent his own pulse of reassurance. "I'm sorry. When you come to my bed, you should be able to leave the worries of the war behind. Even if it's only for a while."

Jaclyn's eyes widened as he tugged on her hand, pulling her onto the bed and into his arms.

"This isn't wise husband. I have a war to fight."

"You're fertile and you wouldn't have come to my bed if you didn't want to breed. Besides, you've always been at war and it didn't stop you the other times. I know you mourn, but you need to breed another child so your house can continue."

"Not really. You have just as much right to the throne. I could put you on it."

"I'd be an even worse king than the one you have now and you know it. Besides, you have both Myra and Liliana by your side as well. Ricardo tells me they are just as able to fight in this war as you are. My fellow husband also told me you are still perfectly capable of being in command, even if you are pregnant. You did so during the war in the land of the trader clans."

As Jaclyn relented, Steven pushed aside further conversations about the war, even though they were increasingly becoming urgent. For now, he'd just fulfil his duty as her husband. That coincidently also helped distract her from the war effort, so perhaps Michael might accept it as an excuse. Even if it was a thin one.

ONE HUNDRED ONE

Michael strode through the camp, ignoring Shaun, the warband leader in charge of the command camp that day. The man babbled at him. Panic and the overwhelming need to make sure Michael understood that none of this was his fault were the predominant emotions he sensed from the man. As he reached Olivia's tent, those guarding the entrance stepped aside, opening the flap for him. Michael held up his hand.

"I'm already aware the incident that occurred was outside your control. There's no need for you to come inside," Michael said as he entered without so much as a second glance at the man.

Michael appreciated it, as the two of Tony's fighters on guard duty adroitly blocked Shaun's path into the tent. Without having to be given instructions to do so. Michael had to admit that having a warband whose entire function was to see to his protection, and to those he nominated, was proving useful. As his eyes adjusted to the dimness of the tent, Michael found his arms filled with Isabella. It startled him since Isabella had remained restrained, keeping herself back from physical contact with others after leaving the Stronghold. Michael hugged Isabella, sending a wave of reassurance to her before carefully releasing her when he sensed she needed him to.

"Olivia won't wake. I transported Olivia here through the grey and then found out Kesha had been sent back to the Smith's residence. I didn't want to risk moving her again. So I brought Kesha here to help as quickly as I could. Now she is sound asleep as well," Isabella said.

Michael's eyes swept over Olivia's unconscious form before he swept Kesha with his powers.

"It's alright, you did just as you should. Olivia will recover, she's healing, and will eventually wake on her own. Kesha is just exhausted after her healing efforts." Michael turned his attention to Vance, who sat on a nearby stool. "What happened?"

"A couple of the Sylannians were much stronger in the veil than we've encountered before. It's no excuse, but the room was crowded and a couple of the men stumbled. I don't know over who or what, but that left Olivia surrounded as multiple of the enemy jumped on her. One of the stronger Sylannians snatched up one of the Smith's blades dropped by one of ours. Olivia took out several enemies as she went down, but the Sylannian with the Smith's blade got lucky. The blade slid between the bands of metal in Olivia's uniform. Olivia's side and abdomen were ripped open. Kesha said several organs were injured on the way through, but the tip of the blade stopped just a hair's width from piercing her heart," Vance said.

Michael rubbed his face with a hand. "You're here in case Kesha wakes and needs more power to continue her healing efforts?"

"Yes, I thought one of us should be. Just in case. I'm sorry."

"For what?"

"I wasn't there. I led the team getting the villagers free but I still feel like I failed. Those with Olivia should have been there when Olivia needed them not tripping all over each other."

"Things go wrong in battle, usually right about at the point we can least afford it to. Olivia will heal. Now go and get some rest. I'll sit and keep watch," Michael said, then he turned his attention back to Isabella. "You too Isabella. I can see you're exhausted. Get some rest. It's not good for those in transition, even those having an easy transition to push their boundaries too far. I know enough now to fill in both Nathanial and your brother when they undoubtedly end up here as soon as they get back from their own attacks."

"Yes Michael, but..." Isabella said, her gaze sliding over to Olivia. "You'll let me know when she wakes?"

"Sorry, it's been a long day. I didn't think. Of course I'll let you know. Don't worry. Olivia's strong, she'll recover. You did well. Both of you," Michael said, then turned his attention to Vance, who stood, hand half raised, to open the tent flap. "Escort Isabella to her tent before you take your own rest, please. Make sure there is a guard detail on her then and advise them no one is to disturb her."

Michael waited until Vance and Isabella left the tent then turned his attention back to the cot where Olivia lay. He reached out with one hand and rested his fingertips on Olivia's temple.

"Don't die on me now my friend. I've just lost father. I can't lose you as well. I don't know if I can pull this off without you." Michael whispered and began to channel energy into Olivia to bolster her flagging strength, willing her body to heal. He could see the signs of Kesha's work and from the looks of it the healer had only just managed to get to Olivia in time. It had been a close call. Much closer than he cared to contemplate.

CHAPTER

ONE HUNDRED TWO

Chelsie panted easing back into the supporting arms of the underwife behind her. The healer at her side blocked her pain and assisted Cheslie's body with the contractions. She hated to think how undignified birth would be in houses that didn't possess those strong with healing talent. Even so Chelsie found the act of giving birth an undignified process.

"Nearly there. One more push and the child will be born," the birth underwife said.

"Wait, just a few more breaths." The healer stroked her temple with one hand, the other rested on Chelsie's abdomen. "Now First, push now."

Chelsie gritted her teeth and pushed even as she felt the healer's power aid her in her efforts. Then she gasped in relief, slumping back as the birth underwife took the baby and passed it over to others for care.

A hearty cry rang out and Chelsie relaxed even further. "The boy lives."

593

"I told you he would First. He may have come into this world early, but you have a healthy baby boy," the healer said.

At a gasp issuing from those tending to the baby, Chelsie's head swung in their direction. She caught the wave of apprehension just before the underwives shuttered their emotions.

"What is it?"

"Nothing First, your son is whole and healthy," the secondwife chosen to nurse her boy said.

"Bring him to me." Chelsie's eyes narrowed as the nursing secondwife swallowed before taking the couple of steps to her and placing the swaddled boy in her arms.

Chelsie looked down at her son as his eyes blinked open to reveal a barbarian staring back up at her. Her face screwed up and she screamed in outrage, thrusting the boy from her to the waiting arms of the nursing secondwife.

"Go. Kill the minor house we marked for destruction and seize the boy child they've birthed. We must have a Sylannian baby to show our husband," Chelsie snapped.

"Yes First. All is in place. The boy will be here by nightfall." The head daggerwife sprinted from the room, gathering her team as she ran down the hallway.

"Take the barbarian boy from my sight!"

"Do you want me to dispose of him First?" The nursing secondwife asked.

"No. I'll try again as soon as I'm fit. It at least is of my blood, even if the barbarian in it is stronger. It will do until I can birth a child whose Sylannian heritage breeds true."

Chelsie leant back cursing that she'd birthed yet another child whose barbarian nature was stronger than it's Sylannian. Her plans would be that much easier if she could birth a child who showed no signs they'd been bred from barbarian breeding stock. With a child that bred true, she could say the child was bred with Samuel. No one could dispute her. With all her children being born with barbarian traits she was still tied to the backup plan. The claim that Tarkhan was from the blood of the Monarch House was shaky at best, but she'd use it if she had to.

CHAPTER

ONE HUNDRED THREE

Isabella walked through the open grounds to one side of the camp between the outer rows of tents and the forest in the distance. She ignored the damp early morning long grass that brushed against her legs. It was one positive thing about wearing the fighting leathers rather than a skirt. The leathers didn't get soaked through to her skin the way her thick skirts would. She shouldn't be out this far away from the others, but the incessant mental chatter of so many people had been driving her mad. It was difficult to re-establish mental shields when you were wound up from everyone else's problems seeping into your mind, day and night. Damien would normally help, throwing up his own shield to protect her until she could calm down and hold her own again, but he was away with Michael. In normal circumstances she could ask Olivia, but Olivia was on orders to rest until she'd recovered from her injuries. Kesha was looking after Olivia, so she didn't want to burden the healer further. Although she doubted the healer would be able to fully shield her mind anymore. In this regard, her strength in the veil was growing stronger every day. So she walked. Far enough away that the

597

random thoughts of others weren't so loud and overwhelming. It was a mental illusion, since being this distance from the tents might stop her physical ears from hearing conversations and whispered words, but it didn't really have much bearing on mindvoices. Isabella smiled. Whatever worked and right now, somehow this seemed to. She had some guards trailing her. She hadn't been that stupid. Not that any of her brother's fellow squad mates would have allowed her to go out unescorted, anyway. They were rather protective. It was unkind of her, but she got the distinct impression they only did so for Damien's sake and not really because any of them truly cared about what happened to her. No matter how many times others tried to assure her she wasn't a burden, even after transporting them all to help rescue the villagers, that is exactly what she felt like. After all. They hadn't really needed her to get them to that village or any other one. They could have just ridden there. All she'd done was to save them time. She squeezed her eyes shut, trying to push out the screaming.

Isabella stopped, her head swinging around and eyes flaring open as she realised the screams weren't mental screams, they were physical ones. Sylannians rode from the forest towards the camp, screaming that undulating cry they made in battle.

"Isabella, we need to get back," one of her guards said.

Isabella turned and started running back towards the camp. She ran with the guards around her, but she knew the attackers would catch them before they made it back. Isabella saw with relief their own forces boiling out of the camp in a belated response. From conversations she'd overheard they shouldn't have been under attack from this direction. Unless the Sylannians had just seized fresh territory that was inland. She stopped as she realised she was running alone and turned to look back. Those who'd come with her had turned to face the oncoming Sylannians.

"Go Isabella. Get back to camp!" a guard yelled at her.

Isabella stood rooted to the spot, staring at the oncoming attack. She was dragging in deep ragged breaths, not just from running but from the sudden screaming in her mind. The guards wouldn't be able to stand against the Sylannians. There were not enough of the guards and too many of the oncoming attackers. As the first rank of the Sylannians crashed into her guards, Isabella screamed, anger burning away the fear that had held her motionless.

"No!"

Hardly aware of what she was doing Isabella sucked in the veil, much as she'd seen Damien and the others do, ignoring the icy burning that ran through her she wrapped the grey around her and jumped the short distance between where she'd been standing and where her guards were fighting trying to protect her. To give her time to escape back to safety. She threw away the obscuring cover of the veil, reappeared right in the middle of the mayhem and screaming, unleashed the power she'd been holding. An almost physical wall slammed into the attackers, several of them falling to the ground as they ran into it. The sky peeled above, but Isabella ignored it and just concentrated on sucking in the veil's power and shaping it, feeding it back into the shield she'd created around them. She could see this bubble of sheer power as it shimmered around their group, and she gritted her teeth, holding it in place. She was aware that her guards had turned to stare at her, but she ignored them. Concentrating instead on what she was doing. Keeping them safe while those outside this little island of calm dealt with the Sylannian invaders.

Blood splattered on her shield, running down onto the ground. Isabella's eyes widened as one of their own outside her barrier collapsed unmoving onto the ground. He was dead. There wasn't even the faintest glow from the veil within the man. Her breathing rate increased as she stared at the dead man. She didn't know him, but she recognised the uniform as belonging to one of their own people, not the Sylannians. They may not have many men in the ranks of their enemy, but they had some, and the dead man wasn't one of them. For a moment, helplessness surged within her. If she dropped her shield, she had no doubt these men and women who were in harm's way because of her would die defending her. If she didn't drop the shield and try to help, many of the members of the warbands would die. Anger flared in her again and the veil responded. The image of the courtyard of the Stronghold where lightning had struck down those who threatened them. She raised her head, eyes fixing on the mayhem that transpired outside her shield. It was a thing that had been tugging on her awareness that she hadn't realised with everything else. The armour the Sylannians wore sung with the veil. Similar to the fighting leathers she and the Unwanted wore. Their own gear had been crafted by the Smith, who had a deep affinity for all things metal. She didn't know what had been used to craft the clothes the Sylannians wore but she was familiar with the feel of the veil that came from it. Distinct from that of the Unwanted. A smile spread across her lips.

"Isabella, whatever you're thinking. Don't. Let the warbands handle this. It's what they're good at."

Isabella heard the words that she was sure contained wisdom uttered by one of her guards. She turned, tilting her head to one side as she regarded him as she considered his opinion. Then she discarded it as her focus was drawn back to the fight beyond. She looked up at the sky, eyes narrowing as she willed the veil to appear. Light traced across the sky, like cracks in a glass that hadn't quite shattered. Then the dark grey poured out of nowhere, building up and appearing just like a front of storm clouds. Blue-silver light traced through the veil of clouds and the world around her rumbled. The power around her flared and bolts of pure energy struck down, clumps of dirt and bodies flying in all directions. She was burning, with the veil pulsing through her, over her, but it didn't hurt, so she discarded the sensation.

Then her gaze fell on the Sylannians and she sucked the veil not only from the world around her, but the power woven into the garments as well.

ONE HUNDRED FOUR

Olivia was doing her level best to rest as she'd been ordered to do. Not an easy thing under the circumstances. There were even guards at the entrance to the tent, allegedly to prevent others from bothering her. However, she had the distinct impression it was also to make sure she stayed put. It was a concession she'd made since Taya had wanted her to go back to the Smith's estate. Given she'd be fine in a few days, it hardly seemed necessary. Oddly enough, even though the healer had fussed to start with, Kesha had backed up her assertion. As long as she stayed put. Despite the circumstances, she nearly laughed because she caught the overwhelming impression the reason Kesha had backed her up was because she didn't want to be sent back to exile at the Smiths residence again either. The healer had gotten into a match of wills with Taya over the issue and won. Isabella and the Unwanted with her made it clear they'd follow Kesha's orders. Since it aligned with what she wanted, Olivia didn't feel the pressing need to reprimand any of them for disobeying orders. She rolled onto her back with a sigh and closed her eyes.

Yelling and the clash of metal caused her to sit bolt upright and roll out of her bed. Even though the sudden movement made her wince. Kesha had warned her the newly knitted flesh would be tender for days. Her hand automatically grabbed her sword from where it lay on its rack as she flung the tent flap open. The guards looked at her. She could see they wanted to run to where the disturbance was but their job was to not only stay put themselves but make sure she did. Since they were members of Tony's warband, she abandoned any hope of them allowing her to go and investigate. Her hope early on that they'd simply attach themselves to Michael had proven wrong. Irritatingly, they'd attached themselves to her as well. It only mollified her a little that they also followed Nathanial and Damien around. They seemed to guess that a new order was coming to their world, at least as soon as this battle was over and were acting accordingly.

"Olivia, don't even think about it. You'll rip yourself open again."

Olivia turned and smiled disarmingly at Kesha, who simply glared at her, not impressed in the slightest.

"I have no idea what you mean."

"Of course you don't. That sword you're carrying just happened to topple out of the weapons rack into your hand all by itself," Kesha said, her hands planting firmly on her hips as she glared.

The yelling and screaming increased. "That's the Sylannians."

"Even more reason why you will not investigate," Kesha said.

Olivia didn't miss that the other woman's eyes flicked over towards the evident sounds of battle occurring on the edge of camp. Her eyes widened as the veil rippled around her, a hollow rushing sound as someone sucked in the veil from all around them.

"Isabella," Olivia said.

She couldn't tell what Isabella was doing, but she was certainly drawing a lot of energy to herself. At first, she thought the girl had gotten out of control, but it didn't quite have the right signature. She glanced up as multiple ruptures seemed to split the sky and the very air around them. The veil spilling out from that other place, boiling up and manifesting as dark storm clouds. As the silver-blue strands of power laced through it, her own abilities responded. The Smith altered metal threaded through her fighting leathers glowed in response and even though she couldn't see them, she knew her eyes also flared with the veil that was living within her.

"Olivia, what are you doing?" Kesha asked.

Olivia drew her attention back to Kesha, as the healer looked around, a hint of concern in her emotions.

"I'm not, Isabella is. The rest of us are just responding to what she's doing. I'd bolster your shields if I were you."

Kesha turned to look at her. "Why?"

"Because with all this power being flung around you, all of you will probably get a reaction headache in response," Olivia said.

Right on queue lightning struck the ground, with peels of thunder and explosions causing the air and earth to vibrate around her.

"What do you mean?"

"The rest of you aren't made to exist with this amount of the veil flooding into the area around us."

"You all are?"

"It affects us in a different way. It always has. Otherwise we would have died long ago, like the multitude of children who died from veil sickness."

Olivia turned, watching the pyrotechnical display. When one of her guards drew her attention by grabbing her arm, she turned her gaze on him. She smiled faintly as he tried not to flinch.

"I think the battle is over," he said.

Olivia sent her othersight out flying over the tents of their camp until she reached the outer edge. She observed the ones she assumed were the Sylannians fleeing back towards the cover of the trees. The Unwanted were easy to pick. With the amount of energy flowing through them, they shone like bright lamps, pushing back the encroaching darkness. They stood in a half circle with a dome of pure white energy at their centre. In the middle of that was Isabella and those who were meant to be protecting her. Although at this moment, it seemed she was the one who'd protected them.

Olivia, a little help? Gavrel said. *We can't reach her.*

Olivia didn't have to ask what they needed help with or who 'her' was. That much was evident.

I'm on my way.

She started walking through the camp, aware of those assigned to be her guards for the day, and Kesha trailed along with her. None of them tried to stop her this time. Still, she didn't run. There was no need to hurry. It wasn't like Isabella was going anywhere right now. At worst, Isabella would pass out, have a splitting headache when she finally woke up after exhausting herself and generally feel lethargic and run down. Of course, it probably wouldn't stop her from overdoing it again on another occasion. They were all gluttons for punishment when it came to overusing their abilities. Although to be fair, at times it seemed like they didn't really have much of a choice but to use their powers. There came a point where if they stopped or were blocked from the veil, they just felt sick. Which was something that Damien had learned the hard way.

Olivia reached the perimeter of the camp and stopped, staring at the scene in front of her. There were the dead and injured, both their own and Sylannians. The members of the warbands that had come out to fight the sudden assault on their ranks were standing around, staring. Then there was the ring of the Unwanted, one and all. They had their backs to her. All their attention focused on a shimmering globe that stood in their middle of the massed fighters.

"What are you doing out of bed?"

Olivia turned her head to gaze at Taya, smiling as the other woman stepped back a step, swallowing. "I was called. Of course, be my guest if you think you can deal with Isabella?"

Taya's eyes widened slightly. "No, that's all right. I was just startled to see you here."

Olivia stared flatly at Taya. "You are warleader right now and don't mistake me. You are doing a good job. But I am Michael's right hand."

"Of course, I didn't mean anything. I'm just concerned about you. We all have been."

"Don't take offence, Taya." Kesha said, her voice soft. "When they are channelling this much power, they can be quite cold. The veil drives all of them when they are like this."

"Do something useful Taya. Get scouts to follow those of the enemy who are fleeing back to their camp, then start recalling the warbands and get them ready for an attack as soon as we know the enemy's location," Olivia said.

Olivia turned from the pair and her guards, along with the assorted others that had come from the camp who clearly hadn't been part of the fight. She dismissed them all. They weren't the ones that mattered right now. Olivia walked forward, the ranks of the Unwanted parting as she approached their line. Reaching out, she touched the shimmering shield of power that Isabella had spun around herself and her guards. Admittedly, she was impressed.

The threat is gone. Let go.

There was no response for a moment, then Isabella's head turned to stare at her through the shield.

I, I don't know how.

Olivia caught the smile and laugh before she uttered it at the girl's plaintive tone. As much as others gathered around outside the Unwanted's ranks might fear her and what she could do. Isabella, as powerful as she was becoming, was just a young woman reacting on instinct rather than with purpose. It was interesting that, unlike Damien, she didn't seem prone to her conscious mind being entirely overwhelmed. Although, unlike Damien, she didn't have much understanding of what she was capable of. By contrast, her brother had soaked up what he'd seen the rest of them do with a nearly instant understanding and, of course, he'd had training. Far more than Isabella had so far. They'd all been far too busy and left the poor girl to stumble along by herself. It was a situation Olivia was determined to change, regardless of the circumstances they currently found themselves in.

Take a deep breath, concentrate on keeping it smooth and controlled. Olivia kept her own mindvoice soft as she willed Isabella to bring down her agitation. *You and those with you are safe. So are our people. The Sylannians have gone.*

Isabella only managed the breathing exercise for a moment or two before her panic rose. *It's not working.*

Shh... trust me, it will. I've been doing this a long time now and helped train a lot of our people. As hard as it is, you need to relax. Olivia increased her own pulses, urging calm. Although she restricted her efforts to soothing Isabella. While Olivia was perfectly capable of compelling Isabella, after the girls' ordeal with Aiden, she was loath to do so. It was the last thing Isabella needed while she was still struggling to come to terms with freedom again. Olivia waited and to her credit, Isabella closed her eyes and started to concentrate on her breathing. *Can you feel the veil around you, no don't reach for more, just be aware of it.*

Yes, there's so much of it. A tremor shook Isabella's mindvoice.

It's always been there, you are just better at sensing it now. Olivia did her best to soothe the other woman's sudden spike of fear. *Now take a breath. Keep concentrating on your breathing and just allow the power to run through you. Don't try to shape it or control it. Just relax and leave it be. Allow your shield to fall.*

Won't it burn me out if I don't use it? Isabella asked.

No, you won't die from what some call veil sickness. You're strong enough to cope with the power level running through you and you've more than proved you can wield it as well. Those who die, for one reason or another, can't. We don't know why, Olivia said.

Olivia waited patiently while Isabella digested the information. With one final shaky breath, she closed her eyes again and concentrated on her breathing. Bit by bit, she released the tight stranglehold she had on the veil. Olivia breathed a sigh of relief as the blackness along with the silver-blue power beating at its heart started to recede. It disappeared back to where the veil normally lived, except in small increments, when one of them called more of it forth into the world. Olivia wasn't sure how they all did that either, and it wasn't something she felt the need to disclose to anyone outside their ranks. It was one of those details she was certain would cause everyone more than a little concern.

Olivia's attention was drawn back to Isabella as the shield she'd raised finally dissipated. As Isabella sunk to the ground, seeming to wilt as the veil fled, Olivia went forward, sinking to her knees and drew Isabella into her shoulder, rocking her gently.

CHAPTER

ONE HUNDRED FIVE

A t a commotion occurring in the camp, Jaclyn rolled out of the bed she shared with Steven. As she wrapped her silks around her, she sensed fear and pain roll over her and tightened the shield she held not only on herself but on Steven's mind as well.

"Stay here," Jaclyn said, the entrance flap hissing aside as she hummed at it.

"First, we need to run—" Reyanna said.

"Calm down and explain. What happened?"

"Three of the sister houses launched an attack on the enemy camp. It didn't go well," Reyanna said.

"When exactly did we locate the enemy war camp?" Jaclyn asked, choosing to ignore the increased agitation. It would take time for the underwives and collared to pack up the camp, so it wasn't like she had to run now.

"A few hours ago," Reyanna said.

"The fools didn't even scout the enemy? They just straight out attacked?" Myra asked, outrage colouring her tone.

"So it seems Primewife Myra. I sent teams out to stop the

611

sister houses as soon as I learned what was happening, but it was too late," Reyanna said.

"The enemy knows we're here?" Liliana asked as she joined them from one of the inner rooms.

"I believe so Primewife Liliana. Reports suggest they're mobilising. I recommend we seek the high ground," Reyanna said.

"Very well, let's get moving. Arianne, you and your team will see to Steven's safety. I want him well away from the battle-front," Jaclyn said.

"I'll keep our husband safe, Firstwife Jaclyn," Arianne said, then issued instructions to her team, who scattered promptly to follow their orders.

"Ricardo, you have your choice. You can leave for safety with Arianne and Steven, or you can ride with me."

"I'd rather fight, live and die by your side than watch it all from afar. Besides, if you died, the mate bond between us will snap back at me. I know you have contingencies for such an occurrence, but we both know it's unlikely I'd survive long after such an event."

"As long as you promise me that if I order you to run, you'll do so." Jaclyn held up her hand, and the protest died on Ricardo's lips. "These barbarians are much better fighters than the trader clans were, and if it comes to that, I'll send Myra with you. She'll protect you from any recoil that would occur from my death."

"Or Jaclyn will run with you," Myra said, a challenge in her voice as she stared unrelentingly at Jaclyn. "Which is the way it should be and you know it, Firstwife."

Jaclyn bottled down her irritation, then waved ascent. Not that she'd liked it any better on the previous occasions either. It was unfortunate that Myra was correct, and she could hardly expect Ricardo to run to safety if she didn't.

"Let's hope it doesn't come to that," Jaclyn said.

Jaclyn strode from the command tent. The camp was a hive of activity with underwives and the collared scrambling to dismantle the camp. There was no running or yelling. Just people moving with purpose and working together. One tent after another collapsed. Horses stamped and snorted as the dagger-wives of her house formed around her. Jaclyn took the reins of her horse and mounted.

"We need to move Firstwife Jaclyn. The scouts have confirmed the barbarian forces are heading in our direction. They're unbelievably fast."

"How?"

"The scout doesn't know, just they are covering a great deal of distance much faster than we can."

Jaclyn spurred her horse. Her house moved with her as they raced for high ground. At least neither she nor any of her house needed to ask directions. They'd done their battle planning and had contingencies in place for different circumstances. Jaclyn deliberately let out a breath. Her anger threatened to boil over at the disobedience of some of the sister houses which put them all at risk. She had to stay calm and in control. With the thundering of hooves surrounding her, Jaclyn was mollified that at least some of the sister houses could follow instructions. At least the reliable sister houses could. They'd mounted and started riding with her house as soon as she'd moved.

Just as they reached the top of the plateau they'd chosen as their fighting ground, Jaclyn reined her horse in and wheeled to stare back. There in the distance dust rose, Jaclyn drew on her othersight and drew those who pursued her into sharp focus. Myra and Liliana issued orders, and the daggerwives formed up around them to face the incoming threat. Jaclyn took a sip of water from her flask, then offered some to Ricardo. Just as she accepted it back, a hollering cry split the air from behind. Jaclyn swore and wrenched her horse around just as metal clashed on metal and answering cries rang out.

"The Monarch House forces," Liliana said.

"Of all the time for them to catch up with us," Myra said.

Arianne, is Steven safe?

We're just supervising the last of the pack up now, Firstwife, then we'll head out.

Leave it, all of it. Get Steven to a safe location.

Are you safe First?

For now. The Monarch Houses forces have launched an attack on us. The barbarians aren't far off.

You'll be caught between them?

Go. Your only duty is to get Steven to safety.

Jaclyn spurred her horse, drawing one of her long daggers as she did so. As she rode down and joined combat against her brother's forces, a steely determination to survive even this betrayal filled Jaclyn.

We may not be as good at fighting on horseback as the Barbarian forces, but against the Monarch House forces, we have the advantage, Ricardo said, grunting as he swung his blade at an attacker.

Jaclyn pushed her fear of his safety aside. Against custom, Ricardo had proven time and time again he could hold his own in a fight.

ONE HUNDRED SIX

Steven watched the entrance to his room for what seemed like the longest time before he finally sat on the edge of the bed. The chaos of the camp being dismantled around the command tent permeated the thin walls. Steven tried not to panic at the sound of fighting outside.

"It's not that close. The daggerwives would have moved me if the fighting was in the camp." Steven whispered to himself.

He said the words out loud in his most reassuring tone. It was unfortunate it did nothing to calm his nerves. It wasn't like they were in the best position, with a fighting force on either side. Both of them were intent on killing Jaclyn and not so coincidentally him. It was a set of circumstances that didn't seem fair, since it was his brother's army on one side and his cousin's forces on the other. Steven lurched to his feet, scrambling back as the tent flap was flipped back, only to wilt in relief at seeing Arianne.

"Come, husband, we need to go." Arianne grabbed hold of his arm. A wave of reassurance flowed between them as she dragged him out of the tent.

"Is Jaclyn alright?" Steven asked.

"Our firstwife is in the middle of a fight but not at immediate risk."

"So, why are we running?"

"Your safety is my concern. Others will protect our firstwife and I'd rather we run from here while we can," Arianne said.

Steven was rather surprised that Arianne answered him so frankly. As they sprinted from the command tent, Arianne's team surrounded them. The echoed death cries ceased as Arianne wrapped her protective shield around his mind. Relief hit him immediately, and he realised that was a part of what had set him off. Then he mentally kicked himself. If he'd realised that the mental barrier that had prevented him from reaching out to his brother was down, he could have called for help. Now it wasn't likely it would falter in the near future.

STEVEN STOOD LOOKING over at the battle raging on the plateau. His heart was in his throat as he watched the milling and screaming fighters. They were far enough away from the battle that he couldn't hear the actual fighting, but that didn't stop his imagination from filling in the blanks for him. Steven bit his lip as he took in Michael's warbands. They held a position just to the rear of where Jaclyn currently fought with the king's forces. He was under no illusion Michael would stay put and not take advantage of the situation.

"Arianne, please let me call Michael."

"Not now Steven. In case you haven't worked it out, we're caught between the king's forces and your brothers. Both parties want us dead."

"Then we have nothing to lose and everything to gain."

"What do you mean?"

"Michael is going to sit back and watch as Jaclyn and the

king's forces fight. Jaclyn can't retreat because Michael and the warbands are right behind her. When Jaclyn and the king's forces are done, Michael will finish whoever is still standing. It shouldn't be hard for him, since his opponent will be weakened after their previous battle." Steven shook his head as Arianne's mouth fell open. "Just because I'm not a good fighter it doesn't mean I don't understand what's happening. Michael doesn't know I'm here. He may not care, but if he does, maybe, just maybe, he'll try to save us."

"You already admitted your brother doesn't like you."

"He doesn't, but no matter how much trouble I got myself into, Michael always got me out of it alive. If I'd been anyone else after all the things I did, he would have killed me. He didn't, even though he should have."

Arianne stared at him, then at the battle that raged in all directions. Steven could feel the conflict she was under as she fought with herself.

"Jaclyn will kill me."

"Even I can see the battle isn't going well. This might be the only thing that saves her. It was possible Jaclyn might survive a fight against either force, but not both at the same time."

"Do it."

As Arianne dropped the shield she held on his mind, Steven flinched as the mental cries of others flooded his head. He didn't wait for Arianne to get second thoughts, instead he gritted his teeth, ignoring the sudden onslaught, and pulled in as much of the veil as he could hold. Then Steven flung his mental voice out, pitched to the one person here he'd known his entire life.

Michael!

Not that I'm not pleased to find out you survived, but I'm a little busy right now.

I know, unfortunately, I just happen to be in the middle of it. Help?

The silence in his mind was deafening, and he shuddered as

his brother's mental presence came closer, shields wrapping around his mind and drawing him closer. As the outward rush of energy to fuel the exchange ceased, he breathed a sigh of relief, aware Michael had taken over powering their conversation.

You're in the middle of this fight?

No. The Sylannian king's wives launched an attack on our estate. Liliana and my daggerwives got me out when the Sylannian king's forces attacked. We ran to Jaclyn. Unfortunately, they followed us.

Steven waited as his brother swore. He had to admit it was rather inventive and quite colourful.

I must admit it is rather refreshing to watch the Sylannians slaughter each other.

Please Michael, they want her dead.

In case it escaped your attention, so do I.

I don't deserve it, but please. I'm a fool and I know it, but she's not what you think. She's just doing her best to survive. Like you did when the Warlord took you. The king's wives won't stop with just killing Jaclyn or me. They'll have to kill you as well. Because of mother you have the same claim to their throne that I do. Steven dredged up the images he'd caught from Liliana's mind during unguarded moments and threw them at his brother along with the emotions and smells. *Before the king's wives came here to kill Jaclyn, they found the refuge where the children of the house were hidden. The king's wives slaughtered the children. All of them.*

Wait.

Sure, it's not like Arianne will let me do anything else.

Steven held up his hand to Arianne, indicating he was fine. While realistically it must have only been minutes, it seemed like a lifetime before his brother's presence focus on him again.

I take it the women who surround you are there to protect you?

They're the team of daggerwives that Jaclyn detailed to keep me safe.

Tell them to stay put. We'll ride around your position. It will look like we are launching a full attack on Jaclyn. Then we'll turn aside and launch an attack on the other force to the left of your wife's army. Some of my other units will come down on the Sylannian king's fighters from the forest on the opposite bank. We'll have them in the position they think your Jaclyn is in now. Do me a favour and tell her not to turn on my forces, or I swear I'll personally take her out before I go down.

It's not a trap. I wouldn't do that to you. However, it is the middle of a battle and I don't know if Jaclyn can coordinate her forces that way. Wait, I'll ask Arianne, Steven said, although he had to admit he didn't know how Michael could either. Pushing the concern aside, Steven relayed Michael's message to Arianne.

Arianne swung around and stared at the battlefield below their position, her gaze taking in the forest over the far side of the mayhem below. As they watched, Michael's forces wheeled around and reformed off to their rear. Steven couldn't hear the communication, but he could tell Arianne was passing on something.

"Tell your brother Jaclyn can do as he's requested," Arianne said, her tone distracted as she continued to concentrate on the battle. "We're linked in a way that is foreign to your people."

"I thought Jaclyn didn't allow all the daggerwives to mate bond with Ricardo?"

"She doesn't, but we're all still linked to each other. It's just not as strong or as all-consuming as the mate bond. We're all close enough that it aids our communication. Tell your brother our daggerwives will move aside as soon as your brother's forces join with Jaclyn's. Our own house and the sister houses have all been ordered not to attack them."

Steven's eyes widened at that little piece of information, and he relayed it back to Michael.

"It's a communication net. Your Jaclyn and those closest to her are quite strong in the veil. I can't believe I'm saying this but do exactly as your daggerwives tell you to and stay out of this fight or you'll get yourself killed."

As abruptly as Michael's presence surrounded him, it was gone. Steven gasped as death cries filled his mind once more, then sagged with relief as Arianne's shield enveloped his mind once more.

"Husband, are you well?" Arianne asked.

"I'm fine, I should have realised Michael was shielding me. To be honest, I didn't notice the silence, so I wasn't prepared when he broke contact."

Steven didn't feel it necessary to pass on Michael's final instructions. It wasn't exactly like he had much choice, but it was a little embarrassing to admit Michael was correct in his assessment of his fighting abilities. Still, Michael needn't have worried. Arianne and the daggerwife team would pick him up and carry him out of harm's way if it was necessary. Steven's gaze was drawn to one side as his brother's warbands picked up speed and thundered around his own position.

Steven flinched and reinforced his shields as the Unwanted joined battle alongside his wife. The very air around the fight below ripped open, and the veil poured through.

He'd read reports describing Michael and the Unwanted in battle. They were compiled from different sources, including those fortunate enough to survive. Watching it was another thing entirely. Arianne started swearing. A hint of awe and fear seeping from her. Steven found he couldn't disagree with her sentiment. It was about time his wives learned his brother was a force to be reckoned with.

ONE HUNDRED SEVEN

Michael sucked in air as an uneasy truce stilled the battlefield. What had been one united warband while they fought separated. Taya yelled orders at the fighters to scour the battlefield and finish those of the enemy, who hadn't had the grace to die already. Michael paid it no mind and instead focused on the woman who stood in the protective centre of her daggerwives. After plucking her image from his brother's mind, he was in no doubt about her identity. Commander Jaclyn. Sister to the Sylannian king who'd just tried to have her killed. Admittedly, if Steven hadn't intervened, he would have been perfectly happy to sit the fight out and allow both Sylannian battle groups to kill each other. Then step in and finish whichever remained.

The sound of his sword scraping as he sheathed it sounded overloud as he strode forward through the ranks. Those in front parted for him. A ripple of movement showed Olivia, Nathanial, and Damien making their way from their own positions to join him. Michael barely restrained himself from sighing as a fourth shuffling of the ranks occurred and Isabella appeared to stand shoulder to shoulder next to Olivia. Michael flicked to his othersight and saw the glowing thick strands of the veil flowing into and through her. There was no sign of the fitful surging of her powers that her brother had suffered. Even though she should be safely behind their ranks, he wouldn't give any enemy watching any sign there might be a weakness in his own lines. As he returned his focus to those he faced off against, the ranks of the Unwanted arrayed behind them.

"Your majesty you can't—"

Michael waved off Harry's objection and stepped forward into the empty space between their ranks. His eyes were on his opposite number. Jaclyn strode through her fighters, sheathing her long wicked daggers as she did so. As Jaclyn came to stand facing him in the clearing, tension filled the air coming from their respective forces.

"Cousin. Or is that sister since you've taken my brother as your husband?"

"Either, or you could just call me Jaclyn, your Majesty," Jaclyn said.

Michael grimaced. "Feel free to dispense with formality and call me Michael. That form of address was started as a joke, but it seems I'm stuck with it."

"I owe you thanks for coming to our aid. If the situation had been reversed, I'm not sure I would have done the same."

"You can thank your new husband. It was Steven who pleaded your case," Michael said.

His warbands tensed as movement occurred from behind the Sylannian ranks and Steven materialised in the middle of the daggerwives detailed to protect him.

"Still, you could have waited and just allowed the fight between me and my brother's forces to do your job for you."

"I probably should have, but I haven't always been wise when it comes to family. There is one tiny detail that remains. I'll need your surrender. You have my word I'll treat you and your fighting forces well if you do so. Once this war is over, you'll be free to return to your homeland as long as you agree to never come back."

"No scion of the Monarch House has ever surrendered," Jaclyn said, her eyes going cold.

"Jaclyn please, for me?" Steven said, taking a step forward only to be held back by the daggerwives that surrounded him. "I promised to be faithful to you and I am, but you invaded the Warlord's domain. Michael's now, I guess, he'll have no choice but to continue fighting if you don't surrender."

"Personally, we'd be perfectly happy to keep fighting and wipe you all out," Khaliun said, the Kallith arrayed around her, bristling at the chance to keep fighting.

"Khaliun, no, not unless I give the order," Michael said.

Michael kept his gaze on Khaliun until she gave grudging acknowledgement of his order, then returned his attention to Jaclyn.

"So this is where the Kallith ended up," Jaclyn said, her tone musing.

Would you like me to extract you from the Sylannian's clutches? I would have already done so but I get the distinct impression you don't want me to, Michael said and catching Steven's stunned expression answered the question his brother hadn't asked yet. *Your protectors left the line of communication open between us in case we need to coordinate more during the battle.*

I didn't notice, although it's probably just as well. I might have distracted you at a bad time. Don't get mad with me but, I've come to care for Jaclyn and all my wives. It's probably best I stay with them. Jaclyn will fight for me, they all will.

I'm not angry with you but regardless of whether they will fight for you. I can extract you and there won't be anything they can do to stop

*me. What do you want Steven? I only ask since it may make a differ-
ence in how I negotiate with the commander going forward.*

*I don't mean to complicate things for you but I'd like to stay with
Jaclyn, as her husband.* Steven said, the words coming out in a
rush.

*Very well. I can't promise anything but I will keep your choice in
mind. A great deal will be determined on the decisions your wife
makes now.*

Michael's attention was drawn by more movement from within
the Sylannian's ranks and a man who Michael assumed must be
Jaclyn's first husband walked forward. He waved off the attempts
of his daggerwives to stop him. At what sounded like an order from
Jaclyn, the guard details around him melted back. Yet even though
they complied, the tension within the Sylannian forces spiked. The
male walked forward a couple of steps, his empty hands raised.

"That's Ricardo, Jaclyn's first husband. The daggerwives are
nervous about him being too close to you even though he's a
much better fighter than me," Steven said.

"I've seen you try to fight, Steven. That wouldn't be a difficult
feat to accomplish," Olivia said, her tone dry.

"Jaclyn, concede. What good will pride do for our people if
you die here on this battlefield? If nothing else, think of the child
you carry. Do it for him," Ricardo said.

"You're pregnant?" Steven's eyes widened and took a step
toward Jaclyn. "You are. Why didn't you tell me?"

Michael rolled his eyes, willing patience on himself. "Don't
tell me it's yours?"

"All right." Steven's gaze slid from Jaclyn to him, his face
going bright red. "But I'd be lying. It was Jaclyn's fertile period,
and it was me she was breeding with."

"Your wife was in the middle of a battlefield and you were
still dragging her to your bed to breed with her?" Michael asked.

"Well, it's my job as her husband, and it's more like she dragged me. She's the commander, but she had to get some rest sometime."

"After you had sex, I take it since it's hardly flattering if she slept during your nighttime activities," Olivia said.

"Well, yes. After." Steven muttered and clamped his mouth shut.

While they'd had the exchange with Steven, two more women had approached Jaclyn and were engaged in a rapid fire conversation.

"I don't suppose you understand what they are saying?" Michael asked.

"No, they're speaking too fast and I only know a little Sylann-ian. Please Arianne, can you translate? We don't want any misunderstandings," Steven said, then stared mutely at the daggerwife closest to him that Michael presumed was Arianne.

Arianne sighed heavily as if put upon and, knowing his brother, it was a sentiment Michael had some sympathy with.

"They are Primewives Myra and Liliana, and they plead for Jaclyn to surrender. After what the king and his wives have done, they call on her to clean the Monarch House for the good of all Sylannians. This is unprecedented. No daughter or son of the Monarch House has bowed to anyone throughout our history," Arianne said.

"Thank you. Will you be in trouble for translating for me?"

"Probably, but no more than I already will be. I'm the one who conceded to Steven's pleas and dropped the mind shield I held on him to allow him to contact you in the first place," Arianne said.

Michael waited as Jaclyn scanned the massed ranks of her fighters. Most nodded at her sharply before ducking their heads. Overwhelmingly, what Michael sensed from the Sylannians was the desire to live, but he got the distinct impression if she called for them to fight, they would die for her.

Jaclyn turned back to him and swallowed. She closed her eyes and removed her blades from their sheathes, then bent and carefully place her daggers on the ground at her feet. As she stood back up, her armour rippled and became soft, flowing silk that fluttered around her in the breeze. Jaclyn took two steps back, raising her hands so he could see they were empty. Her forces, after a brief pause, followed her lead, each of them placing their blades on the ground and stepping back from them.

Jaclyn opened her eyes, and she stared unwaveringly at him. She sunk to her knees, lowering her forehead to the ground. The only other sound he heard was the whisper of silks as all the Sylannians knelt, mirroring her movement. Doing what he'd been told no Sylannian had done in their entire history.

A child of the monarch house and those who followed her surrendered to an enemy rather than die.

ONE HUNDRED EIGHT

Michael stared at the walls of his family estate. He and his team had been in position for the last few days, drawing up their attack plans for the assault. Originally, they'd planned a dual attack on both Vallantia city and the Rathadon estate. After reconnaissance this last week, it appeared the Sylannian king's forces had all but abandoned the city. Jaclyn's guess that they would have sent as many of their dagger-wives and sister houses against her as they could had proven correct.

"Is it wise to have them here?" Khaliun said.

Michael flicked his gaze over to her and grinned, despite the circumstances at Khaliun's grumbling complaint. The *'them'* in question were their prisoners in the form of Jaclyn and her forces, who'd arrived this morning.

"Those assigned to guard the Sylannians report they've been no trouble at all. In fact, I'm told they've behaved impeccably," Michael said, then relented a little as he understood why the Kallith, more than any of them, would rather Jaclyn and her forces were dead. "Besides, once we get this done, Jaclyn and all her forces will be returning to Sylanna."

"Where she plans to take the throne, giving her even more power than she has now."

"Perhaps, except there is a reason she is here and will watch the assault as I take back the Rathadon Estate. It will be in the nature of a further object lesson of what will happen to her if she dares to set foot in my realm again," Michael said.

"You do plan to kill the other ones, though, right?"

"Oh yes, never fear. You and the Kallith can kill as many of the Sylannian king's forces who aren't currently in my custody as you can get your hands on." Michael pinned Khaliun with his glare. "You will heed my order and leave Jaclyn and her forces alone. I have no wish to be at war with Sylanna for the rest of my life. For the sake of all my people, that includes what remains of the Kallith, I want this war done with."

Khaliun held up her hands. "I swear on the honour of the Wolves that none of the Kallith will break faith with you."

"The Kallith will take the field here. You'll need to take out all the Sylannians outside the walls."

"Given what I've seen of the average numbers who ride the road between your family castle and the city, we can manage it easily enough."

"You'll be working in concert with Tony's warband and acting as backup as required if Harry finds he needs help with the rest of the enemy forces in Vallantia."

"Understood Michael," Khaliun said.

"Harry, are you clear on your mission in Vallantia?"

"Damien and Isabella's help the last few days in taking me into the grey place so I could get a picture of what I'm hitting has been invaluable. From what I've seen, I doubt I'll need to call in the Kallith, but it's good knowing I have you to back me up if I need it, Khaliun."

"Good. Damien and Isabella will jump you and Shaun with your warbands along with Lukas to assist you into position tonight. Harry, you have nominal control over the battle to regain Vallantia," Michael said.

"I'll await your signal to launch our attack. Are you certain I'll hear it?"

"Oh, you'll hear it alright. You won't be able to miss it."

"We're going to make quite a spectacle of ourselves."

"Just to be clear, I still don't like this part," Taya said, her tone just as grumpy as Khaliun's had been earlier.

"We won't be at risk."

"Besides the more of them who climb up onto the ramparts to watch, the more of them who will die," the Smith said.

"You still haven't told us exactly what the Smith and his sons are going to do."

"I wouldn't want to spoil the surprise for you."

"I don't like that bit either."

"Relax, Taya. You'll be suitably impressed," Olivia said.

"Or horrified," Nathanial said.

"I'm going for both," Damien said.

"Why does Damien get to know in advance and I don't?"

"Because he and his team will have a position on the walls once we kick off. So he and his team needed to know what they'll be dealing with."

"Remember, don't try that disappearing trick to get into the estate. You don't want to end up entombed halfway through a solid rock wall," Taya said and shuddered.

"Sorry, I did not know someone could get caught halfway through a rock wall," Damien said.

"It's the fault of the idiots who tried to emulate the Unwanted, not yours. Still, it's a new skill even for you lot. You've proven open spaces are safe enough. Let's keep to that and use your skill to just speed things up," Harry said.

"If I'd realised some of those from the other warbands were going to be foolish enough to attempt to copy us, I would have done my best to dissuade them," Olivia said.

"I and the rest of the Unwanted have far more power than the rest of you, but until we've practised more, even we will restrict ourselves to smaller jumps," Michael said.

"Why do you think we have Damien and Isabella taking control of the longer journeys through the veil?" Nathanial said.

"We don't want to end up entombed in a wall any more than you do. Any last-minute questions?" Michael asked, staring at each of his band leaders in turn, satisfied as each of them shook their head. "Everyone, get some rest. It will be a big day tomorrow. Damien, if you and Isabella could assist Harry and Shaun to get into position before you bunk down tonight?"

"Of course, Isabella is waiting for us," Damien said, then turned, leading both Harry and Shaun back through the trees to the clearing where their warbands waited.

Dawn tinged the sky to reveal the unnatural fog that curled around the Rathadon estate. As the enemy troops climbed the walls to the battlements, the coiled anticipation that sang through the veil rose another notch. Michael stood in the grey with Olivia, Nathanial, and Damien beside him. The ranks of the Unwanted arrayed behind them.

Everyone get ready for action, Taya said, her order firm and clear.

Remember, make this as noisy as possible. The idea is to get as many of them as possible on top of the walls to defend the estate, Michael said.

Acknowledgements from his band leaders that surrounded the Rathadon estate followed.

Attack! Taya said.

With the pooled resources of the Unwanted Michael dispelled the mists. A hollow inrush sounded as collectively all the members of the combined warbands sucked in the veil. Ruptures fractured the still darkened sky, and the veil poured in. It seemed to boil and jump from fighter to fighter, coalescing in the Unwanted. Multiple cracks resounded as power struck from the grey into the ground, sending dirt, grass and boulders flying.

A horn sounded and the battle cry of the Kallith rang out, the hooves of their horses thundering across the intervening space as they charged the walls. Arrows arcing across the sky to slam into those exposed on the walls.

The enemy, to their credit, wasn't caught napping despite the hour. Calls rang out from inside the walls of the estate and more of the daggerwives boiled up onto the ramparts.

Smith, now! Michael said.

Just outside the tree line the Smith, Colin and Adam knelt. Their hands splayed with their fingers dug into the ground. Isabella stood behind them, fuelling a shimmering barrier around all three of them. Michael felt it before he heard it. A throbbing beat that resonated in him as the Smith and his sons called to the bedrock beneath them.

In response, a deep percussive beat answered the Smith's call. The vibration coming from the very bedrock and the walls of the ancient keep. With a screech of metal on rock, sparks flew into the air. Metal spikes sprung up along the length of the battlements and out of the outer walls. Blood sprayed, a red haze hung in the air as those who were unfortunate to be standing on the outlets were speared by the metal spikes that punched through them.

In a rush of power Damien's grip tightened, and he hauled all the Unwanted through the grey. As the grey veil was pushed away, Michael's eyes widened at the sight of the spikes that still protruded on the walk of the battlement. Just as metal pricked his skin, the intensity of the deep percussive beat increased. With a screech of metal on stone, the spikes on top of the wall disappeared once more as they fully materialised.

Sorry, the defences impressed into the stone and metal are ancient. With the defences awakened, it took time to convince them to withdraw the spikes.

My fault, I should have checked it was clear before I pulled us out, Damien said, as he launched himself at a nearby Sylannian who stood nearby, eyes vacantly staring at the horror around her.

Go, I've got this side, Michael said.

Damien's power surged once more and all but Michael and his designated team disappeared from view. With his affinity for metal awakened due to the Smith's call, Michael's skin prickled, metal whispered to him and he ducked reflexively. Michael spun, his weapon knocking the Sylannian's blade aside. In one step, he was within his opponent's guard. Michael slammed his enemy's head into the side of the wall.

Michael sprinted along the wall, leaping over a team member of his who was engaged with a Sylannian. He had but a moment to notice Damien had deposited Nathanial and his team at the far corner before he struck out at the next Sylannian, who'd stayed alive after the deployment of the spikes. Michael didn't stop his charge forward. With the strength of the veil running through his muscles, Michael slammed into the enemy. With one shove, the Sylannian stumbled back and over the wall. The scream as she fell cut off abruptly as the body slammed into the ground below.

WITH THE BATTLEMENTS clear of Sylannian's, Michael pulled the veil to himself, wrapping the grey around himself as he took a couple of steps. Then, between one step and the next, pushed the veil aside and ran across the courtyard to the doors of the estate. An inrush of power and a gust of cold, repeated over and over, signalled the Unwanted materialising in the courtyard to form around him.

Michael wasted no time on pleasantries and, drawing from the collective power of the Unwanted, he punched through the front doors of the house. With a percussive explosion, splinters and bits of metal blasted through the entry and down the hall. Michael jumped over the dead bodies of the Sylannians who'd been taken out by the flying fragments of the door. As he approached the broad stairs that led to the upper floors, Michael resolutely kept his focus on his role. Olivia ran forward to clear the ground floor. Nathanial went in the opposite direction.

Keep this controlled and as safe as possible. Let's get this done, Michael said as he mounted the stairs for the upper floor two at a time. While he and his team made their way systematically through this floor.

Everything is under control out here. I'll get the gates open. Kelsie's warband will be in to help you shortly, Damien said.

Michael kept control of his patience as his team systematically cleared rooms. His othersight told him the enemy was in the suite at the end of the hall. The one that had been put aside to accommodate him on his infrequent visits. It was also the largest of the suites on this level. His othersight also told him the end room contained many people.

I was expecting a full battle in here. Are we sure the rest of the enemy hasn't run already? Nathanial asked.

There are some up here unless the Sylannians tied up some servants to keep us occupied. Although admittedly not as many as I thought they would be, Michael said.

Hold for a moment, I'll leave down here to Nathanial and I'll come up and help, Olivia said.

Michael strode down the end of the hall towards where he could sense people were on the other side. He only had but a moment to wait before Olivia joined him. Michael signalled Gavrel, who ran at the door, his power slamming into it moments before he hit it. As the door exploded inwards, the Unwanted were through the door and battling those inside.

Damien watched the battle, what there was of it outside the walls of the Rathadon estate. Taya and Tony's warbands, along with the Kallith, swept around cleaning up teams of Sylannians that patrolled outside.

Tony, wheel around to your left. There's a team of Sylannians just coming out of the forest, Damien said.

Got it, thanks, Tony said.

Damien kept his eyes peeled, looking for trouble outside rather than worrying about the battle inside the estate.

"Damien, there's Sylannians trying to climb out the window over there," Shallan said, her hand pointing back towards the estate.

Damien's eyes widened as he saw Shallan was correct. Women in Sylannian maroon and cream battle armour were climbing out of the window on a landing that ran down the side of the building.

"Keep watch on the battle below and call out any issue to the band leaders," Damien said, then wrapped the grey around himself before Shallan could reply.

Damien kept his eyes firmly on the ledge and ran a couple of steps through the grey and materialised on the ledge. One of the Sylannains jumped and shrieked as she toppled from the ledge. Damien had his sword out, wishing he had more room to manoeuvre.

Michael, I have some of your unwelcome house guests out here on the ledge.

Your life is more important than theirs. Disregard the order to capture the leader alive. Kill them, Michael said.

"Going somewhere?" Damien asked pleasantly.

The Sylannian in front of him screamed what he was fairly certain was abuse and ran at him with her daggers drawn. Damien wound power around his attacker and shoved her from the ledge. Then his eyes rose to catch the gaze of the last remaining enemy on the ledge. Her chin rose as she spoke to him and backed up step by step.

"I'm sorry. I don't speak your language."

"Stop playing with her Damien," Michael said as he leant out the window and shoved the Sylannian off the ledge.

They both watched as the Sylannian hit the cobblestones below with a sickening thump, her head splitting open and blood splattering around her.

ONE HUNDRED NINE

Samuel gasped as Fiona's scream rang in his mind. The image of a cold stone building receding and the sense she was falling. Two barbarian men who flared with power stared down at her. Then the vision cut off as abruptly as it had started and pain shot through him. Fiona was dead. There was a gaping, raw hole where the bond she'd fused into his mind had once been. His bloodwives' barriers flared around him, and the pain bled away. He turned to see Chelsie reel back, clutching at the back of a chair. Other wives doubled over in pain, a few fainted.

"Where was Fiona?" Samuel demanded.

"She was doing her duty."

"You said she'd retreated because of feeling unwell due to her pregnancy. She just died in a foreign land. What was she doing?"

"She was in command of a force to the barbarian lands charged with killing your sister," Chelsie's eyes were bloodshot and wave after wave of rage came from her as she glared at him.

"From what I just saw, the barbarians just killed her."

Triumph shone in Chelsie's eyes. "Given Fiona was heading

to Jaclyn's base in Vallantia, that means your sister is dead as well. So her life was well spent."

Samuel shied away from the possibility Jaclyn was dead. Instead, he clung to the report he'd received that Jaclyn wasn't in Vallantia. According to his sources, Jaclyn had left one of the sister houses to maintain control of Vallantia while she had taken the rest of her forces to push out and conquer more land.

"You had no right to order such a thing without my approval," Samuel said.

The air in the room stilled. It was thick and heavy and he laboured to breathe. The sound was harsh in the otherwise silent room. Samuel's eyes widened and his gaze rose to meet Chelsie's, who's glittered with malice. Her presence swarmed up the primary bond they shared. Samuel closed his eyes and hit the last remaining trigger in his head.

Samuel collapsed, curling into a ball gripping his head between his hands even as he called on his bloodwives for support. Fire raced through his mind, obliterating Chelsie's control bond. As the bond that connected them snapped, power recoiled back into the mind of the person who'd created it. Chelsie screamed as she collapsed onto a couch.

"What have you done?"

As strength flowed into him from Ellith and her team, Samuel turned his back on Chelsie. He went to the open balcony. Although this time, the sight didn't soothe him. Still it gained him some time for the throbbing in his head to recede. As moisture trickled down the side of his neck from his ear, he brushed at it with his fingers. Blood stained his fingertips.

"Confess what you've done and I'll grant you an easy death." Samuel was surprised by his calm tone, despite how tense he was.

"Whatever do you—"

"I remember Chelsie."

"Nothing husband—"

"No longer, I've severed that which was between us. Was it at least a hard decision when you betrayed the Monarch House?"

"I haven't…" Chelsie's mouth parted and horror dawned on her face. "What do you mean severed our bond? You can't, you're subservient in the bond."

"Stop lying. I told you I remember. You grew clumsy in your haste, Chelsie. You triggered one of the failsafe's in my mind."

"Failsafe?"

"My bloodline, male and female, has been somewhat paranoid over the generations. When a son is born with the blood of the Monarch House, the reigning Monarch layers triggers in her son's mind."

"To what purpose?"

"In the event of a king ascending the Throne of a Thousand Islands, the triggers defend against the king's wives from usurping the throne."

"Please Samuel, this is all nonsense…"

"My mother wasn't always mad, and she layered those protections in my mind long before you became my firstwife. You tripped over one of mother's protections. I remember everything, Chelsie. All those things you bid me to forget."

"What do you remember?" Chelsie whispered.

"In a way, it's like I'm viewing a lifetime of someone else's life. There is one thing that is clear."

"What…"

"None of the children of the Monarch House are of my blood."

"Please husband," Chelsie's hands fluttered, and she chuckled, her cheeks flushing red. "Who else could have bred them?"

"I'm sterile. You've always known."

"No, husband, my children are yours. Our child I just gave birth to…"

"Is a child fathered on you by Tarkhan. The wolf warrior from the lost clan of Kallith that you have hidden away here in the Monarch house. Along with a hand full of other males you've brought here. We've had some informative chats, by the way."

The barriers protecting Samuel's mind flared as Chelsie desperately tried to breach them. Samuel watched dispassionately as blood dripped from Chelsie's nose. She swiped it away, then froze, her breath catching as she stared at the blood on her hands.

"You fool. We can't survive this. You've killed us both!"

Chelsie's face turned red, screwing up as she launched herself across the room, daggers rising to strike. At a silent signal, the doors behind him shattered as Ellith and Beth burst through, their daggers flashing in his defence. Chelsie screamed, calling the senior wives to her, while his bloodwives poured in, forming a defensive ring around him.

"It's too late. For the good of Sylanna, I'm taking the Monarch House," Chelsie said.

As secondwives and daggerwives poured into the room, Samuel was struck that their movements were perfectly synchronised. Not just in step, but their stance, the drawing of their weapons and even their breathing. Against all custom Chelsie had exercised control over all the wives that formed the core of his household. All of their minds were intertwined so tightly he doubted they had any sense of self left. The wives Chelsie controlled launched at him without even a hint of hesitation.

"Husband, there are too many of them," Ellith said as they stepped back, step by step, towards the balcony.

As the opposing forces surged forward, Ellith and Beth took one of his arms each and launched them over the balcony. Leaves and branches became a blur as they plunged downwards. Then Samuel hit the first of the web nets spun by the silk spiders overnight. He hummed at the web, which sang back to him as it wrapped around them, slowing their downward plunge. With a twang, the web broke, but they were caught by the next. As each successive net snapped, concern plucked at him until finally their downward momentum was halted as the web bulged down under their weight but held.

"Husband?" Ellith said.

Chelsie peered over the balcony far above them moments before her forces leapt over the balcony. His pursuers climbed down towards him, a red wave that flooded down the ancient monarch trees.

Samuel placed his hand on a nearby strand of web and hummed. A herd of the giant silk spiders appeared from the surrounding canopy and scurried across the webs towards them. He hummed at them and smiled as the greeting returned to him. Minute vibrations ran through the web, answered by increasing numbers of the spiders. The angry cries of wives calling for his death changed to chilling screams. Samuel watched coldly as the wives who'd started to climb down the levels of the palace towards him were surrounded by the silk spiders. The spiders spun their webs, encasing those who tried to pursue him in cocoons. Ellith and indeed all the bloodwives around him were pale as they stared up at the fate their fellow wives were meeting.

"I think that deals with that problem for now," Samuel said.

"Did you know the silk spiders could do this?" Ellith asked.

"What? You thought the silk spiders survived on the veil alone?" Samuel asked, his head tilting to one side.

"Well, everyone knows the immature silk spiders are kept supplied with insects and small animals until they mature, but I was told the mature ones only absorbed the veil."

"They mostly do. It doesn't mean they can't or won't eat flesh if prompted to do so."

Ellith's eyes seemed to pop out of their sockets as she stared at him and she went even paler than she had been.

"You mean you can speak with the silk spiders?" Ellith asked.

"You asked them to kill your wives?" Beth said.

"I can't talk to them the way we can with each other. Their communication is much simpler." Samuel frowned. He'd never really tried to explain this to anyone who didn't have an affinity with the silk spiders. He wondered if the herders had similar problems. "A certain, um, vibration sung to them in the veil or through the web means threat. I just let them know the dagger-wives coming after me were a threat. So the mature spiders responded."

While most Sylannians used spidersilk in one form or another, the silk spiders were taken for granted. Admittedly, the arachnids were tended to by the herders, but it amused him that his people seemed to know so little about them. The herders made sure the immature spiders were well fed until they matured. Adult silk spiders increasingly sucked in the veil but still consumed small insects and bird life. Just because they ate very little flesh as adults, if left to their own devices, they were still carnivores. Of course, he was of the line of the Monarch Blood. One of the little known reasons his ancestors had risen to power in the first place was their control over the silk spiders.

"You knew the firstwife would try to kill you?"

"If you were Chelsie and the fact that you'd been breeding with outlanders to usurp the throne had been discovered, wouldn't you try to kill me?"

"Now that you put it like that, well, yes," Ellith said, although the words were slow and drawn out as if she didn't really want to admit them. Then she looked up. The broken webs they'd fallen through were blowing in the wind and the traitors who'd climbed off the balcony to come after them were encased in giant silver-grey cocoons. Ellith's posture stiffened. "Husband, if you believed your firstwife and the others wouldn't submit quietly, then why did we do it this way? We could have just tried to slip away from the court during the night or hide out somewhere."

Samuel looked down at his feet. "Chelsie wasn't always like this. I had to know for sure."

Ellith's arms wrapped around him, her words a mere whisper in his ear. "I'm sorry, husband, you should never have been put in this position. To find out not only the firstwife, but your primewife and secondwives had all betrayed you must have hurt you deeply. I, all of us, should have done a better job of protecting you. Please let me care for you as I should."

Samuel resisted the urge to give up fighting and allow Ellith and his bloodwives to take the weight of the decisions and the fight to come off his shoulders. It was frightening how tempting the offer was. He sent a thread of gratitude to Ellith for her support. Ellith hadn't fought the bonds he'd bound her with, not even once. With a sigh, he pushed away.

"Thank you for the offer, but I don't have that luxury. Unlike the average Sylannian male, I am the king. It's stepping back and allowing myself to sink into the protective folds my wives wrapped around me that got us into this trouble in the first place. Come, it's time we moved on and got under cover before the traitors above get over their shock and think of another way to come after us."

Samuel thanked the bloodwife who cushioned his fall to the walkway as another hacked through the last of the web that bound him in place. As the light faded, Samuel turned his back to the sight of the palace several layers above the walkways they were now on and led the way deeper into the heart of the island.

ONE HUNDRED TEN

Evan didn't even flinch as the outer doors to the cells opened. He wondered idly if it would be him that his captors dragged out and killed this time. As men and women clattered down the stone stairs, his breath caught in his throat. These people weren't Sylannian. Evan contemplated standing up but decided against it. Besides, he didn't think he'd stay upright even if he got all the way to his feet. As the brown and black uniforms of those who entered the cells came into view, relief hit him, and tears tracked down his cheeks. One after the other, the cell doors opened and his fellow prisoners were assisted from their cells. Then it was Evan's turn. He nearly burst into tears as the door opened and a man and woman came in, one on each side of him as they assisted him out of the cell.

"You're safe now. Our healers will treat any injuries you have and well get you cleaned up and some food and water in whatever order you want. What's your name?"

"Evan, is Ben here? Or Michael? Or Steven?"

"They all are, we were tasked with looking for you. Just lean on us. We'll get you upstairs to the healer."

"I'm fine, just filthy and hungry. They didn't feed us much."

"Michael will have our hides if we don't get the healers to assess you anyway."

Evan would have felt compelled to insist he could walk by himself, except when he contemplated all the stairs they had to climb, he didn't think he could. Instead, he pushed what little pride he still possessed aside and allowed them to help him.

"It took you long enough! This really isn't good enough. I demand to be taken to the Warlord," Peter Kastler said, his strident voice ringing out across the cells.

"The warleader will really want to speak to that one." Evan chuckled weakly then put on his best haughty tone as if he were introducing an important guest to his peers at a ball. "It's my pleasure to acquaint you with Peter Kastler. He staged a rebellion, seized control of Vallantia, imprisoned Steven, Speaker and Lady Rathadon, and was responsible for the re-emergence of the slave trade."

The attention of the warlord's troops shifted. The air around Evan and throughout the cells chilled. Anger radiated from everyone except Peter Kastler, who suddenly reeked of fear.

"No, no. He's lying. I can explain it all!"

"Get back in there. You were on our list as well. The king really wants to have a conversation with you," a fighter said as she shoved Peter Kastler back into his cell and slammed the door shut.

Evan considered he was perhaps being a little petty, but then pushed the thought aside as a surge of satisfaction rolled through him. It was amazing how such a thing as justice being served on Peter Kastler made him feel just that little bit better.

"We're calling the Warlord king now?" Evan asked as his escort helped him up the stairs, wincing and turning his head aside as light from a window spilled into his eyes.

"The Warlord was killed by Aiden."

"Then who's the king?"

"Michael, he wouldn't accept the title of warlord, so everyone kept referring to him as king. Much to his chagrin, it stuck."

Evan blinked as the words sunk into his head. "The Warlord is dead? Michael is king? I missed a lot being stuck in those cells."

"A whole war, in fact, but you experienced your part of it here."

Evan was relieved when his escort ushered him into a room just down the hallway on the ground level, rather than up the stairs to the upper floors of the estate. They eased him into a camp bed and pulled a blanket over him. Despite his protests that he was fine, as his head sunk into the pillow, warm fingers brushed his temple and he drifted off to sleep.

ONE HUNDRED ELEVEN

Michael's eyes narrowed despite his best efforts to keep careful control over his temper. Peter Kastler babbled as he grovelled for his life. Michael gazed around at those who watched on. Of all those who'd been resident in the Rathadon estate, only a handful had survived. Yet they all stood here to witness.

"Is there any rule about kings having to show mercy?" Michael asked.

Jaclyn, who stood over to one side, with Ricardo and Steven on either side of her and surrounded by her daggerwives shook her head.

"Not that I'm aware of."

"You can't listen to her. She's the Sylannian Commander. She's the enemy of all of us."

"Correction. She was the enemy, but it seems we have a common enemy and she knows more about this monarch business than I do. As it turns out, happily, it's not so different from being a warlord and that's a role I'm well equipped to take on."

"Funny how circumstances can change, since dealing with

that mutual enemy could solve the problems afflicting both our peoples," Olivia said.

"But, but she invaded our land. Killed our people, she—"

"Commander Jaclyn was responsible for all those things and more. She did so at the bidding of her king. She was loyal to a fault until he betrayed her," Michael said, astounded that his voice was calm. "You, however, betrayed your own people, and you did it for nothing more than greed."

"You didn't even need the money to survive. You already possessed more wealth than most in this realm," Olivia said.

"Your brother conspired with them—"

"Steven is responsible for many things, but not that," Michael said.

"Steven's association with Jaclyn allowed him to learn many details, which he then passed on to us. At least until Jaclyn discovered what he'd been doing," Olivia said, her gaze sweeping over those watching the events unfold. A murmur of astonishment tinged with awe swept through the watching crowd.

"To Jaclyn's credit, she didn't kill Steven when she found out. Besides, you can't choose your family and it seems Jaclyn and I are related. By all accounts Steven has been extremely busy with all his new wives and before too long I'm told I'll have a whole bunch of nephews and nieces," Michael said, his tone extremely dry as he gazed at Steven where he stood next to Jaclyn. For his part, Steven kept his silence, but turned an interesting shade of red.

"Jaclyn and her forces could have united with the other Sylannian battle group against us, but her forces joined ours and helped to wipe out the Sylannian king's battle group," Nathanial said, his voice pitched to carry.

Michael felt it as the mood of the gathered villagers shifted subtly away from anger at Jaclyn and her daggerwives. As justified as that anger was.

"As king, it's my decision who gets pardoned and who gets punished. So we come back to you," Michael said, allowing the cold of the veil to seep into his veins. "You betrayed your own people, enslaved people for your personal wealth and gain. There was one outcome for such an offence under the Warlord. It's a rule I intend to uphold in my kingdom. The sentence for engaging in the slave trade is death."

As if his words unleashed Damien, a flood of the veil crashed over them all. Damien drew his blade in one smooth motion and struck before so much as a scream of denial could leave Peter Kastler's lips. Blood sprayed, only to be caught against a shield, giving evidence that Damien was not as out of control as some might think. Peter Kastler's head and body toppled to the ground, the head hitting the stones with a meaty thunk. A splatter of more blood sprayed the cobblestone, only to be joined by the blood Damien had caught as he released his shield. Michael murmured his thanks as Damien calmy resumed his place next to Olivia.

ONE HUNDRED TWELVE

Michael stopped in his tracks, his back stiffening. "This is not up for debate, Tony. See to it that Jaclyn is brought to me. Now!"

A hasty bark of orders and running feet told Michael his snap of temper had at least conveyed his irritation.

"All of you, go wait at the garden's entrance," Olivia said.

"Our duty—"

"This entire complex has been searched right down to the smallest pebble. If the garden isn't clear by now, we have even bigger problems," Nathanial said, with an edge to his tone.

"We have matters to discuss that you're better off not knowing," Olivia said.

"It will give you a plausible explanation when questioned," Michael said.

Tony's eyes narrowed, and he ordered the rest of his team members to take posts on the doors to the walled garden, but he stayed obstinately put just a couple of steps from them.

"I think between Olivia, Damien and I we can defend

Michael. At least long enough for you to cross the distance between the entrance and here," Nathanial said.

"You have two options. You can choose to join your team or I'll use force to shove you back not only to the entrance but out of the garden entirely," Olivia said as she positioned herself to face Tony and drew in the veil.

Tony's eyes widened as Michael just smiled blandly. Michael chose to ignore the muttered complaints about their stubbornness Tony made as he strode across the garden to join his team.

"He's going to be even more unhappy when he finds out what we're about to do," Damien said.

An amused glint shone in Damien's eyes and Michael snorted in response.

"Yet another reason to have this conversation out here, away from prying ears," Olivia said.

"Are you sure you can cope with Isabella's presence?' Nathanial asked.

Damien nodded. "She'll only follow if we don't include her and even I have to admit, her powers are stable."

"She'll be an asset, but I'll order Isabella to stay behind if you believe it will be too dangerous."

"We're all jumping into the unknown, so it isn't a reach."

"I know and yes, I want her to be safe, but wrapping her in ignorance and hiding away from the world didn't prevent what happened. The Aiden's of the world will always find victims. I don't want Isabella to be that victim ever again," Damien said, a dangerous glint in his eyes.

Booted feet contacting stone in a measured tread and a rustling of silk brought the conversation to a stop as Jaclyn and two of her fellow wives were ushered into the garden under escort.

"She insisted on bringing two of her companions with her, Your Majesty," one of her escort muttered.

"*Commander* Jaclyn is not armed and while she and her companions might be strong in the veil, we're stronger," Nathanial said.

"In our history, outright warfare has been sparked from something as small as an insult between warlords. Commander Jaclyn is currently our guest and should be shown the courtesy due to her rank while she is with us," Michael said rather proud that he'd kept his tone mild.

The member of the escort who'd spoken blanched as he realised he'd made a mistake.

"You four join your teammates at the door," Olivia said.

The guards swallowed and threw what Michael could only interpret as a grateful look in Olivia's direction before they beat a hasty retreat to stand with their companions. Michael waited until the guards were out of earshot before he turned his attention to Jaclyn and her companions.

"I take it you trust the two you've brought with you?" Michael asked.

"Myra and Liliana are primewives in my house. If either were a spy for my brother or his wives, I'd long since be dead," Jaclyn said.

Michael regarded all three of the women who didn't seem nervous in the slightest. If anything, what he sensed was mild curiosity.

"Have those given charge of watching over you given you access to the garden every day?" Olivia asked, her gaze sliding over to those who stood lined up at the entrance.

"They have, thank you. If this war had turned out differently, it is not a luxury I would have granted you," Jaclyn said, nodding shortly at Olivia before she turned her attention to Michael. "Despite your words of us being guests, I'm well aware I'm alive with your benevolence."

"A situation that galls you," Nathanial said.

"As it would you…" Jaclyn clamped her mouth shut, then a sudden grin lit her face. "Several wives in my household have requested permission to breed with you and Damien. They're a little afraid of you, Your Majesty, or I'm certain they'd happily jump at the chance to carry a child of your stock. So I think all three of you would be far too busy breeding to even think of walking in the garden."

While Damien did his best to keep his face blank, he moved a half step behind Olivia before he caught himself. Nathanial, for his part, was amused, but didn't show his response.

"Of course I'd be dead if you'd won," Olivia said.

"Of course. You'd be far too dangerous for me to leave alive," Jaclyn said blandly. "However, that isn't how this minor dispute of ours turned out, so I doubt you called me into your presence to discuss what your fates would have been if things had turned out differently."

Michael gestured for them to follow and walked in a meandering path through the garden. Anticipation, curiosity and a level of wariness at his motives were rolling from the Sylannians despite their best efforts to shield themselves. As they reached a point where they started fidgeting Michael spoke softly.

"Understand the leniency I'm showing you is for two reasons. You could have killed my parents outright, but I have witness testimony that you didn't."

"Despite the circumstances, your mother was of my blood," Jaclyn said.

"You could have also killed Steven when you found out he was passing on information to me. Yet you held back your blade."

Jaclyn's expression softened. "I came to care for him, as did my first husband, who spoke in Steven's defence."

"I'm prepared to give you and yours two choices," Michael said, taking a moment to consider his words, although he had a good idea which of the options he was going to put to her Jaclyn would take.

"Very well. I won't test your patience by requesting a third option."

"You and your people can have sanctuary here in my kingdom. I'll grant you an estate close by where I can monitor you, but you'll have to swear allegiance to me."

Jaclyn licked her lips, then let out a breath. "The second option?"

"I think killing you would not solve the problem of Sylannians attacking my people. It's just a guess on my part, but I suspect that news of your demise would bring your king great satisfaction. Then the attacks would continue."

"My death will not stop Sylanna from wanting this land. You and I both know attacks on this land by Sylanna have been ongoing for generations."

"Do you have other forces in our kingdom that haven't given up arms yet?" Olivia asked.

Jaclyn shook her head. "As far as I'm aware, you took out my forces in Callenhain?"

Nathanial nodded. "We did."

"My only other forces here were those I replaced your communication network with. I haven't heard from them, so I assume you've killed them."

"I did," Damien said.

Michael smiled faintly at Jaclyn's startled expression and could almost see the wheels in her mind turning as she re-evaluated Damien's position in his party. As all three of his closest commanders nodded, Michael faced Jaclyn.

"The second option is to assist you in taking the Sylannian throne."

Jaclyn stared at him incredulously. "You would do that?"

"I would, but regardless of my brother petitioning me to be

allowed to stay by your side, you need to understand what will happen if you ever attack my kingdom again."

"Trust us when we tell you we all have plenty of experience in warfare. We've known no other life since we were children," Olivia said.

"We'll bring the war to you, and we won't stop this time until it's finished," Nathanial said.

"There won't be a single Sylannian left who can raise your banner of war."

"How do I know you won't do that anyway?"

"You don't, but that doesn't concern me," Michael said.

Michael waited, having no doubt that in the silence Jaclyn was talking through the options she'd been given with Myra and Liliana. He also knew which one she'd pick. The so-called two choices weren't really that at all. There was only one option that someone like Jaclyn would choose.

I still think we'd be better off killing the lot of them, Olivia said.

I would if there wasn't an entire war filled kingdom filled to bursting with fighters ready to descend on us. Otherwise, Jaclyn and her people, despite my brother's intervention on their behalf, would have died on the battlefield. As it is, even if this doesn't work long term. It should give me breathing space to get my kingdom in order.

It strikes me that when she sees what we can really do. That we can end not only her life but her entire house and her husband's and there is nothing she can do to stop us. Well, she'll be inclined to stay away from our shores, Damien said.

Michael felt a pang of regret that the earnest young man Damien had been had long since disappeared. While Aiden's action hadn't been wholly responsible, they had killed any likelihood that the young man would resurface.

He's still in there. Damien just isn't the naïve young man he was when he joined our ranks, Olivia said.

Michael's attention was drawn back to Jaclyn as she cleared her throat.

"Well?"

"My brother's wives will never allow me to live. Here or elsewhere. I'm too big a threat to their interests. As I'm certain you guessed, I'll do my best to take the Throne of a Thousand Islands," Jaclyn said, her chin lifting as she spoke. "With the death of my brother's primewife, Fiona, here in your land, I fear madness is already sweeping the court. Even so, given the losses to my house, it won't be a straightforward proposition getting through the guards and into the Monarch house, let alone winning the fight."

"I wouldn't worry about getting in," Damien said.

"That is where we come in," Michael said, "but once we get you in, the fight for your throne belongs to you."

"You've never been to the court of the Monarch House. How do you propose to get us in there?"

"We leave tomorrow before dawn. Take this night to formulate your plan of attack. You can give me up to two locations within the Monarch House for your attack forces to enter from, unseen and unheard by the current occupants, until it's too late."

Michael ignored the total disbelief written all over Jaclyn's face and gestured at the guards. Jaclyn and her companions left, surrounded by guards without a single complaint being uttered. Although Michael caught the frown that marred her forehead as she disappeared into the confines of the castle.

ONE HUNDRED THIRTEEN

Tarkhan's breath caught as the silks on his bed writhed around him. As pressure grew around his throat, his eyes flashed open to see the Sylannian he'd just bred with that night on top of him. There was a wildness to her eye and her hands squeezed around his throat. Tarkhan rolled off the bed. His hand gripped the side of his attacker's head and he slammed it into the floor with his full body weight aiding the strike. Tarkhan scrambled back and rose to his feet, aware of his breathing, which sounded harsh in the otherwise silent room.

Samuel? A little help. One of your wives just tried to kill me, Tarkhan said he was about to call again when the king's presence filled the room.

I take it you killed the wife you were sleeping with instead? Samuel asked.

Sorry, she was choking me.

Stay alive, I'm coming.

As the king cut the connection between them, a scream broke the silence, closely followed by more and the clash of blades. Tarkhan spun, seeking the source only to realise the sounds of battle were coming from outside. He groaned, pressing his palms to his head, and doubled over as a murderous rage beat at his mental shields.

As screams rang out closer, Tarkhan gritted his teeth and pushed the emotions away. Tarkhan stiffened, his head tilted to one side. For the first time since he'd been taken, there wasn't even a whisper of compulsion. The blind rage he sensed was debilitating if he allowed it to be, but it wasn't aimed at him. He shook his head and backed up a couple of steps before heading to the courtyard door. Tarkhan threw himself at the door, his shoulder slamming into it. As the door and wall around it shuddered, he stepped back and slammed himself into the door again. A splintering of wood rewarded his efforts, and he screamed as he launched himself at the door a third time. The door exploded and Tarkhan tumbled forward. He dropped his shoulder and rolled back up to his feet in a half crouch as he scanned his surroundings.

The garden courtyard was still, but screaming rang out from the other rooms. Tarkhan ran towards the door to Altan's rooms. He skidded to a halt as the door was flung open and a Sylannian glared at him from the doorway. Her dagger rose as she screamed and ran at him.

Tarkhan sucked in the veil and widened his stance, eyes on his opponent as she rushed at him. As the blade wielded by his enemy plunged down, Tarkhan stepped to one side and shoved his attacker away from him with both his hands and the veil. Tarkhan pivoted, keeping her in his line of sight, hands raised in a defensive position.

Doors slammed open and Tarkhan backed up a couple of steps. Two more Sylannians emerged. One from Chengiz's room and the other from Bilguun's. The wives closed in on him to form a half ring around him, bloody daggers clutched in their hands. The three Sylannians launched themselves at him, perfectly synchronised with each other. Tarkhan let loose with a wild blast of power and launched himself to one side. He rolled desperately out of the way and scrambled to his feet.

Tarkhan twisted his head to see where his attackers were as he ran. Relief hit him as the Sylannians sprawled on the ground. Breath exploded from him as he hit a solid object and he twisted wildly to see Sylannians in black and red swarming around him. Tarkhan fell back, his mind blank as hands closed around his arms, preventing him from falling.

"Tarkhan, calm down your safe now, these are my bloodwives."

"Samuel?" Tarkhan asked, wilting in relief.

The sea of Sylannians wearing black and red parted, and Samuel appeared in their midst.

"We need to leave now or we won't stay safe because my other wives are hunting me."

Tarkhan tried to turn back to the other rooms, only to find himself being dragged along in Samuel's wake.

"Wait, the others. We need to take them with us," Tarkhan said.

"They're dead."

Even though he'd barely met his fellow captives, their loss hit Tarkhan like a blow. He stopped struggling, as ineffective as it had been, and started to jog with the group around him. Other than down, Tarkhan had no idea where they were going. He was dragged past a fight between Sylannians in crimson and others in black. As they ran down a wooden pathway, Tarkhan glanced around him, shocked to discover they were on the ground. Giant trunks rose around him, with the under-growth hiding what lay on either side of the path. A scuttling sound drew his attention and Tarkhan shivered, a yelp escaping him.

"That's a spider," Tarkhan said.

"Well done, that's exactly what it is, but there are thousands of them," Samuel said.

Tarkhan realised they'd come to a halt and spun slowly, swallowing against the lump in his throat.

"My mistake, so there are. Why are there spiders?"

"Because we're in the silk spider grotto. Don't worry, stay here. They'll protect you," Samuel said as he strode away.

"Wait, where are you going?"

"In case you didn't notice, there's a fight going on. Goodbye Tarkhan, I hope you survive," Samuel said.

As Samuel and his wives left him, Tarkhan tried to follow, only to yelp and jump back as an undulating mass of spiders crossed in front of him. He clamped his lips, trying not to scream as the biggest spiders he'd ever seen in his life spun webs. Giant leaves and branches were woven together in the webs forming an enclosure around him. His breathing sounded harsh above the scuttling of the spiders as he was plunged into darkness.

ONE HUNDRED FOURTEEN

While there was screaming, yelling and clashing of blades, it wasn't coming from this section of the Monarch House. Chaos rang out, transmitting through the veil. Dread filled her with what they'd find, as the rage and chaotic mess of emotions told Jaclyn she'd been correct. Conflict had found the Monarch House, but it hadn't been her forces that had started it. Unless another house had launched an attack on the Monarch House in her absence, the king's wives had turned on each other.

Still, the further they infiltrated the Monarch House without the alarm going up in their presence, the better. Never in her wildest dreams would she have imagined this battle the way it was occurring. Unseen around her forces, Michael and his Unwanted ran with her. She could, however, see the shimmering shields her ally threw up. Ice filled the seams of the wooden walls. Then at the soft if somewhat creative swearing, she glared at one of the daggerwives nearby, only to see Nathanial finish killing off an opponent before a wash of achingly cold veil rippled over her and he disappeared from view again. The appearance and disappearance of the Unwanted caused an eerie mist to billow around them. It might help hide their progress through the court, but it still made her shudder.

"It's unnerving," Myra said. "If I'd known any of the barbarians could do this, no matter how small a group they are, I would have advised we defy the king and stay in the trader lands."

"If I'd known this. I would have agreed with you," Jaclyn said.

There are two teams ahead, Michael said, his mind voice calm and assured. *We'll take the group in the corridor on the left. You'll have to take the group, six members, on the right.*

Jaclyn barely had time to pass on Michael's message before a flash of a blade gave away that one of her daggerwives responded to a threat. A splatter of blood showing the knife had found its target.

Two daggerwives leapt forward, catching the slumping body and dragging it off to one side while another pair took on more of their enemy. As death cries rang in her head, Jaclyn reinforced her mind shield and hardened her heart. With each ring of metal on metal and each half-uttered death cry, Jaclyn expected it to draw even more of the king's wives to her. As the last of the enemy dropped dead to the floor, another team of her brother's daggerwives came around the corner. Jaclyn's daggers were just a fraction too late to stop the hollering cry that called the alarm.

Jaclyn swayed back instinctively as an opponent's blade came for her throat.

Duck! Nathanial said.

Jaclyn did exactly what she'd been ordered to do. Between one breath and the next, Nathanial appeared on one side of the hallway. The only warning before a hammering blow sent Nathanial's opponents reeling back. Michael materialised behind the team of daggerwives and launched at them from the rear. A hollow ringing sounded from the veil and Jaclyn gasped as strands of the veil streamed from the spidersilk of the enemy, reducing their armour to nothing but silk.

"Thank you Isabella, but stay in the grey," Michael said as he fell on the enemy.

"Help them," Jaclyn ordered.

Her daggerwives, who stood staring in shock at the uncanny demonstration of power, surged forward and leapt into battle at Nathanial's side. With the Monarch House belatedly realising another player had engaged in battle with them, the need for silence was gone.

Jaclyn accepted Myra's hand as the primewife assisted her to her feet. Jaclyn drew in the veil and the others around her responded the same. Now was the time for speed. To wipe out the infection that ran through the Monarch Court like a disease before any could run. As battle raged around her, Jaclyn ignored that part of her mind that whispered to her, but for her brother's warning before he purged the court, this could have been her fate. It did no good for her to wonder if any remained within the heart of her brother's court who still gripped on, however tenuously, to their sanity.

Like insects bursting from a nest that had been disturbed, the Monarch House wives streamed in her direction. Jaclyn ran and fought in the corridors. Not only with her husband and fellow wives but Michael, Nathanial and a team of the Unwanted. Jaclyn sucked in a breath as a dagger sheared off her armour. Myra hummed a discordant tone at her opponent and the armour her enemy wore returned to its silken form. Jaclyn instinctively responded and plunged her dagger into her enemy. As she withdrew her blade, a handful of her daggerwives launched themselves on the enemy, taking her to the ground as they ended her life. Although the reaction of her brother's house was too little too late. Nathanial and Michael stayed on her side of the veil now, holding a line in front of her forces. Their shields overlapped each other, rising and falling as they struck out at the enemy that converged on all sides.

Myra took advantage of the breathing space the Unwanted gave her. The discordant hum Myra sent out pulsed over the intervening space between their groups. The frequency did nothing to the armour of the Unwanted but it did soften the silks of the Monarch Houses daggerwives. Jaclyn stepped forward, her daggerwives around her. Her line joined with the Unwanted. Jaclyn lost herself in battle as her blade sliced across the necks of the enemy as they rose in front of her.

With the floors slick with blood wherever they passed, Jaclyn lost count of the bodies that fell under their blades. Time had passed, and she recognised at some point they'd made it into the very heart of the inner court. The colour of the silks gave away that those that fell under her blades now were her brother's wives rather than just his daggerwives.

Chelsie and the senior wives are ahead. Samuel is in their midst, Myra said.

Jaclyn didn't acknowledge Myra's comment but with a slight change in direction, she headed towards her brother and his firstwife. The wives that tried to hold between her and her brother still fought, but did so badly in a frenzy of slashes and thrusts. Jaclyn's daggerwives countered their opponents easily. Jaclyn observed the flow of battle around her brother and frowned.

Samuel isn't battling with his firstwife. He's in a battle against his firstwife, Ricardo said, a hint of disbelief in his tone.

As dawn leaked through the shutters, the blades wielded by the combatants glinted in the light. Jaclyn froze for a heartbeat. The dance of daggers wove through the air and formed deadly patterns she recognised. Arrayed against Chelsie and her fellow wives wearing the Monarch House crimson and cream were daggerwives who stood out in stark contrast. Samuel was in the middle of daggerwives wearing black spidersilk armour threaded through with blood-red strands, which formed an intricate web.

"Bloodwives," Jaclyn said, her words barely audible above the screams and clash of blades.

"Bloodwives but..." Ricardo said.

"No!"

Jaclyn barely recognised the cry of denial being her own as she crossed the distance between the battle surrounding her brother. Jaclyn threw herself at the wall of crimson and cream. Her dagger struck down into the back of the neck of her unsuspecting victim. Jaclyn's first target had no sooner crumpled to the ground than she launched herself at another opponent.

Jaclyn flinched as a blade sliced down her jaw and then immediately struck. At the strange hollow ringing and the sight of the veil being drawn from the silks of her enemy, Jaclyn shuddered. Uncanny or otherwise, Jaclyn took advantage as the spidersilk of her enemy was reduced to nothing more than plain silk. She screamed as she put her weight behind the hilt. As Jaclyn toppled to the floor with her enemy, hands grabbed her and hauled her back upright. Battle calls rang around her. Ricardo and Myra fought by her side as they had step by step in this bloody task. Chelsie's daggerwives fell, one after the other. Jaclyn adjusted her step as she realised she was advancing over the top of dead bodies towards her brother. Dark stains on Samuel's crimson armour and his blood-soaked hands gave testament to the injuries he'd withstood.

While he still stood and fought in an increasingly small circle of bloodwives around him. The number of daggerwives from her house increased as they poured into the heart of the Court of a Thousand Islands from all directions.

I'm sorry, I tried. Know that the children are not of our blood. Samuel whispered to her. *Save the wolf warrior.*

Jaclyn nearly stopped dead in the middle of the fight at her brother's words.

As Chelsie closed the gap between her and Samuel, she lashed out at the bloodwives nearest her. Samuel screamed in pain as the death of his bloodwife recoiled through him. Just as Chelsie's dagger slammed into the last of Samuel's bloodwives, Jaclyn and Myra lunged. Their daggers took out the final few wives that stood. Jaclyn was close enough that she heard Chelsie gasp as Myra's dagger plunged into Chelsie's throat. As ordered, the daggerwives took down her brother, disarming him and restraining him on the ground. Although he put up no opposition.

Everyone tensed as Jaclyn sunk to her knees next to Samuel. His eyes stared vacantly. Not even a hint of recognition or fear. Jaclyn closed her eyes, plunging her senses down into Samuel's mind to find nothing. There was the older damage caused when a trigger in his mind had been flipped. Then the newer damage. Each of the bloodwives' deaths had recoiled on him until there was nothing left. His body breathed and functioned, but there was no sign of life in his mind.

"I can send for Kesha?" Michael said.

Jaclyn looked up at Michael, not caring about the tears that spilled down her cheeks.

"Don't put your healer at risk by bringing her here. The body might still live, but Samuel is gone."

"May I?" Michael asked, stepping to the other side of Samuel.

Jaclyn nodded, swallowing against unexpected grief. She had no hope Michael would detect any more than she did, but a part of her needed him to try, anyway. Michael placed one hand on the side of Samuel's head and his face went pale.

"How did he function with such damage?"

"Parts of his mind were kept safe by the protections our

mother placed on his mind. It's a temporary measure. A failsafe should the wives of the king try to usurp the throne."

Michael stared at her, the tense silence rippling around those present as he stepped back from the body of the fallen king.

"I'm sorry, I agree with your assessment. Your brother is dead,"

Jaclyn nodded, then raised her free hand to Samuel's temple.

"I'm sorry. You didn't deserve this fate. I promise you, like I did all those years ago when you spared my life, I'll put an end to this insanity our people practice," Jaclyn said.

Jaclyn's dagger struck, plunging into her brother's heart.

ONE HUNDRED FIFTEEN

Damien took one step after the other through the grey, soaking in the comforting cool wash of the veil. His shield interlinked with Olivia's. Between them, they dragged the attack team in their wake. If their shields slipped for even a moment, it was likely those that travelled with them would die promptly. At least Kesha thought they would. She'd told them prolonged exposure in the grey by those whose bodies weren't adapted to utilise high levels of the veil would result in them suffering from veil sickness. It made for a delicate push and pull as they travelled through the veil. Olivia's shield wrapped around the fighting force while his own grabbed all of them in an ethereal net and dragged them with him. While he and Isabella had experimented in the grey, they'd found if they just pushed the veil away from each other, they'd just drop back into the normal world. The Unwanted were right at home in the grey. Unfortunately, on this run, they had a group of Sylannians with them as well.

I'm shielding them as much as I can, but most of them are shrieking in fear, Olivia said. The fear and pain regular people displayed while in the grey universally perplexed all the Unwanted. For all of their own, they felt right at home.

They have the opposite reaction to all of us.

What do you mean?

You've never been cut off from the veil?

No.

Their fear and overwhelming sense of wrongness feels similar to my reaction when I was cut off from the veil. Only for them it's in reverse.

That makes sense, I guess.

We're nearly there. Liliana, are you ready or would you like us to anchor you and your team here?

No, we'll be fine. Just get us out of this place, Liliana said, a shudder and loathing being conveyed with her words.

Just as he started thinning the curtain of the veil that wrapped around them, he stopped. Damien flinched as the terrified shrieks of children filled his mind.

Something's wrong. Get ready to fight, Damien said.

As the curtain of the veil thinned, Damien saw children cowering back against a corner of a room. His mind balked away from the sight of dead children that littered the floor like discarded toys. A child ran. Loud racking sobs tore from her lips and tears streamed down her face as she fled a Sylannian adult. A carved wooden play toy dressed in Sylannian silks flew from her hands as the girl stumbled. As the girl sprawled on the floor, Damien tore the thin layer of the veil that obscured him from view. He stepped over the girl, drawing in the veil to fuel his strength. Damien's sword cleared his hilt and swept up in a continuous movement. His veil fuelled blade cut diagonally across the Sylannian's neck. He ruthlessly shoved his shield out and the body slammed back against the wall.

Another Sylannian reared up in front of him. Her face screwed up as if in pain and her eyes were wide as she snarled and leapt towards him. Damien drew his sword back. Then, as he channelled more of the veil along and through his blade, Damien thrust it forward. There was a brief resistance as his blade encountered his opponent's armour, then Damien gritted his teeth and in the trick Isabella had shown him called the veil he sensed contained in the armour. As the veil streamed out of the foreign armour, reducing it to plain silk, Damien shoved the power that flowed through him into his enemy. The Sylannian screamed as Damien's blade and power slammed through her. His boot shod foot rose, and he kicked her back. As his sword slid free of her body, it swept up in time to parry the daggers of another opponent, just as Olivia's sword thrust into the enemy from behind.

Damien spun, scanning the room with his eyes and his powers. The glowing life signs of his own party and some children huddled in the corner of the room sprung into view. All else was still in the room with the only sound of the children crying. Damien pushed past several of Liliana's daggerwives. Damien sunk down next to the child he'd first seen. Her doll lay on the ground, just out of reach of her outstretched hand. Damien steeled his heart and looked at the still form of the child with his othersight. Relief flooded him as the weak, muddy glow within her sprung to his vision. Damien sent the thinnest thread of power pulsing into her.

Her eyes fluttered open and Damien sent a wave of reassurance to the girl as he stared into her green eyes.

CHAPTER
ONE HUNDRED SIXTEEN

Jaclyn saw the blood and scattered bodies of children and adults.

"I said the children were to be spared."

"We saved those we could," Damien said.

"The underwives were killing the children before we got here," Liliana said her eyes shadowed as she grasped the hand of a little girl and led her across the room. "They were trying to dispose of the evidence."

Jaclyn frowned and then scrutinised the child. Jaclyn tilted the girl's head up, taking in her green eyes.

"The others? Are they all like this?"

"Not as obvious, but yes."

"Is there a problem?" Michael asked as he finished a sweep of this room and those connected to it.

"This child has green eyes."

"I noticed. I'm guessing that has some significance?"

"Have you ever seen a Sylannian with green eyes?"

"Or any hair colour other than black?"

"Skin like a barbarian?"

"Other than yourself and Steven, of course," Jaclyn said.

"Now that you mention it. No," Michael said as he focused on each of the children who'd survived one at a time. "So, you weren't the first member of the Monarch House to breed with a barbarian?"

"These children may have been birthed by my brother's wives, but they are no relation of mine."

"Why would they have taken such a risk?" Michael said, then his eyes widened. "Do you think he found out his wives were cheating on him and that sparked off this insanity?"

"It is possible everything started unravelling because Samuel discovered the truth about these children. Have you discovered where Chelsie and her fellow wives were hiding their barbarian breeding stock?" Jaclyn said, a bite in her tone. "They can't be too far away."

"I think I have. At least I've found a man that doesn't think in Sylannian. Here I'll take you," Damien said.

Jaclyn didn't have time to reply before she was gripped by Damien's power and hauled into the grey place. She shuddered as the bone aching cold seeped into her, then the grey cleared and she stood on a walkway at the lowest levels of the island. Webs strung from tree to tree and Jaclyn held up her hand, humming as agitated vibrations preceded the flow of giant silk spiders in their direction.

"What are we doing in the spider grotto?"

"Sorry, I should have checked our path was clear." Damien said as his eyes tracked the approach of the giant spiders.

Jaclyn was surprised by Damien's calm response, although his hands twitched as if he wanted to grab a weapon he wasn't currently holding. A number of the Unwanted muttered oaths under their breaths and their shields popped into existence.

"Are those things venomous?" Michael asked.

"No, they don't possess venom. They don't need it. They mostly feed on the veil."

"Mostly?" Olivia said.

"They're carnivorous, but don't worry. I won't ask them to eat you."

"Good, because otherwise you're going to be surrounded by a lot of dead spiders," Olivia said, her tone flat.

Nathanial walked over to the side of the walkway and held up his hand. A small glowing ball of power popped into existence, floating just above his palm. Jaclyn watched as two giant silk spiders scuttled forward. They stopped just short of the glowing ball of the veil Nathanial had produced. As she watched, the globe stuttered and dulled as the spiders sucked in the power. Not that she'd ever admit it, but the idea of using a ball of pure power to attract the attention of the spiders had never occurred to her. She'd always hummed at silk spiders to get their attention and as far as she was aware, so did the spider herders. At least the equally astonished expressions on Myra's and Liliana's faces told her she wasn't the only one shocked by the discovery.

"Huh, that's fascinating. They really use the veil." Nathanial turned to her. "So, this is how you produce the silks you wear?"

"Foreigners have been killed just for setting eyes on our silk spiders," Jaclyn said then turned to Damien. "You could hear the spider's song. Is that how you and your sister can destroy the spidersilk?"

"What? Oh, no. Isabella found out she could call the veil that the silk contains to her. She shared the trick with me before we came here." Damien shrugged off the achievement. "The person I can hear is nearby. It's just the webs are blocking our path."

Jaclyn shook her head and gestured to her daggerwives, who sprang forward and started clearing the webs from the pathway.

"These were ordered to protect the one within," Jaclyn said.

"They speak?" Michael asked, as he kept a wary eye on the spiders.

"No, but they can understand simple commands,"

The spiders had bound leaves and branches into their webs, making a shelter of sorts for whoever they contained. It took time to clear the layer upon layer of webs and leaves obstructing the path. As the daggerwives cleared a hole big enough to walk through, Jaclyn peered past them to see a foreigner huddled against the far wall.

"Tarkhan?" Michael said.

Jaclyn spun to see Michael's eyes were wide as he stared past her. The man, Tarkhan stepped forward, eyeing her warily as he walked out, blinking at the sudden light.

"Michael? How? What are you doing here?"

"Ending a war. More to the point, what are you doing here?" Olivia said.

Jaclyn took in Tarkhan's tattoos as the man edged around, putting Michael between himself and her.

"You are one of the Wolf Warriors of the Kallith?" Jaclyn asked.

"I was," Tarkhan said.

Jaclyn stared at Tarkhan. While she had no right to cast judgement on her brother's wives, she did so anyway. She still had a deep-seated distaste for the idea of breeding with foreigners. Somehow she regarded Steven as being Sylannian, at least that is how she justified taking him as a husband. This man, though, was so far beneath the blood of the Monarch, even the thought of her brother's wives breeding with this man appalled her.

"Can you take us all back to my court? We can walk, but your way is quicker," Jaclyn said.

Jaclyn had no sooner uttered the request when the icy grip grabbed hold of her, hauling her and her party into the grey.

ONE HUNDRED SEVENTEEN

A brush of power that ghosted over Michael, which caused him to switch to his othersight. It had taken practice, but he was finally able to see the ghostly presence of Isabella as she maintained her position in the grey. True to her word, Isabella hadn't taken part in any of the fighting, except to destroy the spidersilk armour of their enemy as she'd watched over them all. It had also been Isabella that had pulled them out of trouble on more than one occasion during the battle as she watched over them.

Tarkhan sat in mute silence now that he'd shared his story. Callan and Gavrel stood guard over him, not because there was any risk, but because the presence of the Unwanted calmed Tarkhan.

"Tarkhan would you like to reunite with your fellow clansmen or would you prefer some time at my family estate to recover and adjust to being free again?" Michael asked.

Tarkhan jumped, his eyes sliding over to where Jaclyn stood issuing orders to her daggerwives.

"If you'll accept some advice, speaking as someone who's

spent some time as the captive of another, having some space to recover is beneficial," Damien said.

"You, but, how?" Tarkhan said.

"When everything is settled, we can share a meal and swap horror stories," Damien said.

Tarkhan stood, rubbing his hands against the Sylannian silks he wore.

"Thank you, perhaps to your estate for now," Tarkhan said.

Michael nodded. "Isabella?"

Michael automatically turned to face Isabella as she parted the veil aside and appeared next to him. He placed his hand on her shoulder, sending a wave of reassurance at Tarkhan's sudden fear.

"You'd like me to take them back to your estate?" Isabella asked.

"If you don't mind. Tarkhan, this is Isabella you've never met, but she's Damien's sister. She'll transport you back to my estate and ensure you are safe. We'll talk when I'm free of this engagement," Michael said.

"A moment. There is some business with the Wolf Warrior I need to settle," Jaclyn said before turning and snapping orders to her daggerwives.

"It's alright, you're safe. There's nothing the Sylannians can do to prevent me from taking you safely back home," Isabella said.

"You mistake me. Against all convention, I'm willing to let this man go back to whatever life he wishes," Jaclyn said.

Michael tensed, his shields springing up, until he saw the Sylannian women guiding children into the room. He blinked at the sight of about a hundred children of all ages. The oldest looked about ten right down to a handful of newborn babies.

"Ah, these are the children of your brother's wives who survived the massacre?" Michael said.

Jaclyn waved forward an underwife who carried a baby and gestured over to Tarkhan. As the underwife approached, Tarkhan paled and took a half step back.

"The records of the breeding house show Chelsie bred with you Tarkhan to produce this boy child. There were other wives pregnant after breeding with you, but they died in this battle before they gave birth."

"Mine?" Tarkan whispered his gaze fixed on the baby being held by the underwife.

"It is. Records show my brother's wives used barbarian stock to breed these children. None have the blood of the Monarch House. There will be no place for them here. It will be better for them if you take these children back with you to your homeland."

"I don't know the how of caring for them, but they are children of the People. Can we take them from this place?" Tarkhan asked.

"Not that I'm objecting, but I thought Sylannians had the belief that male children all belong to Sylanna?"

"We do, but you note I'm willing to let you leave as well. They could be trouble for me in the future if they remain here. Think of the boy as being payment for taking all the girls off my hands as well."

Michael spoke rapidly as he saw the outrage on Isabella's face cutting off what he guessed would have been a heated response.

"Isabella, could you transport Tarkhan and all the children back to the estate?"

"Of course."

"Order some guards back there to look after them. Then bring the Sylannian right back here." Michael threw a glance at Jaclyn. "No offence. I don't trust your people that much."

"None taken. As helpful as you've all been, I don't want any of your people staying behind either," Jaclyn said.

Michael waved permission, and Isabella took Tarkhan's hand. Isabella's power reached out, wrenching not only Tarkhan but all the children and their carers into the grey. Michael curbed his impatience and walked out to the balcony overlooking the forest. The serenity of Jaclyn's court was in stark contrast to the bedlam in the Monarch House. From here, it was hard to believe the bloodshed they'd waded through. Most of it committed before Jaclyn and his own forces had even arrived.

"Would that have happened to me? With Aiden in my head," Damien asked softly as he joined him on the balcony.

Michael didn't have to ask what. He'd spent many years at the business of war and he was hardened against all types of depravity. Yet the chaos in the minds of the members of the Monarch House as they fell on each other was disturbing. They'd essentially slaughtered themselves, with the job mostly done before he'd arrived to do it for them.

"Not quite as dramatic, but even you told me you didn't realise it wasn't your own voice you heard whispering poison to you."

"I didn't, right until just before Aiden stabbed the Warlord."

"Imagine not just one voice whispering to you but hundreds. Like a sickness, it spread and jumped from person to person."

"It was foolish of them to send Fiona to your shores," Jaclyn said.

Michael acknowledged her presence with a slight incline of his head. "I agree, but why do you think so?"

"Her death triggered the madness we waded into."

"The breaking of the bond would have recoiled on them all," Myra said.

"Fiona was a primewife. Her mate bond with Samuel was much stronger than those of the daggerwives. Fiona didn't have the control over Samuel's mind that Chelsie had, but near enough," Jaclyn said.

"Does it hurt you when your daggerwives die?" Damien asked.

"I don't have a mate bond with the daggerwives," Jaclyn said, her lips quirking. "Others considered my house to be odd. We followed the old traditions and only I and Myra have a mate bond with Ricardo."

"You're all linked, though." Damien said, his eyes scanning the room around them. "I can see it. Like a fine interlinking web between you all."

Jaclyn's eyes widened. "In a way, as a family, yes, but it's a light touch. It's not possible to control another person through it."

"Ah, it's like the awareness we share among the Unwanted?" Olivia asked.

"I would imagine so. There are just more of us in my family."

"Do you have things in hand here?"

"Thank you for your help. My daggerwives are just," Jaclyn paused, her eyes shadowed. "Just cleaning up. As soon as the Monarch House is secure, the underwives and workers will move in and make it habitable. Then my house will move and I'll assume the Throne of a Thousand Islands."

"Steven, a word," Michael said.

The daggerwives seemed to freeze but stepped aside as Jaclyn gestured to them and Steven joined him on the balcony.

Jaclyn took a steady breath and then backed up a couple of paces. "I will give you some space to speak to my husband, your brother."

"Are you sure you want to do this?" Michael asked.

Steven glanced across at Jaclyn then ducked his head. "Yes. If I remained back home everyone who disagrees with you will try and use me to get at you. It's taken some getting used to but my wives treat me well. I'll be fine here. Besides it's not much different than the contract partnerships among our peers back home. I just have a lot more wives."

Michael stared at his brother then nodded. "Very well. Remember, if you ever change your mind, you will be welcome back. Your actions during the uprising and then the war show a man I'm proud to call my brother."

Steven smiled then stepped forward hugging Michael. "Thank you. I'm sorry for all the trouble I caused you."

Michael noted the relief that radiated from the Sylannians when Steven retreated among them. "You won't mate bond to Steven in the way of your people?"

"I will not. I have promised him I will not do so. It will be my first decree. The mate bonds and mind bonds between my people will cease."

"You'll have a fight on your hands. People don't like change and for Sylannians, forgoing the mate bonds is a major one."

"I'm ready for it. If they don't comply. They will forfeit their ancestral lands to others."

"Fair enough," Michael said, then gestured to the Unwanted before he glanced back at Jaclyn. "Neither you nor any of your people will come against me and mine ever again."

"You have my word. As one monarch to another. Besides, we're family now, you and I."

"The clansmen?" Olivia said, prompting him.

Michael sighed and rubbed his face. "The remains of the People who've settled on my side of the Heights are under my protection."

"I will not seek to reclaim them, but the land, their former homeland and all in it belong to Sylanna." Jaclyn hesitated then added. "Those children I gave to Tarkhan's care will never seek to return to Sylanna or their lives will be forfeited."

"Agreed. Understand if you break your word, having my

brother as your second husband won't protect you or Sylanna. I'll raise the banner of the Unwanted and bring war to you. If you provoke that, there is nowhere you or any Sylannian can hide. I won't stop if there is a next time. I will roll over this entire land and wipe you out."

Jaclyn's face was impassive to the threat but the hard glint in her eyes gave away she took the threat seriously. Michael gestured to the Unwanted, and they all wrapped the grey around themselves to travel back home.

CHAPTER

ONE HUNDRED EIGHTEEN

Tarkhan hugged Kesha and concentrated on how grateful he was to the healer for her care. The complex array of emotions and feelings were easier to convey that way than they were to put into words.

"It was nothing. You did most of the work yourself," Kesha said with a little flutter of her hand. "I know you're nervous but remember it's perfectly normal."

"Thank you," Tarkhan said and at hearing the door open, he took a breath and faced the newcomer.

Damien leant against the doorframe, a grave expression on his face. "Ready?"

"As I'll ever be. Michael isn't coming?"

"He's already in the Heights, along with Olivia and Nathanial. They've been trying to wrangle some sense into your people for the last few days."

Tarkhan stooped over and picked up the small leather satchel, which was filled with a few meagre possessions. Most of which had materialised by themselves while he'd been here at the Rathadon estate, convalescing. The Sylannian silks he'd been

689

wearing when he arrived had disappeared. Thankfully, the silks had never returned. They would have just been a reminder of his captivity. He contemplated the nondescript brown leathers he wore, similar to the fighting leathers the Unwanted wore without the crest. It had been odd dressing in them but Damien had assured him that while they were of excellent quality, no one would even look twice. Even the thought of wearing the traditional hides of the Kallith had made him uncomfortable. It was a sentiment Tarkhan suspected Kesha had picked up on in one of their sessions and right about the time he was ready to move about the estate, these had appeared. Along with a spare set and boots.

Damien reached out, weapons complete with a weapons belt in his hand. Tarkhan stared at the weapons and dropping his satchel on the floor, took the belt and strapped it around his waist. When he was done, he picked up his bag once more and nodded. Before he could utter his thanks, between one breath and the next, he was gripped by Damien's mental grasp and hauled into the grey place. Tarkhan tried to relax. He understood Damien and all the Unwanted felt right at home in the grey place, whatever it was. Yet the sensation unnerved him more than a little.

How did you face it? Tarkan asked.

Face what?

Your squad mates, after what happened to you? I know none of what happened was my fault, but still...

I didn't really have a choice. They rescued me. Twice. The second time was worse after what Aiden and his men did, but somehow easier.

How?

The first time I didn't just give into my addiction, I dived in head first. I was mortified when I came out of the drug haze. The second time, there was nothing I could have done. I was drugged, stripped, tortured and abused. It took time and a great deal of work with Kesha and others, but none of it was my fault.

Tarkhan's breath caught as fragmented images flashed into his mind as Damien spoke. It made Tarkhan feel like a fraud. Here he was whining about what had happened to him while Damien had suffered far worse.

I'm sorry. I was aware something happened to you, but no one divulged the details. It's not like I was forced. Tarkhan's cheeks heated, and he was grateful that Damien wasn't looking at him.

You were captured by the enemy while trying to save your countrymen.

Well, yes.

They took you to their homeland and locked you up.

They used restraints at first, but after a while, they didn't have to even do that.

Were you free to leave?

No. My keeper wouldn't allow that. I had certain freedoms after I proved myself to them, but they still kept tight control over my life. It was easier to give them what they wanted from me. I told myself I was lulling them into a false sense of security, that I'd fight my way out and get back home. It was a lie. I didn't even try to fight.

You were their captive. They messed with your mind. Sylannians are very good at that particular skill. You did what you needed to do to survive. Just because you weren't strung up in a courtyard and tortured during your captivity doesn't make it any less true. Damien paused and reached out to squeeze his shoulder. *Maybe talk to Isabella if you will. It is Isabella's story to tell, but her captivity is closer to your own than mine was.*

Kesha suggested I talk with both Isabella and Nathanial.

Nathanial has his own experience as well. Like Isabella, what happened to him is closer to your own captivity. They're both in the Heights. As are we. Ready?

No, but let's get this over and done with.

Tarkhan heard a faint whisper, like the ruffling of fine lace in the market square when the wind picked up. The grey fog thinned to show a communal meeting tent in the fashion of the People. Only a handful of people were in the tent, they lounged in the cushions off to one side. None of them strangers. Michael's head turned, his eyes narrowing as he looked in their direction and Tarkhan had the uncanny feeling Michael knew that he and Damien stood there. Although no one else reacted. Tarkhan appreciated the chance to orientate himself even if only for a moment before the grey dissipated entirely, leaving him standing in the room, Damien only a step away.

"Tarkhan, it is true. You're alive. I'm so sorry I abandoned you to your fate at Hallaran," Khaliun said, her eyes brimming with unshed tears.

Tarkhan removed the sword he carried from its scabbard and placed in on the rack near the door. Aware he was stalling for time. Even if only a little. Damien placed his sword next to his, then thumped him on the shoulder.

There is no shame, Damien said.

Tarkhan nodded, then turned to Khaliun, closing the distance between them and sunk down onto the cushions opposite her.

"It is true and you have nothing to be sorry for. You followed our plan and clearly got back to safety." Tarkhan said, pausing as sadness flooded into him from Khaliun. "I've been told the clan fractured while I was away."

"The clan imploded while I and the wolves were fighting alongside Michael and his people against the Sylannian invasion. Those left here turned on themselves, feeding on fear. Many of the tribe were killed."

"What were the other leaders doing?"

"Those of the tribes who were leaders and should have stopped the madness sat back and did nothing. After I returned and passed judgment in the reckoning, I was the only leader of the clan remaining."

"They're all dead?"

"Of those who were leaders, only Erden, the one in the centre of all the death, paid for what he'd done with his life. The others have stood down from leadership."

"So what now?"

"I never would have returned here if there weren't so many innocent people of the tribes left looking to me for leadership. To help fix this mess. As it is, I can't abandon them."

Michael cleared his throat. "For your efforts in helping to defend what was the Warlords domain but is now my kingdom, you have my pledge that in the future, when you are ready, you shall have autonomy. However, I don't think you are ready for that yet. You need time as a people to recover and flourish once more. So settle and make this your home in whatever fashion you choose. You'll have two turns of the growing season before I'll expect the tithe to begin. For now, those of you who remain here in the Heights have my protection."

"Thank you Michael," Khaliun said.

"Although you'll be exempt from the tithe, we'll need reports on your progress," Olivia said.

"Once the regular patrols start up again, pass your report onto the band leader who passes through here," Nathanial said.

"Of course. Tarkhan, like me, you are still a leader of the clan. Will you help me pull our people together?"

"I thought, after everything, you'd ask me to stand down. After all, I was a captive of the Sylannians until I was rescued. Hardly a glowing endorsement of a leader of the wolves."

"You are exactly the leader we need. I know Michael offered you a place if you wanted it, yet after everything that's happened, you've returned. No one could blame you for deciding you do not want the stress that is bound to come with resuming your leadership with me."

Tarkhan swallowed past a lump in his throat. "If you and those that were the Kallith that remain will have me, I'll gladly resume my duties as a co-leader of, well, not the tribe anymore, but of whatever it is we will become."

"I think one of Michael's people scrawled the Heights Protectorate on the map when marking out the boundaries of the land we can call our own. I figured I had better things to occupy my time than arguing about a name."

"I'd imagine so, but now I can help share the burden of leadership with you."

Childish laughter floated through from outside and Khaliun suddenly grinned and grabbed his hand, pulling him out the door.

"Come and see the gift you've brought us," Khaliun's eyes shone with excitement. "Batu, can you ask the Children's Enclave to bring out Tarkhan's boy?"

Tarkhan swallowed at the mention of his child but couldn't help the surprised laughter as he allowed his fellow leader to show him through the camp. As they came to a halt, he smiled at the sight of children. Hundreds of them, boys and girls playing a game of team tag. It involved much laughter, cheering, and groans as the opposing team tagged participants out of the game.

"Have all the girls been accepted, despite their mixed heritage?"

"They are children born of war who needed a home. Not one member of our people would deny them the chance to thrive."

Tarkhan took a steading breath as his eyes settled on the baby being carried towards him by a member of the clan.

"That's my son?"

Khaliun rested a hand on his arm. "It is. You don't have to be a father to him if you can't bring yourself to. He'll be raised in the manner of the clan, as will all our children rescued from the Sylannians."

Tarkhan took a shuddering breath then took a step forward, holding out his hands. The carer stepped forward and carefully placed the tightly wrapped bundle in his arms. As the baby's eyes opened and he stared into eyes so much like his own Tarkhan smiled.

"You were born into a world of horror, but everything will be all right my son. All of us will work together to make this new land of ours safe for you all." Tarkhan brushed his lips gently on his son's forehead and a feeling of peace settled on him.

Tarkhan took a deep breath. Kesha had been correct. He was ready to move on. While he had just as much work to rebuild himself as his people did, at least they'd work together to make this place a home.

ONE HUNDRED NINETEEN

Jaclyn rested her head on Ricardo's chest as they stood out on the balcony. It had taken a long time to clean up the mess and dispose of the bodies that had littered the Monarch House. She opened her eyes as Arianne approached, but otherwise, didn't move.

"Your report?" Jaclyn asked.

"The sister houses have reported that only two other houses were showing signs of infection. They have been dealt with and, as per instructions, the children of both houses were spared. As were some of the lower levels of the houses where it was judged the infection hadn't spread yet."

"They will be carefully monitored?"

"Yes, my Queen, they are being detained and the stability of their minds individually assessed."

"The children of the fallen houses?"

"They have been placed into the care of the Underwives of several houses. Initial reports say that although some of the children are traumatised by what they've witnessed, they are otherwise sound."

"Well done, keep me appraised of their progress," Jaclyn said waving dismissal to the daggerwife, then frowned as the woman didn't move.

"There is one more matter, Your Majesty," Arianne said, hesitating as her gaze slid over to where Steven lounged on a couch with Liliana.

"What is it?"

"There is a firstwife, Allani, asking to speak with you."

Ricardo stiffened as he recognised the name, but refrained from commenting. Jaclyn flicked a hand signal to the daggerwives who moved closer to Steven as Liliana rose smoothly to her feet and crossed the room to join her.

As the doors opened, a party walked in with Allani in its midst and a barbarian man at her side. Steven swore and surged up to his feet. The daggerwives surrounding him drew closer to him, suddenly tense.

"What's wrong Steven? Do you know that man?"

Steven came to her, the daggerwives fanning around him as he crossed the room, careful to keep their own line between him and the newcomers. Unlike Ricardo, who appeared regularly by her side while she was holding court, Steven never did. He stayed safely behind in their private section of the palace, surrounded by squads of daggerwives.

"Not well, but yes I recognise him. He's meant to be dead. A fact that I'm certain Michael will rectify if he learns that he lives."

"Your brother would want that man dead?"

"Without a doubt. Jaclyn, Ricardo, Liliana, let me introduce you to Aiden. He bears watching since he killed his father. You would have known his now deceased father as the Warlord."

"The same Warlord who ruled your former homeland before your brother took over?"

"The one and only. Incidentally, the same man that Michael thought of as his father."

"Would your brother start a war over Aiden?"

Steven snorted in amusement. "No. There's no love lost between them. Michael saw the Warlord as his father, but he didn't regard Aiden as his brother despite the Warlord wanting him to."

Jaclyn ran her other sight over Aiden, checking the mind bonds that Allani had him bound with. While Aiden's abilities didn't show the potential of Steven's bloodline, Aiden did have a great deal of power. Although it was oddly muted.

"You believe you can continue to contain this man?"

"Yes, your Majesty. As well as the control I have over his mind, I have this," Allani said, snapping her fingers.

A couple of Alanni's daggerwives stepped forward, displaying some plant cuttings and a flask.

"What is it?"

"A drug and the plant it is brewed from. The barbarian's call it Tiscan. It represses the ability of a person to use the veil when consumed."

Jaclyn closed the distance between her and Aiden. While on the surface he stood passively enough, turmoil was at a fever pitch in his mind.

"You do nothing to ease his fear?"

"No."

The hard edge in Allani's tone piqued Jaclyn's interest. She rested her fingertips on Aiden's temple. Allani opened the shield she held on Aiden and Jaclyn dove into his mind. Jaclyn sucked out memories, her breath catching as the rapid-fire events played through her mind. Her skin crawled at the vile thoughts and actions Aiden had committed. She paused as she recognised the image of the rather terrifyingly powerful girl, Isabella, who accompanied Michael.

Mine! The girl belongs to me, Aiden snarled.

That was all the prompting she needed to suck more information out of Aiden. Jaclyn gasped as she sped through the mistreatment of Isabella and Damien by this man and the ones he led. She shuddered at the vile thoughts and atrocities Aiden had either committed or ordered.

"He's a vile little man," Jaclyn said.

"If it wasn't for his bloodline, I would have ordered his death. I know it goes against our culture, but this man deserves to pay for what he did to Isabella and Damien," Allani said.

"You knew them both?"

"I didn't know Damien well, but he treated us all with respect when the warleader captured my family. Isabella was but a child by the rules of their people. I did what I could to shield and ease the torment of Damien and Isabella during their abuse at Aiden's hands."

Aiden flinched as he stared at something over her shoulder, and a strong sense of fear emanated from him. Jaclyn tracked what held the man fixated and saw immature silk spiders scurrying along the balcony.

"You won't get free of the bonds we place on you. Nor will you know luxury or ease between your duties," Jaclyn whispered while she stroked Aiden's temple, reinforcing his fear of the silk spiders. The spiders scurried across the floor towards them at her call. Aiden's eyes bulged, and he shrieked in terror. Satisfied, Jaclyn stepped back. "Take him to the lower breeding halls and place him in the hands of the underwives. When he isn't being bred, Aiden's punishment will be to clean out the spider grottos. His accommodation and food will be nothing but the necessities. What is it you want in return for this gift?"

"A place in your court in service to the Monarch House. Safety for those of us left of my former house."

Jaclyn weighed Allani's words. Even though Jaclyn's attack on the barbarian lands hadn't gone as planned, Allani had been true to her word. The disgraced firstwife had done everything she'd been asked to do. That the woman had survived frankly astonished her.

"You have it. Go. The underwives will find a place for you. In the meantime, reinforce this man's fear of the silk spiders so he doesn't become accustomed to them and I'll turn my mind to what other functions you can fulfil in my court."

Allani and all her people bowed, then withdrew from her presence, herding the man, Aiden with them. Aiden looked back, staring mutely at Steven, but otherwise didn't speak. It at least attested to the constraints and hold Allani had on her captive.

As the door closed, Steven leant forward and kissed her. Then he rested his hand on her expanding abdomen, a small pulse of power checking the life that grew within her. It gave Jaclyn satisfaction that Steven showed no sign of being unsettled at all in encountering a man from his former homeland. He also didn't seem to care about the man's fate now that Aiden had been taken away. With a twinge of regret, Jaclyn brushed Steven's temple and pushed at his mind.

Forget husband. Your former countryman, Aiden, was never here. Only Allani came into our presence. A disgraced firstwife returned from the war in Callenhain. She begged a place in my court, which I granted.

Steven's eyes widened and his breathing became shallow as she layered what she wanted him to remember over the event that had just occurred. His head sunk to rest on her shoulder as she worked.

Is that necessary? I doubt Steven would betray us, Ricardo asked.

I gave permission for his friend, Evan to visit once things are settled between our nations. It made Steven happy to believe he might see his friend one day. Even if Evan and Michael are the only people outside our house he will ever be allowed to mix with again. Michael also looked at the concession with approval. He believed it was a sign that more of the restriction I impose on Steven's life with me would relax over time. Steven might mention the encounter with Aiden without thinking of the consequences. I have no wish to have Michael go to war with us if Steven is wrong about his relationship with the man.

You're right. It's a small detail that Steven could very well mention to his friend, or worse, Michael. He's better off not remembering.

"The underwives tell me you've settled in well," Jaclyn said, as she finished her work and eased back the compulsion from Steven's mind.

"I don't want for anything, particularly now that I have more places I'm allowed to roam around in."

"What, you thought you'd be living in a cell?" Ricardo asked, a hint of amusement in his tone.

Jaclyn sighed happily. Both of her husbands had settled into an easy friendship.

"Well, no, you told me I'd have some space, but it's like a palace within a palace, complete with my staff and everything."

"I'm sorry for the delay in you moving to your own place. The quarters had to be refurbished and expanded to suit your status."

"You don't need me to attend the court sessions with you, like Ricardo?"

Jaclyn's fingers brushed Steven's temple. "No, there is no need. You will stay safe here in the court for the rest of your life, just as I promised you. My people can stay curious about you."

Jaclyn lightly touched Steven's mind and relaxed, seeing he truly was as at ease as he appeared. More importantly her compulsion over his mind held and there was no sign of the recent meeting with Aiden. Steven plucked at the gold collar she wore around her neck a mirror of the one he and Ricardo also wore.

"So, what are these for?"

"A reminder."

"About?"

"We of Sylanna raided the shores of your homeland and took your people. Slapping our collars around their necks and hauling them back here to Sylanna to serve. It's a reminder to not only to me and all my descendants never to repeat the mistake, but also to all of Sylanna."

Steven cocked his head to one side, then shrugged. "I guess that is a valid point and it's not like the collar hurts. The under-wives gossip. They tell me that many of the collared servers you freed stayed here in Sylanna."

"They have. It doesn't excuse what we did. What I did. It will never happen again, particularly not in your former homeland or I have it on good authority, your brother will wipe us all out."

"If he's said he will, then I'd trust his word. We should keep wearing the collars, it wouldn't do to forget," Steven said.

"Come, it's too pleasant an evening to talk of death. Let's have dinner, then find something else to amuse us for the evening," Jaclyn said.

At Steven's feigned look of shock, Jaclyn laughed and grabbed both Steven and Ricardo's hands, pulling them both towards the low tables off to one side. As she settled back into the cushions, it occurred to her this was the first time in her life she felt content, happy, and safe.

ONE HUNDRED TWENTY

Michael listened to the outraged complaints of his various warband leaders. While he had to admit, at least to himself, they had some extremely valid objections to his disappearing act. It didn't mean he had to like it. His chair protested, scraping against the stone floors as he stood abruptly. Michael turned his back on the leaders who sat around the table and went to the window, gazing out over the forest and the rooftops of Valantia in the distance. It took longer than he thought it would, but the various leaders finally worked out he wasn't listening to their complaints. They petered out and an uneasy silence filled the meeting room.

"I didn't ask for your approval of my plans because I don't need to. You made me your king. Remember?" Michael said, his voice filling the room with ease.

"Michael, you're too important to—" Harry said, cutting off abruptly as Michael raised his hand.

"We did what we needed to do to secure this kingdom," Olivia said.

"The Sylannian king has been defeated and Jaclyn has ascended the Sylannian throne," Nathanial said.

"She isn't likely to forget our capabilities or that perhaps we have abilities she doesn't know about," Olivia said.

"The former Kallith clan has settled back in the Heights. They are now known as the Heights Protectorate. They have some autonomy under Khaliun's and Tarkhan's leadership, but still answer to me," Michael said.

"How does the resettlement of the people dispossessed by the war with Sylanna go?" Olivia asked.

A brief silence met the question, then Taya cleared her throat. "Those who still have a home have returned to them. Those that don't are being housed in tents on the outskirts of Vallantia and at the Smith's estate while the damage to the city is being fixed."

"We received word from Callenhain the other day that normal trade is resuming and Jenna is sending food and supplies to Vallantia to assist those who have need."

"Will you take over in Callenhain?" Michael asked, turning from the window as he regarded Olivia.

Olivia shook her head. "My place, as always, is at your side. I cede the estate house and the lands to the crown."

"I already have my estate here in Vallantia. What need could I have for another one?" Michael asked.

"The hunting and weather is much better in Callenhain during summer than here," Nathanial observed, then brightened. "You could use it as your summer court."

"Taya, you'll keep the title of commander. I hardly think warband or warband leader is appropriate anymore. If you could sit down, with others or not as you choose, and come up with an alternative rank and structure."

"Of course Michael," Taya said.

"Pass whatever you come up with through me for approval," Olivia said.

Michael nodded agreement. The four of them had discussed the potential issues going forward and Olivia, Nathanial and Damien had made it clear that he could continue to lean on them for support.

"You but…" Taya said, stumbling to a halt as her face went red.

"My role as one of Michael's second's hasn't changed, even if the title and number of responsibilities likely will."

"Of course, Olivia. I didn't mean any disrespect."

"You'll also need to come up with a patrolling plan for the entire realm. I'm thinking the units, whatever you end up calling them, should rotate, so there's some flexibility. Turn your mind to that as well and run your ideas through Olivia."

"We'll be considering the tasks the leaders and their troops should have to complete on their rounds. I'll fill you in on those responsibilities once we've had time to come up with a list," Damien said from his place sitting on the window seat off to one side.

Given more than one person around the table jumped when Damien spoke up, Michael gathered that in their shock at how the meeting had departed from their agenda, they'd forgotten Damien was sitting there. Michael shared an amused glance with Damien, who appeared perfectly at ease in assuming responsibilities.

"You'll want me to consider the Unwanted in my plans?"

"No," Nathanial said. "The Unwanted will remain in place. Wherever Michael is as our king, the Unwanted will be. They will have the job of keeping our king safe."

"The Unwanted will continue to take their orders directly from us and no one else," Damien said, his gesture including both Nathanial and Olivia.

"I have a kingdom to shape. You are all some tools I will command to make it. There will be rules and they will be mine and mine alone. My country will not slide back into a realm of barbaric feudalism. I won't permit it. I think you have enough to think about and do for now, so unless there is anything else?"

"You'll need an heir…" Isabella said, pausing as her words caused the heads of everyone in the room to swing abruptly in her direction. "Well, he will. Michael is the king. Unless we want war to break out and in fighting about who will take control when Michael dies, he needs an heir."

Michael wanted to be outraged, but instead, he threw his head back and laughed. Isabella had an irrepressible nature and even though she hadn't been invited to the council session, she'd invited herself. While the various warband leaders had stared at him when she'd come in, since he hadn't objected to her presence, no one else had gotten up the nerve to ask her to leave.

"I'll give that little detail consideration as well. I'll leave you all to your work." Michael walked to the door, with Nathanial, Olivia and Damien falling into step with him, then paused, half turning. "Come on Isabella, unless there are further instruction you can think of for that lot. I have a kingdom to run, and it seems you have just volunteered to assist me with this lot to run it."

Isabella grinned, then smoothed her face in an attempt to appear responsible. She pushed her chair back and joined them. A wave of incredulousness followed their departure from the room. He'd enjoyed disrupting the warband leader's plans for him and his kingdom far too much. Michael would wrestle them kicking and screaming from the path of warfare, whether they liked it or not.

This kingdom and its people deserved peace, and Michael intended to give it to them.

About the Author

Catherine M. Walker was born in a small country town in Western Australia but now resides in Perth, Western Australia.

Defiance is the third and final book in Catherine's second epic fantasy series Emergence.

If you'd like to know more about Catherine's work, including following the progress of her new series visit:

https://www.catherinemwalker.com